Heaven Right Here

Also by Lutishia Lovely

Sex in the Sanctuary
Love Like Hallelujah
A Preacher's Passion

Heaven Right Here

LUTISHIA LOVELY

KENSINGTON PUBLISHING CORP.
www.kensingtonbooks.com

This book is dedicated to everyone who believes
they can experience heaven . . . right here, right now.

ACKNOWLEDGMENTS

First and foremost, I thank Spirit, the connecting force in all of us.

As always, a huge thank-you to Selena James and the entire Kensington crew, my agent Natasha Kern, and all of the fellow writers who help make this a journey where one can always expect the glorious unexpected.

In addition to Kensington's Adeola Saul, I am happy to have the support of publicist Ella Curry, whose company, EDC Creations, and the BAN Network Internet radio show are vehicles through which writers thrive. And to Debra Owsley, your Simply Said reader aids are simply wonderful. These products are excellent additions to the writer's arsenal of promotional and marketing materials. My readers love them, and so do I.

A special *I love you* to Pat G'Orge-Walker and Naleighna Kai. Good looking out, ladies! I also want to give a thumbs-up to West Coast Biz, a hard-working up-and-coming writer who in his own words knows how to "push a pen." I agree—your street lit drama kept me turning the pages, and I look forward to future works.

To all of the book clubs, Internet radio shows, and bookstore owners—especially the independent Black bookstores, which sadly are too few and are growing fewer. You were there for the African-American writer from day one, and I pay homage to your tenacity, strength, and courage in the face of a changing global marketplace.

I am continually amazed at the power of the reader in spreading the word about this series, whether it be within an organized format such as a book club, reviewers who take the time to post their comments on Amazon or other Web sites, or individuals who make my cause their own by telling all their friends and family about what they've just read. This word-of-mouth sharing is truly love in action, and I feel it. Your thoughtfulness and active participation propel me as, with your help, I continue to write and grow as an artist. I couldn't do it without you . . . and I am very grateful.

Now, sit back, turn the page, and indulge yourself in a little *Heaven Right Here.*

Heaven Right Here

1

Baby Daddy

Stacy Gray, Hope Taylor, and Frieda Moore sat enjoying the breeze coming off the Pacific Ocean. Stacy's son, eighteen-month-old Darius Crenshaw Jr. sat cooing and clapping in his high chair, obviously enjoying the early November weather as well. Stacy and Hope belonged to the same church and saw each other almost every week. Hope and Frieda were cousins. But it was the first time in months that all three of these thirty-something ladies had hung out together. The good food and great conversation was just what the doctor ordered.

"I don't care about what she did—I love *Conversations with Carla*. That sistah keeps it real!" Frieda jabbed a fry in the air for emphasis.

"I like her too," Hope said. "I'm just saying it's amazing how someone who fell so low could rise again so quickly."

"I'm with Frieda," Stacy added, taking a napkin and wiping mashed potato from her son's face. "She did wrong, and she was punished. She lost her husband, her ministry, dignity, respect. No one on the outside looking in will ever truly know how much her present success cost her."

Minister Carla Lee Chapman had paid dearly for the scandal she had endured a year and a half ago. A secretive, short-term affair with a church associate had become very public via a cuddly, late-night photo and tell-all article in *LA Gospel*, a Los Angeles–based magazine targeting the Black church community. Her husband had promptly divorced her and married the woman who had revealed Carla's secret. Carla's base of Christian women supporters—that had once numbered in the hundreds of thousands—dropped to four figures, and all but a handful of Christian bookstores pulled her DVDs. But now, less than six months after her nationally syndicated television show debuted, Carla was attracting a following that promised to eclipse that of her former popularity—a new popularity that included women of every race, religion, and socioeconomic status. Her Dr. Phil–style directness and Oprah-like warmth, combined with her religious sensibilities and Southern charm, had endeared her to the masses. Fortunately for both her and the MLM Network, her scandal and shame had garnered sympathy from the secular public. They embraced the contrite woman whom the religious community had ousted. The show's sky-high ratings were her final vindication.

"Did you see the girl on there the other day?" Frieda asked. "The sixteen-year-old who already had two kids? I wasn't expecting Carla to get with girlfriend like she did, but telling that little sistah to put a closed sign on the punany was real talk!"

"She said that?" Hope exclaimed.

"Pu–na–nny. On national TV. That's why women love her."

"What did the girl do?"

"Boohooed and then promised Carla she'd put her stuff on lock and focus on taking care of her kids."

"What I liked," Stacy interjected, "is that Carla offered to be her personal mentor—that she cared enough to get involved with a guest like that."

Stacy and Frieda kept talking, but Hope didn't hear. Idly twirling a strand of jet-black, shoulder-length hair, she tried to stave off the wave of depression that often accompanied any talk about babies. She and her husband, Cy (pronounced like the *sigh* his fine frame evoked from most women), had been trying for almost two years to get pregnant. She'd gone to several doctors and gotten mixed diagnoses: one said she was fine, another that her uterus was tilted, and a third said something about low-producing ovaries. Her first lady at church, Vivian Montgomery, had told her she just needed to relax and stop *trying* to get pregnant. But Hope had just turned thirty. She and Cy wanted at least two children. It was time to make it happen.

"I know one thing," Stacy was saying when Hope finally began to listen again. "If Darius thinks he's going to force me to have my son stay in that den of sin he and Bo call home, he'd better think again."

"But he the daddy, girl," Frieda reasoned. "Let that boy get to know his father and his 'uncle,'" she said with a wink, referring to Darius's lover, Bo Jenkins.

"You can't keep the boy away from his father," Hope agreed. "A child needs both parents."

"Yeah, well, his *father* should have thought about that before he chose Bo over me!"

Stacy flung her black, sixteen-inch Indian Remy weave away from her face so hard the hair slapped the face of the man sitting at the table behind her. He turned and glared, but Stacy didn't notice. She was too busy looking at yesterday.

Time had not dimmed her resentment at the way Darius had chosen to end his bigamous ways—to remain in the civil union with his male lover and have his marriage to Stacy annulled. It hadn't helped matters that his subsequent coming out hadn't received the backlash she'd hoped it would. Granted, it had generated all types of controversy in religious circles, and he wasn't getting many requests to play in churches, but his concerts were selling out, and his attempt to cross over from gospel into R & B was proving successful.

"Having a child is a blessing, Stacy," Hope said softly. "Don't miss out on the joy of it by holding on to anger. I'd do anything to have a baby right now."

Just then they were interrupted by a well-dressed man stepping up to their table. "Stacy Gray?" he asked, looking from one woman to the other.

"I'm Stacy."

"This is for you." He handed her a large envelope. "You've been served," he added brusquely and quickly walked away.

"What the . . ." Instead of finishing the sentence, Stacy put down her drink and tore open the envelope. Her eyes scanned the papers quickly.

"Oh, my God, I don't believe this crap. He cannot possibly have this kind of nerve." She flipped through the pages quickly before throwing the document on the table. "He's out of his ever-loving—"

"Calm down, Stacy," Hope interrupted, putting her hand on the woman about to go postal. "What is it?"

"It's Darius, acting like the asshole he is," Stacy responded, her eyes welling with tears. "That fool is taking me to court. He's suing me for full custody of my child!"

2

Too Much Drama

"Let me see that," Frieda quietly demanded as she subconsciously ran her hand through the short pixie cut that emphasized a narrow face and high cheekbones. She read parts of the document aloud—paragraphs outlining charges of slander, malicious intent, and willful disregard of joint custody arrangements previously set up by the courts after Darius and Stacy's marriage had been annulled.

"How often does Darius get to visit his son?" Hope asked as she reached over to Darius Jr. and took the spoon that had become an annoying drumstick against the wooden highchair. Before the child could inhale enough breath for an all-out wail, she'd replaced the noisemaker with a quieter, crowd-friendly pair of plastic straws. She was rewarded with a gummy grin, signaling that all was forgiven. *If only adults could forgive and forget as quickly,* she thought.

"Often enough."

Hope pushed the issue. "As often as the court dictates?"

Stacy's facial expression made words unnecessary. She apparently was not keeping up her end of the custody arrangements.

"All I asked was for him to keep Bo out of our business. I did not, and do not, want that man influencing my son. But does Darius listen? No! He acts like he can't walk without Bo saying which leg goes in front of the other. I think he clings to Bo just to piss me off."

Frieda chuckled. "Girl, he clings to Bo because he's in love."

Stacy rose from her chair and lifted a stained but happy toddler from the highchair. She methodically cleaned mashed potatoes from his hands, toes, shirt, and pants as she continued. "It's simple, really: if he wants to see Darius more, make sure I see Bo less. There," she added, referring both to her cleaning job on her son and also to her son's father. "I'm not asking too much, am I, little man, huh?" She nuzzled his neck as he emitted peals of laughter. "I'm not asking your daddy for too much."

"I say let the child see his father," Frieda said. "I know you don't want to hear this, Stacy, but the man pays child support. He has a right to see him. So what if his booty-bumping buddy comes along for the ride. Hell, I say the more love, the merrier. Besides, if you'd let the man see his son more often, we probably wouldn't be sitting here looking at court papers." Frieda ignored Stacy's venomous stare and continued. "Look, I'm your friend so I'm going to call it like I see it. Darius doesn't want drama right now. He's probably just doing this to make a point. Go home, give the man a call, and work on an arrangement you both can live with. You might even be able to get some more money out of the deal, and you might be able to put in a request for solo visits—visits without Darius's 'husband'—into the actual custody paperwork. Because unless that madness about you not wanting Bo around your baby is not only legal but justified, Darius will do a Kevin Federline–style drive-by, and they'll be sitting over in Bel Air talking about 'And baby makes three.'"

Hope agreed with Frieda but wisely chose to keep this information to herself. "What are you going to do?" Hope asked instead.

Stacy swung the diaper bag over her shoulder and positioned Darius on her hip. Her stance matched the attitude that poured from her lips. "I tell you what I'm not going to do. I'm not going to let some fake faggot pseudo-celebrity run my life. This is my child, and his welfare is my business. Darius wants a fight? Darius wants to do battle in court? Well, I'm going to call his sorry ass and tell him it's about to go down!"

Hope watched silently as Stacy navigated around filled tables and raised eyebrows, crossing the patio with her head held high. *She's about as big as a minute,* Hope thought as she watched her five-foot-three, size-four friend walk away. *But if she ran into them, I think she could kick both Bo's and Darius's butts right now.*

Frieda shook her head once Stacy had turned the corner. "That's the very reason why I will never have two things—a child or a husband. Unh-unh. Too much drama." A beep alerted Frieda that she had a text message. She looked at her Blackberry and typed in a quick reply, speaking to Hope as she did so. "It's about time Giorgio got his butt back on this side of the country."

"Giorgio? I thought that relationship played out a while ago."

"It did. But he's still a friend . . . with benefits."

"Too much drama, huh?"

Frieda winked at Hope and then reached for the wallet inside her purse.

"No, no—my treat," Hope insisted. She pulled out her black Centurion American Express card and motioned for the waitress. Then she returned her attention to Frieda, who was busy texting away. "What happened to Jonathan? I thought things were heating up with you two."

"That's who I'm texting now," Frieda said without missing a stroke. "I'm moving our date to tomorrow so I can pick up Giorgio from the airport." Her eyes widened at Hope's exasperated expression. "What?" Frieda asked in as innocent a voice as she could muster. "Giorgio always gets Saturday nights if he's in town. That man loves to party and knows some of everybody who's anybody." She continued typing as fast as her thumbs could move.

"You know what? You keep saying you want to find a good man and settle down, and every time we talk you're mentioning a new name . . . or, in Giorgio's case, bringing up an old one."

"Good man? Settle down? Didn't you hear what I just said about marriage? Besides, how am I supposed to find a good man without looking for one?"

"If all you were doing was looking, and if it were only one, we wouldn't have a problem."

"We don't have a problem now. But I hear a sermon coming, and it's nowhere near Christmas or Easter—my official dates with the Lord. So hold that thought, cuz. I gotta run."

Frieda gave a stunned and still seated Hope a quick hug. "Thanks for lunch and your wonderful company." She hurried across the patio and threw a quick "Love ya!" over her shoulder before finishing her grand exit.

Hope's smile lingered after Frieda had gone. This was her crazy "I am who I am" cousin, and one thing was for sure, what you saw was what you got. As much as she chided Frieda for her fast-lane lifestyle and questionable dating etiquette, she also admired Frieda's ability to live life to the fullest and on her terms. As Hope prepared to leave the restaurant and signed the receipt, adding a twenty-dollar tip to the fifty-dollar total, she decided to do more of that herself—live a full life—beginning with doing whatever it took to become a mom.

A smile spread slowly across the face of the person who sat directly behind the table just vacated by Stacy, Hope, and Frieda. She couldn't believe her good fortune on hearing the juicy drama that had just played out. She always knew Stacy had had that child to try to trap Darius, just like she'd always known he'd never stay with her. And not for one minute did she believe that her idol, the man of her dreams, was gay. Everybody knew Bo was Darius's business partner, and that gay chitter-chatter that had been all over the news had been planted by Darius simply to keep people like Stacy away from him.

"What are you smiling about?" her date asked. He gave her a seductive gaze, and hoped the smile was for him.

It wasn't, as her next words confirmed. "I'm smiling because what we just heard puts me one step closer to what I want. And I *always* get what I want." She rocked her leg and twirled the straw in her drink as she pondered which plan to put into play. Then the smile faded, her eyes narrowed, and the young, determined woman made a declaration: *Darius Crenshaw is as good as mine!*

3

Babies Are Blessings

"Are you sure you don't want to fly over here? My business wraps up in a couple days. We can take an extended European tour and then go down under for the Australian Open." Cy's voice dropped to a near whisper. "Maybe sneak into the stadium at midnight and make love on the main court."

Hope smiled as if Cy could see her face through the phone. She knew her six-foot-two, one-hundred-and-eighty-five pounds of caramel goodness would do anything to make her feel good, which is why she tried to put on a happy face around him and now respond with a cheerful voice.

"That would give new meaning to tennis balls, now, wouldn't it?"

"Not to mention the things I'd do to you with my racquet," he said, laughing. "But if we continue this discussion of racquets and balls much further, I'll have to cancel the rest of my meetings and fly home now."

"Promises, promises," Hope countered. "I love you, baby, but handle your business. I'll be here, ready and waiting, when you get home."

"Last chance for this first-class ticket, baby." Cy's *want* to see his wife had turned into *need*. "Especially since your mom canceled her trip. And speaking of, how's Earl? Still improving?"

"Daddy's much better. In fact, Mama said he may be released in a couple days. Thank God this wasn't an actual heart attack. It was a warning, though. Mama said she and Lena are joining forces to play food cop. Of course, Daddy was in the background begging for smothered pork chops."

"If Earl's joking around, he's definitely on the mend. That's good to hear, baby. Maybe you should fly there instead. I can even meet you in Oklahoma if you want."

"That's a good idea, Cy. Maybe I will. I'll either call or e-mail you as soon as I make any plans."

They shared a few more naughty innuendos before Hope gently placed the receiver in its cradle. She fought to maintain the lightness and joy that had transpired during the conversation with her husband. The happiness lingered briefly, especially as she thought of her mother and father genuinely getting along for the first time since they had divorced more than a decade ago. Hope felt a small sense of pride knowing their attendance at her and Cy's wedding had been the catalyst to her parents' platonic reconciliation. Lena was a big help too. She and Earl had recently married, and Lena had immediately offered her friendship to Hope's mother and Earl's ex-wife. "We're all family, Pat," she'd said. "You loved him then, I love him now. So we've already got something in common." When Earl complained of chest pains and couldn't catch his breath, Pat's was the second number Lena dialed, after 911.

That's some kind of woman, Hope thought as she flipped through hundreds of television channels. Her mother was the kind of woman Hope doubted she could be. If she and Cy ever divorced, heaven forbid, could she be friendly toward his new wife? Hope felt she would have to try, for the sake of their children . . . if there ever were any.

Children—what Hope wanted more than anything in the

world. The second of her two-pronged, decade-long prayer to God. He'd already answered the first part. Cy Taylor was everything she could ever want in a husband, lover, and best friend. When she thought about Frieda, Stacy, and the hordes of single women at her church, Kingdom Citizens' Christian Center, her gratitude intensified. Frieda changed men like some women changed hairstyles. *And just look what Stacy is going through.* Hope felt guilty for wanting more. She and Cy had been trying forever to get pregnant. Aside from when he was out of town, theirs was an almost daily effort to welcome in a Cy Jr. or little Hope. Would she ever wipe mashed potatoes from the mouth of her own bundle of joy?

I don't know if or when I'll do that, Hope thought. But what she wasn't going to do, she decided, was sit in a three-million-dollar penthouse suite overlooking the Pacific Ocean with a five-karat diamond on her hand, food in the refrigerator, money in the bank, and have a pity party. She could almost hear the response if her mother knew Hope was feeling sorry for herself: "Girl, you better add up your blessings before the Lord starts subtracting!"

Her mother would be right. She was too blessed to be stressed, and she decided to start acting like it. Hope went online, booked a Monday morning ticket to Tulsa, phoned her mother with her travel plans, and sent Cy an e-mail. She felt better after talking to her mother. After fixing herself a snack tray, she hunkered down for a marathon viewing of the *Conversations with Carla* television shows she'd Tivo'd the week before.

The first two shows—on religion in the workplace and life after sexual abuse—were interesting but didn't hold Hope's genuine interest. She was about to come to that same conclusion about Wednesday's show, "Today's Working Woman," when—after hearing from a bank executive and a woman who owned her own catering business—Carla introduced her next guest.

"For some of us, being the wife of a successful man can feel like a full-time job," Carla joked with her usual warmth. "Juggling his needs with those of the children can sometimes get tricky, especially for new mothers. Here to share her story, as well as tips on how to succeed in this balancing act of motherhood and ministry, is the wife of an international business entrepreneur and pastor, a woman successful in her own right, Millicent Kirtz."

Hope froze, celery stick in midair, blue-cheese dip dripping unnoticed on the plush, silk divan. Surely this wasn't the Millicent she knew, the woman who'd stalked her husband and almost ruined New Year's two years ago. *There's no way God would bless her with a child before me,* Hope thought.

But she thought wrong, because onto the stage walked a poised and radiant Millicent Sims Kirtz, looking as beautiful as ever. Hope dared not think, let alone state the obvious, that motherhood agreed with her. Not that anyone would ever look at her and assume she'd had a child. No, Millicent was still model thin, even on television, which supposedly added ten pounds. Her cream-colored dress, belted at the waist, complemented her lithe, five-foot-seven frame and accented her perfect pooch of a derriere. The strappy jewel-colored sandals she wore were Giuseppe Zanotti originals. Hope knew this because a similar pair was in her closet. But Millicent's excellent taste in footwear wasn't the problem. What had taken away Hope's appetite was hearing the words *Millicent* and *mother* in the same sentence.

Millicent's makeup was flawless. It brought out the gold undertones of her café-au-lait skin, and if girlfriend had any blemishes, no one could see them. She wore her naturally long, dark brown hair in a cascade of curls. The soft-looking ringlets bounced slightly as she rocked to and fro in Carla's plus-sized bear hug of an embrace. It was the way Carla greeted most of her guests, as if they were long-lost relatives. Her unbridled show of affection made the guests feel right at home, and most ended up talking to her as if that were true, spilling secrets as if it were just the two of them curled up in the living room sipping tea.

Hope moved from the divan to the floor, directly in front of the sixty-five-inch flat-screen television. A surge of jealousy rose up before she could stop it, and at that moment, if she could, she would have reached through the television screen and slapped the happy off Millicent's face. She almost couldn't bear to watch, yet couldn't turn away as she listened to Carla and Millicent go on and on about the joys and challenges of motherhood.

"I think it helped that little Jackson was a total surprise," Millicent said in response to Carla's question. "He came along as quickly as my marriage to his father at an impromptu ceremony in Mexico. And just like that unplanned, spontaneous occurrence, our son has brought the greatest joy."

"Wait, hold up, I think I just heard another storyline. I know we're talking about motherhood, but your wedding wasn't planned?"

"Not exactly," Millicent answered, nonplussed. "Jack and I had already planned to get married; we just hadn't planned to marry so quickly. And, no, I was not pregnant before the wedding," she deadpanned directly into the camera. "Jackson was conceived three months *after* we returned to California."

Carla also spoke into the camera, directly to the television audience. "Did y'all hear that? Millicent got pregnant after she was married."

She eyed a few women in the studio audience and spoke conspiratorially, again as if they were the best of friends. "You know how lies get started, so when you repeat this story, tell the truth and shame the devil." Carla's laughter tempered her not-so-subtle message to gossipers, particularly those in the Kingdom Citizens congregation, where Millicent had once been a member. Then Carla turned back to her guest. "So here you are, juggling your duties as a pastor's wife and in-demand marketing consultant, and here comes a baby. Oh, my!"

"Exactly. I was shocked but pleased. Jack has two children from a previous marriage, but we always talked of having one of our own."

"So he's, what, hitting those terrific twos now?"

Millicent laughed. "I remember you calling them that, Carla—the terrific instead of terrible twos. And, yes, Jack and I, along with his children, Sarah and Thomas, are enjoying those moments right now . . . immensely."

Millicent winked at the audience to underscore her sarcasm. They laughed along with her, feeling a part of the camaraderie Carla had created onstage.

"Babies are blessings," Millicent went on, ironically spouting the same phrase Hope had earlier said to Stacy. "Ultimately even the challenges with Jackson are a gift."

Hope watched the rest of the segment through a sheen of tears. Millicent Sims Kirtz was a mother. Millicent had a child who was two years old. Millicent had gotten pregnant without even trying, three mere months after marrying her husband.

The irony of life wasn't lost on Hope. When she'd married Cy, she'd gotten what Millicent had long desired. And now Millicent had something Hope desperately wanted. Check, and checkmate.

Hope reached for her purse and pulled out her cell phone. With Giorgio in town, she wasn't surprised to get Frieda's voice mail. Hope only hoped they'd made it to a hotel and weren't humping like two love-starved teenagers in a rented SUV on a dark side street.

She waited for the beep. "Frieda, why didn't you tell me Millicent had a baby? I know you knew; you never miss Carla's show. Call me when you get this message. I don't care what time."

Hope hung up, dialed Stacy, and also got voice mail. *It's probably just as well,* she thought, hanging up the phone without bothering to leave a message. Stacy probably couldn't care less that Millicent or anybody else had a baby. She was dealing with enough baby-mama drama of her own.

4

Baby-Mama Drama

"Who was it?" Darius asked as Bo placed the phone back on the receiver and his arm around his husband.

"Baby-mama drama," Bo said simply. Enough said.

It was almost a week to the day since Stacy had been served the custody papers, and she'd been calling Darius ever since. After their one and only conversation had turned into a shouting match, Bo had suggested any further communication happen through their attorneys. Bo had been right, as was often the case when it came to all things Darius. And while Darius knew his attorney had not only phoned Stacy repeatedly but also e-mailed a proposed child-support increase that could result in Darius dropping the lawsuit if she complied, Stacy was still acting a fool.

Darius sighed. "Hell hath no fury like a woman scorned."

"A scorned woman *is* hell," Bo corrected. "But we both know what this is about, and it's *not* about a baby. It's about you."

"I know. And don't even go there with another round of 'I told you so.'"

"I wasn't," Bo lied even as he almost choked on the litany of ways he'd tried to discourage Darius from getting involved with Spacey Stacy Gray. He'd known she was trouble the first time he'd laid eyes on her. But with Bo, anybody remotely interested in Darius was trouble until thoroughly investigated and proven otherwise. Not that it mattered. Darius had finally seen the light, ended the sham of a marriage he'd had with Stacy, and come home to his heartbeat. He and Darius had been enjoying life ever since. Not only that, but after Darius had come out of the closet, his already successful music career had soared. The numbers he'd lost in judgmental church members had been more than made up by new fans in ever-growing gay America. That was one thing about the homosexual community—those birds of a feather definitely stuck together.

Bo lazily ran his hands across Darius's closely cropped hair, rubbed his broad shoulders, and admired the smooth, chocolate skin. "Uh-huh, tight as a drum, just as I figured. You can't get all stressed out with this Stacy business."

Bo stood, stretched his lithe, light-skinned, five-foot-nine body, walked behind the couch, and reached for Darius's shoulders. He was as good a masseur as he was a business manager. Darius began to relax immediately.

"Dang, baby, you're almost better than Ching," Darius said, referring to the licensed practitioner he saw once a week when his schedule permitted and he was in town. He rolled his neck from left to right, no longer feeling the kinks that had been there moments before.

"Almost? Ching wishes he could knead a muscle like I do, and he'd like to knead one muscle in particular, if you get my drift. At least he's not in the band," Bo finished quietly.

"Contrary to your popular belief, my dear man, everyone is not after me sexually." Darius chose not to respond to the band reference. Randall, his six-foot-one bass guitar player, rumored to swing in both directions, had sent Bo into a tizzy from the moment he'd been hired a month ago.

"Uh, did I say everyone? 'Cause I could have sworn I just said Ching." Bo recognized that Darius hadn't taken the band bait and wisely dropped it.

"Okay, more specifically, Ching is not trying to have sex with me. He has a girlfriend."

"Is her name Stacy?" Bo asked. His skepticism was obvious. "I rest my case."

Once again ignoring Bo's jab, Darius rose from the couch and pointed to where he'd been sitting. "Let me return the favor."

Darius's strong fingers were soon working their magic. Bo moaned his appreciation until his cry was an exaggerated wail.

"You nut," Darius said, laughing. "It sounds like you're about to climax."

"No, but I'm hoping *that* will be happening within the hour."

Darius figured this somewhat happy mood was as good a time as any to spring on Bo the news that would surely upset him—as anything upset him that Bo didn't control. As it was, Darius had kept the secret for almost a month, a rarity for this partnership where everything was shared.

"Oh, hey, I've got some news."

"Aw, hell." Bo sat up and turned to Darius. "What?"

"Relax, baby," Darius said, continuing the massage. "This is lightweight. A fan club."

"A fan club? Says who?"

"Says me, that's who!"

"Okay, cool, but where did this come from all of a sudden?"

"From the Andersons' daughter. You remember them, right? Clyde and Bernadette?"

"How could I forget their homophobic asses? Those are the ones who accosted us in the parking lot, right? The woman with a face like old cottage cheese telling us what we were doing was an annihilation?"

"Abomination, nut. But, yes, that's them." Darius rejoined Bo on the couch and put his arm around him. "It seems their daughter doesn't share those archaic views. In fact, she's a computer whiz, and, according to her, my number-one fan. She wants to head up a fan club for me. I don't see a problem with it."

"Yeah, neither did Paul Sheldon."

"Who's that?"

"From that movie, *Misery*, with Kathy Bates. He didn't see a problem either until his 'number-one fan' pushed his ass down a set of stairs and *then* broke both his legs. Of course, I'm sure the leg Miss Thang is interested in isn't the one you walk with."

"Her name is Melody."

"That light-skinned, loud-mouthed girl with a booty the size of our widescreen?"

"Her booty isn't that big."

"Oh, so you've been looking."

"No! Stop trying to start an argument. I'm not interested in that girl—I repeat, *girl*. She's sixteen years old."

"I don't care if she's sixteen *months* old. She's got a va-jay-jay, and so I say nay-nay. She can be a member, but let somebody else head up your fan club. What about that old chick who wears those outlandish hats? I like her."

"Mother Moseley?"

"Yeah, let Mother Moseley head it up."

Darius rolled his eyes. "Bo, I like her too, but she's seventy years old!"

"Okay, caller, what's your point?"

"My point? Let's see. I'm sure her computer skills and Internet knowledge are up to par: e-mail, Google, Twitter, the works. She probably even has a MySpace page."

"I can't deny she might have problems navigating the net. So let Mother Moseley be the official head, and let Melody be her assistant."

"It's kinda too late for that," Darius sheepishly admitted.

"Kinda why?"

"Because I kinda ran into her—*okay, last month, but who's*

counting—and I kinda told her she could do it. Look, her parents are old and strict, and their bible beating is draining the life out of her. This will be a way to put some of it back. And she can do it from the bedroom she calls a jail cell. If she's home managing the fan club instead of trying to run the streets, maybe her parents will give her a break."

"Yeah, until they find out she's cavorting with the enemy."

"They won't find out. Besides, I have a soft spot for the girl. I've known her since she was eleven or twelve years old. She used to bug us to join the choir. And before I came out, her parents were friendly toward me—especially Clyde. He even confided in me that he was in a doo-wop group when he was a teen, something that holy-rolling Bernadette knows nothing about. It'll be okay."

Bo bit back yet another argument, deciding that this particular battle was not one worth fighting. Melody Anderson's naive act might work for Darius, but she didn't fool Bo for one hot minute. *She might be the biggest fan with the grandest plan, but I'll be damned if she messes with my man. She'd better not want anything more than to mail out some glossies, pass out a T-shirt, and update his fan-club database,* Bo thought testily. Because Bo Jenkins, who didn't miss much, would be watching.

5

Let It Go

"Where's Frieda?" Stacy asked after she'd entered the Taylor penthouse. Immediately the living room's color combination of various blues, off-whites, and luxurious sienna splashes enveloped her in an atmosphere of calm. She and Darius had dined there as a couple, and she'd visited many times, but the home's beauty never ceased to amaze her.

"Giorgio extended his visit," Hope replied. "Chances are we won't see her butt until he leaves town."

"That heifah. I thought we agreed that Saturday lunches would be our catch-up time. And look at her, standing us up already."

"Yeah, well, you know how plans can change with Frieda, especially if there's a man involved. Where's the baby?"

"With his aunt Tanya, and if I know her, probably at his daddy's house or on the way there. I told her I didn't want him around Bo. But Darius is her favorite brother, so . . ."

"I thought Darius was her only brother."

"No, Tanya's father has a son by another woman. But it wouldn't matter if she had a dozen brothers; she'd still worship the ground Darius walks on."

"He does seem to have that way about him," Hope mumbled.

"What did you just say?" Stacy was pure attitude. "I know it wasn't what I thought I heard. I may have loved him, Hope, but he was never my idol."

"I'm sorry."

"You should be. But apology accepted. And what has you so snappy anyway? I could feel your foul mood over the phone."

"I know I shouldn't be, but I'm still tripping over Millicent being a mother. I've tried to let it go, but it's been on my mind since last Saturday."

Stacy joined Hope, who'd flopped down on the couch. "I know I'm the last somebody to tell you to stop trippin', but thinking about Millicent is totally unproductive. Besides, you acted like you were over it the day I called and you were at your mom's in Oklahoma."

"I was. For the three days I was there, anyway. Mama can relate to my anxiety because of how bad she wanted another baby after her miscarriage. She never got the second child she wanted. So she understands how bad I want my first."

"But does she understand this fixation you have with Millicent being a mother?"

Hope shrugged. "Y'all are all on the same page with that one, and I admit I need to leave it alone. I *want* to leave it alone. But now every time I watch *Conversations with Carla*, I remember Millicent sitting on the couch."

"Well, switch to *Oprah!*" Stacy exclaimed. "Do whatever you need to do to get past this. Bless that woman and her baby and then focus on Cy and creating a family of your own."

"That's all I've been doing for the past two years!"

"Well, maybe that's the problem."

"What?"

"Maybe you're focusing on it so hard you're stressing yourself out. It's not that you can't get pregnant, am I right?"

Hope nodded.

"And what did Sistah Viv tell you?"

"To let go and let God." Those words from her first lady had been comforting a year ago, but not only could Hope not seem to let this Millicent news go, but the information had caused her to pick up a burden she'd put down.

"Maybe we should think about fertility drugs," Hope said aloud, even though she was talking more to herself than to Stacy.

"So I can become an aunt to sextuplets? I don't think so. One is hard enough to handle, believe me. It's going to happen, Hope. Remember, God's timing is perfect."

Both women became silent, thinking the same thing: that that was the exact same advice Hope had offered Stacy when Stacy was chasing Darius. Trust God's clock. There was no way Hope could have known that Stacy was already pregnant by the time they'd had that conversation. Stacy knew that had she waited for Darius, her current life would look different. But she probably wouldn't have her son, and he alone made all the challenges she now faced worthwhile.

"What are you going to do about Darius seeing his son?" Hope asked.

Stacy immediately became defensive. "The question is what is he going to do? You think my position has changed since last week? Just because his punk ass served some papers? He can see Darius whenever he wants to, just not with Bo."

"But is that really reasonable, Stacy, considering their union is legal? You may not like it, but Bo is in Darius's life, and for the time being, it looks like he's there to stay. Perhaps you should try to find a way to make your peace with this fact and with Bo. You told me the two of you were friends once, remember? When he helped you during your pregnancy? You told me about the meals he prepared, the comfort he offered? You know how much he loves Darius, which means he loves Darius's son as well. Maybe if you change the way you look at the situation, the situation will change."

"Wise words, Mrs. Taylor, but you might want to take your own advice. What are *you* going to do about this unproductive jealousy you feel toward Millicent? How are you going to change *that* situation?"

6

Long Time No See

Cy Taylor's harried spirit calmed as soon as he stepped into the lobby of Hotel Parisi near the shores of La Jolla, California. Perhaps it was the combination of modern designs mixed with Mediterranean old-world charm, or the feng shui practiced throughout the establishment. Perhaps it was the original artwork or the custom designed sculptures and rich walnut furniture. Then again, it may have been the coolness of the marble floors and the tranquil, undisturbed atmosphere that almost caused one to whisper. Whatever it was, Cy was grateful, both for the ambience and for the fact that this was the last appointment on a rarely worked Saturday. He tried to keep weekends free for him and Hope, and he couldn't wait to head home to his lady love and dinner with two of their favorite people—his pastor and first lady, Derrick and Vivian Montgomery.

Cy had just taken a seat on a sofa near the fireplace when his cell phone rang. It was his appointment, Charlie Seagram, who was stuck in 405 freeway traffic and running late. Cy was tempted to reschedule, but because this was to be one of the last meetings before deciding whether he was going to become a silent partner in Seagram's construction company, he decided to wait the half hour Charlie said it would be before he arrived.

He hit number one on his speed dial. "Hey, baby."

"Hey, love! I just got off the phone with Vivian. She invited us to bring our swimsuits and said their grilled patio feast will be followed by decadent homemade ice-cream shakes enjoyed in their Jacuzzi. I told her it sounded wonderful."

"You told her right. Besides, you know I never pass up the chance to see you in your famous thong bikini."

"Uh, right. Flashing my brown cheeks in front of my pastor is sure to win points with his wife, I'm sure."

"She's got a pretty good-looking set of cheeks herself; she won't mind."

"Since when are you checking out Vivian's booty?"

"Since never." Cy wasn't even going to go down that road. "I'm just assuming that because they're universal, she too has a behind."

"Okay, Mr. Taylor, I'll let you slide this time. But if I see your eyes wandering away from my conservative one-piece, you're going to have some explaining to do."

They continued talking for a few minutes until Cy looked up and saw a familiar face coming toward him.

"Look, baby, I have to run. Tell Derrick and Viv we might be a little late. I'll be home as soon as I can."

"Considering Derrick's always full schedule, I'm sure they'll understand. I'll call them now."

Cy's smile was genuine as he rose from the sofa with hand outstretched. It was immediately batted away and replaced with a heartfelt hug. They hadn't seen each other in a long time.

"Cy Taylor," Millicent said, smiling. "What are you doing in my neck of the woods?"

1

Mysterious Ways

Cy and Millicent exchanged cordialities and sat on the sofa.

"Millicent Sims . . . or, actually, it's something else now, Millicent . . . ?"

"Kirtz," she replied.

"That's right. Your husband is the man we met in Mexico." Millicent nodded. "Jack Kirtz."

"That name is familiar. Isn't he the one heading up that international alliance to stop genocide in Darfur?"

"Jack represents our ministry, Open Arms, as a very active board member. He's especially concerned about the effect of those horrible atrocities on that country's children and more specifically is working to set up adoptive homes for some of those orphaned. We've even discussed perhaps adopting a daughter."

Cy sat back and got comfortable, crossing his right foot over his left knee as he eyed Millicent intently. "No offense, but I never really saw you as the mothering type."

Millicent laughed. "None taken. Until I met Jack, I wasn't. But look what God can do. I've been married for just over two years now, with a son and two nearly grown stepchildren. Much different than the Millicent you remember, huh? The one who stalked you relentlessly for years."

"Look, I—"

"Really, Cy, it's okay. I've prayed for this moment actually, a chance to see you face-to-face . . . and apologize. I embarrassed both of us, and I am truly sorry. I was a different woman then, obviously disillusioned. Looking back, I simply cannot believe I did the things I did. Thank God my mother was right: time and God have healed those emotional wounds. And I no longer have regrets. Everything in my past has led to my present—a wife and mother with a wonderful husband, delightful child. . . ."

Cy's heart warmed as he looked at Millicent. This self-assured person he saw now was the one he'd admired years ago, the reason he'd asked her out. She was smart, sensitive, and, yes, beautiful. He was genuinely happy for her happiness. And glad she'd finally left him alone.

"I guess I owe you an apology too," Cy said, changing the subject. "I was pretty forceful with you that night we ran into each other at the resort in Riviera Maya. I was sure you were stalking me, had followed me there."

"I had," Millicent admitted. "I found out you and Hope would be vacationing at the Rosewood Mayakobá resort."

"How?"

Millicent held up her hand. "Don't ask. Let's just say that where there's a will, there's a way. I don't know what I had in mind exactly, except to try to get you back. I was so jealous of the fact Hope had you and I didn't.

"God works in mysterious ways," Millicent continued. "Unbeknownst to me, Jack's travel agent had booked his vacation at the very same resort. He had no idea I'd be there. In fact, I'd lied to him and said I would be vacationing in Hawaii. But after he arrived, he spotted me sitting at the bar in the restaurant. At God's urging, he decided to keep an eye on me. And he did. You might remember how shocked I was to see him. That was not acting."

"Interesting," Cy said, rubbing his chin. "Unbelievable."

"Now I can honestly say I'm happy for you and Hope. If

your marriage is half as much a blessing as mine is to my savory Scot, you are two very blessed people. I'm sure it's just a matter of time before you'll be adding some little Taylors to your household."

"In God's time," Cy replied before quickly changing the subject. His comfort with Millicent did not extend to talk about his fertility issues. "So Jack is Scottish?"

"Among other things. His great-grandparents were from Sweden and England. But the Scottish blood on his grandfather's side is where he gets his fire." Millicent blushed, again murmuring her husband's pet name. "My savory Scot."

Seeing the obvious love she felt for her husband, Cy relaxed even more. "What are you doing here at the hotel?"

"Meeting with our church's woman's group, the Divas of Destiny. We meet here once a month—love the ambience. And you?"

"Meeting a prospective business partner."

"Regarding real estate? You know, Jack has quite a substantial holding of properties in this area."

Cy immediately thought of his and Hope's plans to build a dream home. "Actually, I am looking for property in this area, something near the ocean."

Millicent pulled a card from her briefcase. "This is Jack's number. You might give him a call. His properties include some exquisite oceanfront tracts of land, and he's recently talked of developing some of it. Maybe he'd be willing to sell you a few acres."

Cy had been researching property in the area for the past twelve months and, even with his deep pockets, had seen how difficult it was to acquire pristine, unobstructed oceanfront land. It would be the height of irony if the spot for his dream home came by way of his former nemesis. But as Millicent had said, God worked in mysterious ways.

Millicent looked up to see a nice-looking older man with

thick salt-and-pepper–colored hair heading in their direction. He waved his hand to Cy in greeting. Cy waved back.

"Sorry I'm late," Charlie said before he'd fully reached the now standing couple.

After handshakes and introductions, Millicent turned to Cy. "It was great to see you again, Cy. Please keep in touch. I'm sure my husband will be delighted to hear from you."

Just over an hour later, Cy rolled down the 405 in his brand-new cream-colored Azure Bentley convertible, the sounds of vintage Miles Davis pouring from the top-of-the-line speakers. True to his word, he'd phoned Jack shortly after his meeting with Charlie had ended, and as Millicent had anticipated, Jack was very interested to discuss real estate and possibly other business ventures, including rebuilding communities for the displaced in Darfur.

Cy's stomach growled as he anticipated what was sure to be a delicious dinner flawlessly prepared by Derrick's wife. He couldn't help but smile as he imagined their varied reactions to his surprise meeting with Millicent and of God's sense of humor when he disclosed that his newest business partner may be one they'd never guess . . . her husband.

8

The Devil's Playground

Hope's reaction was not as he'd imagined. Granted, he knew Millicent was not her favorite person; he hadn't thought she'd do cartwheels over hearing he'd run into her. But neither had he expected the anger she was now displaying in front of their hosts, not even hiding her immense displeasure for the sake of appearances.

"I can't believe her nerve, though I shouldn't be surprised," Hope spat out between tightly clenched teeth. "Coming up to chat as if you were friends. Will that bi—*witch* ever be totally out of our lives?"

A subtle look passed between Cy, Derrick, and Vivian. Vivian took a sip of tea before responding. "Given your history, I can understand your reaction, Hope. But God expects us to forgive. It's obvious she's moved on, and I, for one, am happy to see that."

"I am too," Derrick quickly added.

Cy, wisely, remained silent.

"Once you forgive her, Hope," Vivian continued softly, "you'll be able to truly wish her happiness and find your peace as well."

"Look, I've forgiven her, okay? But I'm not going to sit here and act like I like her. And since you haven't been through what I have, Vivian, maybe you should keep your holier than thou opinions to yourself!"

Vivian's brows raised in surprise, while Hope's unapologetic glare dared a response. Her sharp retort to Vivian was uncharacteristic, not to mention disrespectful. Cy looked at Derrick, who subtly shrugged his shoulders and continued eating. For a moment, silverware clinking on china was the only sound heard.

"This chicken is grilled to perfection, baby," Derrick offered. "Was there lemon in the marinade?"

Vivian nodded but didn't yet trust herself to speak. She sympathized with Hope as well as all the other women with issues she faced through counseling the congregation. But even Jesus got angry. And that Hope dared to check her while sitting at her table eating her organic food . . . well, it was almost too much.

"I love these grilled vegetables," Cy said. "What's all in here, Vivian? Zucchini, squash, and what's this?"

Vivian chewed and swallowed her forkful of food. "Eggplant," she said simply.

Figuring a joke about how eggs get planted might not be appropriate, considering the circumstances and his wife's fertility issues, Cy instead tried to right the nearly derailed train of civility by replacing their own drama with another ongoing KCCC feud.

"Were you surprised to see Shabach at church last Sunday?" he asked Derrick. "Or had his office phoned?"

Derrick wiped his mouth with a napkin. "I knew he'd be there. His management called the office and asked if Shabach could sing a song or two. But the Musical Messengers were already booked. You know, Hope, it was at the midnight musical you coordinated in Kansas that I first heard those cats play. I told Vivian then that we'd see the Musical Messengers one day on the national stage. Did you have anything to do with getting them more exposure?"

Hope had calmed down and knew Derrick was trying to

coax her back into the conversation. "Not much, other than recommending them to any and everyone who'd listen. I heard an agent was at Noel Jones's church when they played there and that's how they got a deal."

"You know, baby," Vivian began, "it's not right that this ridiculous feud between Shabach and Darius is keeping us from extending the same invite to him that we do other gospel talents."

Derrick leaned over and kissed his wife. "That's why I love you, woman. You keep Big Daddy in check. But I'm a step ahead of you. I've scheduled a meeting with Darius to discuss this very issue because Shabach's people let me know he'll be back in our area around Thanksgiving, and I've given them an open invite to sing at the church."

The feud between Shabach and Darius was legendary, going back to when both were unknowns trying to come up. The rivalry was constantly fueled by rumors, lies, and half-truths of each trying to sabotage the other's career.

"It's about time someone stepped in to squash that beef," Cy added. "There's enough money, fans, and success out there for everybody."

The discussion flowed from the constantly dueling recording artists to the changing landscape of gospel music and of music in general. From there the topic switched to the success of Carla's talk show and what everyone was doing for the holidays. By the time dinner was over, their usual camaraderie had returned. The Taylors said yes to the decadent vanilla dessert, but Hope asked if they could take a rain check on the swim and Jacuzzi.

A half hour later, Derrick and Vivian walked Hope and Cy to the door.

"All right, my man," Derrick said as he gave Cy a brother's handshake. "Are we still on for basketball later this week?"

"I hope so," Cy answered. "All this delicious food has me watching my waistline."

Meanwhile, Hope hugged Vivian. "I'm sorry for snapping at you, Vivian," Hope said softly. "I didn't mean what I said. I value your opinion . . . always."

"All is forgiven," Vivian said. "What are you doing Monday?"

Hope thought for a moment. "I have a few errands to run in the morning and a Pilates class in the early afternoon. After that I'm free. What's up?"

"I was hoping we could meet. I have an idea I want to run past you."

"Why don't you come over to my house, say, around four o'clock?"

"I'll be there," Vivian said and then added, "But I'm coming in my tennis shoes and without my earrings so that if you go off on a sistah like that again, I can give you a Madea-style beat-down!"

The comment elicited the laugh Vivian had hoped for. The women hugged again, and both couples waved at each other once more as the Taylors walked to their car.

Vivian's smile remained in place until their guests' taillights had disappeared down the drive. Then her brows furrowed. She was concerned about Hope and what her obsession with Millicent and motherhood was doing to her spirit and to her chances of getting pregnant. Mother Moseley said an idle mind was the devil's playground. Maybe Hope had too much free time on her hands. Vivian hoped involving Hope in her plans for ministerial expansion would give her friend and valued church member something else to think about.

9

Family Feud

Hope was thinking, all right, and the devil was busy. The joy from Vivian's joking had dissipated before the Bentley exited the driveway, replaced by the anger that had simmered since Cy's "You'll never guess who I ran into" surprise. The drive from Beverly Hills to the marina was a quiet one. A bewildered Cy waited for an explanation for the night's uncharacteristic behavior.

"You could have warned me," Hope said finally. "You could have told me privately that you'd seen Millicent. Why did you wait until we were at their house?"

Cy didn't answer immediately as he tried to discern both the spoken and unspoken questions. "I didn't think it necessary to tell the story twice and was honestly expecting a variety of humorous reactions. I never would have mentioned it if I'd known you'd get this upset."

Hope snapped her head around to look at Cy. "Oh, so you would have kept it a secret?"

"Don't twist my words, Hope, and don't assume the worst about me. I meant I would not have mentioned it in front of D and Vivian." A frustrated Cy eased his foot off the gas and tried to calm his now rising temper. "I don't get all this anger anyway. Millicent has been out of our lives for years now; she's married, a mother, happy. Why are you so upset?"

"Because I don't want to hear about her *happiness*, that's why!" Hope replied in a raised voice. "And I don't want you talking to her either, understand? She's caused us enough trouble."

"Look, if you want to make a mountain out of this molehill, go right ahead. But you need to understand this: you don't dictate who I can and cannot talk to. You're acting like this was some sort of clandestine rendezvous. She saw me waiting for Charlie in the hotel lobby and came over to speak to me. End of story." Cy took a breath and spoke in a more soothing tone. "More than anybody, you should know how much of a non-threat Millicent is. She's never held a candle to you. You know that."

"That was then; this is now. Before, there was the thrill of the chase to keep you interested, the anticipation of having something new. We've been married two years now. Men . . . men's feelings change."

Cy looked hard at Hope. "You can't be serious."

Hope knew she was being irrational, but she went on in spite of herself. "I'm very serious."

"You think I'm less interested in you now than before we were married? You think I'm getting bored with you, that the thrill is gone?"

Hope shrugged.

Cy sighed. He didn't know whether Hope was on her period or the moon was full, but his normally even-tempered, perpetually positive wife was flat-out trippin'. "I don't know what all this is about, Hope, but if I'm missing something, I'd suggest you enlighten me. Now."

Hope's response was to cross her arms, turn away from Cy, and spend the rest of the drive home seething as she stared out the window. This was their first real argument since becoming

Mr. and Mrs. For it to be about Millicent made it even worse in Hope's eyes. She refused to admit that pride prevented her from telling Cy the truth: that she was jealous of his former fellow church member, envious of the fact that she had a child, and frustrated beyond measure that their attempts to conceive had been unsuccessful. Stacy had warned her to not keep these feelings from her husband—to share her feelings. But Hope never thought her feelings about Millicent would be an issue with her husband. She was a part of their past, not their present, wasn't she? Hope knew one thing: she definitely didn't want Millicent Sims Kirtz to be a part of their future.

10

Darius's Crew

The Sunday crush at Kingdom Citizens Christian Center was more dense than usual, partly because of more than fifty newcomers crowding the already overflowing foyer. Greg, the church's manager of security, barked orders into his cell phone, rounding up additional personnel who were working the parking lot to help maintain order.

Greg turned to Melody Anderson, the obvious ringleader of nearly one hundred hormonal teenaged females all decked out in Darius's signature colors—chocolate brown and mint green. Their outfit bottoms varied from mini to maxi skirts and pants of different material, but the tops were the same: a mint-green satiny poly-cotton blend with the initials D.C. emblazoned across the front in multicolored crystals. It was obvious who they were there to see, and it wasn't Jesus.

"I think I've secured a place for your group in the balcony," he said. "But you'd better be glad you got here early, and even so, we don't usually seat a group this large without prior notice. It's great you invited your friends to church, Melody, but next time make sure you clear a group this large with the office."

Melody cocked her head to the side and fixed Greg with a youthful smile. "I'm sorry, Greg," she said with mock humility.

"I'm just so glad I got my friends to come and praise the Lord!"

"Praise the Lord, huh? Well, if that's so, shouldn't the initials on your T-shirt be J.C. and not D.C.?"

"Jesus doesn't need a fan club," Melody replied, her smile turning to a pout. "And we came here to praise the Lord, not Darius."

"Just so you keep that in mind," Greg replied with restrained patience.

Two of the men from Greg's security team walked up, and after a short conference with the balcony ushers, the group was led upstairs. Melody took a seat front and center on the first row of the balcony. Once seated, she decided this was better than being downstairs. What a picture she was sure Darius's fan club made, all decked out in their green and brown! He was sure to be surprised when he looked up—and hopefully pleased.

Melody was proud of what she'd been able to accomplish in such a short time. In less than two weeks she had coordinated this local fan group, Darius's Crew, and signed up almost five hundred people to his newly redesigned MySpace page. Melody aspired to a career in show business and, after the painful acknowledgment that she couldn't hold a note in a bucket, had decided that her path to success would be from the business end. This fan club was only the beginning, simply the door by which she'd enter a celebrity filled, illustrious future. And get her man.

Darius walked over to the musician's platform and joined the drummer, saxophonist, and guitar player already set up and tuning their instruments. He immediately went into a jazz-infused remake he'd charted of the Edwin Hawkins gospel classic, "Oh Happy Day." Soon the buzz of conversations from the almost-two-thousand-person-strong congregation occupying a standing-room-only sanctuary was replaced by clapping, rocking, and well-remembered song lyrics: *". . . When Jesus washed . . . He washed my sins away. . . ."*

Derrick Montgomery entered the pulpit, followed by Vivian; his assistant, Lionel; Cy Taylor; and four other associate ministers. Hope, Stacy, and a decked-out Darius Jr.—in a pinstriped chocolate-brown suit and mint-green shirt—took reserved seats on the first row of the center section while Bo Jenkins occupied a seat on the second row in the far right section, directly in line of sight of where Darius played keyboards.

Stacy glanced over at Bo and cut her eyes. "I see his bitch is here," she whispered to Hope.

Hope jabbed Stacy with her elbow. "You are in God's house," she hissed. "Show respect."

"Forgive me, Lord," Stacy whispered. She knew Hope was right, but something about Bo rubbed her the wrong way, something like . . . everything. Especially the fact that he was "married" to the man she once loved. She was also still upset about the previous week's meeting with her attorney and Darius's legal lackey, otherwise known as his representation. The fact that he hadn't even thought it worth showing up for his son's mediation hearing should have told the legal teams something about how interested he was in being involved in Jr.'s future.

It didn't matter that she was in violation of the joint custody arrangements they'd made when Darius Jr. was six months old, or that Darius had offered to increase her monthly child-support payments from nineteen hundred to four thousand a month. According to Stacy, it wasn't about the money. At least, this was what she'd conveyed to Hope as they'd lunched the day before. And it wasn't about getting Darius back. She didn't want him back. Or so she had tried to tell herself. Even looking at him now—fineness personified in his chocolate suit—and then looking at her son—who looked more and more like him with each passing day—she denied that her heart was still hooked on all things Crenshaw, and that if he said the word, crooked his finger, dialed her number, or called her name, she'd run back to him in a heartbeat. She would never, ever admit that as crazy as it may seem to some, there were times when she even longed for the duplex days, when love had made strange bedfellows, and when she and Bo had been neighbors.

Stacy's heartbeat quickened as she watched Darius look out into the congregation. His face showed no emotion as he looked at her, but his eyes twinkled at his son, who cooed in return. He looked toward the back of the church, and his smile widened. She covertly followed his eyes. Her own eyes widened and then narrowed as she took in the obvious groupies filling the balcony. Their ages varied, she guessed, but none looked legal. *Perhaps they're from some high school,* she thought.

She scanned various other faces as she rocked a fidgety son who was obviously not wowed by his father's playing. Every brother in the band was getting their fair share of attention, but she correctly deduced that most eyes were on her ex-husband. When she made one last visual sweep across the congregation, she met Bo's unreadable stare. He gave her a curt nod and then smiled pointedly at the man he now called husband—and legally so.

"I'll be back," Stacy said, shifting Darius into her other arm and reaching for her baby bag. "I'm going to take him to the nursery."

"You want me to?" Hope asked.

"No, I need the break," Stacy replied honestly. She needed a word from God even more, a message to soothe her troubled soul. But she knew that with her eyes on Darius, and with Bo's eyes on her, she wouldn't hear a thing.

11

All These Things

Pastor Derrick Montgomery took the podium, as aware of the hidden and not-so-hidden dramas as he was of the Spirit. He winked to Vivian and nodded at Darius to finish the song. Offering had been lifted, the choir had sung its last selection, and now it was time for the Word. Having watched the triangular interplay between Darius, Stacy, and Bo, he almost smiled at the message that had been laid upon his heart. God indeed "sat high and looked low," as Derrick used to hear the old people say. Translated, that meant God didn't miss anything; He saw and heard all. As Derrick began the scripture reading of his sermon, he hoped that all who needed to would heed the Word of the Lord.

"Seek ye first the kingdom of heaven and its righteousness," he said slowly, clearly, in a raspy voice considered sexy by some, not the least of whom was the adoring wife hanging on to his every word. "And all these *things* will be added unto you."

Derrick took a moment to look around the congregation, waiting, hoping the message would sink in. He knew from the way some females were ogling him that everybody would undoubtedly *not* get the message. Still, he finished the text and began the message entitled "All These Things."

An hour and a half later, he sat in the large corner office of the executive suites. He'd removed his jacket and loosened his tie and was slowly sipping a large mug of tea, a blend Vivian had personally concocted that was supposed to soothe his throat and revitalize his vocal cords. The taste was delicious, and his throat did feel better, so for the second time in less than eight hours his wife had made him feel good.

Vivian arched a brow as he continued to stare at her. "Tasty?" she asked.

"Delicious," he said softly, his eyes drinking her in. "And the tea is good too."

For a moment, Derrick and Vivian forgot all others in the room. She knew the message in those eyes; he wanted another taste.

"Where are my manners?" she said, breaking eye contact with her husband of eighteen years who could still make her tingle without a touch. She turned to Cy and Hope, who were also in the executive offices. "Would you two care for something to drink?"

Their answer was interrupted by a knock on the door, followed by Lionel's entry. "Greg needs to see you, Rev. And you've got quite a crowd in the conference room. The Musical Messengers and their posse and a few other celebs are waiting for you. The councilman is back, and he wants his wife to meet you. How do you want me to handle the flow?"

"Escort the Messengers to the private suite. I'll greet everyone else in the conference room. Oh, and if the councilman is still here, ask if he and his wife would like to join us for brunch at three."

Lionel opened the door to exit, and yet another couple from the inner circle entered.

"Hey, Pastor," Darius said. "You've got a crowd out there. Hey, Cy. What's up, Hope? You're looking good."

"Hello, Darius. Hey, Bo," Hope answered. "You were great today, as always. I didn't think you could do any better than 'Possible,' but your new song is stellar, for real."

The men greeted each other and shared light conversation. Vivian took that opportunity to speak to Hope.

"How are you doing, sistah?" she asked, sitting in the chair Cy had vacated.

"I'm okay," was Hope's reply.

Vivian looked into Hope's eyes, wishing she could erase the sadness she saw, the feeling that even an Yves Saint Laurent suit and Jimmy Choo pumps couldn't cover.

"Are we still on for tomorrow? I know you said four, but I'd like to move it up an hour if that works for you."

Hope nodded. "That's fine, unless you want to discuss whatever it is now."

"In all this chaos? No, tomorrow's fine. I've wanted to spend some sistah-girl time with you anyway."

"I'm okay," Hope repeated and added a smile. "It's just that . . ." The door opened yet again, and Greg walked inside.

"You're just the man I want to see," Greg said to Darius. "Why didn't you tell me your posse was coming to church?"

"Hey, it wasn't me," Darius said, raising his hands in mock defense. His comment immediately elicited others from the brothers surrounding him.

"The brother's coming up! Has a whole cheering section now!" one of them said.

"Just watch out." Cy punched Darius playfully. "Sixteen will get you twenty."

"Seriously," Derrick said to Darius. "It would probably be a good idea to let a more mature woman of God get involved with . . . who are they calling themselves, Greg?"

"Darius's Crew," Greg said, laughing.

"Yeah, well, we want to make sure your crew's main criterion is Christ," Derrick replied.

"I told him the same thing," Bo interjected. "I suggested Mother Moseley."

"Suggested me for what?" Mother Moseley was preceded into the office by a twelve-inch black feather bobbing from a canary-yellow hat with a mesh veil and felt-covered foam canary perched on the brim. It was the perfect complement to her canary-yellow suit and platform shoes.

"Howdy-do, everybody!" She walked over and gave Bo a kiss on the cheek. "Hello, Mrs. Crenshaw," she cooed. Clearly her personality was not the only thing colorful about her.

That this seventysomething, staunch Christian woman from the South had embraced Bo and Darius's relationship had endeared Faye Moseley to Bo forever. Her philosophy had been simple: "If that murdering David got into heaven, with his hundreds of wives and thousands of concubines, who am I to condemn you to hell?"

Her outward acceptance warmed some of KCCC's frigid fellowshipping saints, and little by little, Bo was accepted—for the most part. He worshipped the ground she walked on.

"Aw, get out, Mama Mo," he said. "And you better wear that yellow and give the sun some fierce competition."

"Flattery will get you everywhere, son." Mother Moseley beamed. "Now, suggested me for what?"

"We'll discuss it over dinner," Vivian said as she hugged the woman who was like a second mother to her. "And anyway I have someone else in mind to oversee the group." She winked at Hope before joining her husband on the other side of the office.

Hope shook her head. She wasn't in the mood for a bunch of fast teenage girls chasing a grown man. In fact, the only children she wanted to be bothered with at this point were her own.

Her vibrating cell phone interrupted her thoughts. She checked the ID—Stacy. She walked out of the office and into the hallway.

"Yes," she said, knowing the question before it was asked. "He's in here."

"Both of them?"

"Yes."

"Well, tell Darius I'm not giving the child to Tanya. He's the father, and he should be the one I deal with."

"You come tell him, Stacy." Hope wanted to throw the phone. Here was a woman who had a beautiful healthy son and a father who wanted to be a part of the child's life, and she was letting jealousy and pettiness overshadow the blessing.

There was a pause before Stacy answered. "Excuse me?"

"You heard me. *You* come deliver that message or, better yet, let me pass the phone to Sistah Viv to see if she wants to carry the news. I'm not going to get in the middle of your mess."

"Look," Stacy replied, ready to go off. "I'm asking you as a friend—"

"And I'm telling you as a friend. Give Aunt Tanya her nephew and then come over to brunch. The councilman and his wife have been invited. I'll make sure his handsome assistant and a couple other cuties get invited as well."

"Yeah, whatever."

"Whatever what?"

"Whatever, I'll be there, that's what." Hope and Stacy often bickered but could never stay mad for long. "I saw Tony Johnson when I was going to the nursery. Give him a personal invite."

Hope said she would and smiled as she ended the call. Mission accomplished. As Frieda always said, nothing could get you over one man faster than getting under another one. Especially a fine, fit, successful one like veteran pro football player T.J. the Tackler. And rumor had it the football field wasn't the only place he could make some moves.

12

Delicious Chocolate

They said the road to hell was paved with good intentions. Hope didn't know about that, but she sure knew the road to the Montgomerys' brunch resembled that heated path. Things started out beautifully. The spread was exceptional, as always: spicy red snapper alongside rib-eye steak, fresh green beans, new potatoes, rice pilaf, stuffed artichoke hearts, and Vivian's famous salad bar and dessert table adorned with nothing other than Mother Moseley's famous German chocolate cake.

The company and conversation were equally delicious. Tony Johnson indeed brought his fine self to the Montgomery Mansion, as the church members jokingly called their first family's large and elegant Beverly Hills home. Stacy was there as well, and Hope didn't miss that she'd gone home and changed outfits. No one would have guessed her boyish frame had ever born a child. The soft knit dress made the few curves she did have stand out, not to mention the larger breasts and booty the pregnancy of little Jr. had thankfully left behind postdelivery. Tony wasn't the only one who'd noticed. So had Councilman Jeffries's assistant. Granted, he wasn't pulling down the same amount of paper as his athletic competition, but he cut a mean portrait in his navy suit and ice-blue tie. He was charismatic, well-mannered, and obviously interested in Ms. Stacy Gray.

The feeling was mutual, and Tony's recognition of the competition stirred the interest pot. Hope couldn't have been happier as she watched the men's subtle posturing for Stacy's attention while Stacy genuinely enjoyed it. Either one of these men could make her all but forget about one Mr. Darius Crenshaw, Hope concluded. Maybe there could finally be a happily-ever-after to the soap-opera-style drama involving Stacy, Darius, and Bo.

Hope turned her attention to the devastatingly handsome Cy Taylor, who in his black Valentino suit with stark white silk shirt provided a touch of *GQ* class to the dining room. He was laughing with Mother Moseley, who was being her usual humorous self.

"So this little child loved Vacation Bible School and was running as fast as her legs could carry her to get there. She was *fervently* praying to the Lord, 'Please don't let me be late, please don't let me be late.' Girl got almost to the church when she tripped and fell. She got up, brushed herself off, and frowned at the sky. 'Lord, please don't let me be late,' she repeated again as she ran toward the church doors. 'But please don't push me either!'" Mother Moseley's eyes twinkled as she delivered the punch line, and as the others joined in, her laugh was the loudest.

"You're too much, Mother Moseley," Vivian said.

Before long Derrick joined in with a joke of his own, and soon multiple conversations sprang up around the table. But Stacy didn't hear any of them. Her focus was on Tony, who'd gently touched her arm to get her attention.

"Are you a member of Kingdom Citizens?" he asked.

"Yes. Where do you normally go to church?"

"I normally go to City of Refuge, Noel Jones's church. You familiar with it?"

"Of course," Stacy responded. "Everybody knows Noel Jones."

"Did you know his sister is Grace Jones?"

Stacy nodded as she finished her bite of perfectly baked fish. "And he loves his sister too!"

"That's right," Tony agreed. "Nobody better come up to him with a bad word to say about Grace, man—he'll set 'em straight."

"I think that's one of the reasons his ministry is so successful. There's room for everybody in his church."

"Your church seems like that too," Tony countered. "Just like that Darius dude—Darius Crenshaw. The fact that he came out and your pastor still lets him lead the choir?" Tony shook his head. "I don't know of too many churches that would do that."

Now why did he have to go mention the D-word? Stacy hadn't thought about Darius since Tony had sat down beside her. The moist morsel of fish now felt like sawdust in her mouth.

"Whoa, did I say something wrong?"

Stacy sipped her soda and collected herself. "No, not really. It's just that Darius is a sore spot with me. He's my son's father."

"Oh," Tony said, his eyes widening. "It's like that, huh?"

His reaction was so innocent, Stacy couldn't help but smile. "It was." She felt her good mood returning. "But that's in the past."

As she continued the conversation, intermittently between Tony and the councilman's assistant, Stacy started to believe those words were true.

And then the past rang the doorbell.

"Greetings, greetings," Darius said cheerfully as he rounded the corner. Seeing Stacy, he cast a hard look at Mother Moseley. Undaunted, she cast one right back. As though she needed more leverage, which she didn't, she rose to her full five-feet-nine inches, without heels, and placed her hand on a still strong, three-score-and-ten-year-old hip.

"Don't you go looking all haughty at me, boy. I didn't know she'd be here. And it shouldn't matter. We are *all* God's children, and we should *all* be able to get along!" She stared boldly at Darius for a full five seconds before turning the "I dare you to defy me" look on Stacy. She rolled up her fist. Guesses around the table on whether she was joking or serious was around fifty-fifty. "Now, is there gonna be a problem here?" she asked loudly. "Because if so . . . I'm getting ready to be the problem solver!"

Vivian saw Mother Moseley's cheeks coloring red. *Lord, let me calm this woman down before she has a stroke.* She placed a comforting hand on Mother Moseley's arm.

"No, Mother, there will be no problems. You're right. This is the Lord's day, and we're all family. In my home, everyone is welcome." She shot a subtly compassionate look to Stacy, who didn't meet her eyes.

Mother Moseley sat down and wiped her face with a napkin. She took a few deep breaths before she spoke. "Y'all done gone and raised my blood pressure. Pass me that Tabasco so my mouth can get as hot as my anger right now."

"You want some more iced tea, Mother?" Vivian poured, not waiting for an answer.

Mother Moseley took a drink but wasn't quite cooled down. "Acting like fools," she mumbled. "'Bout to make me curse up in here on this Sunday afternoon, and I ain't done that since Brother Jackson's brother's nephew's son wrecked his motorcycle in my rosebushes!"

"Didn't he break his leg in that accident?" Derrick asked.

"Yeah, and after I saw my crushed perennials, I almost broke the other one!"

That comment effectively calmed the brewing storm, and everyone tried to act civil. The Montgomerys' dining room table seated twelve, which kept the warring factions a good ten feet away from each other. Though not as free-flowing as before, conversation resumed. Her heart was no longer in it, but Stacy now flirted more openly with Tony, a change in behavior he neither missed nor appreciated. Tony turned and began talking business with Cy, even as the councilman's right-hand man charmed a sincere smile or two from the lips he'd love to kiss . . . Stacy's. But then Councilman Jeffries—whose cousin had been a famous singer in the seventies and knew firsthand how crazy the music industry could be—had to bring up just that fact with Darius.

"How do you resist the temptation?" Jeffries asked sincerely. "And remain a Godly man in a devilish world?"

That's when Stacy snorted. "He takes his bodyguard," she said in a matter-of-fact tone. "No one can get close to Darius with his 'protection' there."

Vivian nudged Stacy under the table. Hope kicked Stacy's foot. The councilman missed the look that passed between Derrick and Cy. His assistant didn't, partly because he already knew about Darius's marriage. Not surprisingly, he didn't point out this fact, and he didn't think anybody else at the table would either. He was wrong.

"Most of the people with access to me know I'm married," Darius said, his eyes fixed on the councilman but his mind on the thrashing he wanted to give Stacy.

"And that stops them from chasing you?" Councilman Jeffries exclaimed.

"No," Darius countered. "It stops me from being caught. Could you pass the rolls?"

"Oh, Lord, these rolls sure are good," Mother Moseley exclaimed. "I wonder who made them."

"You know you did," Vivian said, glad for the subject change. She prayed Stacy would take the hint. She didn't.

"Oh, he gets caught sometimes," Stacy said to the councilman, her voice dripping sweetness. "He doesn't always get away."

"And how would you know?" Councilman Jeffries asked, curious to learn more about the drama sizzling around him.

Stacy ignored jabs, nudges, and narrowed eyes and continued. "Darius is my son's father and my *ex*-husband."

"Well, since he's your *ex*," Bo said calmly. "I guess he gets away eventually."

"Yeah, well, you would do well to keep that in mind, you blabbering idiot."

"Huh! I got what you wish you coulda kept, you crazy butt of a baboon."

"Hey, hey, hey! We're not going to have that in here," Derrick said firmly.

"I'm sorry, Reverend," Bo said sincerely. "I'm sorry, Stacy. That was out of line."

All eyes turned to Stacy. She stood. "I'm sorry for bringing my drama to your dinner table, Pastor Derrick, Sistah Viv." She turned to Darius. "Where's my son?"

"With Tanya, getting his picture taken."

Before she could stop herself, the anger flared again. "Isn't that something you should do? Serving me with—"

"Stacy," Vivian said calmly. Her eyes said much more.

Stacy threw her napkin on the chair and reached for her purse. "This isn't over," she said to Darius. "I'm taking my son home after church tonight."

Darius's voice was as low and as calm as Vivian's. "You'll get him back on Tuesday, as we agreed."

Stacy stared at Darius a long moment. "We'll see." She curtly nodded to the Montgomerys and left.

Hope rose to follow her. "Wait a minute, Stacy."

Hope and Stacy's lowered voices were heard before the front door closed. Once again the room was quiet, much like the stillness in the air after a tornado has swept through.

"Are you okay?" Vivian asked Darius.

Darius sighed. "I'm fine."

"He *sho'* is," Bo piped in without missing a beat. "That's why we've got baby-mama drama."

"Now, you just behave," Mother Moseley said. "You're just as much to blame as Stacy; and you're not too big to get a whuppin'." Her voice was gruff, but her eyes twinkled.

And Vivian's narrowed. She wasn't altogether sure about Mother's innocence in inviting Darius. She had been in the office when Hope had mentioned that Stacy was coming, but half a dozen other people had been in there too, so maybe the church matron hadn't heard. But Vivian knew that one Sistah Faye Moseley could be a little messy at times. That twinkle suggested Mother may have secretly enjoyed the excitement, though she'd never admit it.

"Ah, Mother Moseley, I don't mean no harm." Bo rose, kissed her on the cheek, and strutted to the buffet. "Are we ready to cut this cake? I know you put your foot in it, Mother, and Lord knows I could use some oh-so-delicious chocolate right about now."

More than one person guessed it, and an absolutely certain Darius hid a smile. *That's why I love this nut,* he thought. Bo's chocolate reference wasn't about Mother Moseley's cake.

B

Cheering for God

Vivian stood at the floor-to-ceiling windows of Cy and Hope's high-rise penthouse and marveled at God's handiwork. It was a brilliant mid-November afternoon; the various shades of blue, from the sky to the ocean, were breathtaking. The white foam of the waves contrasted sharply with the light brown sand, forming a border for a body of water that went on forever.

"Here's your tea, Viv," Hope said as she wheeled in a tray. "I know you said you weren't hungry, but I brought out these freshly baked, homemade, white chocolate and pecan cookies, just in case."

"Well, Lord knows I can use me some chocolate right about now," Vivian said, mimicking Bo's bodacious line. The women laughed. "I couldn't believe he said that," Vivian continued. "That Bo Jenkins has some kind of nerve."

Hope poured tea from the pot into their cups. "I can. Nothing Bo does would surprise me."

"You can't help but like him though."

The women were silent as they prepared their tea—lemon and sweetener for Vivian, vanilla-flavored creamer for Hope.

Hope took a swallow of hers and set the cup on the coffee table. "Stacy's calmed down."

"I was going to ask if you'd spoken to her since brunch yesterday."

"I called her last night, just to check on things."

"Did she have Darius?"

"No, he's still with his father."

"Thank goodness," Vivian said. "It's especially important for a male child to bond with his dad." She bit into the cookie. "It can't be an easy situation," she added thoughtfully.

"That's an understatement. I can't imagine anything harder than having your husband choose his male lover over you."

Vivian nodded.

"Do you think it's a sin, Vivian? Homosexuality?"

Vivian sipped her tea and pondered the answer. "Honestly, Hope, I don't know what to believe. The bible is clear—at least from all the interpretations I've heard and from what I've studied—that yes, it is a sin. And while we all sin and come short of God's glory, people who live homosexual lifestyles don't turn away from that sin. Someone very close to our family was a homosexual," she continued. "And before meeting him, there was no doubt in my mind that people who lived this way were going to hell. But then I got to know . . ." Vivian hesitated, looked at Hope thoughtfully, and decided to be truthful. "But then I got to know Derrick's uncle, Charles Montgomery. That's when everything I thought I knew changed."

Hope didn't try to hide her surprise. "The man who died two years ago, the one Derrick still speaks of with so much adoration?"

"Oh, everybody adored Uncle Charlie," Vivian said, a warm smile spreading across her face. "He was the kindest, funniest, most compassionate and generous person I've ever met. He loved God fiercely and loved Derrick like a son. He exemplified the meaning of being a Christian . . . Christ-like. Derrick owes a big part of why he's in the ministry to the encouragement—emotionally and financially—his uncle gave him. I remember a brief conversation we had—a time when I asked him why he chose to be gay. I'll never forget the look he gave me. He said, 'Vivian, if you knew the hell my brothers go through, the pain, isolation, and guilt we suffer, that *I* suffered before I was sure God loved me just as I am, you'd know this is something no one would ever choose.' So my position is that of my husband's and Mother Moseley's. If it is a sin, I'll love the sinner and leave the decision of where he spends eternity to God Almighty." Vivian finished her tea and sat back on the sofa. "Now, the reason I'm here."

Hope groaned. "Those fast hussies panting after Darius?"

Vivian laughed. "Well, don't sound so enthusiastic or skeptical. I personally think you'd be perfect to work with Melody and this group. As I watched them yesterday, executing their choreographed clapping and moving to Darius's songs, I thought maybe somehow they could be incorporated into our youth ministry."

"I'm not so sure how much interest we'd get there," Hope said. "It seemed pretty clear those girls were there to cheer for Darius."

"Maybe," Vivian admitted. "But with a little training from the right teacher," she looked pointedly at Hope, "they just might end up cheering for God."

Vivian and Hope spent the next half hour tossing around ideas about how they could encourage these teenagers by expanding the outlet for their talent and energy and redefining the object of their affection. No one was more surprised than Hope at the enthusiasm that began to build as they continued talking.

"I've told you this before, but I never forgot the performance by your dance troupe when we attended Mount Zion Progressive's conference a couple years ago," Vivian said. "When we returned home, I toyed with trying to reproduce a similar group at Kingdom. With all the other responsibilities on our youth minister and director, I couldn't bear to give them yet another task. But you'd be perfect, Hope. Will you think about it?"

"I will, and I'll discuss it with Cy. Maybe this is just what I need, something else to focus on besides myself . . . and my problem."

"Oh, you've got a problem?" Vivian bellowed, this time mimicking Mother Moseley's gnarly tone. "'Cause I'm a problem solver!"

Hope laughed until her sides hurt. When Vivian left a short time later, after Vivian's fervent petition to God for Hope's peace and patience to wait on Him, not only her mouth but her heart also was smiling.

14

Show and Tell

The warm and fuzzy feelings from Hope's meeting with Vivian continued into the evening. Cy knew something had shifted as soon as he walked in the door. Soft jazz played, candles flickered, and the tantalizing smells of good home cooking wafted through three thousand square feet of silk walls, marble floors, and upscale everything.

"My baby's home," Hope sang from the kitchen.

Cy began walking in the direction of her voice. The sight of Hope rounding the corner stopped him dead in his tracks. His abrupt halt caused Hope to stop too.

She wore a white, dolman-sleeved, shear midriff with white silk boy shorts that showed off her 36-26-38 curves to perfection and contrasted sharply with her smooth, dark brown skin. The outfit left little to the imagination, revealing part of her butt cheeks and dark nipples that hardened under Cy's intense stare. Her shoulder-length jet-black hair was pulled back in a simple ponytail, further highlighting her deep cocoa, slanted eyes, prominent cheekbones, and full lips set in a heart-shaped face. She wore three-inch silver sandals that laced up to mid-thigh. That this woman could believe it possible for him ever to lose interest, or to find somebody new, Cy thought was beyond ludicrous. For him there was only one woman, and he was looking at her.

He stared at her a beat longer, then licked his lips. "Come here, my beautiful ebony queen."

Hope's heartbeat quickened as she closed the distance between them. Cy loved it when she dressed provocatively. His reaction was just as she'd hoped. "Thank you."

They kissed passionately, leisurely as Cy's hands sculpted the body on which his eyes had feasted. He placed his hands on her bottom and lifted her off the floor, molding her to his muscled frame, letting her feel the evidence of his desire. He broke the kiss, lowered her back down, and took her hand. His pupils darkened as he gazed at Hope through nearly closed eyelids. He licked his lips again. Hope became wet.

"Come . . . sit with me," he whispered. He took her hand and started for the sofa.

Hope knew that sitting was the last thing on Cy's mind. It was definitely the last thing on hers. But the plans she'd formed this afternoon could not be hurried. She hadn't been the best company lately and had come up with several creative ways to apologize.

"I need to check on dinner," she said even as Cy tweaked her nipple through the gauzy fabric. This simple touch rocked her core, and a shiver tore through her. "I . . . I . . . Do you want me to . . . Ooh, Cy, I can't think when you do that."

Cy had slipped his hand under the top and now gently outlined her nipple with his thumb. He looked at her as if she were the meal. "That's fine," he said, his voice low and sexy. He continued to touch her with expert strokes.

Hope closed her eyes as Cy's large hands slid over her body. He cupped her cheeks, massaging bare flesh. They kissed again, his tongue now joining the dance of his fingers. Hope hugged Cy's hard body, outlining his shoulders, squeezing his tight, round butt.

Finally she managed a coherent thought and reluctantly

pulled away. "I've got to check on dinner before it burns. Every-thing's ready for you to take a shower."

Cy shook his head. "No, I'll wait and take one with you."

A short time later, they sat shoulder to shoulder, dining on fricassee of lobster over homemade goat-cheese ravioli. The food was delicious, but neither noticed. All of their senses were focused on each other. Cy battled the desire to clear the dishes and ravage his wife on the dining room table. Hope wrestled with thoughts that needed to be shared with her husband be-fore they left the room. They hadn't talked Saturday night, and yesterday had been filled with church stuff. By the time she'd finished the hour-long conversation with her much improved father in Tulsa, it had been too late to get into it. But the Mil-licent matter had to be dealt with. Hope had to make peace before they made love.

Cy slid a gentle finger along Hope's cheek. "You're quiet."

"I know. It's because I want to clear the air between us." Hope turned and faced Cy more directly. "I want to talk about Millicent."

Cy nodded. He rose and placed his hand on Hope's chair. "Let's go sit on the balcony."

The sound of the waves lapping against the shore matched the cool breeze that greeted them as Cy opened the sliding door. "Let me get a cover for you," he said before ducking back inside.

Wrapped in one of Pat's homemade quilts and the security of Cy's love, Hope began. "I want to apologize for the other night. How I acted when you mentioned Millicent."

Cy's reply was swift. "Of course I forgive you." He knew there was more and waited for Hope to continue.

"I'm jealous of her," she said softly.

Cy wrapped his arms around Hope, kissed the top of her head. "Why, baby?"

Hope told Cy about seeing Millicent on Carla's show and how it had affected her. "I know it's crazy," she concluded. "I know you love me, and I trust God that we'll have a family. Honestly I'm surprised at myself for how the news affected me. I've never been much of a hater—I normally wish other sisters well. But my reaction made me admit how obsessed I've been with getting pregnant. And I know that stress can't be good for my chances at conception. Vivian was over today, talked to me, prayed with me. That helped a lot." She went on to tell Cy about the plans they'd discussed for Hope to mentor Melody and possibly revive her praise dance troupe at Kingdom Citizens.

"What do you think about that?" she asked.

"I think it's excellent; you're an exquisite dancer. That's when I lost my heart to you, when you danced before the Lord that night at King's conference." Cy closed his eyes and remembered. "There were eight of you in these white, flowing dresses. Your arms lifted in praise as you twirled around. But I can't tell you a thing about what the other ladies looked like—the only one I watched was you."

"And I was so mad when you called the next morning," Hope said. "I thought Millicent was your fiancée, and you were trying to get some out-of-town nooky right under her nose!"

They laughed and reminisced about their first unofficial date, when Cy had folded his tall frame into Hope's small MG, and they had toured the sites of Kansas City. Hope admitted that even after their wonderful time together, she'd doubted anything serious would come of their meeting. She admitted how perfectly suited she'd thought Millicent was for Cy: tall, lean, light-skinned, long-haired, the kind of flawless beauty Hope usually saw on the arm of successful Black men.

"I didn't dare believe someone like me could have someone like you," Hope said softly as she watched the moon's dancing reflection on the dark waters.

Cy placed a finger under Hope's chin, raised her face until her eyes met his. Hope could have drowned in the amount of love she saw there.

"I want to tell you something, and I don't want you to ever forget it. God sent me you. There's no one else for me. I knew it the moment I laid eyes on you. You'd haunted me in my dreams, woman. The minute, the very second, Hope, that I saw you . . . I knew."

"What do you mean, you dreamed of me?"

"Exactly that. It was a rather, um, explicit dream. I was making love to an exotic Nubian angel on the white sands of a tropical island. The dream was so real I woke up with a hard-on, my arms aching to hold you. Instead it was a pillow I clutched. When you walked into the church, with that gold shimmering suit that fit like a glove, the dream came back to me. And I knew I was looking at my future wife."

Tears shimmered in Hope's eyes as she looked at him. "For real, Cy?"

He brushed his lips across hers. "Cross my heart."

They kissed tenderly and spent a few moments in companionable silence. "Tell me more about the dream," Hope said finally, burrowing herself closer into Cy's embrace.

"Let's go inside," he suggested as he lifted her into his arms. "I can show you better than I can tell you."

15

Still in Love

Stacy looked at her watch as she chatted with Hope on the phone. *Where is Darius with my child?* "I'm sorry, Hope. What did you say?"

"I said you were right."

"About what?"

"About how I should talk to Cy about Millicent. My jealousy at her being a mother and everything."

"Did you?"

"Uh-huh."

"And?"

Hope resisted the urge to purr like a kitten. Her cat was still tingling from the lavish attention Cy had given it the previous night.

"Well, let's just say Millicent is no longer an issue, and Cy and I are all the way back on track."

"Oh, so he must have hit it really good last night, huh?"

Good doesn't begin to describe it. "We, um, enjoyed ourselves."

"Ooh, you make me sick. Over there getting it good and regular while the only penis I'm seeing these days is two inches long. I'm about to climb the walls."

"What about Tony? I saw y'all flirting at Pastor's on Sunday."

"Naw, girl. I think Darius messed that up."

"Darius messed it up? How so?"

"Okay, more like I did. Acting a fool when he showed up. I think Tony figured out I was flirting with him just to make Darius jealous. He hasn't called."

"Were you?"

"Not at first. Tony is fine; who wouldn't love to spend some time with that brothah? But after Darius and his 'wife' showed up, I did start overdoing it. Tony changed after that, started talking to Cy."

Hope paused. This was old ground she and Stacy were covering, and she didn't know if her two cents would be of any value. She plunged in anyway. "I'm doing so much better today because I listened to you, Stacy. Maybe it's time you take some of the advice that's been offered where Darius is concerned. Bo and Darius are together, professionally and personally. They love each other. Like it or not, that's how it is. It's also obvious that Darius loves his son, and so does Bo. And that little boy is crazy about his father. It seems the only one truly miserable in this situation is you."

"Well, what do you expect me to do?" Stacy's voice became agitated. "Hand my son to him on a silver platter? Let Darius grow up thinking it's okay to be a faggot?"

"That's wrong, Stacy."

"Oh, please, don't even start. This isn't some show where I'm trying to be politically correct; this is my life, my son's life!"

"Do you really think little Darius will become gay by simply hanging around his father? Do you truly believe that, Stacy?"

Silence.

"Well, do you?" Hope repeated. When Stacy didn't answer, Hope continued. "Let's talk about what's really going on here— the real reason why you're keeping Darius from his son. It's because even though you won't admit it, and after all that's happened, you're still in love with Darius Crenshaw. Isn't that what all this is really about?"

The doorbell rang. Stacy didn't have to look out the window to know who it was. "I gotta go," she said to Hope. "This asshole should have had my son here an hour ago!"

Stacy walked through the living room of the three-bedroom split-level Darius had purchased for her, flung open the door, and crossed her arms. "You're late."

Darius stood there, determined to be calm, with little Darius in one arm, and several shopping bags and a diaper bag in the other. "We were shopping; time got away from me."

Stacy reached for her son. "He's wet."

"Um, I don't think so. I just changed him." Darius took a deep, quiet breath. *Don't let her get under that gorgeous skin of yours, baby. That's what she wants.* Darius remembered Bo's parting words before Darius had dropped him off at the Starbucks down the street on their way over, an action done to avoid yet another ugly scene. He followed Stacy inside the house.

"They had a sale at Baby Gap," he continued pleasantly. "And then we stopped at another shop where they were rocking baby Sean Jean. Little D is set for the ladies now!"

Stacy had checked Darius's diaper, and indeed he was dry. She talked to her son and ignored his father.

Maybe this is best, Darius thought. He'd take the silent treatment over screaming any day. "Well, I guess I'll see you Sunday then. Will you be at the eleven o'clock or early morning service?"

"What difference does it make? Won't you be at both of them?"

"Stacy, why does this have to be hard? Why do we have to continue to bicker and fight, have all this drama? We were friends once, remember?"

"Oh, I've got a ton of memories, Darius. How you played me for a fool to further your career and your heterosexual persona, how you married me knowing that for you it was just a front, how you chose your lover over me. And you expect me to invite you in like we're friends? Ask you to sit and share a glass of wine?"

"Merlot, if you have it," Darius said, attempting humor.

Stacy glared.

"I'm not asking us to be best friends, Stacy. I just want us to be civil. Darius picks up on all this—"

"How do you know what my son picks up on?" Stacy screamed.

Little Darius started to cry and reached for his father.

"That's how I know," Darius said in a quiet voice. "Come here, little man." He stepped toward the couch.

"I can handle Darius," Stacy said, moving the child out of reach. "Just get out of my house."

She cooed and rocked Darius Jr. and then walked into the kitchen and got him a bottle. When she walked back into the living room, Darius's back was to her as he eyed a grouping of family pictures hanging on the wall. Most were of his son.

Stacy tried to maintain her anger and view him dispassionately. But somewhere between the perfectly shaped head; strong, broad shoulders; narrow waist; and butt she'd used to squeeze in the throes of passion, her ire faded. By the time she'd admired the strong, thick legs that stood firmly apart and the brand-new Nikes that covered Darius's size-twelve feet, she'd admitted to herself what she'd refused to acknowledge to Hope. She still loved this man.

"I'm coming to early morning service," she said, placing little Darius on the floor. He immediately half waddled, half crawled over to his father.

Darius picked him up, kissed and hugged him, and put him back down. "Okay, then, I'll make sure Bridgette is there to take care of him while I'm working."

Stacy nodded.

Bridgette was the Belizean nanny Darius had hired to help care for Darius Jr. Stacy had demanded the right to interview her and had begrudgingly given her approval and eventually her admiration to the woman who treated Darius Jr. as if he were her own child.

There was an awkward moment as Darius fought the urge to bring up the custody hearings. Better to continue letting his attorney handle it, as Bo had suggested. He knelt down and kissed his son again. Rising, he looked at Stacy. He noticed the vulnerability in her eyes, the flicker of desire before she tucked it away. He wanted to comfort her somehow, hug her, kiss her, make the hurt go away. He knew he couldn't. It would send the wrong message. But she looked so lonely standing there. And so cute in her pink ribbed tank top and low-rider jeans that exposed the outward navel he'd used to flick with his tongue. They continued to stand there.

"Look, Stacy—" Darius began.

"Do you want—" Stacy said at the same time.

Inside Darius's pocket, his Blackberry vibrated. *Bo.*

Darius glanced at his watch. "I have to go," he said quickly, covering the distance to the front door in three long strides. "I'll see you Sunday, okay? Take care, Stacy."

Stacy watched Darius stroll to his shiny black Navigator and step inside. She saw him punch his Bluetooth device before the car was fully backed down her driveway. Stacy would have bet money on who'd been calling. But it did her no good to think about the constant barrier between her and her man.

"No," Stacy said aloud, forcing a change in her thoughts. She said it so loudly Darius Jr. looked up from his toys. "Not you, baby," she said with a smile. She stood a while longer, watching her son pound his toy piano. *He's so much like his father. But his father is not here,* she thought. *And I need to stop hoping that one day he'll come back.*

16

Friends for Now

Later, after Stacy had fed, bathed, and put Darius to bed, she retrieved the card Tony had given her the previous Sunday. With just slight hesitation, she dialed his number.

"Hello?"

"Tony. Stacy."

Pause.

"From Sunday brunch at the Montgomerys'."

"Oh, what's up, Stacy?"

Stacy noted a lack of warmth in his tone, definitely not the flirty voice he'd used as they'd discreetly teased each other at the dining room table. "Is this a bad time?"

"No, I've got a minute."

Tony was not going to make this easy. Stacy understood and decided to cut to the chase. "I'm sorry about my actions on Sunday. My ex gets under my skin sometimes, and I lose my temper."

"Why do you think that is?"

What was this, Get Stacy to Face the Truth day? Was it time to put on Usher and sing "this is my confession"? First Hope, now Tony. Was she so obvious that everyone knew what, until now, she'd refused to admit?

"It's because at one time I had deep feelings for him. Had. Past tense."

"Past tense, huh."

"Yeah."

"Are those past feelings why you started flirting so openly all of a sudden after your boy showed up with his dude?"

"It was childish and stupid, and I shouldn't have done it. There's a lot of bad history there. But I'm ready to move on." Stacy hesitated, waited for Tony to speak. When he didn't, she continued. "I was hoping that maybe the move-on could be with you."

Tony cleared his throat. "Look, Stacy, I think you're cool and all, and you've definitely got it going on in the looks department, but truthfully? I don't think I'm the one for you right now. I went through a messy divorce a couple years ago, and I just got things on the right track with my first child's mother. I almost lost my mother last year, and now I'm sidelined with this knee injury. What I'm trying to say is for the first time in a long time, things are relatively calm in my life. I don't need or want any craziness in my life right now."

"I don't want that either."

"I believe you, but sometimes we're not totally in control of that situation. I think you've still got some unresolved feelings for your boy. So it's just not a good time for you and I right now."

What could she say? Tony was right. Stacy knew this, and even though his words weren't what she wanted to hear, she appreciated his honesty and told him so.

"One thing the past few years have taught me is that life is short, and, unlike football, it is not a game. You deserve the best, Stacy, and one of these days, when you're ready, it will come to you."

"Listen to you, sounding all intelligent. You know ball players have low IQs."

"Aw!" Tony bellowed good-naturedly, liking the change in tone. "You hit below the belt, girl."

Stacy laughed. Once they shifted away from the topic of romance, conversation became easy. They talked about church, family, Tony's NFL team—the San Diego Chargers; their interplay came easy for the woman who'd grown up with four athletic brothers.

"I'll give this to you, Tony Johnson: you make a woman feel good. So don't let me catch you in a dark alley somewhere; you just might get accosted."

"I can think of worse things," he responded with a smile in his voice.

"So, friends for now?" Stacy asked.

"Why not?" Tony asked as much to himself as to Stacy. "Friends for now."

17

Church Girl

Frieda crossed her legs and smoothed her A-line, turquoise Smitten dress over her curvy, five-foot-five frame. It was a present from Giorgio, and running her hands against the soft viscose and spandex fabric helped her not miss him as much.

"Where are we going?" she asked with chagrin.

Joe, a coworker and good friend, slid her a sideways glance. "Look, don't get all testy with me, Miss Thang. I can't help it that your man left you, *again*, for the bright lights and big city of New York."

"Giorgio's my favorite lickin' stick; I can't lie about that. But you know your girl—out of sight, out of mind."

Frieda adjusted the passenger mirror and reapplied her lipstick. She hardly noticed the shrubbery and hidden mansions as Joe navigated through the rich, exclusive neighborhood of Holmby Hills. Giorgio had left that morning, and while he'd reiterated his open invitation for her to join him in the Big Apple, winter was coming, and if Midwest-born-and-bred Frieda never traipsed through snow again, it would be too soon. But she missed him, and Jonathan giving her the heave-ho after finding out why she was MIA all week only added to her need for diversion.

"Who lives here?" she asked as Joe turned onto a dead-end street.

Joe chuckled. "You'll see."

"You get on my nerves. I don't know why I bother with you."

"I'm your rebound friend; I can set my watch to when Giorgio leaves town by the time you call me to hang out. You like to act as if you're footloose and fancy free, but I know better. Giorgio has that meow on lockdown. All he has to do is show up!"

Frieda uncrossed her legs to give said feline, sans panties, access to air. "Why are you telling me what I already know? Hell, yeah, it's locked down for the G-man. I ain't ashamed of where my affections lie. If he called right now I'd tell you to stop, put me out on the side of the road, and I'd hoof it back to Baldwin Hills in these four-inch Guccis. You feel me?"

Joe laughed. "I feel you, Frieda. At least you don't bullshit. That's why we're friends."

A few seconds later, Joe pulled up to an imposing, gold-plated, wrought-iron fence and announced his name to security. After checking the guest list, the guard buzzed them in, and Joe swung his BMW into an empty parking space.

"Damn," Frieda said, eyeing the huge home spread out before her. "You sure know how to make a sistah forget to be sad." She eyed Joe for a moment, ready to get emotional, and then quipped to stay the tears, "I think I'll keep your Pillsbury Doughboy ass around!"

Joe simply winked at her, recognizing her sarcastic affection. "I thought so."

Inside the mansion was an all-out party. The music pulsated, liquor flowed, and everyone in attendance belonged to the Beautiful People Club. Frieda wasn't intimidated; she knew she looked good. Besides the designer clothing, her beautician had styled her short hair to within an inch of its life. She was bathed in Escada and dripping in Swarovski crystals she'd stack against diamonds any day. Fuck the bitch who thought sporting yellow sapphire made her special. Did she have a mouth and a pussy that gripped like a vacuum? Frieda didn't think so, and that's what kept her at the top of the player game.

She lifted a glass of bubbly off the serving tray, and after she and Joe coordinated a mutual meeting spot for later, began surveying the layout of the land. Right away she saw some people she knew: rappers, actors, ballers, including that prime rib Tony Johnson. By the time she finished her second glass, she'd made her way to the second floor of a home that could have doubled as a mini mall and found the usual goings-on: sex, drugs, and enough silicone to keep the *Titanic* from sinking. Frieda loved the excitement of the Hollywood lifestyle, but after living it almost nonstop for a week with Giorgio by her side, it felt empty without him. She walked through a room where a small group was watching videos and found solitude on a small balcony. Relishing the night air on her skin, she tossed her head back and inhaled deeply.

"Hold that pose, lovely. That's a pretty picture."

Frieda slowly brought her head down and opened her eyes. She turned and saw a man with a body that could have been featured in a workout ad. A baseball cap covered his nearly bald head, designer jeans rode low on his hips, and an unbuttoned shirt revealed abs toned to perfection. Once Frieda's neck-and-down perusal was finished, she raised her head to catch his eyes.

"Damn, baby, did you like the journey?"

Frieda was nonplussed. "You know I did. That's why you spend so much time in the gym, for sistahs like me to dig it. Why you trying to come off all fake cool and shit?"

The machismo brother was taken aback but recovered quickly. "That's what I like, a woman with balls."

Frieda invaded his personal space and boldly put her hand on his thigh, precariously close to his manhood. "And this is what I like."

Her prey's pupils dilated. "Do you know who I am?"

"Of course I know who you are, Shabach. And I was wondering what a good gospel boy like you was doing in a bad-boys place like this." In her wanderings, Frieda had found out that the home belonged to Murder He Wrote, the preeminent A-list thug of hip-hop.

"I can be in it and not of it, can't I?" he asked. He made no move to remove her hand.

Frieda smiled seductively. "That's a question for you to answer."

She removed her hand abruptly and waltzed away. Shabach stared after her for a long, long time.

Frieda maneuvered her way back downstairs and joined the throng of beautiful people gathered around Murder's Olympic-sized pool. Four blue-and-white-striped cabanas anchored each corner. In one, a near naked stripper lap danced a well-known billionaire's son; in another, drugs such as coke and ecstasy covered the table. The third one housed a Middle Eastern business-man being fanned by two six-foot, blond-haired, blue-eyed Amazon women. And in the fourth, Tony Johnson held court. That's where Frieda stopped.

"Ah, man, there's no way Williams is gonna rush for one hundred yards a game," Tony said. He paused to puff on a premium-packed Tatuaje Havana cigar. "He didn't do that at Grambling, and he sure as hell isn't going to do it for the Jets. They're trying to prop up a weak offense, but that's not going to happen. Watch what I tell you. They'll be lucky if they make the playoffs, let alone the Super Bowl."

"What about the changes at quarterback?" a burly, bald-headed brother asked.

"Man, Favre can't save the world. If your line is breaking

down every time the ball is snapped, what's the quarterback gonna do besides get sacked?"

A spattering of laughter broke out at this comment, and the crowd shifted. That's when Tony noticed Frieda.

"Hey, beautiful, who are you?"

Frieda dropped her head shyly. *There's all kinds of money in the house tonight,* she thought. *If I play my cards right, I might actually come up from this evening. At least get a couple Gs, a trip to Europe or something.* She'd thought this when she'd recognized Shabach. Tony was more her physical taste, but he was injured. Paper disappeared quickly when an athlete stopped playing and the endorsements dried up. Shabach wasn't as big a name as Darius Crenshaw, but he had hella game. Plus there was a rumor Shabach was breaking into the acting biz. In the end he might be the wisest of choices. But a woman couldn't be too hasty.

Tony pushed back his chair and stood. "Show's over, gentlemen," he said with authority. The crowd dissipated as if the pope had spoken. Frieda liked that.

"Now, what can I get for the lady?"

Frieda sat down, exposing smooth, waxed skin as she leaned back and crossed her legs. "Maybe you."

From the other side of the pool, Shabach discreetly observed the goings-on, especially what was happening in cabana number four. Women threw themselves at him all the time; it had been a while since one had left him wanting and he'd felt the thrill of the chase. He turned to one of the guys he'd come with. "Hey, any of y'all know that girl over there?"

Several pairs of eyes turned to check out Frieda. A short, stocky man with two-karat diamonds in each ear nodded slowly. "Ain't that the girl who hangs with that punk Darius's baby's mama?"

Hearing the name of his number-one archrival put Shabach instantly on alert. "Oh, yeah?"

Shorty shrugged. "I think so. I think I saw her at church one time with what's-her-name—Stacy—and the fine chick who married the millionaire."

"Was it Montgomery's church, Kingdom Citizens?"

"I think so, man. Either there or Logos Word. But don't quote me, brothah, it's been a minute. But I think that's where I saw her; you don't forget that vision quickly."

Shabach rubbed his day-old stubble thoughtfully. The vision of loveliness who'd handled him like she'd known what she was doing had just gotten more intriguing. A courtesan-acting female who was also a church girl? To say the least, Shabach was interested. Very much so.

Shortly after midnight, Frieda met Joe at their preestablished rendezvous point. "Hey, man, you ready to bounce?" she asked.

"Why? It's not even late yet."

"I know, but I haven't gotten much sleep lately, and I have to be at work early tomorrow."

"All right, *mamí,* let's blow this joint."

Frieda was almost to the front door when she felt a strong hand on her shoulder. She stopped and turned around, her face inches below that of heavy-lidded Shabach. She watched his tongue as he licked his lips and then looked down at the card he held out to her.

"Call me. I want to get with you."

Frieda cocked her head. "I might," she said with a smile and then walked out the door.

18

Follow the Leader

Hope turned into the church lot and parked her Lexus convertible next to Vivian's 700 Series BMW. She turned off the engine but remained in the car, enjoying the groove of Darius's latest hit, "Looks Like Reign":

> *"How does it look to be a kingdom citizen?*
> *How does it look to bear His royal name?*
> *I think it looks like we are more than conquerors,*
> *It looks like blessings falling, in fact it looks like reign.*
> *Reign over troubles, over doubts and fears, reign, reign . . ."*

This is the one, Hope thought as she reached for her briefcase and opened the door. *This will be the song the church troupe dances to.*

Hope had called Vivian the Wednesday following their Monday meeting and agreed to work with Melody and members from the fan group, Darius's Crew. By Thursday, Vivian had orchestrated a conference call with herself, Hope, Darius, and Bo to develop a basic outline for aligning the group with KCCC's youth department. Everyone agreed the fan club wouldn't fall directly under the KCCC ministry, but rather that Hope would serve as a liaison between the two, overtly providing creative direction for the group's expansion and covertly monitoring the girl's activities. Darius was KCCC family, and if there was a way the church could help protect him from overzealous female teens, they were ready to do so.

Hope greeted the security guard as she walked up the sidewalk to the executive offices. "Hi, Greg."

"Hello, Mrs. Taylor. You're looking nice today."

"You are too funny. How many times do I have to tell you to call me Hope?"

"No, you're too fine for me to get familiar. I'd better stick to Mrs. Taylor." Greg winked. "That way I stay reminded."

"Well, in that case, I am *definitely* Mrs. Taylor to you." Her phone rang as she stepped inside. "Hey, Frieda, what's up? I'm just getting ready to go into a meeting."

"Oh, that's why you're not available for lunch today? And you were the one squawking the loudest when I canceled on y'all to be with Giorgio."

"Yeah, but this is different. I'm not canceling because of a man; this is God's business." She explained briefly about Vivian's request for her to teach praise dancing. "I'll call you later."

"You do that because I want to invite you to church tomorrow."

Frieda's words had the desired effect. Hope stopped dead in her tracks. "Oh, wait a minute, something must be wrong with my cell phone. I know I didn't just hear that *you* were going to invite *me* to church?"

"Yes, I'm coming to Kingdom Citizens tomorrow."

"And it's not a holiday? I better say my prayers real good tonight because I know Jesus is coming."

"And if he isn't there, Shabach will be. We went out last night."

"Shabach? I didn't even know you knew him. Look, I can't talk now. I'll call you when I get out." She entered the meeting room, turning off her cell as she did so. "Hello, everybody."

Hope joined Vivian, the youth director, the youth minister, Melody Anderson, and Melody's best friend, Natasha, who was also a member of Darius's Crew. After exchanging cordialities and saying a prayer, Vivian began the meeting.

"I want to start by saying I have spoken to Darius, and while we're not sure he'll be able to join us today, he's in full support of this meeting and the plans Hope and I would like to share with you."

"Darius is going to be here?" Melody asked.

"He *may* be here," Vivian emphasized. "And he is very excited about what we're here to propose."

Melody and Natasha exchanged excited glances.

"First of all, Melody, I'd like to commend you on the excellent job you've done organizing such a large group of young people to support one of our own. And so quickly! Darius tells me you just started this club, what, about a month ago?"

"Three weeks," Melody corrected proudly.

"The club has almost five hundred members on MySpace," Natasha offered.

"Seven hundred and fifty," Melody corrected once again after shooting Natasha an annoyed look. "We added another couple hundred this week."

Vivian continued, telling the group about the dance troupe Hope had coordinated before she relocated to Los Angeles as a member of one of Kansas City's premier churches, Mount Zion Progressive. Vivian shared the vision of using resources from the fan club—those who were members of KCCC—to be the core group of the dance troupe, while the primary dancers would perform with the church's main choir, the Kingdom Citizens Chorale.

"Mrs. Taylor," Vivian concluded, "is a talented performer with a heart for God. She has the experience and the passion to help lead this group to the level of greatness God intended."

Melody sat up in her seat. "Wait a minute! *I'm* the leader of this group."

Vivian nodded. "I understand. But when your group performs under the umbrella of the ministry, Hope will be in charge. Do you have a problem with that?"

Melody looked at the youth pastor but didn't respond.

"What do you think, Natasha?" Hope asked.

"Hey, I think it's cool," Natasha said. She ignored the evil eye Melody gave her and continued. "You got it going on, married to a millionaire and stuff. So you must be doing something right. Maybe there's a thing or two we can learn from you." Natasha shot a cautious eye toward her best friend. "I mean, Melody is the leader and stuff, but . . . you can help us, that's all I'm saying."

"And that's all we're saying, Melody," Vivian said. "It's clear you're president of the fan club. Mrs. Taylor will be in charge of incorporating some of you into our worship arts ministry. What do you think about that?"

"I'll tell you what I think about it." Darius had opened the door unnoticed and now strolled over to the conference table to sit down. "I think it's a fabulous idea. Hello, Pastor, Hope, ladies," he said, winking at the girls.

Melody showed all thirty-two pearly whites in appreciation, her sulky mood quickly forgotten with Darius's entrance. "Yeah, Darius. I think it will be cool for Hope—uh, Mrs. Taylor—to lead our dance troupe; that's what I was just thinking when you walked in."

Darius simply smiled.

Hope took over. "So now that that's settled, ladies, here's the deal. I want to start right away with eight dancers and choreograph a routine to 'Looks Like Reign.'"

Natasha was obviously excited, and while Melody tried to hide it, her eyes held a certain sparkle as well.

"Sister Vivian wants us ready to perform at the New Year's

celebration." Hope turned to Melody. "I'd like you to help me during the auditions for the eight initial dancers. Do you have some girls in mind?"

Melody slid a sly look at Darius before answering. "Well, Natasha and I," she began. "And then there's Tanishia and Shaira, Valencia, Micah . . ."

19

Sixteen Will Get You Twenty

Within fifteen minutes, the first meeting of the newly minted dance group, the Kingdom Crew, had adjourned. As soon as the youth minister's prayer ended in an enthusiastic "amen," Melody was by Darius's side.

"Hey, D," she said, a broad grin adorning her face. "Did you see us last Sunday?"

"I did, and you all looked great," he said.

Melody moved closer to him, her arm lightly brushing his. In her nervousness, she stated the obvious. "We're gonna be your dancers now."

"Don't you have to audition first?"

"Not me," Melody said with confidence. "I'm the leader. Plus, I'm the one who did all this for you. We've got almost a thousand members on your Web site already."

Darius looked down at a woman-child whose feelings were written all over her face. There was absolutely no attraction, so the words were unnecessary. But still, Cy's recent admonition floated up in his mind: *sixteen will get you twenty.*

He reached around and hugged her as an uncle would a niece. "Bo and I appreciate everything you're doing," he said. "Sometime in the next couple weeks, you need to meet with him. He has some ideas for giveaways that will give the fans in the club something to look forward to. Oh, and I almost forgot, this is for you."

Darius reached into his pocket and pulled out a necklace. Groupings of multicolored crystals formed the letters *D* and *C*, held on a silver chain. "These are going to be marketed with the next album," he explained to an enthralled Melody. "Because of all your hard work with the fan club, you get one of the first."

"Oh, thank you, Darius," Melody said, reaching up to hug him fiercely. She hugged him tighter still, reveling in the moment she'd dreamed of each night—being in his arms.

Darius became aware of young, tender breasts pressed against his hard chest, and the faint wisp of M by Mariah Carey mixing with his Bvlgari pour Homme Soir.

"I have necklaces for all of you," he said as he disengaged from Melody and hugged Natasha. Belatedly he realized how Melody had misinterpreted his innocent gift.

He looked at his watch and began walking toward the executive offices. "All right, girls, you be good."

He knocked and stepped into Derrick's office. He'd barely sat down before Derrick spoke. "Shabach is performing Sunday—here at Kingdom."

Darius looked at Derrick. His frown said it all.

"Why have him here? In my church?"

"This is God's house," Derrick countered. "And I'm not going to let what's going on in the streets affect what's happening in here. His staff called me two weeks ago and specifically asked if Shabach could minister this coming Sunday. He hasn't been here in two years, and that's long enough for whatever is going on between you to be over."

"It'll never be over," Darius grumbled.

"It can be over as soon as you decide it is," Derrick countered. "It can be over on Sunday when you step up, be the man I know you are, and show Christ's love. Will you try to do that?"

Darius nodded and left the room. He needed Bo . . . and a drink.

20

Chocolate Twinkies

The next day, the after-church KCCC crowd in the executive suites was the usual controlled chaos, made even more frenzied by Shabach's presence and everyone vying for a chance to say hello. Shabach was comfortable holding court. Frieda, who'd been standing by him initially, walked over to the other side of the room where Stacy, Hope, Vivian, and other guests conversed in a circle.

Hope turned and hugged her cousin. "I called you back."

"I know. It was late when I got your message."

Hope looked from Frieda to Shabach and back again. Clearly, getting her cousin in the church building was only the beginning to getting her saved. "Well, I'm glad to see you in church."

"Did you enjoy the message?"

Frieda leaned in even closer. "More like I enjoyed the messenger," she whispered. "Sistah Vivian better hold on to that chocolate Twinkie."

Before Hope could respond, the door opened, and Darius and Bo walked in. Darius walked directly up to Shabach and held up a fist to give him some dap. Shabach hesitated, looked at Derrick, and held up his fist. They tapped lightly.

"You were the heat in there," Darius said sincerely. "Were those LA-Gritty's beats on 'Sanctified'?"

Shabach nodded.

"Thought so. Those were tight."

"Yeah, Grit added a little sumpin'-sumpin' to the flavor, for sho."

Seeing there wasn't going to be WrestleMania in the place of worship, the room exhaled, and conversation around the duo resumed.

Darius remembered what his pastor had said about being the bigger man. "Listen, man, I know we've had our squabbles and everything, but your nabbing the Stellar and me getting a VH1 nod . . . Both our careers on the rise and whatnot, I figured maybe now is the time to squash our decade-long fight. You down with that?"

"I ain't down with nothin' but making sure I get mine. That's the only thing I'm focusing on . . . ever!"

"I hear that, dude, but I'm just saying as for my part in the madness, I'm making our peace part of my New Year's resolution. I'm going to let bygones be bygones. That's where my head is at . . . just so you know."

"Okay, man, yeah, we cool." Shabach signaled Frieda, and she walked over to join them.

"You know Frieda?" he asked Darius.

"Yeah, I know her. What's up, Frieda?"

Stacy took her son from Mother Moseley and joined Frieda with Darius and Shabach. Meanwhile, Melody and Natasha finagled their way into the room on the coattails of Melody's parents, the Andersons. Melody tried to get some one-on-one with Darius but as soon as her mother saw Darius and Bo, she made a face and motioned Melody to follow them back out of the office. It was just as well. Bo was on Darius tighter than a fat woman's girdle, but Melody would be as patient as she needed to be. It was rare, but she did agree with one thing her mother often said: Good things come to those who wait.

21

No Ill Will

Cy finished knotting his tie as Hope came up behind him. "What did I do to deserve you?" she asked, running her hands down the length of his fine, wool-covered thighs.

"I don't know," Cy answered as he turned around and cupped her butt. "But if you don't stop all that rubbing, you're going to get something else you deserve." He kissed the top of her head and left his dressing room.

"Do you want breakfast?" Hope asked, following him as he walked through their master suite and into his office.

"No, baby, I'm running late already. My meeting is at eleven, and you know how unpredictable the 405 is."

Hope eyed the clock on the wall. "It's not even nine o'clock."

Cy placed a final folder in his briefcase and snapped it shut. "My meeting is in San Diego."

Hope's heart skipped a beat. "With who?"

Cy hesitated just a fraction of a second before he answered. "Jack Kirtz."

Hope tried and failed to keep her voice light and nonchalant. "Why are you meeting with him?"

"Remember the home we rented last year, the oceanfront property in La Jolla? Jack owns land in that area, the same area

I've been trying without success to get a piece of. Word has it he's ready to sell." He left out the details of how he'd gotten this information.

Hope wondered if Millicent had had anything to do with this knowledge. She tried to remember that it no longer mattered, that there was no ill will or hard feelings, no jealousy or anger where Millicent was concerned. So why was her heart beating faster? And why, out of all the land in California and all the Realtors in the world, did the property Cy want belong to Millicent's husband?

Cy saw her discomfort. He stopped, put down his briefcase, and walked over to her. "If you have a problem with me doing business with him, just say the word, and it's over," he said softly.

"No, it's okay," Hope lied. But what else could she say? That he couldn't potentially make millions of dollars with Jack because of her insecurities? She took a deep breath, reached up, and kissed her husband. "It's okay, Cy," she said, with more conviction this time. "I hope the meeting goes well."

A few minutes later, Hope stood on the balcony with a cup of tea, watching choppy waves that resembled her emotions. She recalled the conversation when Stacy had told her to "bless that woman and her baby and then focus on Cy, and creating a family of your own."

Hope realized that's exactly what she needed to do. "Bless Millicent, God," she said to the ocean. "Bless her child and her husband and bless the business deal between Cy and Jack."

The phone rang, and Hope answered it. "It's about time you called," she said when she saw it was her cousin. "You've got some Monday morning 'splainin' to do."

"Look, I haven't let him hit it yet," Frieda began.

"Well, thank God for small miracles," Hope responded.

"But I let him, you know, dibble-dabble a bit, take a dive at the Y."

"That sounds like some hittin' going on to me," Hope said in response to Frieda's reference to oral sex. "How'd you meet him anyway?"

"That party I went to with Joe on Wednesday, after Giorgio left."

"Frieda, what are you going to do with all these men?"

"What do you mean 'all these'? There are only two!"

"Uh, are we forgetting Jonathan?"

"I'm sure trying to. We broke up. He got mad because I was with Giorgio."

"And you're surprised?"

"It's not like we were exclusive. Men get on my nerves. It's all right for them to play the field, but when a woman does it, they can't stand it. He wasn't that good anyway. Had a little dick."

"Girl, shut up."

"It's the truth," Frieda said, laughing. "You know I can't do nothing with a number-two pencil! I mean, really, when you have to ask if it's in yet . . ."

Hope's phone beeped. She looked at the caller ID. "Hold on, it's Stacy." She clicked over. "What's up, Stacy? I've got Frieda on the other line."

"Darius is what's up," Stacy said. "I think he wants to get back with me."

"Hang up," Hope said, not trying to hide the chagrin in her voice. "So I can do a three-way."

"Look, hussies, unlike y'all ladies of leisure, I'm at work," Frieda said when they were all on the phone. "So make it snappy."

"Say it, Stacy," Hope prompted. "What you just told me on the phone."

Stacy did, recounting the evening a week ago when Darius had dropped off his son and the vibes had been floating in the air before he'd gotten a phone call. She then told of a conversation with sexual undertones they'd had the previous night.

"I think he was getting ready to ask me to, you know—for us to get together."

"And?"

"And I want to be with him. I haven't had any in forever, and he was there last week looking fine and smelling good. It's not like he hasn't had it already. Hell, we have a child together!"

"But you know you can't be with him without feelings getting involved," Hope said.

"That's real talk," Frieda concurred. "And after all the fighting y'all have been doing over little Darius, I can't even believe I'm hearing this come out of your mouth!"

"I know," Stacy said. "But it felt different this time."

"Uh, yes, Mr. Langley, I'll make sure he gets the message. You're welcome. It's no problem. Thanks for calling."

Hope and Stacy heard a click in their ear and knew the deal; Frieda's boss had entered her vicinity, and she had hung up.

"Stacy, why do you keep chasing that married man? Darius is not going to leave Bo!"

"How do you know what Darius is going to do? You weren't at my house the other night."

"Look, I'm just trying to keep you from getting hurt again. But if you like it, I love it. Far be it from me to try and help a friend."

Both women were silent a moment. Stacy knew Hope was right, and Hope knew Stacy had a right to her feelings.

Hope sighed heavily. "Life is so crazy."

"I know, but I'll survive."

"Yeah? Well, I don't know if I will."

"Why?"

"Cy is on his way to meet a potential business partner—Millicent's husband." She told Stacy about Cy's interest in investing in La Jolla real estate—land that just happened to be owned by one Jack Kirtz.

"Okay, that *is* crazy. I can't believe he'd do that, Hope,

knowing how you feel about her." Stacy paused. "He does know how you feel, right?"

"Yes and no. I told him about my jealousy issues."

"And?"

"And he said he wouldn't do business with him if it bothered me."

"Then I don't get it? Why is he still meeting with him?"

"I told him to, Stacy. How can I let this jealousy nonsense get in the way of his business? I'm being ridiculous, and I'm determined to get over it."

"I'm sorry, Hope. Life is messed up sometimes, isn't it?"

"You know what they say: it's a small world."

"What are you going to do?"

"Oh, nothing too serious. Just invite them over for a nice, cozy dinner and then put some strychnine in her food."

"You know I've got thugs in my family—they could get you some!"

Hope laughed. "Thank you, sistah. It's good to know you've got my back."

22

Forgiving Ain't Forgetting

"Thanks, Millicent. Lunch was delicious." Cy wiped his mouth and placed his napkin on the table.

"Anytime, Cy," Millicent answered, shifting Jackson from one hip to the other.

Jack stood, walked over, and placed a kiss on his child's forehead and his wife's lips. "I agree, honey. You are amazing, as always."

Millicent's eyes twinkled as she absorbed Jack's praise. She leaned in for another kiss, and Jack obliged. Cy watched, both amused and amazed at the transformed woman who stood before him.

"I'm headed over to the church after this," Jack informed Millicent. "Will you be able to live without me for a few hours?"

"I'll try. Oh, and remember: Sarah's plane gets in at two. She's getting a ride with a friend from LA and should be here by seven."

Jack nodded. "I'll be back by then."

Moments later, Jack and Cy were buckled into Jack's black Cadillac, headed toward the other end of his property on La Jolla's shoreline. During lunch, the conversation had centered around business. Jack now steered it toward more personal matters.

"You know, Cy Taylor, in a somewhat indirect manner, I have you to thank for my present happiness."

Cy shifted in his seat and looked at Jack. "How's that?"

"If it weren't for what happened between you and Millicent, I may have never met her."

Cy turned back to face the road. "Is that so." He didn't know what or how much of their history Millicent had shared, and decided to tread lightly.

Jack laughed. "Oh, you can relax, man. She told me everything. After the infamous run-in between the four of us in Mexico, she and I had a good ol' heart-to-heart. She didn't want anything to do with church, much less a pastor," he continued. "But I'm pretty irresistible when I put my mind to it, and pretty determined when I see something I want. I was willing to wait a lifetime for that woman."

"It seems fortunate for both of you that you didn't have to. I've never seen Millicent happier." Suddenly, a thought came to Cy. "I guess you wouldn't be doing business with me if you had any reservations . . . about Millicent and my shared past and her old feelings about me."

"If I thought there was any chance that Millicent was still in love with you, we wouldn't be doing business. And if I didn't want to do business with you, you wouldn't be in my car."

They rode along in silence for a while before Jack spoke again. "The fact is, Millicent has forgiven herself for what happened, but I think she still feels bad about it, wishes there was some way she could make up for the trouble she caused you and your wife. Plus, she respects you as a person and as a businessman, and after doing my homework, I know that her respect is well warranted. So from a strictly business point of view, I'd be crazy not to want to partner up with someone of your caliber, and character. On a personal note, I think it would make my wife happy to know she was able to help you and your wife. She knows how scarce the real estate is in this area, and I know how hard it is to find good men with whom to do business. I think our potential partnership is a win–win for everyone. What about Hope? Is she okay with us working together?"

"Yes, she's given the partnership her blessing." Even as he said this, Cy remembered her apprehensive look when he mentioned coming to San Diego. If what he had in mind was going to work, he had to be absolutely certain Hope's resentment toward Millicent was over.

Cy and Jack's conversation returned to real estate and ministry. A few miles later, after traveling along the pristine, unobstructed ocean view, Jack turned into a partially obscured driveway. He punched in a code, and the heavy, steel gate slowly swung open.

The pathway was lined with lush greenery, creating a canopy over the cobble-covered roadway. The atmosphere was at once tranquil and serene, giving one the feeling of being enfolded in beauty.

"These trees are almost a hundred years old," Jack explained. "My great-grandfather planted them not long after he arrived in California from England and fell in love with the place."

"This is your family's property?"

Jack nodded.

"And you're actually going to sell it?"

"Just a couple dozen acres," Jack answered. "We'll still have over a hundred more to pass down to our children. The Word admonishes us to be charitable with our bounty. You're a good brother in the Lord, and it's a pleasure to share some of my blessings with you."

"Charitable, huh? So that means I'll get this land at well below market value."

Jack smiled. "The Word also says, 'Wisdom is a shelter as money is a shelter, but the advantage of knowledge is this: that wisdom preserves the life of its possessor.'"

Cy laughed. "So you intend to share possessions, but keep possessing—is that it?"

Jack nodded. "You got it."

Later that evening, Jack sighed contentedly as he wrapped his arms around Millicent. They had made love—slowly, sweetly—and were now resting in the afterglow.

After a few moments of companionable silence, Jack spoke. "That Cy Taylor is quite the businessman."

"Umm," Millicent replied. "I take it he liked the plot of land you showed him?"

"Surely you jest."

"Of course I do. Anyone would be crazy not to purchase any part of this property they could get their hands on." Millicent leaned over and kissed Jack's cheek. "Thank you, honey."

"For what?"

"For everything. I know you're doing this largely for me. To help me right a wrong. I appreciate it . . . and you."

"I'd sell my entire inheritance to make you happy. I just hope . . . well, never mind."

"No, darling, what were you going to say?"

"I just hope his wife is really okay with the idea."

"Of his buying property? Why wouldn't she be?"

"Cy is buying this land for personal reasons. He thinks it's a perfect place to build his and Hope's dream home."

"Oh, Lord," Millicent said, immediately wondering if Hope was aware of Cy's plans, and what she'd have to say about the four of them becoming neighbors.

23

Dreams

"Baby, you're late," Hope said, greeting Cy with a kiss as he entered their home. "How are you feeling? I bet you're starved."

Cy took a moment to enjoy Hope's soft curves. "I'm better now," he answered. "Plus, I had a big lunch."

"Ooh, don't tell me you ate at Roppongi's." Hope's mouth watered at the thought of delicacies from their favorite sushi bar.

Cy walked around her and headed for the bedroom. "No, I ate at Jack's. They've got a beautiful home, complete with a top-of-the-line, forty-nine-foot sailboat docked about fifty feet from their front door."

Hope was glad Cy's back was to her. That way he couldn't have seen her initial pissed-off reaction. When she spoke, her voice was light, airy.

"Oh, you had lunch with the Kirtzes?"

"Yes. They've extended an open dinner invite to the two of us, whenever we can." Cy walked into their dressing room.

Hope followed, unable to staunch her curiosity. "How was Millicent?"

Cy turned and peered at his wife. Satisfied that this was simply a routine question and not the beginning of an interrogation, he answered easily. "She's great—obviously in love with her husband and child."

Hope ignored the pang that comment caused and continued. "You saw their son too?"

"Jackson," Cy said, smiling as he undressed. "Rambunctious little kid. His skin is darkly tanned, but his eyes are blue. I think he's going to be a heartbreaker. Come on, let's see what's behind that tantalizing aroma that has me salivating in here . . . besides you."

Hope followed Cy while trying to reconcile the way she should feel—happy and content—with the way she actually felt—anxious and angry. Why couldn't she get over this envy where Millicent being a mother was concerned? And why couldn't she get pregnant?

Theirs was a companionable silence as they fixed their plates for a casual dinner on the balcony. As they walked through the sliding glass doors, Cy spoke his mind.

"I'm so glad we're back on track, baby, and that you no longer harbor ill feelings where Millicent is concerned. I think we're going to love living in that area; I'm even going to move our main office there and keep only a branch office here in LA."

Hope nodded and smiled. It was the best she could do. She'd been ecstatic when they vacationed in La Jolla, had said it was a slice of paradise and she wanted to live there. But that was before she knew Millicent lived there. *This is a test,* she thought. *A test of my faith and my true forgiveness.* San Diego County wasn't as big as LA, she reasoned. But it was fairly large. Chances were, aside from an occasional business dinner, she'd never even run into Millicent.

"I can't wait to see the property, baby," Hope said sincerely.

"And I can't wait to show it to you."

Cy's eyes sparkled with excitement. He'd initially had reservations, but tonight's conversation allayed his doubts. Now he could confidently move forward with his plans—to build his and Hope's oceanfront dream on the ten acres he'd already agreed to purchase from Jack Kirtz.

24

Grown-Folks Business

"Darius! Wait up!" Melody scampered across the church parking lot, careful to swing her tender hips and bob her breasts as she ran. She feigned a trip and thrust herself in his arms.

"Whoa, slow down now, you're going to run over me!"

"I thought I was going to miss you," Melody gasped. "I sent you an e-mail on MySpace. Did you get it?"

"Baby girl, I don't check those messages. An assistant at the label does that."

"Oh," Melody said in a dejected tone. "We have almost two thousand fans for you. And I have all these ideas about T-shirts and contests and stuff to, you know, keep people all hyped about you. I was hoping you'd e-mail me so I could tell you."

"Well, you're telling me now. And that's real sweet, Melody. But are you sure you have time for all this, with school and all? What are you, a junior?"

The last thing Melody wanted to be reminded of was that she was in high school. "I'm graduating early," she said. "Besides, I've got my eyes on bigger, better things. I got goals and stuff."

"What higher goal can you have besides getting your education?"

You! "I'm going to do that too. I'm going to major in business so I can do what Bo does."

Baby, you'll never be able to do what Bo does. "This fan club should give you some good experience then."

"So can I, like, you know, hang out with you guys . . . you and Bo? Maybe he can show me the ropes, give me some pointers to help me out. He must be good at what he does. Look at you!"

"I don't know if that will be possible," Darius began but reconsidered when he took in Melody's crestfallen face. "What's your cell number?" He took out his Blackberry.

Melody's eyes lit up as he punched in her numbers and her phone suddenly rang. "Hello?" she answered shyly.

"Now you have my number," Darius spoke into the phone, playing along with an obviously smitten fan. "If I start getting calls from high school females, I'll know where they got my number. My number will get changed, and you'll get booted out of the fan club you started." He laughed to take the sting out of his warning.

"I won't tell anybody," Melody promised. "I'll even save it under a code." She punched her phone's keypad. "One more thing. Can I bring a couple friends with me to your party?"

"On Thanksgiving weekend?"

"Or just me and Natasha is cool!"

"Oh, you can't come to that, baby girl. Grown-folks business will be happening, and you're underage."

"I'm almost seventeen!" She'd actually just turned sixteen, but who was counting?

"Grown is eighteen." Darius began walking to his Navigator; Melody was hot on his trail. He popped his lock and stepped into the vehicle. "I'll have a group of you girls over some other time."

Melody knocked on his window, determined to get her way.

Darius frowned slightly and then slid his window down. "You know, Melody. There's a fine line between being ambitious and obnoxious. If you want to make it in the game the way you say you do . . . you'll do well to learn the difference."

Melody smiled and waved as Darius exited the parking lot. She stared at his Navigator until it disappeared around a corner. Not at all dissuaded by his mild rebuke, she rechecked the code name she had assigned to his number. She concluded it was perfect and mouthed it again as she stared at the screen. The code was one simple word: *mine*.

25

Just Maybe

Darius clenched his teeth as he navigated traffic, trying to hold on to his temper as Bo rattled away on the phone. This was what he both loved and detested about his partner: his obsession with people he *thought* wanted to come between them.

"You haven't mentioned him in weeks. I thought you'd come to your senses." Darius paused, and when Bo said nothing, continued. "Randall is purposely pushing your buttons. Why do you let him get under your skin?"

"Because he's trying to get under yours, that's why!" Bo hissed. "Why don't you fire him and hire Evan?" Evan was safe—married with kids.

"Because Evan is Shabach's guitarist, and I'm not stealing personnel. I'm trying to get along, remember?"

"And Randall is trying to get you. I'll see you later." *Click.*

Darius continued to Stacy's house, totally frustrated. Being under the microscope with the record company and the church community was enough pressure. He didn't need Bo's subtle nagging, his doubts about their union. Especially now when he *did* find Randall attractive and his body was once again responding to Stacy Gray.

Minutes later, Darius pulled his sleeping son from the car seat and headed up the walk to Stacy's home. The perky smile and twinkling eyes that greeted him immediately warmed his heart and eased his troubled conscience. "Hello, Stacy."

"Hey, Darius." Stacy eyed her sleeping son and pointed to the stairway. "Take him upstairs and put him down. If I'm lucky, he'll sleep another hour or so until I finish dinner and can clean up. You hungry?"

Darius hadn't realized he was until now. "Something smells good," he replied over his shoulder.

Stacy smiled. She'd been thinking about Darius all week, ever since she'd seen him at church. They'd talked several times over the phone, about their son mostly. But Stacy found reasons to call him, and he always made himself available. That had to count for something, didn't it?

She hadn't told anyone about her plan to get back with the father of her child. She didn't want to entertain the naysayers—not until she made progress. Hopefully this dinner would be a start. Baked barbecue chicken was Darius's favorite meal. *If I'm lucky,* she thought, *his sauce-soaked fingers won't be the only thing he licks tonight.* As he came down, she met him at the bottom of the stairs with a glass of wine. "You look frazzled."

Darius took the wine. "A little bit." He took one sip and then another. "This is good, thank you. Is that barbecue chicken I smell?"

"It sure is."

Darius smiled. "Woman, you know the way to get to a man's heart."

I hope so, Stacy thought. "It was the only thing thawed," she said.

They ate quickly and mostly in silence, except for casual conversation about KCCC, their son, and the possibility of dissolving their court case.

"You know I only did that because you had me so frustrated. I love that boy like I love my life and know what it's like not to have a father. I refuse to do that to him."

"I know," Stacy said softly.

"So do you think we can put the court case and the drama behind us?"

Can you put Bo behind you? No, Bo would probably like that. Out of your life? "We'll see."

That was as close to a yes as she'd come, and Darius decided he'd pushed enough, for now. "I can't believe how he gets bigger every time I see him. And he's already talking up a storm! I think he's going to be a singer like his dad. You're an excellent mother, Stacy."

"I try," Stacy said, warming all over at the compliment. "And being around other kids has been good for him too. I started taking him over to a friend of mine's day-care center just so he could hang out with other children."

"Well, whatever you're doing, it's working. And speaking of work," Darius looked at his watch, "I probably should be going. Bo is probably pacing the floor wondering where I am already."

Stacy hid her disappointment. "I made dessert."

"Some other time," Darius said. He rose from the table. "Dinner was great, Stacy. Thanks."

Stacy walked with him from the dining room through the living room, wondering how she could prolong the stay without seeming desperate. They were at the front door before she'd come up with any bright ideas.

"Uh, you know about the party we're having Saturday," Darius said. "After Thanksgiving?"

"I heard about it."

"Well, you're welcome to come if you'd like. And of course," Darius hesitated, "you can bring a date."

"I don't know, Darius. Bo and I . . ."

"Hey, I know y'all aren't each other's favorite people. But you guys got along for a hot minute. When you were pregnant you were thicker than thieves and regular partners in crime when you united against Shabach. I'm just extending the invite—a little reprieve for the holidays, that's all."

"I'll think about it."

There was an awkward moment as they looked at each other. Darius opened the door.

"Darius," Stacy began.

"What?"

"I have something for you." Stacy stood on tiptoe and wrapped her arms around him. Soon their bodies meshed and tongues swirled. Her nipples hardened, and she could feel something pressing against her stomach.

"Stacy, I can't," Darius said, his breathing labored.

"But you want to."

"I don't want to hurt you."

"I hurt already."

Darius stared deeply into Stacy's eyes, then turned and left without another word.

Stacy closed the door and rested her head against the cool wood. A myriad of emotions flowed through her; desire simmered, aroused and unanswered beneath her clothes. Darius hadn't totally embraced her, but he hadn't pushed her away.

26

True Ecstasy

Darius wasn't the only one exasperated that week. So was Hope. She paced the length of her bedroom as she reasoned with Frieda. "This guy at church *likes* you, girl. He specifically asked where you were and if maybe the four of us could go out tonight."

"I already told you. He's too goody-goody for me," Frieda countered. "I'm a freak."

"Goody-goody? What's wrong with that? And how would you know? You won't even take the man's number.

"He's a good catch, Frieda. A solid, educated professional, not to mention very attractive. Who is causing you even to think twice about this? Giorgio—whose new mistress is the runway—or Shabach—who's known all over America as a big church ho?"

"Now, don't be too hard on hos," Frieda said with a smile in her voice. "Some people could use that label on me."

Hope didn't dare respond to that.

"Besides, I feel more comfortable with the Giorgios and Shabachs. Your church friend is out of my league."

"Do you really believe that, Frieda? That you're not good enough for a certain type of man?"

A flicker of pain crossed Frieda's face, but just as quickly disappeared.

"I've already told Shabach I'd go to Darius's party with him. You and Cy should come too." Frieda resorted to her usual humor. "Maybe y'all could take some ecstasy and get your freak on."

"When it's right, cousin," Hope said softly, "love is the only ecstasy you need."

There was a slight hesitation before Frieda answered. "Whatever, Hope. I'm out."

Hope pushed her luck once more. "Will you be at church again tomorrow?"

"I should have told you last Sunday that that wasn't going to become a habit."

"Even if you and Shabach get serious?"

"That's not going to happen. He's just a good time."

Again Hope was struck by the fact that Frieda refused to go out with an interested, potentially long-term mate in favor of a "good time." What was that about?

"All right then, girl. Be safe."

27

LA's Finest

By nine PM, Bo, the caterers, and decorators had transformed the ten-thousand-square-foot Bel Air estate into a classy party central. Instrumental remixes of Darius's music, interspersed with jazz and hip-hop beats, provided a fitting backdrop to the upwards of seventy-five people mingling in the place Bo and Darius called home. Groups gathered in the theater room, den, and living room, and conversed in small groups in and around the pool and Jacuzzi. Darius strolled comfortably through the different sectors represented: celebrities, athletes, recording artists, a few gay members from KCCC, and many mutual friends from the gay community sprinkled among LA's finest partygoers. Darius saw that one of his guests was gaining his share of attention from male and female alike: his bass player, Randall Smith. He slid open the patio door and stepped out to the pool area, where Randall lounged on a chaise, surrounded by admirers.

But not everyone was in awe. Bo stood just to the right of the patio doors, able to take in the scene without being seen, nursing a Courvoisier and trying to calm the possessive tendencies toward Darius that even by his own standards had gotten out of hand. He attributed his heightened sensitivity to the custody battle with Stacy and hoped that what Darius believed was correct—that she was ready to cooperate with Darius regarding proper visitation rights with his son.

One of the brothers from Kingdom Citizens sidled up next to him. "That's a nice slab of bacon there," he said, nodding toward Randall.

"Yeah, and he can sizzle his Oscar Meyer ass right out of our house!" Bo hissed.

"Calm down, wifey." His eyes feasted on Randall. "That black is all that, but green does not become you."

Bo's response was eyes rolled back in his head.

"C'mon, girl, you need a shot of Alizé!"

"Chile, I just need a shot of Darius *alone*. I'll be all right."

Bo pushed his gay friend away in an annoyed manner, but truthfully the playful exchange had calmed his ire. *I need to get a handle on my emotions and chill the bump out,* he thought as he refreshed his straight-no-chaser glass of liquor. The truth was, Darius had done everything possible to make Bo feel secure. Just this morning they'd returned from a trip to Las Vegas to celebrate their wedding anniversary—a trip taken on a chartered jet, the night spent in a Caesars Palace penthouse, front-row tickets to Céline's latest show, and a private dinner catered by the renowned Wolfgang Puck. He had everything—and the man. And here he was, about to let jealousy get in the way.

"Shiiiit," he said, slamming back another shot of Courvoisier. "Why am I worrying. . . . I got this."

Frieda had something too—a hotshot gospel star on her arm—and she was loving every minute of it. From the time they had stepped through the door, glances had slid their way, the question of the identity of the lucky woman with Shabach no doubt on many of their minds. Frieda knew her dress was perfection: a skintight black mini with silver zippers by European designer DSquared. This was paired with a thigh-hugging

pair of four-inch, shiny black boots, which, along with her
Frederick's of Hollywood push-up bra, revealed just enough
toffee skin to send the men salivating. Her hair had been moussed
to spike in places, and she'd applied her makeup in a dark, exotic fashion. Large silver hoops completed the ensemble . . . if
you didn't count her major accessory, Shabach.

As for this accessory, Shabach did not disappoint. His ap-
pearance looked casual but had been carefully thought out:
black Rocawear jeans with a dazzling white tank top, a perfect
backdrop for the twenty-karat diamond S—similar to the Super-
man logo—that swung from a thick rope chain. He'd had his
hair cut close to the scalp, a move that brought out his deep
brown eyes and high, arching eyebrows. Ironically, from a distance, he and Darius bore a resemblance. But their close-cropped
black naps, dark brown skin, and even, white teeth was where
the similarities ended, unless one counted the streak of com-
petitiveness that kept them both aiming higher and higher,
when even the top wasn't high enough.

After greeting a few friends and even more fans, Shabach
and Frieda took themselves on a self-guided tour through the
estate. They walked through two living rooms, a great room,
den, theater, library, dining room, and tea room, before reaching an atrium. Shabach said little as they passed room after luxuriously appointed room.

"You know, this house is leased by the record company,"
Frieda said casually.

"How do you know that?"

"Stacy told me." Frieda sidled up to Shabach and put her
head on his shoulder. "You know there's no way he could have
something better than you without help."

Shabach nodded. "True dat."

He pulled Frieda even closer to him, and she smiled. *Stroking
a man's ego works every time,* she thought, staving off Shabach's bad
mood she felt developing with every square inch of marble on

which they walked. They continued in a maze of twists and turns, chatting easily before reaching a wing of the home that was locked.

"This must be booty-bumpin' headquarters," Frieda whispered. "For D and his 'girl.'"

Shabach reached around and grabbed Frieda's backside. "Yeah, and here's a booty I want to bump right now." He captured her mouth in a hungry kiss, even as his fingers ventured past the fabric to tear at the wispy thong underneath her short dress.

"Ooh, baby, you know the right button to push," Frieda panted. She pressed herself against his hardening erection as he pushed up the dress to expose her entire backside for his pleasure. He kneaded her cheeks and groaned.

"I want you now," Shabach demanded.

"Come on," Frieda prompted. "Let's find a room so we can have our own private party!"

They found a guest bedroom and closed the door. Meanwhile, the front door of the house opened, and in walked Hope and Stacy. The almost-never-sick Cy had caught a bug, so Hope had canceled their dinner plans with the Montgomerys. While Stacy would never wish illness on anybody, she was glad Hope was there. She just wished Bo wasn't.

"Maybe Tony's here," Hope said as she and Stacy walked farther inside the massive living quarters.

"Maybe," Stacy answered. She'd told Hope more than once that she and Tony were just friends. That didn't stop the eternally matchmaking Mrs. Taylor from wishing for more.

They'd dressed to impress, and while Hope's chocolate-brown CK pantsuit was decidedly more conservative than Stacy's electric-blue suede jumpsuit, both ladies turned heads as they entered. After accepting wine and sparkling water from the floating waiter, they headed toward the floor-to-ceiling glass panes and the pool beyond.

"This is stunning," Hope said as they passed through the massive foyer and into the living room.

"It's okay," Stacy said. "Stunning" would be when hers was the name on the letters coming in the mail.

Hope cut her eyes at her downplaying friend. "Well, 'okay' looks like it could fit our penthouse inside three times."

They reached the sliding doors as Darius was walking in. "Ladies!" he said with sincere enthusiasm. He hugged them both, and before he could blink, Bo was standing beside him.

"Hey, Hope. Hey, Spacey," he cooed while placing a possessive arm around Darius.

Stacy played it cool. "Hey, Little Bo Peep."

Darius let out the breath he'd been holding.

"Can I take you ladies on the grand tour? Of course, Stacy's been here before, but what about you, Hope?"

"Oh, no, see to your other guests. Stacy and I will just make ourselves at home."

"So long as you don't wear out your welcome," Bo mumbled.

"We can't wear out what's already worn out," Stacy replied.

Hope tugged on Stacy's arm before World War III broke out. "Where's the food?" she asked Darius.

"There are waiters throughout. And if you follow the hallway to the other side of this wing, there's a large spread in the dining room." Darius smiled at Stacy. "If you don't see what you like, find me. We can have Chef fix whatever you'd like."

Stacy's smile lasted until they'd turned the corner. "Maybe I shouldn't have come," she said.

"If you want to leave, we can," Hope readily replied.

Stacy was about to say yes, when two hundred and twenty pounds of "maybe not" walked toward them.

"Hey, Tony!" Stacy said brightly.

"Hello, gorgeous." They hugged.

"You remember Hope Taylor."

"Of course. How are you, Hope?"

"Good. And I'll be better with a little something in my stomach. Why don't you two catch up while I find something to eat?"

There was a moment of awkward silence as Stacy watched Hope's retreating form while Tony watched Stacy.

"You look very nice tonight," he said to break the quiet.

Stacy looked into dark brown eyes surrounded by tightly curled lashes. A well-groomed mustache framed cushy lips. "You do too," she replied. While they'd talked on the phone, she hadn't actually seen him since dinner at the Montgomerys'. *Was he this fine before?*

"I'm sur—"

"How do you—"

They laughed at their obvious nervousness.

Tony bowed his acquiesce. "Ladies first."

"I was asking how you knew Darius."

"I've seen him at a few parties. Backstage a couple times. Here and there. I'm kinda surprised to see you here, to tell you the truth."

"Why, because you think I'm still drooling over his receding back? Darius and I will always be bonded because of our child, Tony. But as I tried to explain to you, I've moved on."

The speech was so good that for the moment, both Stacy and Tony actually believed it.

"What about you?" she continued. "That big, strong arm looks like it should be around a pair of soft shoulders. Where's she at?"

"I'm rolling solo tonight," Tony countered smoothly, not fielding the obvious query as to his single-or-not status. "Are you hungry?"

Stacy's one-word answer had two meanings. "Yes."

28

Marital Privileges

The chicken wasn't the only thing packing heat in the house. While Tony and Stacy went to assuage their appetites, there was another feast of love going on. On the other side of the house, down another hallway, and behind one closed door, two sweating bodies caused bedsprings to creak.

Frieda grabbed the headboard as Shabach continued his rhythmic assault.

"Who does this belong to, huh? Whose is this?" he asked.

A prolonged moan was the only answer.

Shabach delivered a final thrust. Frieda chirped like a parrot as an orgasm rocked her center. Shabach's release quickly followed, punctuated by a hiss and a low growl.

"Girl, you're going to get me addicted to this," Shabach teased once he'd caught his breath.

Frieda said nothing, dealing with the dueling emotions she often felt after being with a man—happy she'd been able to turn a brothah out, and sad that afterward she felt so empty. Just like it had always been, from back in the day . . .

Before her mind could roll back the clock to a time best forgotten, Frieda sat up and gazed at Shabach's smooth, round cheeks backlit by the lamp on the nightstand. She reached out a finger to outline the symbol tattooed just above his buttocks.

"What's this?"

"Huh?" Shabach moaned and barely stirred.

"This." Frieda's fingers danced along the raised outline.

"Girl, stop, that tickles." Shabach rolled over. "It's a combination of the Chinese signs for peace, prosperity, and power."

"You've got a tatoo promoting peace, yet you're fighting with D? That's jacked up, Shabach."

Shabach rolled over and walked toward the bathroom. "That's over, girl. Now get in here and take a shower with me. It's time for me to get back out there and meet my public."

Stacy sat in a corner of the plush ballroom, feeling rejected. After about ten minutes of pleasant conversation, a very attractive sistah with whom Tony was obviously friends had butted into their conversation and asked if she could steal him away and introduce him to someone. Instead of passing on the invite, he'd turned, held out his hand, and said, "Take it easy, Stacy." Now all she wanted to do was take her butt home.

So here she sat, watching Darius hold court as if he were royalty and Bo flit around as if he were Darius's shadow. Throughout the night, she'd tried several times to talk to Darius. Their conversation had been pleasant but continually interrupted. Hope had met a junior partner in a real estate firm who'd done business with Cy. This mutual interest had paved the way for a conversation between them that had lasted until now. And after two hours in the home of the man she loved but seemed unable to have, Stacy was ready to go. She decided to use the restroom before wrangling Hope away from her new friend. After a few moments, she found a bathroom near her. As she reached for the handle, the door opened.

"Frieda! Are you just getting here?" Stacy asked.

Frieda would have blushed if she could. "No, I've been here a while. Have you been able to play footsie with Baby Daddy?"

"Don't I wish. I can barely get near him without Bo hovering like a mother hen.

"It was crazy of me to think I could get some real alone time at a party Darius was hosting anyway. I'm not the only one Bo is fighting off. I saw him giving the evil eye to Randall a few times."

"Girl, stop! Don't tell me that fine, tall drink of hot chocolate is gay?"

"Okay, so I won't tell you. Rumor has it, though, that he swings both ways."

"That is wrong on so many levels. He is too fine to be wasting that stick on another man."

"Don't even get me started on that subject. Anyway, I'm getting ready to leave. Just decided to use the restroom before hitting the freeway."

Frieda looked at Stacy's tired red eyes. "You're not drinking and driving, are you?"

"No, I'm here with Hope. You know she barely drinks. I think she made it through half a glass of bubbly before she switched to sparkling water."

"Cy's here? Now, that's a surprise. I don't see Darius and company as his kind of crowd."

"Cy is home with the flu. Hope and I came all by our lonelies."

"Well, good for her. It's about time she stopped acting like an old married woman."

Just then Shabach turned into the hallway. "There you are, woman. Come meet my manager." He sidled up to Frieda and whispered loudly. "Then I might be ready for an encore."

Before Stacy could form a hello, much less a question, Shabach had whisked Frieda down the hall and around the corner.

That girl can get any man she wants, Stacy thought glumly as she closed the bathroom door behind her. *While the one man I want is in love with another one.*

A little while later, Hope and Stacy said their good-byes. Stacy made it a point to find Darius, confirm their arrangements for little Darius tomorrow, and give him a hug—in front of Bo—to show that she was not intimidated by their wedding rings or Bo's shriveled thing. She waved at a few others and chatted for a brief moment with one of the brothahs from KCCC. As she made these rounds, a pair of eyes followed her intently. He discovered that once she was gone, she wasn't easily forgotten.

Hope tiptoed into the master suite and walked directly to her large walk-in closet and dressing room. More than once she'd marveled that her old apartment's living room could almost fit inside here. She shut the door, turned on the light, and undressed quickly. Naked, she exited the dressing room and turned into the master bath, which was right next door. Dreaming of sleep, she made quick work of her shower and then donned a thigh-length nightgown and slipped into bed.

Once her head hit the pillow, however, it was quickly revealed that someone else had other plans.

"Mmmm, you're so soft," Cy whispered as he cuddled up behind her, spoon style. "And you smell so good."

Hope responded by wiggling her booty against him, grabbing his arm to place it around her, and burrowing her head deeper into the pillow.

"Did you enjoy yourself?" Cy persisted.

"Mmmm-hmmm."

"Well, can I enjoy myself now?"

Hope smiled and pulled his arm tighter. "I'm sleepy, Cy."

"Okay," Cy said. "I understand."

He rolled over and got out of bed.

Poor baby, Hope thought. *Having to watch TV so he can fall asleep.* Fighting off guilt from not giving her man what he wanted, she reasoned to make it up tomorrow night—give him a double dose of loving.

Suddenly Hope felt a current of air on her lower leg as the comforter was lifted up from the foot of the bed. Seconds later, the feeling of air was replaced by that of Cy's tongue slowly circling her big toe while his hands roamed her legs.

"Cy!"

"Just lay back and relax, baby. I know you're sleepy."

"Cy, I can't go to sleep with you . . . ooh!"

Cy had found her sensitive spot, a little nook at the back of her knee. From there his tongue traveled to her inner thigh, while his fingers found paradise and worked magic. Against her will, Hope found her legs opening wider, her moans becoming louder. By the time Cy's tongue replaced his fingers, Hope was wide awake and a willing participant.

Once she'd been thoroughly satisfied, she became the aggressor and returned the oral favor. She gingerly and teasingly took Cy's manhood into her mouth, lavishing it with all the love she felt for God's gift to her. She went on and on until Cy's moans matched her earlier ones. She used techniques she'd picked up in a DVD that had been a surprise gift from none other than first lady Vivian Montgomery. Hope had called her shortly after viewing it, filled with a mixture of embarrassment and excitement.

"No wonder you and Derrick are still on your honeymoon," Hope had shyly gushed.

"Baby, the marriage bed is undefiled. Derrick and I take *full* advantage of our marital privileges."

"How is it that I love you more each time?" Cy asked as he retook the lead and slowly sank himself into the warmth of Hope's love nest. "Hmmm?" he asked again as he withdrew to the tip and then plunged back in with long, measured strokes.

Hope couldn't answer because she couldn't think. There were too many emotions clouding her head and her heart: joy, ecstasy, gratitude, love. So many that she couldn't separate them or verbalize them. She could only feel, and she tried to communicate these feelings with each upward thrust, with the widening of her thighs, with her legs wrapped around Cy's buttocks, with her tongue swirling in Cy's ear and mouth and the kisses that covered wherever her mouth landed.

The dance went on as the ecstasy went higher. Hope answered the call for heightened pleasure when Cy switched positions and they opened themselves to all aspects of sensual gratification. As they raced toward their mutual climax, Hope's tears mixed with Cy's, and their voices blended together in thanksgiving and praise to the God who had brought them together—the God who'd created this timeless, unsurpassed expression of marital joy.

29

Watch Your Man

Hope rolled over and stretched lazily. She felt like a contented cat, and if not for all the purring she'd done into the wee hours, she'd be tempted to do so right now. *Is it really possible for this much happiness to be in one woman?* Hope laughed aloud as she bounded out of bed. Not only was she physically satiated but mentally satisfied as well. God had answered her prayers, and she no longer felt depressed. It felt good to truly feel like herself again.

She was tempted to join Cy in the shower, but she knew he had a meeting with Jack Kirtz, and she didn't want to make him late. Instead she decided to prepare breakfast. She pulled on a pink silk kimono, placed her feet in rhinestone-covered slippers, and, after a quick wash-off, headed toward their newly remodeled, ultramodern kitchen. Passing Cy's office, she decided to quickly shoot off an e-mail to Vivian, deciding it may be too early to call. But she wanted to change their plans for a noon lunch to one o'clock and hoped to catch her before other plans were made. She pushed the SEND button and rose from the chair when Cy's Blackberry rang. Hope rarely answered his phone and only gave it a casual glance as she walked from behind the desk. But the name caught her eye: Jack Kirtz. She figured the call was about their meeting.

"Cy Taylor Enterprises. Hope speaking."

There was a short pause before Millicent responded. "Hi, Hope, it's Millicent."

Hope willed herself to remain calm and reminded herself she was no longer depressed, or jealous. It wasn't out of the question that Millicent would place a call for her husband, just as Hope had answered Cy's phone.

"Hi, Millicent."

Another pause followed. "Well, this is rather awkward, isn't it? I, uh, I've been thinking of talking to you and of what I'd say when the time finally came."

Hope remained silent.

"This isn't the time or place for the type of discussion I'd like to have," Millicent continued slowly. "But I've apologized to Cy and want to do so with you. I am sorry for the hurt and confusion I brought to you and his life. Obviously we've both moved on, but I just wanted you to hear from my own mouth that I repented for what I did and now ask your forgiveness."

Hope closed her eyes and forced the words from her heart and through her mouth. "I forgive you, Millicent."

"Thank you, Hope. Because everything does work together for good—we're both married and happy now. And did Cy mention that we've invited you two for dinner? Now that our husbands are going to be working together, I thought it would be a good idea. I mean, I'm not expecting us to become best buds or anything, but a cordial relationship might be nice."

Cy walked into his office. His brows furrowed slightly when he noticed Hope on his phone.

"Millicent, Cy just walked in," Hope said. "We'll talk again soon."

Hope handed Cy the phone and walked into the kitchen. Her mind was a flurry of thoughts as she started the coffeepot, put eggs on to boil, and took out bagels and a fruit salad. She then reached into the cupboard for the SuperFood capsules she and Cy had started taking daily. She placed his dosage next to a glass of freshly squeezed orange juice and then swallowed the two green pills with a long swallow of her own. Before she'd had a chance to organize her thoughts, Cy joined her in the kitchen.

"Oh, baby, I love you so much," he said as he joined her at the counter. He placed a quick kiss on her forehead before downing his capsules with a long swig of juice. "God sure has a sense of humor," he continued as Hope walked over to the coffeemaker and poured them both steaming cups. "If anyone had ever asked whether you and Millicent would ever speak to each other in this lifetime, I would have hedged my bets. And now her husband and I are partners. Imagine that!"

"Yes, imagine that," Hope said, hoping the laughter in her voice reached her face.

Cy shook his head and smiled to himself as he sat at the breakfast bar and opened the *New York Times*. He quickly scanned the front page, financial, and sports sections before Hope set a plate in front of him.

They chatted amicably during the quickly devoured breakfast, and minutes later Cy was giving her forehead one last peck before he strolled out the door.

"What time will you be home for dinner?" Hope asked.

"I'll call you," Cy replied just before the elevator door closed.

Hope busied herself the rest of the morning. Instead of leaving the housecleaning for the maid, she washed and put away the breakfast dishes, made their bed, and readied the laundry for wash. Then she took a long shower, dressed in a casual, tan-colored velour warm-up with brown lace-up sandals, pulled her hair back in a ponytail, and, after phone calls to her mother and father, left to do some quick shopping before meeting Vivian for lunch.

As she navigated traffic from the mall to the restaurant, she finally gave the morning's main event the attention it deserved. Yes, she thought, there had been a moment of discomfort when she'd heard Millicent's voice on Cy's phone, but it hadn't lasted long. More importantly, the jealousy that usually came when Millicent's name was mentioned, let alone when her voice was heard, had not been as strong as before. Perhaps the intense lovemaking session from the night before had released any lingering ill feelings she'd had where Millicent was concerned. She sure hoped so. Because if she was going to actually break bread with the woman she at one time wanted to break the neck of, she'd best have any and all negative feelings under control.

This was primarily what she relayed to Vivian after they'd settled in with soup and salad at the Souplantation in Beverly Hills.

"I'm proud of you," Vivian said once Hope had finished talking. "Look what God has done. In just a little over a month, He's helped you replace anger with forgiveness and worry with the peace that passes all understanding. And you know what else?"

"Hmmm?" Hope responded around a mouthful of vegetable soup.

"This is the first time in a long time in which pregnancy hasn't been the main topic of conversation. God is going to bless you, Hope," Vivian continued. "Just continue to believe."

Hope's phone rang shortly after she started her car and headed back to the marina. "Hey, Frieda! I heard you were at Darius's party! We looked all over for you after you'd bumped into Stacy."

"Yeah, well, it is a big house," Frieda said.

"Yes," Hope admitted. "It's gorgeous. Where were you?"

"Here and there," Frieda answered elusively. "You know Shabach had to make his presence known to all the partygoers—let everybody know he was in the house."

"So you and Shabach . . . do you think it can get serious?"

"I'm just going with the flow, girl, taking one day at a time. That man sure can fuck though."

"Why do you insist on talking like that?"

"It's who I am and what Shabach and I did when he put the bat in the cat. What do you think we did, 'made love'?"

Hope sighed and then stopped before she began her "safe sex/less promiscuity" message. Instead she told Frieda about the conversation with Millicent.

"You'd better watch that heifah," Frieda warned.

"Now, don't you start," Hope countered. "Millicent is very much in love with her husband. Anybody who saw her on Carla's show could see that. And Cy confirmed it—said you could feel the love they had for each other when he was in their home."

"Cy was at her house?" Frieda asked with incredulity.

"Cy was at her and Jack's house," Hope corrected. "Having a business lunch."

"Is Millicent part of his business?"

"Look, I'm not even going to go there with you. I've just released the demon of jealousy, and I'm not going to go back and get it."

"Whatever, Hope. Just watch your man, that's all I'm saying."

"And so you've said, cousin."

The conversation changed to that of family, Frieda's thoughts on changing jobs, Hope's update on how her dad was doing, and hearing Frieda's mother's latest dating dilemma. By the time Hope pulled into the condominium complex parking lot and headed for the elevator, she tried to convince herself her heart still felt light. And true, there were still no jealous feelings regarding her former nemesis, Millicent. But the depressing pangs of longing were creeping in, courtesy of Vivian's light-hearted comment shared earlier. As soon as she entered the house, she walked straight to the computer, pressed a search engine, and began looking up info on fertility drugs.

30

Lord, Help Us

Cy sighed as yet another call lit up on his dashboard. It had been a crazy morning, with one unexpected event after another. He hoped this wasn't yet another one.

He flicked the speaker button. "Yeah, Charlie. I'm just now leaving LA—should be there by one o'clock."

"That's fine, Cy. But hopefully you won't mind moving our meeting until four. Our partner's connection was delayed in London. He probably won't touch down at LAX until noon. Security, customs—it'll be four at least before he gets here."

Damn. "Okay," Cy said after a long pause. As crazy as his day had been, he could hardly fault someone flying in from Switzerland for a delay that was beyond their power to control. "I'll see you then."

Cy voice-activated a call to Jack.

Millicent answered. "Hey, Cy!"

"Hey, Millicent. Jack around?"

"You can catch him on his cell. He took Jackson on a tour of his inheritance."

Cy smiled. "Okay, fine, I'll call him."

"Cy?"

"Yes?"

"I don't mean to pry into Jack's affairs, but weren't you guys supposed to meet this morning?"

"Yes, but this has been a crazy Monday. We pushed back our meeting, and it looks like I need to push it again."

"Oh, shoot."

"Why, do you think that's a problem?"

"It's just that we had dinner reservations at Panuche's for the three of us."

"Panuche's? Even with my connections, Hope and I couldn't get reservations until three months out."

Panuche's was the latest southern California restaurant sensation: an upscale bistro with arguably the best Italian chef and unarguably the highest prices. The service was beyond stellar, with personal waiters for each of the twenty tables in the cozy establishment.

"We've waited six months for this one." Millicent paused for a moment. "Hey! We could always make it a reservation for four—oh, but Hope probably has dinner plans."

"Don't worry, she'll understand. I wouldn't think of having you cancel your reservations, and quite frankly, I've heard too much about this chef to pass up an opportunity to get inside. I'll call Hope and let her know I'll be home after dinner if you'll do me a favor and call Jack. What time are the reservations?"

Millicent smiled as she hung up to call Jack. She'd always treasured Cy's friendship, and was glad to be experiencing it once again.

"You're what?" Hope turned away from the sauce she was making and placed her hand on a peeved-off hip as she spoke into the phone to Cy.

"It couldn't be helped, baby. My schedule has been screwy all day. Jack and Millicent already had reservations, so—"

"Millicent? Why is she attending a meeting between you and Jack?"

"They've had the reservation for months. I didn't want them to cancel on my account."

Hope could barely hear Cy's answer for Frieda's words ringing in her ear. *Watch your man.* And she could have sworn what she did hear came precariously close to an insult.

"You've been gone all day, Cy. Why couldn't you guys meet earlier, in Jack's office?" *Without Millicent!*

"Hope, unless you've made dinner plans for us, I don't see why you're upset."

Frieda's words continued as a litany in Hope's mind: *Watch your man, girl. Watch that heifah. . . .*

"Who says I'm upset? Why should I get upset because you leave for San Diego first thing this morning, and then call me tonight telling me you're having dinner with Millicent? I thought your partnership was with Jack. If this is going to be a husband–wife venture, then I need to match my calendar with yours and become a part of the project!"

Cy took a moment before he spoke again. Until this year, he and Hope had rarely debated and never argued. He didn't like this side of Hope and begrudgingly admitted their marriage might be entering an "or for worse" period. He'd told Hope that Millicent would be at the dinner because he never wanted any secrets between them. So he decided on full disclosure.

"Look, baby," he said finally. "Jack and Millicent have reservations at Panuche's. You know how long one has to wait for those tables—it was either cancel the meeting or join them. It's obvious we need to talk about this. I'll be home as soon as I can. Okay, baby? Baby?"

Cy looked at the dashboard. His eyes narrowed when he realized why Hope didn't answer. Because she had hung up.

★   ★   ★

"Mama, I don't know what's wrong with me!" Hope paced the floor of her living room. The crisp December day gave a perfect backdrop to the plush shade of navy Hope had recently added to the living room's color scheme. The bright sunlight danced off their handscraped bamboo flooring, an art that dated back to the artisans of the Ming dynasty, but its richness was lost on Hope's dark mood.

"Why can't I get past it?"

"Because you aren't being honest with yourself, or with your husband. You keep saying you've forgiven Millicent, when you haven't. And that you're okay with his business dealings with her husband, when you're not. But I don't think this is just about Millicent." Pat took a deep breath and continued. "When I had my miscarriage, I went into a deep depression. I tried hard to hide it from your daddy, and thank goodness you were too young to remember, but times were touch-and-go with me for a while, to the point where Earl and my mama seriously considered, you know, putting me away for a while."

"Putting you away? As if you were crazy?"

"As if I were mentally unstable, which I was. Even now, but especially back in those days, Black folk just didn't admit it if they were having mental problems. We couldn't afford to be depressed or to have a bad day. Bad days were just part of living, and no matter what happened, we were expected to get over it. I mean, heck, we'd been through slavery, Jim Crow, the Civil Rights Movement. We weren't supposed to get too bent out of shape over something we couldn't control. And even though I knew in my head that the miscarriage was not my fault, I couldn't get my heart to believe it."

"So what did you do?"

"You remember our old neighbor, Miss Susie? The one who used to bake those pies for us all the time?"

Hope smiled through her tears. "Who could ever forget Miss Sue?"

"Well, unbeknownst to me, she'd been watching me, took

special pains to pay attention after I'd lost the baby. One day she saw me wandering around in the backyard; she said I was just kinda going in circles. She came over, and we had a long talk. She told me about a doctor she'd gone to one time after her mother died and she thought she'd lost her mind. He helped her. I went to him. He helped me too."

"You think I'm going crazy, Mama?"

"I think you've put yourself under a lot of pressure trying to get pregnant, and you've been trying to deal with it by yourself."

"I've been getting counseling. Sistah Viv is very aware of what's going on."

"Yes, but, Hope, it might be time for you to go to someone besides your pastor. Now, I'm not saying God can't fix it, because He can fix anything. I'm just saying He might want you to use a method other than the one you're using. Will you think about it?"

Hope promised her mother she would, but she knew she wouldn't. As hard as she tried, all she could think about was Millicent spending the evening with Cy. She didn't include Millicent's husband in the picture she painted—which, had she thought about it, may have been why her imaginings made her hurt so much.

Cy walked into the penthouse several hours later. The lights were out, yet when he went into the kitchen he found a pot of cold sauce and another pot of rice on the stovetop. He looked in the oven. Two fillets of salmon sat in an ovenproof pan. He frowned, put the food in storage containers, and put the containers in the refrigerator. After placing the cookware in the dishwasher, he walked into the bedroom.

Hope was lying on the comforter, fully clothed and sound asleep. Cy sat down gingerly, his look a mixture of love and concern. He placed a soft finger to Hope's cheek, noting the dried tearstains that had streaked her makeup.

"Hope?" he called out softly. He called again, but to no avail. Hope was sound asleep. Cy removed his shoes, suit, and shirt and crawled on the bed in his underwear. He didn't want to bother his sleeping princess and therefore simply cuddled Hope tightly in his arms.

He stared into the distance as he leisurely stroked Hope's hair.

"God, please help Hope. She's the love of my life, and she's hurting. If it is Your will, please help us start a family. A child will make all the difference. Help us, Jesus."

31

Like Paradise

Vivian sat back in her office chair, a calm expression hiding an inner turmoil. She was worried for Hope and not at all sure how best to help her.

"Did you and Cy discuss things this morning?"

"Somewhat."

Vivian was silent until Hope went on.

"He told me he was canceling the partnership with Jack. That it wasn't worth the effect it was having on me."

"How did you respond?"

"With the truth. I admitted that while I'd forgiven Millicent in my head, it hadn't yet occurred in my heart. And that that was precisely why he shouldn't cancel the partnership. I believe God has brought Millicent back into my life for a reason, probably several. Mama helped me realize that it's not about her, it's about me, and my need to deal with issues that until now I've ignored or set aside."

"Such as?"

"Along with jealousy and envy, insecurity and self-esteem challenges are rearing their ugly heads. And then there's the baby issue. But I'm getting ready to fix that. I've scheduled an appointment with a fertility clinic."

"And Cy is in agreement?"

"He doesn't know yet. I'm just going there to find out more about their treatments, exactly what they entail. Then I'll share it with Cy. I don't want to stop his dreams—our dreams—because of my issues. Almost from the time we were married, Cy has talked about expanding his business into San Diego County and northern California. He's told me how hard it is to buy into the coastal properties along La Jolla's seacoast. You should have seen his face as he described the land he's buying from Jack. He makes it sound like paradise. So I told him to hold off on ending the agreement."

"California is a large state," Vivian said matter-of-factly. "There are other paradises. But I am proud of the way you're facing your issues head-on, refusing to give the devil the victory."

Hope nodded.

"Maybe in addition to talking to the fertility specialists, you should take your mother's advice and speak with a therapist or mental health professional as well. There's no shame in reaching out for help and at the very least knowing exactly what is going on."

"Maybe I should," Hope whispered, the shame she shouldn't feel about to suffocate her.

Vivian's intercom interrupted their discussion.

"What is it, Tamika?" Vivian responded.

"Melody and the dancers are here. Should I send them over to the youth hall?"

Vivian gave Hope a questioning look.

Hope straightened her shoulders and answered with a firm nod.

"Yes, Tamika. Send them over to the hall. Hope will meet them there shortly."

For the first time since Hope had accepted Vivian's request to teach dance at Kingdom, Hope was truly happy for the diversion from her drama. She drew strength from the teenagers' high-level energy, and even the usually snooty Melody didn't get on her nerves. In fact, Hope admitted she was impressed with the choreography the girls had created to the chorus of Darius's chart-topping "Looks Like Reign":

"Reign over troubles, over doubts, over fears, reign, reign
Reign through the heartaches, through the pain and the tears,
God reigns
Reign like you know your breakthrough's already here, and
just reign
Made in His image, you reign . . ."

After two hours, the girls were exhausted, and Hope was pleased. She'd also been uplifted. The words penned by Darius had ministered to her mind and soothed her spirit. If she would simply let go and let God, as Vivian had said, reign as if the breakthrough, her pregnancy, was already here, everything would be all right.

As for the girls, there was no doubt the group would be ready to perform at the Kingdom Citizens New Year celebration, where for the first time in a very long time, Darius and Shabach would share the same bill. All in all, Hope should have been acting like a woman on top of the world because she was, indeed, blessed beyond measure. She felt she needed to apologize to Cy, yet again, for her erratic behavior. And she'd seriously think about what her mother had said and seek professional help if it came to that. Because she would let nothing, and no one, come between her and her marriage.

Cy was determined not to let anything come between him and Hope either, which was why he was on the phone to Jack Kirtz.

"I'm really sorry," he said. "But it's a personal matter, nothing at all to do with you and your business dealings. They've been exemplary."

Jack paused, framing his words carefully. "I know Millicent and Hope have a—how should I say this—interesting history. And I totally understand if their past issues are what has caused you to change your mind. I won't deny the fact that I was looking forward to being almost neighbors, and I hope this decision won't prevent us from perhaps partnering on other deals in the future."

"Absolutely not, Jack. Like I said, I—oh, hold on a minute. Hope is calling. Let me just take this quickly." Cy pushed the cell phone's FLASH button. "Hey, sweetheart. I've been thinking about you. I'm on the other line; can I call you right back?"

"Sure, baby, but I just want to say this quickly. I'm sorry. I'm really, truly sorry, and I'm okay, and please, please, please don't let me come between you and Jack's business dealings or any other thing you're working on. The devil has been busy, and this is a test. But I have the victory, Cy. *We* have the victory. I love you, baby. Now, go get 'em."

Cy heaved a heavy sigh as he switched back over to Jack. "Women—I'll never understand them."

"Is everything okay?"

"Everything's better than okay." Cy smiled. "The deal's back on. I'm going forward with the plans to surprise my baby with the home of her dreams."

32

No More Tears

Stacy gave herself a last look in the mirror and was pleased at her reflection. She liked her new, shorter weave. The curls came to just above her shoulders, framing and softening her angular face. Normally not one for makeup, she'd enhanced her brown eyes with black mascara and enhanced her cupid-shaped lips with beige gloss to match the tight, beige tank top she wore over cream-colored jeans.

She walked from her bedroom to the living room and stopped at the stereo. She chose a mix of jazz, hip-hop, and R & B for the five-CD changer and pushed PLAY. The sounds of Alicia Keys filled the room as sandalwood, one of Darius's favorites, floated up from the tan-colored candle in the middle of the coffee table.

With one last glance around the living room, Stacy proceeded to the kitchen. Not wanting to appear overly presumptive, she'd kept the menu light, just in case Darius was hungry: homemade chicken salad with kaiser rolls fresh from his favorite kosher bakery, homemade potato salad, and an ice-cold chardonnay. After taking the wine out and putting it back and taking it out again, Stacy decided to open the bottle, have a glass, and calm her nerves. Tonight was the night things were going to get back on track with Big D. . . .

Stacy carried her glass of wine into the living room, dancing around to the musical groove: *"No one, no one, can get in the way of what I'm feeling. . . ."*

"That's right, Alicia," she said to the empty room. "Sing it, girl!" She danced over to a picture of little Darius being held by his father. "Nobody can stop what I'm feeling for you, baby!"

Stacy picked up the picture and twirled around the room, sipping wine and dreaming of "one big, happy family." She replayed the events of the past few weeks and the undeniable attraction she'd once again felt with Darius. She *knew* she wasn't the only one. He had to be feeling it too! The ringing of the doorbell signaled Darius's arrival—and with it . . . her future.

Stacy stopped just before she opened the door. She took a deep breath.

"Hey, D," she said, trying to sound casual as she smiled at father and son. "Come on in."

Darius could smell sandalwood before he opened the door. He immediately recognized Alicia Keys, noted the diamond earrings he'd given Stacy two Christmases ago, and picked up the scent of Issey Miyake's Reflections in a Drop perfume he'd raved about the first time Stacy had worn it. *Uh-oh.*

Stacy's come-hither smile widened. "What are you standing there for? Are you going to drop our son on the doorstep and run?" She left the door open and walked toward the kitchen. "Want a glass of wine?" she asked over her shoulder.

"Uh, no, thank you. I'm on my way to a meeting." Darius walked over to the couch, unstrapped his son, and lifted him out of the carrier.

"How long has he been asleep?" Stacy asked.

"Not long. Fell asleep on the ride over."

Good. Maybe Little Man will give me and his daddy a couple hours of quality time. Stacy held out a glass of wine from the crystal set Darius had purchased shortly before Darius was born— the ones they'd used to cheer his birth.

"Here—it's best to drink it while it's chilled," Stacy said.

Darius reluctantly took the glass. "Thanks," he said. He took a large gulp.

"Whoa, hold up, baby!" Stacy laughed. "Remember what you showed me? You're supposed to swirl it around and then take a small sip. And then you're supposed to savor the flavor, appreciating the taste of each ingredient as it goes down." She paused and demonstrated. "Like this, remember?"

Darius remembered. That was one of the good months, when he, Stacy, and Bo had been getting along. They'd taken a trip to Napa Valley and toured wine country. Stacy was about seven months pregnant then, so she'd merely taken a sip of two or three of the premier wines. But he and Bo had gotten ridiculously drunk, and they'd stayed up all night singing bubblegum soul from their childhood days at the top of their lungs: Cameo, Ready for the World, and Bo's hilarious, screeching rendition of Karyn White's "Superwoman."

Stacy's eyes sparkled. "You're remembering the wine country, huh? When we spent the night under the stars and made love in the grove by the grapevines?"

Darius simply smiled and nodded. His fondest memories were actually of him and Bo and the stolen moments they'd enjoyed.

"Let me take him upstairs," Stacy said. "Sit and relax. I'll be right back."

"Really, Stacy, I—"

"I'll be right back!" She was already up the stairs before he could reply.

When she came back down she went straight to the kitchen and brought out the bottle of wine. Amid Darius's protests, she refreshed both their glasses and then joined him on the couch, practically sitting on top of him.

"I've been waiting for this all day," she said and began kissing him without preamble.

When Darius opened his mouth to protest, Stacy slid her

tongue inside. All of a sudden, she was on fire, the months of celibacy exploding in a torrent of emotions and passion that left her breathless.

"Come on, Darius, you know you want to," she panted even while she tore at his shirt and fumbled with his jeans zipper. "Let's finish what we started last week."

"What we—Stacy, stop!" Darius pushed Stacy away from him and stood up in one motion. Silence descended on the room as they both caught their breath. "Look, Stacy, I'm sorry about that kiss last week. I never should have gone there."

"I wanted it; we wanted it. Don't tell me you haven't been feeling something these past weeks. Didn't you say you wanted us to be friends again, to stop all the fighting and haggling over Darius and all get along?"

"Yes, I said it, and I meant it too. But *friends*, Stacy, not lovers."

"And your comment the other night . . . about my lips."

"Stacy, it was a genuine compliment, nothing more."

He took a step toward Stacy. She turned her back to him.

Darius walked to within a foot of where she stood and began again. "There'll always be a bond between us, Stacy, because of our son. And I will always love you as his mother. I don't know how to make you understand . . . especially since my love is for another man, but . . . I'm in love with—"

Stacy held up her hand to interrupt him. "Don't . . . don't say his name." Against her will, her eyes began to water.

"Stacy . . ." Darius took the final steps and pulled her into his arms.

That's when the doorbell rang. Stacy's brow creased, angry at whoever had such a bad sense of timing. At this point and time she'd take a charity screw. All she could think of was getting rid of whomever as fast as she could so she could make Darius feel sorry for her and kiss her "boo-boo" so she could feel better.

She walked purposely to the door. Darius was right behind her. Without looking through the peephole, she opened it quickly.

"What the hell are you doing here?" she demanded.

Bo crossed his arms and drew himself up to his full five-foot-nine. His attitude was as starched as his shirt, and Stacy almost gagged at his profuse use of Unforgivable cologne.

Ignoring her, Bo called over her shoulder. "Baby, we're going to be late."

Stacy turned to Darius. "Oh, so this was your meeting? Why did you lie? Why didn't you just tell me you had a date with your wife? Damn, Darius. Does it do something to your ego to make me look like a fool?"

"Stupid is as stupid does," Bo mumbled.

"Look, asshole, nobody asked you."

Bo ignored her again. "Baby, we've got to go. People are waiting."

"Excuse me, Stacy," Darius said calmly.

After a few tense seconds, Stacy moved away from the door.

Once out, Darius turned back to her. "I'm sorry for the misunderstanding," he said as his eyes pleaded for peace. "If you'd like, I can pick up Darius next Saturday, give you and your friends a chance to go out . . . or whatever?"

"Don't worry about picking him up next Saturday or Sunday. I guess our little cease-fire was temporary. I'll be calling my lawyer tomorrow."

Stacy slammed the door and stood in the middle of the floor trying to catch her breath. How had she gotten it so wrong again? Especially when she knew the signs, had watched this movie again and again. Darius had been a reluctant participant at best, much like the first time they'd slept together. Darius couldn't have been plainer if he'd placed an ad in the *LA Times*: he didn't want her!

She downed her glass and then reached for the one Darius had barely touched. She gulped it down too, determined not to cry. She'd cried a thousand tears for Darius Crenshaw, and enough was enough. Finishing the glass she'd poured for him, she poured the remainder of the bottle into her glass and set the glass down on the table with a loud *clunk*.

"Am I stuck on stupid or what?" she yelled.

The sound woke up little Darius, who started yelling for his dad, of all people.

"Dada! Dada!"

"Your daddy ain't here!" Stacy yelled back as she stomped up the stairs to get her son. She walked into his room and turned on the dimmed light beside his crib. "Your daddy ain't here," she repeated. "It's just me and you, little man."

She almost choked on that line, but instead of crying, she bit her lip until she tasted blood and then redirected her attention to Darius's wet diaper and his need for a bath. As she washed his tiny brown body, the same skin tone as his father, she finally let the tears come.

But not for long. Stacy angrily wiped them away and forced herself to face reality. Darius would always be a homosexual, and she would never be his wife.

She put Darius to bed, and although it was barely eight thirty, she put on a pair of flannel pajamas and climbed between the sheets. Her head throbbed, both from the wine and from the reality of her self-deception. She thought about how different things might have been if she'd played it cool at the dinner when Tony had seemed genuinely interested. He seemed to be a good man and had become a regular at KCCC. But as had happened for the past four years, she'd bypassed all others for the singular goal of Darius Crenshaw. And for what?

Stacy tossed and turned as the thoughts refused to leave her. The next time she looked at the clock it was almost eleven. She was all cried out, yet sleep continued to elude her.

Then she remembered something, remembered the one thing she had never done. She'd asked God a zillion times to help her get Darius; she hadn't once asked Him to help her get over him.

Scurrying to the edge of the bed, she threw back the covers and got down on her knees, another thing she hadn't done in a long time.

"Father God," she began, as new tears threatened to erupt. She took a deep breath and began again. "God, I want to change. I don't want to keep wanting Darius, to keep needing him in my life. Help me get over him, God. Tell me what I need to do; give me some direction. Help heal my heart, God. And help me, please, help me move on."

Stacy stayed on her knees for a long time, not knowing whether or not her prayer had been answered, yet not being able to think of anything else to say. Finally she dragged herself off the floor and again folded herself underneath the covers. This time, sleep came quickly. And there were no more tears.

33

Thank You, Lord

"Hey, girl, how you doing?"

"I'm okay."

"You don't sound like it. Stacy, what's wrong?"

"I'm fine, Hope, just a little tired. Darius kept me up last night." She didn't feel the need to tell her friend which one.

"Is he sick?"

If you had a man who left his wife and child for another man, wouldn't you say so? "No, just a little cranky, maybe constipated or something. He's all right now. What's up?"

"I called to see if you wanted to go to church with me tonight."

"To bible study?" At one time, Stacy had never missed a Wednesday night at Kingdom Citizens. But she couldn't remember the last time she'd gone. "I don't know, Hope."

Hope persisted. "I don't usually go either, but I just found out we'll have an unexpected guest tonight. Rev Thicke will be there. Remember the preacher out of Texas, the one who has the prophetic ministry?"

Stacy remembered—another fine, unavailable Christian man. She didn't know if she was up to an evening of lusting after someone she couldn't have . . . again. And she definitely didn't want to see Darius.

"Thanks, Hope, but I think I'll pass."

"Please, Stacy. My life's been crazy lately. I prayed to God for a word from Him. And now the prophet is coming. Maybe he'll have a word for you too. So, will you come? Cy is in New York today, so it'll just be me and you."

Hope rarely asked Stacy for anything. A couple hours in the house of the Lord was the least she could do for her friend. "I guess I'll go. Though I doubt there's anything Rev Thicke can tell me I don't already know."

The buzz about Rev Nathaniel Thicke being at KCCC had the pews filled early. Stacy and Hope walked to a row reserved for ministers' wives. Right away, Stacy's eyes landed on Darius, front and center, as always, playing lead keyboards for the praise and worship team.

Stacy felt the familiar flutter associated with seeing her man. "God, you promised," she whispered.

"Huh?"

Stacy just shook her head. *Help me get over him, Lord, please.*

Hope looked at her another moment, then at Darius, then back at her. She said a silent prayer for her friend.

Both prayers were answered as a man who could help any woman get over anybody walked into the pulpit. Thoughts of other men fled when a woman looked at Rev Nathaniel Thicke, the thirty-year-old senior pastor of the Gospel Truth Church in Palestine, Texas. Reverend Thicke was new to the Total Truth Association and to the national stage, having joined the organization two years ago. He'd caused a female frenzy when he'd spoken for the first time at Kingdom Citizens during the annual Kingdom Conference. News had spread like wildfire about this "fine young preacher from Palestine."

Nathaniel stood six feet, three inches tall in his deep chocolate glory—"blue-black," as his hue was defined in the Texas countryside. He licked thick lips surrounded by a dimple on one side and small mole on the other, his creamy, smooth complexion thankfully devoid of hair, scars, pimples, or anything else that would take away from his beauty. His texturized hair was immaculate; cut to just above his ears in front, grazing the top of his tan-colored designer suit collar in the back, with groomed sideburns just long enough to make one know he was his own man with a sense of what worked for him and what didn't. On someone else, the sideburns would have looked tacky; on him, they just made you want to smooth them down with your tongue.

After briefly scanning the congregation, Nathaniel stood with eyes closed, swaying softly to the instrumental music Darius played in the background. He licked his lips once again, causing a flurry of fluttering heartbeats, and began to sing softly: *"Thank you, Lord; thank you, Lord; thank you, Lord. I just want to thank you, Lord."*

The band immediately switched to accompany him, and a spattering of congregants who knew the song joined the choir, who backed the visiting minister effortlessly. Nodding his head, Nathaniel began again, a little louder, as he opened his eyes, left the podium, and began walking back and forth in the pulpit.

"That's it, son of God, daughter of the Most High, give him thanks and praise tonight!" The sound got louder as more and more worshippers joined in. "You've been so good. You've been my friend," Nathaniel continued, each phrase repeated like the first. The song was simple, yet powerful, giving God the praise. By now most of the congregation was on their feet, some swaying, others with hands upraised, while still others cried openly and wiped tears from their eyes as they remembered reasons to be grateful.

Stacy was not one of these congregants. She folded her arms as Hope stood, trying hard not to have an attitude. She'd asked God to deliver Darius Crenshaw from homosexuality, but He had said no. She'd asked for God to send her someone

else, and He had said no. What made her believe He'd help her
get over him?

But as the saints continued to sing, Stacy's heart softened.
She knew she had plenty of reasons to be thankful: a healthy
son and mother and brothers who'd do anything to keep her
safe and happy; friends like Hope and Frieda; and a church that
preached the unadulterated Word of God. Stacy knew she was
being unreasonable, but sometimes reason flew out the window during that time of the month. She'd gotten her period
just this morning, and that—not seeing Darius looking good
as ever—was the excuse she used for her fairly foul mood.

Nathaniel stopped singing and motioned to the musicians
to continue playing softly.

"Now some of you in here are wondering 'What do I have
to praise God about?' You've got bills due; your child is sick.
Some of you have prayed for a mate, while others have prayed
to be rid of the mate you have!"

Laughter filtered through the audience.

"Some of you need a job; maybe others are trying to maintain your college GPA. You're having problems with your kids;
your parents just don't understand you; gas is high; pay is low;
God hasn't come through, he hasn't answered! Why, you ask,
should I thank God? We're going to go into detail tonight, on
prayer, and getting yours answered, but for now, just know this:
It's not what you pray, but how you pray, that determines the
kind of answer you get. It's not simply the words you speak, it's
the feeling that's in your heart that determines whether your
supplication will reach the throne of grace. And then there's
one more thing beloved . . . you have to believe.

"Matthew 21:22 says *'All things,* whatsoever you shall ask
in prayer, *believing,* you shall receive,' you shall have. In Mark,
chapter eleven, Jesus says, 'Whatever you say to the mountain.'
Now, mountain can be perceived as any problem you have, but
Jesus says if you don't doubt in your heart but believe that the

things you say—translated, pray—shall come to pass, you shall have whatever you say. Dearly beloved, what I am saying is exactly what Jesus said in Mark 9:23: 'if you can believe, all things are possible.'

"So let's sing this song again. And this time, sing it like you believe God has already answered your prayer, that you already have the victory. Close your eyes, and in your mind's eye see that thing already done. And then thank him now like you'll thank him later, when the desire of your heart has come to pass. Thank him now as if what you've prayed for, you've already received."

Darius and the band bumped the music up an octave as the musicians showed why they made the band. Randall plucked his bass guitar strings as if each note were a hallelujah, while the saxophonist and drummer put the *P* in praise. Blending it all together was Darius's soft and steady tickling of the ivories, his head nods serving as direction for the band and for the choir who once again lifted their voices. *"Thank you, Lord, I just want to thank you, Lord."*

This time Stacy stood, joining a tearful, already standing Hope, who sang with her arms outstretched to heaven. Stacy could just imagine the baby Hope pictured, for she was sure there was an infant somewhere in Hope's prayer to God. Stacy began singing softly as she closed her eyes and imagined how it would feel to be able to totally let go of Darius and have someone in her life who would return her love. And even now, someone was looking at her with adoration in his eyes.

Stacy left church feeling better and thanked Hope for the invite. Driving home, she realized she had heard a Word from the Lord: to be thankful and to believe that what she wanted had already come to pass.

Once home, Stacy decided to pamper herself with a bubble bath. She poured a liberal amount of Bath & Body Works Coconut Lime Verbena into the tub and added a handful of bath salts. While the tub filled, she walked into her room and put on a CD Frieda's friend from Kansas City had sent her, a phenomenal female guitar player named LadyMac. As the sounds of the CD's first cut, "After the Rain," began to play, Stacy took off her clothes and walked naked into the bathroom. She lit two white candles, turned off the lights, and gingerly sank down into the steamy, hot water.

After thoroughly washing her body, Stacy continued to gather bubbles and run them over her body with her hands. With eyes closed, she explored her body, running hands over thighs, stomach, breasts. She lifted an arm out of the water and placed it behind her, examining her breasts as she did regularly when bathing.

After finishing with her left breast, she changed arm positions and continued the examination on her right breast. As she pressed lightly on the outer portion of the tender flesh, her eyes flew open. She sat up in the tub, raised her arm and felt again. Her heart began beating faster, seemingly of its own volition, as Stacy felt a definite lump about the size of a quarter.

Probably nothing, she thought as she quickly exited the tub, toweled off, and went to her master bedroom's full-length mirror to further examine the area where she'd felt the lump. She couldn't see anything, but she definitely felt something.

Stacy forced herself not to panic and calmed herself by saying the Lord's Prayer. But her mother's words came in louder than thoughts of thy kingdom come. "The Lord helps those who help themselves."

Stacy concluded her mother was right. She vowed to make a doctor's appointment first thing in the morning.

34

Watch Your Man II

"Hey, baby, I'm home." Cy walked into the living room late Thursday and found a sleeping Hope on the couch in the living room. Instead of watching television, the television was watching her.

Cy smiled softly as he put down his briefcase, turned off the television and lights, and then scooped up his sleeping beauty and headed for the bedroom. Hope woke up in his arms.

"Hey," she whispered.

"Hey, baby. You were out like a light. Long day?"

"Not really. But I took a Tylenol PM—premenstrual cramps." She yawned into his shoulder.

Cy entered their master suite and lay Hope on the bed. "Well, mine was a long day, not the least of it being the five-hour flight that was part of that weather delay in New York. And I need to be in San Diego first thing tomorrow morning. So I . . . Hope? Hope, are you listening?"

The soft sound of light snoring was his reply.

The next morning, Hope stumbled into the kitchen as Cy finished the glass of orange juice he'd used to down his Super-Food pills.

"Good morning, Sleeping Beauty. Feeling better?"

"I don't know. I'm feeling discombobulated. That's it for me and those pills." Hope looked at the clock on the kitchen wall. "No wonder I still feel sleepy—it's seven o'clock. Where are you going so early?"

"Meetings. I'll be home around seven or so, in time for dinner. Or we can go out if you'd like." Cy walked over and kissed her forehead. "Take it easy today, baby. We can't afford to have you sick during the holidays."

Though tired and a bit jet-lagged, there was a bounce in Cy's steps as he waited for the valet to bring around the Azure. Plans were proceeding quickly on his and Hope's dream home. After today's meeting, he could implement the next steps in the process—meeting the construction company the architect had recommended and clearing all zoning and construction concerns with the city. Then the stage would be set to make the home he and Hope had long envisioned a reality.

Initially, Cy had really wanted Hope to see the property, make absolutely sure it was what she wanted. But after at first insisting on doing so, Hope later refused, saying it was time she put total trust back into him and the marriage. Now, he was glad she hadn't seen it. It would make the final unveiling that much more spectacular.

After Cy left, Hope fought the urge to crawl back into bed and instead stepped into a hot shower. Once done, she put on water for tea and then dressed in a casual, black warm-up with butterfly flip-flops. It had been a long time, but she planned to push any remaining cobwebs from her mind with a long walk on the beach.

Hope flavored her green tea English style, with vanilla creamer and raw sugar. She was on her way to check e-mails on her computer when the phone rang.

"Hi, Mama."

"Hey, Hope. Just calling to check on you. How's everything?"

"Okay, I guess. It's that time of the month, so I'm pretty moody. Plus I took a Tylenol PM last night that still has me feeling like I'm underwater. I don't think I'll take those again."

"But other than your period, you're feeling better?"

. . . *as if what you've prayed for, you've already received.* Hope would fake it until she made it.

"I'm fine, Mama, really."

She spent the rest of the conversation talking about Dr. Thicke's sermon and her father's ever improving health.

After pouring another cup of tea, Hope walked into the den where she'd last used her laptop. Touching a button to prompt the screen, she quickly typed in her Yahoo address and hit ENTER. Nothing. *Oh, no, not again,* she thought. Her laptop had been acting up the past couple weeks, but every time she thought of taking it in for repair or replacing it, the machine would act right for a few days. But here again, the screen was frozen. With an exasperated sigh, Hope turned off the computer, picked up her tea, and headed for Cy's office.

The screen came on to Cy's inbox. Hope sat down, clicked on the address bar, and was just about to type in Yahoo when a name in her husband's inbox caught her eye: Millicent Kirtz.

Before Hope had time to think about it, she clicked on the e-mail. It was short and to the point. She read it twice to make sure she'd read correctly:

Hey, Cy:
Change in plans. I'll meet you at the Hotel Parisi.
Love, MK

Hope stared at the message as thoughts raced through her head. The first thoughts were rational: *Don't trip, Hope. He's doing business with Jack. Millicent is probably just . . .* Then the devil on the other shoulder took over. *Yeah, just doing what? Screwing your man, that's what.* Frieda's mental mantra was the final straw. *Watch that heifah . . . watch your man.*

Hope pushed her chair back from the desk and stood abruptly. After retrieving her cell phone from the bedroom, she called Stacy. The call went to voice mail. She started to punch in Frieda's number and then changed her mind. By the time her cousin got through adding her two cents to the situation, Hope would be really jacked up.

She walked back to Cy's office and read the message a third time. Why would Millicent be meeting Cy? Why didn't the e-mail mention Jack? Hope was determined to find out, now, before the devil could steal her joy. Hadn't she vowed last night to believe God's promises? She couldn't get to the phone fast enough.

The first time, Cy's phone went to voice mail. She left a quick "call back" message, hung up, and texted him: **Where are you? Call me.**

After waiting five minutes, Hope decided to leave the house. She was too wound up to stay inside. She retrieved her purse, phone, and other necessities from the bedroom and headed for her car.

As soon as she'd exited the parking garage, she dialed Cy again.

"Hey, baby, I was just about to call. Is something wrong?" he asked.

"I couldn't reach you. Where are you?"

"Headed to San Diego. I told you last night."

Hope didn't remember him saying anything. "Another meeting with Jack?"

Cy didn't want to give too much away; he planned to surprise her with a mockup of their mansion next week.

"I'm meeting with, uh, Charlie and some other construction companies. Boring stuff, baby. You wouldn't be interested."

You're meeting with Millicent! Hope fought the urge to scream what she knew. He was ninety miles away from her and could easily deny it. She had a better plan.

"Baby, I have another call. See you tonight?" he said.

"Sure," Hope said and disconnected the call. He'd see her, all right. Hope switched into the turn lane and merged onto the southbound 405.

35

Right Now

Stacy nervously twisted her purse strap as she waited in the screening room where the nurse had left her. She wished she'd remembered to bring a magazine from the waiting room— anything to take her mind off of the lump.

The nurse performing the mammogram had been reassuring: most lumps were found to be benign, especially among Black women, who seemed to have "lumpy" breasts more frequently than their counterparts. Stacy remembered hearing something like that before, but she couldn't remember where.

What's taking them so long? Stacy thought as she looked at the clock to see if the second hand still moved. Had it really been only five minutes? Now she was second-guessing her decision to come to the hospital alone. *Maybe I should have called my mom or Hope.* But she didn't want to involve anyone in what would probably turn out to be a routine procedure. *Most of these tests usually come back benign.* Stacy tried to calm herself with a litany of the nurse's words. And then she remembered the sermon from two nights ago and the prayer she'd prayed again and again since feeling the lump. *Lord, please let me be all right.* She took a deep breath and then took comfort in the minister's words. God's Word would not return void, and what He promised, He would do.

Stacy's phone rang. As she reached for her purse, she remembered it had rung earlier while the nurse had been performing the mammogram. Suddenly she wondered if it was about her son. Was Darius all right? That was the last thing she needed, she thought as she raced frantically to find the phone that somehow always ended up at the very bottom of her purse. By the time she found it, it had stopped ringing. *Hope.* Stacy breathed a sigh of relief. Just as she was about to dial her number, the nurse came back into the room.

"Sorry that took so long," she said. "We're understaffed today."

The nurse took another look at Stacy's chart and then noticed her patient's steady foot tapping against the floor. She sat down next to her and put a soft hand on her arm.

"Please try not to worry," she said sincerely. "Most of the time, these tests prove to be nothing more than lumpy tissue. Having said that, we would like to biopsy the lump as a precaution and have the tissues sent to our lab for processing. The radiologist is with another patient right now, and the procedure itself will take about thirty minutes. Do you need to call your employer?"

Stacy's fear returned, tripled. "You want to do it right now?"

"Yes, we believe the faster a diagnosis is determined, the better for everyone. If it's benign, you can have the reassurance of the test, and if for some reason we get another result, treatment can begin as soon as possible. Okay?"

"I guess so. So you're going to actually cut off some of my breast? I may need to call my mother."

"No, Stacy, what we're going to do is a minimally invasive procedure called image-guided needle biopsy. It's an alternative to surgery that employs the use of ultrasound. It's basically painless, treated with just local anesthesia. You'll be fine."

The rest of the visit passed in a fear-induced mental fog. The nurse brought Stacy a stack of magazines, but later Stacy wouldn't have been able to tell anybody what she'd read. It took almost an hour before the radiologist got to her and another hour for the procedure. The nurse had been right—except for the prick of the initial needle to deliver the anesthesia, the procedure hadn't really hurt at all. It looked like the most painful part would be waiting for the results. It would probably be the longest five days of her life.

36

The Tea Party

The closer Hope got to La Jolla, the stupider she felt. *What in the hell am I doing?* She knew it would be good to get another opinion, but Stacy wasn't answering her phone, and she wasn't sure she wanted Frieda's advice. She thought about calling Vivian but just as quickly dismissed that idea. She didn't want to come off looking like a weak, paranoid woman, which was rather how she was feeling right now. In the end, she decided it was better to look foolish now than to wonder later.

"Exit La Jolla Village Drive," the GPS computer voice intoned. Hope veered onto the exit ramp to follow its instructions. A couple turns later, a beautiful, boutique-style hotel was in front of her. It looked expensive and Mediterranean and . . . romantic. Hope waved away the valet, parked, and walked into the hotel.

"Oh, Cy, forgive my unprofessional bare feet. But I've been in these heels all day, and my feet say enough!"

Millicent walked past Cy into the large, well-appointed suite. She carried a couple of paper bundles and a briefcase.

"Here—let me help," Cy said, taking the bundles out of her arms.

"Whew, thanks. I never thought I'd like staying home rather than being full time in the workplace, but I can't say I miss it. Especially wearing heels all day every day. But it makes a difference. Our church is very casual, so I hardly wear heels now unless Jack and I go out."

"Your life sounds so different than your Kingdom days," Cy said as he unrolled the bundle of papers to reveal several separate sheets of what were clearly floor plans. "*You* are so different."

"And that's a good thing. By the way, Jack should be here in about ten minutes."

"No worries at all. In fact, I just ordered room service. Nothing fancy, just sandwiches and something to drink. I didn't know how long this would take, but I'm anxious to get this part done so we can build the model and I can finally let Hope in on the surprise."

"Goodness, she doesn't know?" Millicent frowned slightly. "I don't know, Cy. Most women I know would definitely want to be in on the planning of their home's design."

Cy shook his head. "Oh, no, the house layout won't be a surprise. We've discussed it in-depth. And we both agree on building here in La Jolla. She just doesn't know the land I purchased was for our dream home, or that it is six months away from completion. I'm hoping to give it to her as a birthday gift or for whichever holiday is close to the time it's completed. Do you think she'll be pleased?"

"If you two have already agreed on everything you're building, I think she'll be thrilled."

Cy said nothing but just nodded his head as he scoured over the plans Millicent had brought.

"I hope you don't mind that I volunteered to bring the plans over. Jack was going to have his assistant do it, but honestly, I wanted to talk to you."

This time Cy looked up. "About what?"

"I don't miss my old life, but I do wonder what's going on with everybody. I know I should call Vivian and a few others, but it seems the longer you go without calling, the harder it is."

"I'm sure Vivian would love to see you guys, Millicent. Derrick too."

"And I'd love to see them. And believe it or not, I really want to get to know Hope better. She seems like a woman with her head on straight, and now that you and Jack are in business together, well, I just hope we can put the past in the past and embrace this wonderful now."

"I want that too."

"So tell me, how is life at good ol' Kingdom Citizens Christian Center?"

"Steady growing, as usual. We're behind on the building of the new sanctuary but—" A knock at the door interrupted him. "Excuse me. That's probably room service."

It was, but the person standing behind the rolling tray was not who he had expected.

"Hope! What on earth are you doing here?"

"I could ask you the same question!" She almost ran Cy over with the cart. He jumped out of the way as she barreled into the room, having given the waiter fifty dollars and a smile to let her "serve her husband."

Once inside, she wasted no time ripping into an incredulous Millicent, who'd been stunned into silence.

"You just can't give up, can you? Just can't let it go. Even a husband and a baby isn't enough. Being first lady isn't enough!"

Millicent finally found her voice. "Hope, please this is totally not what you—"

"Baby—"

"Don't you dare!" Hope said as she whirled around to face her husband. "You lied to me!"

"Hope, I—"

"Lied! Time and time again. I asked you point blank this

morning where you were going. Uh, let me see, if I recollect correctly, that answer would have been 'a meeting with Charlie?' Well, unless Charlie has turned from a White man into a Black woman, you've got some explaining to do. No, never mind. On second thought, a picture is worth a thousand words."

Cy was still so shocked he could barely think. But he knew Hope was an intelligent, logical woman who would listen to reason. And truth. It was time to let her in on what was going on.

But he didn't get a chance to. As he walked over to the table where the plans lay, Hope walked over to the serving tray.

"You're still chasing after him, still have the hots for my man?" she asked Millicent on her way over. "Well, maybe this will cool your adulterous ass down."

And with that she threw the full pitcher of Numi certified organic Rainforest Green Mate Lemon Myrtle Green Tea into Millicent's shocked face.

Some of the tea splashed into Millicent's open mouth. She sputtered and spit, even as she tried to recover from the shock of Hope's attack. She tried to speak, but no words came out. So she just stood there, dripping, and looking at Cy like WTF?

Cy was even more shocked than Millicent. Hope was almost to the door before he recovered and went after her.

"Hope—now, you just wait a minute!"

Hope flung open the door and ran into the hard chest of Jack Kirtz. "Whoa, there, little lady. Where's the fire!"

It took him a few seconds to realize there had actually been one. First, Cy pushed past him and ran down the hall after said little lady and then he walked into the suite to see his dripping-wet wife looking lost and forlorn in the middle of the living room.

"What in God's name is going on here?" Jack asked. He rushed over to his wife. "Millie, honey, are you all right?"

"I'm fine, Jack."

"What happened? Did Cy do this?" Jack turned to leave the room. "Why, I'll—"

"Jack, no, it's not Cy's fault. Please, just come help me."

Cy caught up with Hope at the elevator. Grabbing her arm, he turned her around forcibly. "You are not going anywhere until you learn the truth about what's happening here."

Hope snatched her arm out of Cy's grasp and glared at him.

"Hope, what is wrong with you? This is nothing like what you're imagining." When she continued glaring but said nothing, Cy took a deep breath and continued. "It's about us, Hope, and what I was trying to make a surprise. When you come back to the suite, you'll see floor plans for our dream house. Jack recommended the architect. Charlie is doing the construction, and yes, he is coming to this meeting, and because Jack was delayed by a meeting at his church, Millicent simply brought the plans over for him. She knew how excited I was to get started on . . . on my gift to you."

As if on cue, the elevator dinged, and the door opened. Out walked a cowboy-hat-wearing Charlie Seagram, being his usual, jovial self. "Well, my goodness," Charlie said when he saw Cy by the elevator. "I know I'm special, but really, Cy, you didn't have to wait by the elevator. I would have found my way to the room." He turned to Hope with an outstretched hand. "Charlie Seagram, ma'am. Pleased to meet you."

Hope felt as if she were waking up to find herself in a bad dream. She looked at Charlie blankly and then at Cy as tears began shining in her eyes.

Charlie looked at the couple and finally picked up on the tension he'd missed earlier. "Uh, Cy, is everything all right, here?"

"Jack's in the suite," Cy answered. "The last door on your left."

Charlie looked from Cy to Hope and back again before he turned and walked down the hall.

"I am so sorry, Cy," Hope said softly. "I read an e-mail Millicent sent you and—"

"You're reading my e-mails? After all this time, all the talks, you *still* think something is up between me and Millicent?"

"No, I just—I mean." Hope swallowed and began again. "You know how my computer has been locking up. I went into your office to check my e-mails, and when the screen came up, your inbox was open. I saw her name and clicked on it. It was wrong. I shouldn't have. I'm sorry."

Cy vacillated between pity, incredulity, and straight-up pissed. He shook his head. "I don't know what's going on with you, Hope, but this woman here? She's not the one I married. We need to figure this out, but first, we need to go back and try to undo the damage your assumptions and ill-conceived actions have caused."

Hope followed Cy like a recalcitrant child. She couldn't have felt worse if he'd called her a *b* or a *ho* and told her she sho' was ugly. She would almost have preferred a cussing out. His controlled patience underscored her having been out of control. Hope always prayed against experiencing an earthquake, but now, as they walked down the hall, she hoped that one would happen right now, if only where she was walking, so the earth could swallow her up and deliver her from the mess she'd made.

As they turned the corner to the suite, Millicent was coming out. Millicent hesitated a moment when she saw them walking toward her and then straightened her back and began again with renewed resolve.

Hope started talking while there was still distance between them. "Millicent, I'm so sorry."

"You should be, Hope."

Millicent turned to Cy. "I told Charlie I tripped. Your professional reputation is still intact."

"I'm very sorry, Millicent," Hope said again. Her emotions were still roiling; it was the best she could do.

Cy stepped in. "Please tell me what I can do to remedy this situation."

"It's okay, Cy. I'm okay, really."

He reached into his pocket and pulled out several hundreds. "At least let me handle the cleaning bill and your hair . . ."

"You just take care of Hope. I'll be fine." Millicent continued on toward the elevator.

"We'll be in touch!" Cy called after her.

They both watched as Millicent continued down the hall, head held high, wet blouse clinging to her back. Once she turned the corner, Cy and Hope turned toward each other.

"I think I need to see a doctor," Hope blurted.

"I don't know what to say, baby. But whatever is going on with you, it needs to get handled."

"Mama told me depression runs in our family. I've tried to deny something was really wrong, but . . . Cy, I am truly, really so sorry for everything: not trusting you, looking at your mail, not asking point blank about you and Millicent. This is just so wrong, and it's my fault."

Cy looked at his watch. He had an appointment after this one, and it could not be postponed. "We'll talk when I get home. Are you okay to drive?"

Hope started to cop an attitude and then changed her mind. When you acted like you were insane, this was how you were treated.

"I'm fine, Cy," she said softly. "When do you think you'll be home?"

"I don't know."

With that, Cy turned and walked toward the suite of the new infamous LaJolla "tea party." He did not look back.

37

Life and Death

"I think I just ruined my marriage." Stacy had finally answered when Hope called.

"Girl, now you're sounding as dramatic as Frieda," Stacy said dryly.

"No, Stacy, I'm serious." Hope relayed the day's events in minute detail, so someone would have to pay Stacy not to understand how serious this was.

"Things could be worse," Stacy said after Hope's long diatribe.

That's when Hope knew something was not right. The woman she was talking to didn't have Hope's toe, knee, or pinkie finger, much less her back. "Did you not hear what I just said? I poured a pitcher of tea over Millicent Sims's head!"

"Payback is a mutha—" Stacy mumbled.

"It wasn't payback, Stacy. I thought that she—wait a minute. Something's wrong. What is it?"

"Nothing. Not yet anyway."

"What am I supposed to make of that cryptic answer? Is this about Darius?" Hope asked that question to be polite; with Stacy it was hardly ever about anything else.

"I found a lump in my breast."

It was the first time Stacy had said the words aloud, and it stopped conversation on both ends for several seconds.

When conversation restarted, it was Stacy who spoke. "Two nights ago, after the prayer service with Rev Thicke, I went home, took a bath and, while sponging myself, felt this lump, about the size of a quarter, under my left breast."

"Oh, my gosh, Stacy!" Hope was quiet a moment. She didn't know what to say. "Did you go to the doctor?"

"That's where I was when you were blowing up my phone. They did a biopsy on me and sent the tissue to a lab. I'm supposed to know in three to five days whether it's benign."

Hope was quiet. There was life and death in the sense that she didn't think she could live without Cy. And then there was *life and death,* as in cancer, the word both women had thought but neither had yet said.

"Look, Stacy. I'm almost back in LA. Why don't you come over?"

"Naw, girl. It looks like you've got your own set of ugly going on. Plus, I stopped by my mother's house when I left the hospital, and nothing can make you feel better than a mama. She helped me put this whole thing in perspective and told me not to focus on something that isn't even fact yet. The nurse said most tests come back benign and that probably mine will too. I tell you what, Hope. It just makes me more thankful of everything, you know? Here I've been fighting with Darius over whether he should see his own son, and with Bo, who has legal claim to somebody who doesn't even want to be with me. What have I been thinking the past two-plus years? I haven't been thinking—that's the problem. I think this little scare is simply God's way of getting my attention. And I'm listening. It started the night Rev Thicke spoke, and it was just reemphasized today. From now on, there's no more half stepping when it comes to my faith. From now on, with my whole heart, I'm living for God."

★　★　★

It was after nine PM when Hope, waiting in the sitting area of their master suite, heard the elevator doors open to the penthouse. It was a moment she'd both been anticipating and dreading with equal measure. She already knew there was no excuse she could offer, no argument she could make, that would defend the day's actions. So she was willing to offer her sincere apologies and ask for forgiveness, and then it would be up to Cy from there.

She waited, hearing Cy move around in the living room and then in the kitchen. She heard the television turn on and then off. She thought she heard him in the office. He was in no more of a hurry to face the inevitable conversation than she was. So, taking the lead, she got up from the sitting area and walked toward the door. Cy was coming in at the same time.

"Oh, excuse me. I, uh, thought I heard you come in," she said.

"Yeah. Honestly I was avoiding this moment. And then I realized how silly and immature that was. I love you, Hope. You're what I have most wanted in this world. That's when I knew I had to stop dodging you and come in here to have a straight-out conversation. I need to know what is going on and how I can help you."

They walked back into the bedroom together. Cy took off his suit jacket and lay it across the bed. He loosened his tie and unbuttoned the first few buttons. Hope watched his actions while clasping and unclasping her hands. Finally she walked over to the suite's sitting area, where he joined her.

"Would you like some—" She almost choked on the word *tea* and changed the question. "Something to drink?"

Cy almost smiled. Sharing a cup of chamomile or passionfruit or one of their other favorite flavors was almost a nightly ritual. Now it would forever be linked to an ice-cold pitcher tossed in a hotel suite.

"No, I'm fine."

Hope began. "I talked to Vivian on the way home and made an appointment to see a therapist she recommended."

Cy eyed her critically. "That's good."

"And I talked with my mom. I thought it might be good to get away for a few days, but we've got rehearsals for the dance troupe."

"Nothing is more important than you being okay, Hope. I couldn't care less whether you finish the dance for Darius. In fact, maybe that responsibility is too much right now. Maybe it's too soon."

Hope nodded. "Maybe. I'm having lunch with Vivian next week after I see the therapist."

Cy steepled his fingers under his chin and looked at Hope for another long moment. "You and I need to talk about all this right now."

"Cy, I don't have anything for you other than 'I'm sorry.' This was without a doubt the stupidest thing I've ever done. I didn't listen to rhyme or reason, just went off half cocked the way I've seen other women do. The way Millicent did at Kingdom. I've always said I could never understand what would drive a woman to do such crazy things. Well, now I know.

"And even more than throwing that tea on Millicent—and I truly hope she forgives me for that—I'm sorry that I ruined your surprise to me. You've been working so hard, all these meetings and long hours, to give me exactly what I wanted. And here I go and ruin everything with my jealousies and insecurities, emotions I keep saying are under control . . . but they're not.

"Cy . . . can you forgive me?"

At any other time, this would have been the moment in which Cy walked over, scooped Hope up in his arms, looked into her eyes, and melted her soul with an "Of course, baby." Now, however, was not one of those times.

Instead he got up and began taking off his shirt. "I forgive you, Hope. But this can't be forgotten; it has to be dealt with.

Let's see how things look after you've met with the therapist. Now, it's been a very long and trying day for the both of us. I'm going to take a shower, and if you don't mind, I think I'll sleep in the guest room."

Hope's look was crestfallen. She and Cy had never been under the same roof and in separate beds.

"I'm sorry, but it's just the way I feel right now. I love you, Hope, but I need space."

38

Tempt a Godly Man

The *clickity-clack* of Vivian's heels on the church parking lot pavement was in stark contrast to the unusual quiet of this sunny and warm southern winter Saturday, Cali style. It was as if the entire neighborhood had embraced the first lady's somber mood, reflective and introspective, balancing a myriad of challenges on the shoulders of her St. John suit.

The quiet was almost thankfully broken up as she entered the youth center, where the sound of Darius's "Looks Like Reign" bounced off the rafters. Melody, the obvious troupe leader in Hope's absence, was front and center, executing an intricate step-and-turn movement for the other dancers to follow. They all stopped as they saw their first lady approach.

"Hello, ladies," Vivian said.

A variety of responses followed. "Hello, Sister Vivian."

"Hi, Mrs. Montgomery."

Finally, a shout-out from the ringmaster. "Hello, Lady V. Where's Ms. T?" Melody said, referencing the nickname they'd given their unasked-for chaperone.

"That's why I'm here. She had an emergency and won't be here today. She asked me to send her love and to tell you she has full confidence that we can carry on in her absence. I'm hoping her faith in you was not misplaced."

Again, a variety of responses ensued, the totality of which amounted to "We got this."

"Is Hope—I mean, Mrs. Taylor—I mean, Ms. T—going to be okay?" one girl asked.

"Just a little family business," Vivian said. "So here's what I need you to do. I need you ladies to start from the top and show me what you've got. If things look as though they've progressed sufficiently, I'll leave you to rehearse on your own."

The girls lined up quickly. They couldn't wait to show their first lady how tight their routine was. Melody stood in the center and counted off. Vivian pushed the PLAY button, and "Looks Like Reign" once again filled the room.

The first verse of the song accompanied Melody's solo dance. It was a combination of passion and raw talent, and Vivian could see where some of Hope's signature moves were being incorporated into the group. Halfway through the verse, Natasha joined Melody. The six remaining young women moved in sync during the chorus, and this sequence continued through the second verse. During the song's bridge, Melody was once again featured.

> "Reign: realizing everything's in God alignment . . . reign
> I'm in Him, and He's in me, and there is no denying
> I have the victory as long as I believe, come what may,
> That when the morning comes my life will look like reign. . . .
> Reign over trouble, over doubts over fears . . . reign, reign . . ."

When the ladies finished their routine, Vivian clapped politely. She could see from the expressions on their faces that they were quite pleased with what they'd created. Vivian was too, for the most part.

"Great job, ladies," she said sincerely. "I especially like the sign language that's been incorporated. Very nice." Vivian knew that this too was Hope's signature. But she wisely kept the praise generic.

"Melody, may I speak to you for a moment?"

Melody followed Vivian to a corner of the center.

"You really liked it, huh?"

"I loved it. You ladies will soon exemplify the godly woman God exalts. But there's something, Melody, that I want you to be acutely aware of."

The slightest frown scampered across Melody's youthful complexion. "What's that?"

Vivian decided on a direct approach. "You are a very attractive young lady, rapidly becoming a woman of God. Your body is reflecting these changes, so it is imperative that you are conscious of the signals you are sending with your movements."

"What's that mean?" Melody asked in a sulking tone.

Oh. She wants to play boo-boo the foo-foo. Well, here we go. "It means that when you stick your breasts out like this," Vivian demonstrated, "or your butt out like this," she mimicked Melody perfectly, "that movement may tempt a godly man in a way he doesn't want or need to be tempted."

"Was I doing that?" Melody asked the question, knowing the answer as it escaped her lips.

Vivian let her know she knew it too. "Look, girl. I know you find it hard to believe, but I was once your age. And I wanted to make sure the boys noticed me. Now I'm not saying this is your MO, but because you are such a beautiful girl, you may get a type of attention you don't want. There is a difference between performing and praise dancing," Vivian continued. "You are dancing for God, and your body is His temple. So make sure the moves you make are ones for which He gets glory. Understand?"

Melody nodded, her eyes downcast. *Forget you, witch. I'm not dancing for you or God. I'm dancing for Darius.*

"Okay, good. Now go work on your steps. You're an obvious leader and doing a good job. I'm proud of you."

Yeah, whatever.

Vivian realized how important it was to instill self-esteem

in these ladies and to offer praise so they didn't go looking for validation in all the wrong places. Still, she made a mental note to talk to Hope about implementing the praise-dance training courses that had preceded the Angels of Hope praise troupe's debut at Mount Zion Progressive, the church run by Vivian and Derrick's best friends, the Brooks.

"What did she say?" Natasha asked as Melody joined the girls in the circle.

"She just told me how good we were," Melody responded. "C'mon, y'all, let's hurry up and finish this so we can go over to Darius's house."

Thirty minutes later, that's where they were. True to his word, Darius had finally made good on his promise to have the girls over. It was almost unheard of for Bo not to cook, but he didn't agree with Darius's befriending of Melody. A dozen boxes from Pizza Hut was the silent protest Bo had had delivered before retiring to the bedroom.

Melody was in seventh heaven as she soaked in her surroundings—the landscaped backyard, complete with pool and Jacuzzi. If she played her cards right, all this could be hers. And she intended to play the bump out of her deck of cards. She waited until the other girls were deep in discussion about who said what about whomever, and then she sidled up to Darius, who was checking his e-mails.

"I did something for you," she whispered. "Can I show you?"

"What is it?"

"Our latest dance video. I hope that if you like it I can maybe be in the next one you make. But can we go to another room? It's kinda bright out here."

Darius eyed Melody before replying, "Come on in, ladies, I'm getting ready to watch your routine."

How am I going to seduce him if I never get him to myself? Still, she pasted a smile on top of her carefully cultivated carefree attitude and followed Darius into the house. They walked through the sunroom and down the hall to the combined library and theater. Melody felt as if she had died and gone to heaven as she watched the man of her dreams in his low-riding shorts and black tank top. He looked the part of who he was— a superstar.

They entered the room, and Darius asked for the DVD. He pushed a button, and the watercolor painting lifted to reveal a large flat-screen. He went into a small room just off the main area to insert the DVD, and soon the rough sounds of girls talking filled the room. Darius adjusted the volume as he joined Melody on the couch. She was thrilled he'd chosen to sit next to her!

Melody squelched the urge to watch Darius instead of the video. She wanted to know if he was focused on her. She didn't have to wait long to find out.

"That was good, y'all," he said once the song had ended.

"You really think so?" Natasha asked.

"Yes, I do. In fact, if y'all keep behaving yourselves, I just might put you in a video."

"All of us?" one of the girls shouted.

"We'll see," Darius responded. He pushed a button on the remote to stop the DVD and another to shut off the television. The watercolor picture slid back in place, and Darius stood. "Okay, ladies, I've got work to do. Hope you enjoyed yourselves."

Various answers rang out as the girls thanked their host. Melody hung back as they walked toward the door. She didn't want to leave.

"Can I stay a little longer, by myself?" she asked boldly. "I want to talk to you about the fan club and about becoming a part of your business. The other girls are just doing this because I asked them. But I seriously want to help you."

Darius looked at the sincerity on Melody's face and almost felt sorry for her because, one, she actually thought he needed her help and, two, she thought there might be more than one way she could help him. Didn't she know he was gay? And what was it about straight women who felt they could make a gay man straight? At the end of the day it didn't matter. Even if she wasn't too young, which she was, Darius wasn't interested.

"Thank you," he answered as he gently led her around him and out the door where the others stood waiting. "But Bo is all the help I need."

39

Guys and God

It had been a while since Stacy had gone to the early morning service, but on this slightly cool December Sunday, she was one of the first to arrive. In her heart she knew that the change to live for God had come before she'd felt the lump, but she had to admit her fear of having cancer definitely made her all the more determined. She turned the corner to the nursery and was surprised to see Vivian coming down the hall.

"Good morning, Stacy. You're here early."

"Good morning, Sistah Viv," Stacy responded.

"Is everything okay?" Vivian asked.

Stacy hadn't meant to share anything with her first lady, but before she could form a yes with her mouth, tears threatened.

"Get Darius settled and then come in my office," Vivian said.

"It's okay, Sistah Viv. I'm okay."

"Did that sound like a question, Stacy Gray? Now, don't make me come look for you if you're not down there in five minutes!"

Stacy managed a weak smile with her okay.

A half hour later, Stacy entered the sanctuary feeling grateful that she'd bumped into Vivian. The first lady had helped to calm her fears and then prayed with her. Stacy informed Vivian that she wanted to get more involved in the ministry. They discussed her rejoining the choir, helping with the Sanctity of Sisterhood seminars, or participating in an area of the worship arts. When Pastor Derrick spoke on the fruitfulness of forgiveness, Stacy knew God was talking to her and vowed to do one more thing before leaving church.

Hope walked over to her pew as soon as church was over. "Hey, girl. I called you this morning. Wanted to invite you out to eat after service."

"Over at the Montgomerys'?"

"No, Cy and I have been wanting to try this new soul-food restaurant. The menu is completely vegetarian, but people swear it tastes like real meat."

"Yeah, the only people who think soy taste like meat are vegetarians who haven't eaten meat in years."

Hope laughed. "So you want to come?"

Stacy looked up and saw Darius walking toward the side door that led to the executive offices. "Hold up. I need to do something."

Hope looked in the direction Stacy had fled. She fought the urge to roll her eyes. *Girl, when are you going to stop chasing after Darius?*

Vivian walked up. "Hope, can you come back to the office for a moment? There's something I need to discuss right quick."

Hope reached for her phone. "Let me tell Cy where I'm at."

"No need to. He's already back there with Derrick. Come on."

Instead of going to Derrick's office, Vivian walked into her smaller one just down the hall. Hope quickly texted Cy that she was in the suite and then sat back to hear what was on Vivian's mind.

She didn't have to wait long. "I'm afraid I made a hasty decision I now need to retract," Vivian said as she sat down next to Hope. "It's the dance troupe. We're moving too fast. The girls need to be taught before they perform. They need to understand the difference between dancing for guys and dancing for God."

Just outside the executive office entrance, another type of understanding was taking place.

"Just what exactly are you saying, Stacy?"

"I am saying you don't have to continue the lawsuit. I won't fight you anymore in spending time with your son. And I won't come between him and his inevitable relationship with your—with Bo. He's your child, and he needs to be in your life. He needs to know his father, and I need to get out of the way of your relationship."

Darius raised his brows with a skeptical look. "What brought on this change of heart?"

"A lot of things. But mostly that what I was doing wasn't right." Stacy looked directly into Darius's eyes, her own shining with sincerity. "I had my priorities all out of order. But I'm changing that. I've been waiting on God for things to get better, and He's been waiting on me. And I'm sorry, Darius, for everything."

"I accept your apology, Stacy. And of course I'm ecstatic to know I can have a relationship with my son without all the drama. It's all I've ever wanted, you know, to be able to have a civil relationship and help raise our son."

"Well, from now on, you'll have that." Stacy turned to go before tears threatened to fall.

"Wait a minute, Stacy. Is there more to this story? It's like you . . . Are you okay?"

Why does everyone keep asking me that? Do I look like I have cancer? Stacy chose attitude over fear. "Why? Don't I look okay?"

"Sure, it's just that . . . Never mind. Is Little Man in the nursery?"

Stacy nodded.

"Okay. I'll see you on Tuesday."

Stacy left the sanctuary and headed for the parking lot. She wasn't in the mood for food or company. Try as she might, she couldn't stop thinking about the test results and what would happen if the biopsy was malignant. Would they have to do a mastectomy? And what if it had spread to the other breast or other parts of her body? A cancer diagnosis was serious. People died.

After she'd driven a while, she had second thoughts. Maybe being by herself was the last thing she needed. There was too much time to think. She needed somebody to take her mind off her troubles, and she instantly knew who to call.

"Y'all heifahs about to feel my wrath," Frieda said upon answering.

"What?"

"What?" Frieda mimicked. "You cows forget about our weekly powwow? I couldn't catch you or Hope yesterday!"

"Oh, what's the matter, Shabach back in Atlanta? 'Cause that's the only reason you'd be trying to have lunch with your friends."

"Forget you, heifah."

"You know I'm right."

"Damn skippy, and I won't even lie about that. And to be honest, I'm glad he's gone."

"Why, what happened?"

"He's about to turn a sistah out. He eats the va-jay-jay like it's his last meal."

"You're so silly."

"I ain't lying! Before he left, he sucked my nub so hard it swelled up like a grape. I had to walk gap-legged for two days!"

Stacy burst out laughing. "Girl, you know you're a fool!"

"And that's why you love my crazy ass. Now meet me over at Aunt Kizzy's. Now *I'm* in the mood to suck on something—like a rib!"

Stacy laughed again as she headed down Slauson Avenue to the 90 freeway. She did love Stacy's crazy butt. Not just because she'd put a smile on her face, but because she had sense enough to know the terms *vegetarian* and *soul food* didn't belong in the same sentence!

40

Don't Get Played

Stacy walked over to the mirror where Hope was holding a black silk mini up to her body.

"That's cute."

"It is, huh? I think I'll try it on."

Stacy continued browsing while Hope went into the dressing room. Stacy didn't know what she'd be doing for the holidays, but whatever it was, she wanted to look good. She casually reached into her purse when her cell phone rang.

"Hello?"

"Stacy Gray, please."

"This is Stacy."

"Stacy, this is Cedars-Sinai Medical Center. We're calling because your test results are in. Could you come in this afternoon?"

The results are back already? Stacy's heartbeat raced. "Can't you just tell me over the phone?"

"No, ma'am. You'll need to come in. Will three o'clock be okay?"

Stacy agreed and hung up. She was too stunned to think. Why had the tests come back so fast? And why did she need to go in to get the results? This did not sound good, and that was what she told Hope when Hope twirled out of the dressing room.

"Don't go assuming the worst," Hope said. "They rarely deliver any kind of news over the phone anymore. Continue to believe and remember God answers prayer." Hope looked at her watch. It was a little before two o'clock. "Wait for me while I change."

"I think I need to head on over there."

"Not by yourself you don't. Just wait until I get changed. I'm going with you. We'll come back for your car later."

Forty-five minutes later, Hope and Stacy sat in the hospital waiting room. Conversation had been limited on the drive over, and now that they were at the hospital, it had ceased entirely. Both women busied themselves by turning magazine pages neither was reading. Hope prayed silently, Stacy too.

At barely five minutes past three, Stacy's name was called. She stopped and looked at Hope briefly before following the nurse behind the door. As she walked into the office, she tried to gauge the results by the nurse's actions. It was the one who'd been there when she'd had the biopsy, but she didn't seem to be as open and friendly this time. *Didn't she talk more the last time I was here? And why won't she look me in the eye?*

"Do you know my results?"

The nurse gave Stacy a small smile. "The doctor will be in shortly. He'll explain everything." And then she left.

When the door opened about five minutes later, Stacy looked up into the kindest eyes she'd ever seen. The doctor was younger than she'd imagined he'd be, and he was Black, which also surprised her. His smile was warm and genuine as he stretched out his hand.

"Hello, Ms. Gray, I'm Dr. Livingston."

"Hello."

He sat down and opened her chart. "How are you today?"

"I'm okay. Just anxious to hear the results, that's all."

"I totally understand," he said in a voice like syrup—soft and warm.

Stacy's eyes went from his bespectacled brown eyes to his tapered nose, which was lightly sprinkled with freckles. His light-skinned complexion had a red tint, and his curly hair was naturally brown. His look was more nerd than handsome, but his calm bedside manner was reassuring.

"Ms. Gray, we're very glad you took it upon yourself to come in and that you had been performing self-examinations regularly. Most people run into trouble because they come in too late."

The door opened and the nurse returned to the room. Dr. Livingston continued. "Malignant cells were found in the tissue samples you submitted, but we're confident . . ."

Stacy heard nothing past the word *malignant*. Why in the hell did he keep talking? She knew what that meant. She had cancer!

"I have cancer?" she interrupted. "Oh, my God, do I have cancer?"

"Please, Ms. Gray, try to stay calm. Because you came in when you did, we see you making a full and complete recovery."

"Recovering from what?" Stacy was becoming more upset. "Am I going to lose my breast?"

"Please, Ms. Gray, this is understandably upsetting, but I assure you, you will be fine."

"Excuse me, doctor, but she came with a friend." The nurse turned to Stacy. "Would you like for your friend to come in here for support?"

Stacy nodded.

Hope's prayers faltered as she followed the nurse through the hallway to where Stacy was. If they were calling her to come back, she thought, it couldn't be good. This thought was confirmed as she stepped into the room.

". . . and so with this procedure, you're home the same day.

Recovery is normally rapid, and, most importantly, based on your concerns, the breast remains largely intact." The doctor turned to Hope. "Hello, you must be Hope."

Hope stepped forward to shake his hand. "Yes."

"Well, that's quite an appropriate name for your friend, Ms. Gray. I'm Dr. Livingston."

They were at the hospital another half hour as the doctor answered more of Stacy's questions and paperwork was done, scheduling her surgery for a week from today. The doctor wanted to get in and get the cancerous tissues removed as soon as possible. Stacy didn't want a delay either; the quicker she had the surgery, the quicker this nightmare could be over.

"How are you doing?" Hope asked again as they drove into the mall parking lot. "You sure you don't want to spend the night at my place and pick up your car tomorrow?"

"Thanks, Hope, but no, I think I'm all right. I'm going to go by my mother's, and then I really need to be with my son tonight."

"I understand," Hope said, but she really didn't. She only wished she knew what it was like to be comforted by your child. "Well, if you need anything, call me."

Stacy called Darius on her way to her mother's and told him she'd pick up little D on her way home. The normally re-served Mrs. Gray offered sympathy and compassion and assured her little girl that everything would be all right. At her mother's insistence, the two brothers who were in town came over and lent their support. They made her feel so special. She knew if either one of them could have, they would have taken the cancer themselves, as well as the radiation treatments Dr. Livingston had said would follow the surgery. She floated on their cloud of love as she left her mother's and picked up her son.

She didn't tell Darius Sr. After she left, she wondered why she wouldn't tell the father of her child what was going on. She really didn't know. *Maybe,* she thought, *I don't want his pity.*

Maybe I don't want him to know I'm suffering. I always want him to see me as the perfect woman.

But little Darius and his unconditional love gave her the balm she needed. When she got home, she fed and bathed him and put him to bed. It was as though he knew something was wrong, because he kept cooing, saying "Mama" and smiling. She stared into his little chocolate eyes, and at one point she could have sworn she could *feel* the love flowing from his heart to hers. And, tucking him in, she knew she'd live. There was no way God would give her little Darius and then take her away from him.

Stacy went to bed but was too keyed up to sleep. She looked through her DVD collection and then remembered a book she'd recently purchased by a new author, Zuri Day. It was called *Lies Lovers Tell,* and it sounded like just the type of escapist reading she needed to forget her own troubles by delving into someone else's. She fixed a cup of hot chocolate, fluffed up her pillows, and had just begun reading the first chapter when her cell phone rang.

Stacy looked at the number and almost didn't answer. But then, on second thought, she punched the TALK button. "Yeah, Tony, what do you want?"

"Dang, girl. What kind of greeting is that?"

"An honest one. What's up?"

"Wow. Can't a brothah call just to check on a friend?"

"I guess so," Stacy replied without enthusiasm. She regretted that she'd changed her mind and answered the phone.

"Well, it's obvious you don't feel like talking," Tony said. "I just thought I saw you at the hospital today and called to see if you were okay."

"Yeah, I'm all right."

"So that was you at the hospital?"

"Yeah."

"But you're okay."

"Yeah."

"You might be, Stacy, but you sure don't sound like it. I guess you don't want to talk about it, though, so . . . I'll hollah later."

"Wait a minute, Tony. Don't hang up." Stacy took a deep breath and continued. "You're right. I'm not okay. I found a lump in my breast a couple weeks ago and got the results today. I have can"—*No! Don't claim it!*—"the tissue was malignant."

"Stacy, I'm really sorry to hear that."

"Me too."

There was a moment of silence, and then Tony spoke again. "Who's there with you?"

"My son."

"Who else? I mean, who's there to comfort you?"

"God is my comfort and my refuge. His unconditional love shines through in the love of my son."

"Wow, that's beautiful, Stacy. You're a strong woman. And I didn't mean to imply otherwise, I just know at times like this it's nice to have someone around."

"How would you know?"

"Because cancer is how I almost lost my mom. So I can tell you from personal experience to be encouraged. With God, you will get through this. My mother kept telling me that while she was going through her illness, and there were times I thought we'd lost her. But she kept telling me the earth had no sorrow that heaven couldn't heal."

"Hmmm. Did she go through radiation and chemotherapy?"

"Yes."

"Was it hard?"

"She never complained, but it couldn't have been easy. But if I were you, I'd try not to focus too much on the negative aspects of your situation. What happens for one person might be different for another. Try to keep positive; that's what I'd do."

"Tony Johnson, when did you get to be so smart?"

They talked a bit more, about Tony's family, his returning

to the NFL, and his getting his knee x-rayed—the reason he had been at the hospital. Just as they were saying their good-byes, Tony switched the subject yet again.

"So you're still seeing Darius?"

"I'm not *seeing* anybody. The only connection he and I have is our son."

"Oh, so you brought your son to his party? That's why you were there Thanksgiving weekend?"

"If I didn't know better, I'd say you were trying to get in a sistah's business."

"What, am I out of bounds?"

"I don't know, are you trying for a touchdown or a field goal?"

"Let's just say I'm on your team, and players look after each other."

"Oh, so you're a player, is that what you're saying?"

"No, I'm a cautious brothah, making sure I don't get played."

41

Why I'm Here

Dr. Elliott Whitmore's West Hollywood office was vastly different than the waiting room at Cedars-Sinai. Instead of stark white walls and fluorescent lights, this room was decorated in warm earth tones of brown, tan, and cream with punctuations of bright orange and vivid blue from pillows and wall art. Low lighting with an amber glow came from two colorful Tiffany lamps flanking a dark wood credenza. A gurgling fountain of a goddess or guru provided serenity, while a large white candle burning on the credenza emitted a faint, floral odor. A Middle Eastern–sounding instrument played in the background, and a plaque directly in Hope's eyesight read THOUGHTS BECOME THINGS.

Vivian, who'd recommended the office, had said Elliott was not a typical therapist. She said he used alternative treatments, read a person's energy and vibration, and believed that factors such as diet and surroundings largely influenced a person's mental state. If his waiting room was any indication of how he worked, Hope would have to agree with the first lady.

Following her episode with Millicent in La Jolla, Hope had called Millicent to apologize again. She had found Millicent to be cordial, reflective, and the possessor of a dry sense of humor—much different than the person she'd expected.

"Millicent, it's Hope," Hope had said.

"Hope, I'm so glad you called."

"You are?"

"We're concerned about you. Jack and I."

"I expected anger, not concern, and you have every right to be furious. I am truly, very sorry, Millicent. I don't know what came over me. The person you encountered in that hotel room is not who I am at all."

"Look, as someone who could be described as the poster child for losing it, I'm the last one to hold a grudge. And honestly I was too shocked to be angry for long. I knew why I was there and how excited Cy was about surprising you with the house. I didn't know you two were having problems."

Hope had quickly squashed any such notion. "Cy and I are not having problems. I am the one dealing with something right now. It's personal, and I don't care to get into it. I just called to apologize and ask your forgiveness."

"I forgive you, Hope. And our offer to have you two over for dinner still stands. I think it would be good for all of us to have at least one open, honest conversation. A lot has happened between the four of us, and we've never talked about it, not all together. Look, I'm not asking to be your best friend, and at this point I'm not even sure if Cy and Jack will continue being business partners. I'm just saying if you need me, I'm here."

Hope's thoughts were interrupted as the inner office door opened to reveal a man who seemed as unconventional as his office space. He was younger than she'd imagined but probably older than he looked. His long blond hair gave him a boyish air, as did the gold hoop earring and hippie sandals. He wore a tie-dyed dashiki over khaki pants. His twinkling hazel eyes and bright smile put Hope immediately at ease.

"Hope? Dr. Whitmore, but please call me El. Come right this way."

They entered his office where the unconventional decor continued. Instead of a desk and chair—or a couch, as movies portrayed—there was a tan love seat, two brown leather chairs, and a pair of brightly colored beanbags occupying a corner. A low-slung file cabinet braced the far wall, where steam from a boiling kettle wafted toward the ceiling.

"Would you like some tea? Or water?" El asked.

Hope hadn't been able to drink her favorite brew since it had ended up on her husband's ex-stalker.

"Nothing. I'm fine," she answered.

After offering her the love seat and sitting across from her in one of the chairs, El reached for a yellow notepad and grabbed a pen from his shirt pocket.

"So, Hope, why don't you begin by telling me why you think you're here."

Twenty minutes later, Hope felt she had adequately described the series of events that had led to her depression. El had encouraged her to start at the beginning, and she had, beginning with her years-long desire to be married and start a family, her celibacy while she had waited on God to send her mate, Cy's fairy-tale courtship, their wedding, and the past two years during which they'd tried unsuccessfully to get pregnant.

"What are your doctors saying? The medical doctors?"

"Different specialists say different things. I have a tilted uterus, which makes conception more difficult, but all the doctors agree both me and my husband are capable of making a baby."

"Tell me about the symptoms you believe are a result of being depressed."

"Dr. Whitmore—excuse me, El—I've always been an upbeat person, the one whose glass is half full. But lately I've been moody, easy to snap at people, and can cry at the drop of a hat. Becoming pregnant has become an obsession. And then there was an episode last week where, in a fit of anger, I doused a woman with a pitcher of tea!"

"Well . . . was she thirsty?"

It took a moment for Hope to realize El was joking. "After I finished with her," Hope replied, "she was simply wet."

"Tell me about this woman and your relationship with her."

Hope gave the doctor an abbreviated version of their strained relationship. "Even though I forgave her," Hope concluded, "I obviously am still hanging on to anger and resentment. But I've never been violent to anyone in my life, not even as a kid. This is starting to affect my marriage. That's why I'm here."

The doctor jotted several notes on the pad and then stroked his chin as he looked thoughtfully at Hope. He closed his eyes for a moment and then placed the pad and pen on the ottoman in front of him.

"Here's what we're going to do. I'm going to have my assistant run a series of tests to determine your blood work, hormone and sugar levels, and your blood pressure. It's a bit unorthodox, but I'm sure Vivian told you I'm not a typical therapist. I believe in a holistic approach to mental treatment, and once these tests are performed, I'll have a better idea of what type of treatment will work best for you. I'll send Amy right in."

Dr. Whitmore's assistant was friendly and efficient. After she'd administered the tests, she told Hope to "sit tight" in the doctor's office while the results were obtained.

About fifteen minutes later, El returned to his office. He carried a long computer printout with what Hope assumed was a workup of all that was wrong with her.

"So, doctor, what's the verdict?" Hope asked as El once again took a seat across from her. "How crazy am I?"

"We still have to conduct further tests to adequately gauge your mental state. But what I'm certain of right now is that one of your worries is over. You're going to have a baby."

42

Baby Mama

It took several seconds for the doctor's words to sink in.

"I'm pregnant?"

El smiled and nodded. "While I advise a visit to an obstetrician, I am ninety-nine point nine percent sure you are with child. The mood swings, bouts of depression—all common among some women in the early stages of pregnancy."

"But that's not possible. In fact, I just had a period last week."

"Continued menstruation in the early months, or for some women throughout their pregnancy, is not uncommon. The test is conclusive, Hope. You're going to have a baby."

Hope walked out of the doctor's office in a fog and dialed Cy as soon as she left the building and could get a signal.

"I know why I went off on Millicent!" she blurted as soon as he answered the phone.

"I take it you just left your appointment with the therapist?"

"Yes! And I know why I've been acting all crazy: the mood swings, the depression, the bitchiness, everything!"

Cy was unconvinced. "He gave you a complete diagnosis in an hour, in one visit? Wow, he must be some kind of doctor."

Hope reached her car and got inside. She was bursting to

tell him the news. But for years she'd planned how it would happen—with candles, dinner, Stevie Wonder's "Isn't She Lovely" playing in the background.

That's what I'll do, she thought as she eased into traffic on Wilshire Boulevard. *I'll make us a nice dinner and buy some non-alcoholic bubbly.*

"I'm pregnant!"

Wait, did I just say something? Did "I'm pregnant" just fly out of my mouth?

"You're . . . what . . . baby! Are you sure?"

Dangit, I must have said it! Who is this walking around in my body, and where is the disciplined, controlled old Hope Jones?

"Oh, baby. I didn't mean to blurt that out. I had it all planned how it would happen."

"Well, you know what they say about that, right?"

"What?"

"That life is what happens while you're making your plans. Wait a minute, how am I standing here talking to you calmly? We're going to have a baby!" They'd waited so long for the news, Cy thought he was dreaming. But surely she wouldn't say she was pregnant unless there was not a single shadow of a doubt. "Baby, what did you do, a home pregnancy test?"

"No, the doctor Viv recommended is a licensed medical doctor as well as therapist and works from a holistic view-point—you know, mind, body, spirit. So before prescribing any medication he does this whole physical workup as well as mental. The last thing I was thinking about when the assistant asked for a pee sample is that it would be used to detect pregnancy. He told me he was checking my hormone levels!"

"And you're absolutely sure?"

"I'm getting ready to be. I'm heading over to the hospital right now so I can get tested again, by an obstetrician this time. I don't want to take a chance with a home pregnancy test. Oh, Cy, I can't believe it! We're getting ready to have a baby!"

All of a sudden the reality of being pregnant hit her, and Hope broke down into an all out boohoo.

"Baby, where are you? Is it safe for you to drive?"

"I'm just so happy," she forced between sobs.

"Pull over, baby. Maybe I need to meet you and drive you to the doctor myself."

"I'm okay, baby. I'm just so overwhelmed."

"I just don't want anything to happen to you, baby. Especially now. You're carrying our future."

Hope pulled over to wipe her eyes, blow her nose, and pull herself together. Three hours later she pulled into the circular drive of their condo's front entrance. Having gone to the hospital, where they confirmed she was indeed pregnant, and then to the bookstore and the gourmet grocery shop, she needed help carrying her purchases. She had no problem carrying the night's dinner—it was the almost twenty baby books she'd purchased that were the backbreaker, the ones that should take her from birth until when the child was eighteen!

She entered the penthouse and was surprised to hear music. Turning to the doorman who'd helped her carry the books, she asked, "Is Frieda here?"

She'd called her cousin, mother, Stacy, and Viv, and while Frieda hadn't mentioned anything about dropping by, she wouldn't have put it past her.

"No, the lovely lady hasn't been by today."

Hope frowned. "Okay, well, maybe I accidentally set the radio timer." She tipped the concierge assistant, closed the door, walked toward her bedroom, turned the corner, and got the shock of her life.

The floor of their master suite was covered in orchid petals. Candles were burning, a mound of presents covered the king-sized bed, and the sounds of Eric Benét drifted toward her ears. Cy stood to the left of the bed, leaning against the wall with his arms folded, looking finer than she'd ever seen him.

"Cy!" Hope gushed, tears already streaming down her face. "What are you doing home? You told me you had important meetings. What's all this? And you're playing our song!"

Hope knew she was babbling, but she couldn't help it. She rushed over and folded herself into his arms. He lifted her off the floor as he devoured her mouth in a kiss.

"This," he said, as he planted kisses all over her face and neck before setting her down on the edge of the bed, "is for the mother of my child."

"But when did you have time?"

"I've got connections, woman. And no part of my business is more important than this moment."

Cy walked over to the sitting area where a bottle was chilling in a silver bucket. It was then that Hope noticed the massive floral arrangement on the coffee table. It contained her favorite, bird-of-paradise, and other exotic flowers. She couldn't stop the tears.

Cy popped the cork on a bottle of nonalcoholic champagne and poured the bubbly into two crystal flutes. His eyes devoured Hope as he walked to where she sat. He sat beside her.

"First, I want to thank God for answering our prayers. I want to thank Him for His faithfulness, and for the amazing blessing He has given us."

"Thank you, God," Hope whispered.

"Thank you, Father," Cy said. "And now, I want to thank you, Hope, for giving me everything I've ever wanted and so much more. I love you with my whole heart, baby, and I'm going to devote the rest of my life to taking care of you and our family. I love you."

They drank the champagne, their eyes never leaving each other. Cy took Hope's hand and stood. "May I dance with my baby's mama?"

His words made Hope's heart dance with joy. She smiled and melted into his arms as their anthem played:

"Can we just feel this way together till the end of all time, Can I just spend my life with you?"

43

The Glamorous Life

Stacy smiled as she sipped hot cocoa and watched Darius play with large foam building blocks. She was so happy she'd decided to postpone her surgery. Even though Dr. Livingston had assured her the invasion would be minimal and that he instead of a radiologist would do the procedure, Stacy didn't want to deal with recovery and chemotherapy during the holidays.

It was amazing what a reminder of one's mortality could do. Since getting the diagnosis, all of Stacy's priorities had shifted. The week after hearing the news, she'd gone over to Bo and Darius's house and made a peace pact—with Bo. A couple days later, Darius dropped his lawsuit. Thrilled not to have to shelve out thousands for lawyer fees, he gave Stacy an all-expenses-paid Caribbean cruise for Christmas. She and Frieda had a ball, so much so that at times Stacy forgot about the lump.

Darius Jr. spent Christmas with his father and came home with so many presents Stacy joked about having to add on a room. Tony called regularly to check on her; she appreciated the thought. Every day Stacy counted her blessings; so much so that she wasn't even tripping that she had no date for New Year's Eve. Instead she was going to be the third wheel with Frieda and Shabach, going to the Kingdom Citizens celebration and then to a private after party at the home of one of the record execs.

"I'd better call her," Stacy said aloud. She wanted to find out what Frieda was wearing.

As she reached for her phone, it rang.

"Happy New Year," Tony said cheerfully.

"Happy New Year's *Eve*," Stacy replied.

"Yeah, auld lang syne and all that."

"So, Mr. Johnson, what's up?"

"Well, uh, that's what I called to find out."

"Nothing much. Watching my son play, chilling out. What about you?"

"Just sitting here chillaxin'. I'm surprised you're not out getting a mani-pedi and whatnot, at the hair salon or something."

"What are you trying to say, that my hair looked jacked Sunday?"

"Naw, naw, but I'm sure you've got some hot date tonight, somebody to kiss when the clock strikes twelve."

"No, little Darius will probably be asleep by then. At any rate, I'll be at Kingdom Citizens. I'm going with Frieda."

"I was thinking about going to that. Darius and Shabach will be playing, right?"

"Uh-huh. It's going to be a jamming show. You should come."

"Can I come with you?"

"Ooh, Mr. Johnson, are you asking me out?"

"I don't know that I'd call going to church a date exactly. But, yeah, it would be cool to hang with you if Frieda doesn't mind."

"She won't. You know she's seeing Shabach."

"Yeah, I heard. So, hey, should I come pick you up instead?"

"I have to drop Darius off at his father's, for the nanny."

"That's cool."

"Okay, see you around eight thirty."

★ ★ ★

"So, Melody, are you going or what?" Natasha had had just about enough of her best friend's pouting, even if it was over the phone.

"Who cares about that stupid service!"

"You care, that's who. You're just mad that Hope and Miss Vivian canceled our dance routine."

"She makes me sick. I'm not taking no kind of classes just to get to dance in their church. Trying to take over everything . . . I'm the one who got Darius's club together. I'm the one who has his MySpace page blowing up. And I'll still get to dance, only it will be on MTV and BET. And later tonight, if I'm lucky."

"Okay, girl, what are you talking about?"

"I'm talking about bringing in the New Year with my man, that's what!"

"Please, you know Officer Anderson ain't gonna let you out on New Year's Eve. You better come to church if you want to see your man."

"I know how to handle my mama, trust. But I do need a little help though. This is what I want you to do for me."

As she laid out her plans, Melody's voice dropped to a whisper, even though she was the only one in the room.

Frieda walked into the bedroom and closed the door against Shabach and his noisy crew. Since moving her into a roomy, two-bedroom apartment last week, he was trying to act like he owned the place—and her. Frieda liked Shabach, but it wasn't like they were married. She knew it was time for them to have a talk. *But,* she thought, *no need to mess up the holidays.*

"Hey, girl," she said when Stacy answered the phone.

"Frieda, I was just getting ready to call you."

"Well, here I am. And with good news. Shabach ordered a

Hummer stretch for us to ride in to the concert. So can you meet us over here?"

"Are there going to be any hardheads? I'm asking because Tony just called and wants me to ride with him."

"I knew he wanted to hit that."

"Girl, everybody isn't always after the nana. Tony is more serious about God than I am. We are just friends."

"The only way a man is just friends with a woman is if he's gay. And sometimes even that don't work, as you well know."

"Whatever, Frieda. Like I told you. I'm living for God now. There's no more time for foolishness."

"I hear you, Stacy. You're right." Frieda decided to back off from teasing her friend. Ever since Stacy had told her about the cancer, Frieda had become aware of her own mortality. She'd even demanded Shabach start wearing a condom again. As long as he lived in Atlanta and she lived in LA, there was no way she was going to chance getting a present another bitch had left him. "So, you down for the limo?"

"Let me call Tony. I'll call you back."

Stacy hung up and immediately called Tony.

"Don't tell me you've changed your mind," he answered.

"No, I'm just calling to see if you want to ride in Shabach's limo with Frieda and his crew."

"Uh, that would be a pass."

"Why?"

"The Word says yield not to temptation. And that's Shabach's middle name. I hope your girl knows who she's dealing with."

"Tony, what do you know?"

"Probably nothing you don't. Shabach is a ho, smokes weed, and is in deep with the hip-hop thugs. That's not the type of Christian I want to hang around. And you shouldn't either."

Stacy couldn't argue. Tony was right. She'd have to pass on Frieda's invitation to the glamorous life.

44

Party Over Here

Frieda leaned into Shabach as she finished off another flute of Cristal.

"You were great tonight, baby," she said before trailing her tongue around his ear.

Shabach played off the compliment by pushing her away, even as he shifted to give his stiffening shaft room to grow.

"Frieda's right, dog," Shorty agreed. "Tonight was fire! You took Darius to school and showed old boy how it's done in the big leagues!"

Shabach finished off a shot of Patrón and melded himself into the limo's plush leather. He had to agree, the night's show had been tight. Darius had been on point too, but Shabach would never admit it out loud. D's bass player, Randall, had been especially good. Shabach rubbed his chin as he plotted how to pull one of LA's best bass players away from the comp.

The limo pulled past a gate into a circular parking lot filled with Maybachs, Rolls-Royces, Bentleys, and stretch limos. An inebriated crew of seven spilled out onto the cobblestone drive, ready to finish the party that had begun earlier at the Palladium, the place Kingdom Citizens' Christian Center had rented out for their New Year's Eve celebration.

Music and chatter competed for dominance as Shabach

and Frieda walked through the door of the after party. Almost immediately she spotted Darius and Bo being openly affectionate as they cuddled on a love seat in the living room. The room was filled with beautiful people, and Frieda knew she fit right in.

"Baby, I'm going over to the buffet, I need something to soak up this champagne."

Shabach made his way through throngs of people in the fifteen-room mansion belonging to Darius's record exec. *So this is the house that Darius built,* he thought as he made his way through the rooms. The longer he stayed in California, the more he was convinced that his beautiful four-bedroom, five-and-a-half-bathroom home in Atlanta wasn't enough. He wanted to be here, in Beverly Hills, where the movers and shakers moved and shook.

"Hey, Shabach, you were great tonight!" a young fan gushed.

"Thanks, baby girl. But if you don't mind me asking, isn't it a little past your bedtime?"

"Not unless you're going to get in the bed with me," Melody pouted before turning to sashay away, showing him the luscious backside that always caught men by surprise.

She walked around the corner and ran into Darius's guitar player. Once again, she went into flirt mode. "Dang, you're tall, but cute though."

Randall looked at the tempting morsel presenting herself like an appetizer. "Little girl, you better go home before you get into trouble."

"I wouldn't mind getting into it with you."

"Is that right?" Randall said, already walking around her. "Well, you take care, trouble."

Melody huffed, walked into the bathroom, and checked the makeup she'd had professionally applied at the Mac store. It made her look older and sophisticated, or so she thought. *I'm a woman, damnit!* And before the night was over, somebody was going to recognize!

Melody gave herself a long, hard look in the mirror. She jiggled her young, tender breasts, prominently displayed courtesy of a push-up bra. She rearranged her curls to cover one eye and formed her mouth in what she felt was a luscious pout. After turning to make sure her mini skirt fit perfectly over her onion and applying another coat of devil-red lipstick, she sat on the commode, pulled out paper and pen, and put part two of her plan into motion.

Back out in the dining room, Frieda was stacking her plate with a variety of delectable goodies: teriyaki shrimp, sirloin tips, and a mound of caviar on top of her rice pilaf.

"Hey, girl, you're going to mess up that figure," Darius teased as he sidled up beside her.

"No, *mami's* gonna stay tight, believe that."

"Where's your friend?"

"Who, Stacy?"

"Uh-huh. I thought she'd be here with you."

Frieda didn't know how much of Stacy's business she should share with Darius. Then again, she couldn't help but be a bit messy. "Oh, you didn't see her at the Palladium? She had a date."

"Oh, well, that's cool. I'm glad to hear she's enjoying herself, what with the diagnosis and all."

"Darius, trust me. The last thing Stacy is thinking about tonight is a diagnosis. But I'll give you this. You got the *D* right."

With that, Frieda disappeared into the crowd.

Before Darius could process what Frieda had meant by her last statement, a stranger walked up to him.

"Someone told me to give you this," the attractive Asian woman said with a mild accent. Before he could question her further, she was gone.

Darius smiled as he read the note:

*Meet me in the room at the end of the north hallway. I've got
what you need.*
Your Biggest Fan

Darius refolded the note and put it in his pocket. Bo knew
how to get him turned on. It had become a regular game of
theirs to make love in strange homes, and parties were a favorite. He took a few bites from the plate of food he'd made,
washed it down with a glass of pinot noir, and then set out to
find the north hall.

It wasn't too hard to find. Darius passed three other doors
before he lightly tapped on the door at the end of the hall,
opened it, and went inside. It was dark, but with the aid of the
moonlight and the pool lights beyond the house, he could make
out a four-poster bed with someone, apparently naked, lying in it.

"Bo," he called out.

The figure shifted. Darius smiled. He began stripping off
his clothes as he crossed the room. Once he got to the bed, he
crawled onto it.

"Hey, baby."

"Hey, Darius. I've been waiting for you."

WTF? Darius jumped off the bed. "Who is this?"

"Darius, it's okay. It's me, Melody. Don't be scared."

Darius began dressing at a furious pace. "Melody, what are
you doing out at this time of night? Does your mother know
where you are?"

Why does everyone keep treating me like I'm a kid! Melody ignored Darius's question and adopted the most adult, come-
hither voice she'd ever heard in a video. "Come here, baby. I've
got something for you."

"Yeah, and I've got something for you. Go home, Melody.
Before you get hurt!"

Darius fumbled his way to the door and slammed it behind
him.

Melody lay naked, totally still, on the bed. She allowed herself to feel the softness of the silk comforter beneath her as sounds of music and conversation drifted underneath the door.

This is it. This is where I want to be, she thought as she rubbed the comforter between her legs. She was in the multimillion dollar home of a record exec, an exclusive party with some of the biggest headliners in the game.

"I'm so close," she whispered into the darkness. And she'd promised herself that tonight would be the night. Melody lay there, daydreaming.

Just then she heard a click as the door opened. Once again the man on her mind entered and stood just inside the room for a long moment before he began stripping out of his clothes. Once naked, he walked slowly toward the bed.

Melody could not believe her good fortune. She dared to blink, lest the vision dissipate once her eyes were closed. But she did close them and opened them quickly. The vision was still there and coming closer. Once he was right beside the bed, he cuddled his large manhood.

"Is this what you want?" he asked.

After a moment she answered. "Yes."

Their conversation was brief because before too much time had passed she'd done as she'd been instructed, and as she'd seen in the videos Natasha had stolen from her uncle's house. She reached out, enveloped his shaft in her hand, and pleasured him.

45

Nothin' Nice

"Look at him, look at little D," Bo exclaimed as his husband's son bobbed his entire body to the music. "Go, D, go, D," Bo exclaimed as he danced around little Darius, who, like Whitney, wanted to dance with somebody.

"Baby, he's looking more like you every day," Bo said. He scooped up his "nephew" and joined Darius in the kitchen. "I still can't get over you trying to cook for me."

"It's about time, wouldn't you say? You are undeniably the one who can throw down in the kitchen. But you're always serving me. I just want to pamper you for a change."

Bo walked over and kissed Darius on the cheek. "Careful, boo, I just might get used to this."

A little while later the three men, one in a high chair, sat at the kitchen's breakfast nook enjoying brunch. For a beginner, Bo conceded Darius hadn't done half bad even though the hash browns were from a package and the waffles from a box. The bacon was nice and crispy, and the eggs were fluffy, made just the way Bo had instructed. The scene was a picture of domestic bliss.

"Baby, I still can't believe that wench tried to seduce you last night. You know what this means, don't you?"

Darius nodded. "Yes. I've already decided to replace her as

head of the fan club. If she acts crazy, as I suspect she will, I'll just have you start another one and get an official MySpace page.

"You kept telling me that girl was just trying to get me in her panties. And once again, I didn't listen. It just seemed crazy to think the daughter of the sanctimonious Andersons would be so scandalous!"

"I don't know why you're surprised. Those sheltered kids are the worst ones. Parents think they're doing their child a favor by not discussing the birds and the bees. And next thing they know the kid has flown the coop and ended up making a nest in some man's bedroom. And it sounds like she did more than that."

Darius didn't respond. He and Bo shared almost every-thing, but he didn't feel like having a fight this morning. And if he told Bo the whole story, that's exactly what would happen—that and that Bo would drive over to the Andersons' house and confront Melody himself. No, best to just cut the situation off before it got worse. Darius already had a call in to Vivian. He would let her know he was through with Darius's Crew, and then hopefully Melody would find another fixation.

"Baby, what about us taking little D to Disneyland?"

"I don't know, Bo, it might be crowded on a holiday."

"When did a crowd ever stop you? Come on, let's go have fun. Maybe you can even call Spacey and see if she wants to go. Since she has finally decided to come around and act like she's got some sense . . . I might actually start to like her again."

Melody opened her front door and then closed it quietly behind her. She peeked around the corner to see if anyone was in the living room. Breathing a sigh of relief, she walked to-ward the stairway. It looked like the coast was clear.

"Melody Elizabeth! Get in here, and I mean right now!" Mrs. Anderson's loud voice could have woken the dead.

"I, uh, I gotta use the bathroom, Mama," Melody cried, determined to get to her room before her mother could see her.

Mrs. Anderson came barreling fast as lightning around the corner, which at five-foot-six and two hundred fifty pounds, wasn't the easiest thing to do.

She grabbed Melody's arm, huffing and puffing to regain her breath. After a couple deep inhales and exhales, she spoke, slowly and carefully, as if she were talking to a mentally challenged child.

"Where have you been?"

"What do you mean where? Over at Natasha's!"

Mrs. Anderson squeezed harder. "Girl, don't lie to me and don't make me have to beat the truth out of you. You wasn't over to Natasha's this morning, and you didn't go over there last night. Now you got about two seconds to tell me where you were!"

"Mama, I was! Did you talk to Natasha? We stopped by her house and then we went over to Danielle's. You can call and ask her!"

"I don't have to call no-datgum-body. You lied to me!"

"Mama, I—"

"Mama, I nothing. Just get on up those stairs and stay in your room until your father gets back here. You are getting ready to be dealt with, young lady, and it ain't gonna be nothing nice!"

Melody stood at the bottom of the stairs waiting for her mother to turn to leave. Mrs. Anderson stood staring at Melody, wondering what was taking so long for her order to be obeyed.

"I'm not going to tell you again, Melody."

"Yes, ma'am," Melody uttered in a childlike whisper. For someone always trying to act grown, Melody could have easily passed for about two right now.

Mrs. Anderson planted her legs apart, crossed her arms, and waited for orders to be obeyed.

"Dang, Mama, are you going to stand there and watch me take every step?"

Melody thought her old-fogy mother was stuck on stupid, but Mrs. Anderson had enough smart for the both of them. "That's exactly what I'm going to do. Now get moving!"

Melody knew she had no choice but to climb the stairs with her mother watching. She took a deep breath and climbed the stairs one at a time, trying to keep her legs together and to ignore the throbbing going on between them.

"What is wrong with you, Melody?" her mother asked.

"Nothing!" Melody shrilled.

"Girl, who are you hollering at?" Mrs. Anderson demanded. "And why are you taking the stairs like you can barely walk?"

"It's nothing, Mama," Melody answered. "I just hurt my leg dancing over at Natasha's."

"I thought you were at Danielle's."

Mrs. Anderson's eyes narrowed as she continued to watch her daughter climb the stairs. Something definitely was not right. She was just about to walk away when something caught her eye as Melody took the last step.

"Melody Elizabeth, get back down here! Is that blood on your clothes?"

46

There Is a God

Conversation had been stilted at first, especially after orders had been taken and casual conversation about menu options had ended. In the ensuing silence, Hope wondered if she'd done the right thing accepting Millicent's dinner invitation. They'd decided to meet at a restaurant instead of at the Kirtz home, which helped, but now that they were here, she wasn't so sure this was a good idea.

Cy and Jack talked easily about church, Darfur, real estate, sports. Millicent and Hope made small talk about the restaurant decor, each other's clothes, the weather. But after dining on the first course and waiting for the second to be served, Cy took the proverbial bull by the horns.

"I think we all know why we're sitting here, and it's way past time we had this conversation. Millicent, Jack, thanks for the invitation. Hopefully after tonight we can truly put the past behind us."

"I really want that," Millicent said. "Sure, there's a lot of unhealthy history between us, and while we may never become the best of friends, it would be great if a certain amount of civility—cordiality, even—could exist between us." She looked at Hope but said nothing more.

"There are some things that aren't my business but that I'd

like to know," Hope said after a lull. "I think the more we leave this table tonight with all questions answered and curiosities assuaged, the easier it will be for us to truly move forward."

"I agree with that," Jack said, placing his hand over Millicent's. "Don't you, honey?"

"Absolutely. Hope, ask whatever you want."

Hope glanced at Cy and then continued. "It's about when we saw you in Mexico. Cy believes you and Jack went there together, but I'm convinced you were there for Cy. Which of us is right?"

"You both are," Millicent responded. She then told Hope the same story she'd told Cy, and Carla when she'd appeared on television. "Jack and I never meant to become intimate in Mexico," she finished. "It just happened. It was right after we'd finished a conference at our church, one for a young women's group called Divas of Destiny. Ironically, their first conference centered around remaining chaste until blessed with a God-sent mate. And then we found ourselves together in the Caribbean, and, honestly, a sacred connection was made even before intercourse happened. The next day we talked about the irony of it all and how hypocritical it would look for us to carry on a relationship, even secretly, having called on the young women of the church to make a vow before God.

"If you ask me, I think Jack had planned it all along. He always wanted me." Millicent laughed to show she was partially kidding. "But by then he didn't have to work too hard. I'd fallen in love. We found an official on the island and got married right there in the hotel garden. It was spontaneous and romantic and the best snap decision I've ever made in my whole life."

"But you still loved Cy then. How could you be so sure it was love when you'd flown down there to be with another man?"

Millicent was given a moment's reprieve while the soup

was served. Hope's questions were tough but justified. They caused Millicent to ask herself some very tough questions, ones she had no intention of sharing with anyone at the table.

"It was how Jack loved me that made me fall in love with him, Hope. He kept coming back when I pushed him away, refused to believe I had no love left. He saw me at my worst, chasing a married man, and he still loved me. Yes, I flew to Mexico to be with Cy, but God orchestrated the trip so I could marry Jack."

"So there's no doubt, you love Jack. You're in love with your husband, not mine."

"Hope . . ."

"No, Cy, it's okay." Looking at Jack, Millicent answered Hope. "I love and am in love with Timothy Jackson Kirtz. There is no other man for me, and there never will be."

Hope witnessed the way Millicent looked at Jack and truly relaxed for the first time all night. Maybe it was true, that she'd been tripping all along and the long chase by Millicent for Cy was really over.

Millicent put down her spoon and leaned back. "Now may I ask you something? Is that why you drove down here the other day? Because you thought I still loved your husband?"

"Obviously."

"There was no other reason? I'm sorry, I don't mean to pry. I just got the feeling there was something else going on with you."

Cy and Hope looked at each other. "Do you want to tell them, baby?" Cy asked.

Hope nodded.

"We're pregnant." Anyone watching closely would have sworn Cy's chest grew. "Saying I was hormonal that day would be a gross understatement," Hope added. "And while it in no way excuses my behavior, at least I have reason to believe my insanity will be over in nine months."

Now it was Millicent and Jack's turn to look at each other.

"No," Millicent said as her eyes twinkled. "You haven't seen crazy until you start raising a child."

As the couples enjoyed their third, fourth, and fifth courses, a miracle happened. The Kirtzes and Taylors enjoyed an evening they never thought they'd experience, one that was both civil and cordial. *Indeed,* Hope thought as they headed back to Los Angeles. *There is a God.*

47

Come Over

"Everything's going to be all right, Stacy." Frieda hugged her friend before Stacy followed the nurse through the double doors. "Remember, we're right here. It'll be over before you know it."

Stacy tried to remain calm as she waved at her mom and then followed the nurse into the room where the lumpectomy would be performed. One would have thought she would have been perfectly fine, with all the prayers that had gone up the previous week on her behalf. Her mother had an Internet prayer circle going that stretched across continents, and Pastor Derrick and Vivian had made a personal stop by her house to pray the previous night. Even Darius had called to let her know he was praying for her. If prayer indeed worked, she had absolutely nothing to worry about.

The door opened, and Stacy turned to see the doctor who would be performing the procedure. Her eyebrows shot up when it was Dr. Livingston who came through the door.

"Surprised to see me?"

"Actually, yes. They told me you'd been called away on an emergency and another doctor would be performing this procedure."

"Another doctor became available to perform that surgery. So here I am. Hope you're not too disappointed."

"I'm grateful. I'm sure all the physicians are competent, but you've been here since the beginning. I trust you."

"Very well then. Let's begin."

Later that night, Stacy lay recuperating in her living room. Her mother had brought over a pot of beef stew and a key lime pie, Bo had fixed chicken and dumplings and homemade muffins, and Tony had had a gourmet pizza sent over. There was enough food to survive an earthquake. Stacy was grateful and tired.

"I think I'll go up and lie down a while," she told her mother after she'd eaten some of the stew and a slice of pie.

"Call me later," her mother said. "I want to hear from you before I go to bed tonight."

"I'll call. Promise."

Stacy kissed Mrs. Gray on the cheek, gingerly hugged her brother, and walked upstairs. Minutes later, Frieda followed.

"Can I get you anything? Water, juice, some Tanqueray with lime?"

"You know you're trippin'. I told you I don't drink anymore."

"Didn't Jesus turn water to wine? Don't you think if the man had a problem with alcohol he would have zapped it into grape juice?"

"It probably was grape juice and the translators got it wrong."

"Girl, now you messing with Jesus's miracle. You *must* be tired." Frieda helped Stacy get into bed and then sat on the side. "I see you've been holding out on your friend."

"What?"

"You didn't tell me about that fine doctor who's been stroking your titties."

"Dr. Livingston? You think he's cute?"

"In a light-skinned, Urkel sort of way. Plus, he's a doctor.

Enough zeros in the bank account makes anybody look fine. Just look at Eddie Murphy and Chris Rock."

"Don't even go there, Frieda."

"What? You know they ass was tore up before they got paid!"

"That statement is wrong on all seven continents."

"It might be wrong, but is it true?"

"Frieda, leave me alone so I can sleep."

"But about the doctor. Is he married?"

"How am I supposed to know? This may surprise you, but I had other things on my mind besides his marital status. Like my life!"

"Haven't you hung around me long enough to know you can't ever take your eye off the prize? You slippin', sistah, you really are slippin'. If you need anything, I'll be downstairs."

When Stacy awoke, the morning sun was streaming through her window. She struggled to a sitting position and looked at the clock. It was a little after seven. She couldn't believe she'd slept all night and so peacefully.

She rolled out of bed and walked into her bathroom. After splashing water on her face and brushing her teeth, she took one of the pain pills the hospital had prescribed. Then she walked down the stairs to get something to eat. All that sleeping had worked up an appetite.

"Frieda!" she called out as she entered a still dark living room. She heard pans clanking in the kitchen and walked toward the sound.

"I should have known you'd be with the food," she said, rounding the corner.

"I didn't know you knew me that well," Tony said, smiling at Stacy's surprised expression. "Frieda had to work. I told her I'd take care of you. I hope you don't mind."

"Tony Johnson? What are you doing in my kitchen?"

It was too late for Tony to hide his food-laden plate, so he grinned sheepishly. "I, uh, heard you needed help eating all this food?"

Stacy leaned back against the door jamb. "Uh-huh."

"No, seriously, I called earlier, and Frieda answered. She said you were sleeping and that she would be leaving soon. I offered to come over so you wouldn't be alone when you woke up."

"Oh, Tony, that was sweet. Thank you."

Tony and Stacy settled in the dining room with their plates. "Mmmm, this is good. Who made these dumplings, your mother?"

"No," Stacy said. "Darius's wife."

Tony's fork stopped in midair. "The dude?"

"Bo Jenkins, Darius's legal partner. I know you're shocked. But a brothah can throw down. He learned from his Aunt Gladean."

"Wow, I never would have thought. So if you don't mind me asking, how did you get involved with Darius if he's gay?"

"That's a good question and a long story. Suffice it to say the end result was a blessing. I love my son more than anything in this world."

"Where is your son?"

"At his father's. Now what about you? I really don't know that much about you outside of the sports world and church."

"What do you want to know?"

"About your ex-wife, for instance. The mother of your child."

Tony wiped his mouth and took a long swallow of soda before answering. "I have two kids," he began finally. "Shea, my daughter, was born when I was still in college. She's ten. My son, Justin, is four. I met his mother when I was at the height of my career. She's a model. A friend of a friend introduced us, and we got married about a year later."

"Why did you two divorce?"

Tony's countenance changed, and for a minute, Stacy didn't think he'd answer. But he did.

"She cheated on me with a teammate."

"Ouch, Tony, I'm sorry."

"So am I. I really loved that girl, and in the end, she loved my money more than me. That's why I can't handle any more drama when it comes to my relationships. I'm looking for a Godly woman, someone with integrity and a conscience."

"And you think that's me?"

"Girl, nobody said nothing about you being who I'm looking for. You must still be under that anesthesia."

"Forget you, nuckah," Stacy said, laughing. She was glad Frieda had answered her phone and that Tony had come over.

48

If It Don't Fit . . .

Darius waved his hand to stop the band. He turned to the choir. "I want to hear the words crisply. Overenunciate so each syllable rings true in and of itself." He separated the phrasing until the five syllables of the song's first two words stood on their own. "That's better. Now, once again, and keep going this time."

"Blessed assurance, Jesus is mine.
Oh, what a foretaste of glory divine."

"Okay, sopranos, sing 'I'm an heir' alone and then everybody else come in on 'of salvation.' Let's hear it!"

The choir ran like a well-oiled machine. Many of them had been singing together for at least five years. One or two times was all they needed to hear the instruction, and then it was off to the races.

"This is my story, this is my song. Praising my Savior all the
day long."

"Sing it like you mean it!"
And they did.

"Much better, guys. We want to make sure we don't lose any of the parts on that chorus. Altos, tenors, make your voices heard. And second altos, don't get lost in there. Your part is important. Act like you know."

Security man Greg walked up to Darius and whispered in his ear. Darius frowned and then turned toward the choir. "Okay, Randall, take over for a minute. I'll be right back."

Darius left the choir area and followed Greg down the aisle into the large foyer. His frown deepened when he saw three serious-looking men in business suits standing near the church entrance.

"Yes, what can I do for you?"

"Are you Darius?"

"Yes."

"Darius Crenshaw?"

"That's correct. What is this about?"

"This is about the statutory rape of a minor. You are under arrest, Mr. Crenshaw. You have the right to remain silent. Anything you say can and will be used against you in the court of law."

"Wait, wait. There must be some mistake. I'm married. I haven't had sex with anyone except my partner."

"We'd advise you to come willingly, Mr. Crenshaw. The security guard convinced us not to make a scene in the church, but there are armed officers waiting just outside. Now let's go."

As the men led Darius out, they continued citing his Miranda rights. "You have a right to an attorney. If you do not have an attorney . . ."

Darius's mind was in a fog. He could not believe this was happening. It was a huge, grievous mistake. At the last minute, he yelled over his shoulder to a bewildered Greg still standing by the door of the church. "Call Bo! Let him know what's going on!"

Several hours later a bedraggled Darius, accompanied by an attorney and a guard, came out of the holding cell. Bo met him on the other side of the desk.

"I brought a change of clothes, baby. I know you want to throw these away."

"You know me as well as I know myself. Let's get out of here. I'll change as soon as I can so I can be rid of any and everything that reminds me of that place."

As soon as Bo and Darius had settled in the back of the limo, Bo raised the privacy glass and turned to his partner.

"What happened?"

"Melody Anderson is what happened. That girl is lying, saying I raped her. New Year's Eve at Brandon's party. Bo, I never touched that girl, I swear on my life, baby. When I walked out of that room, I left her looking the same as when I came in."

"I believe you, baby. But for them to arrest you, they must think they have something. Do you know what that could be?"

"I've been racking my brain all day. Okay, Bo, there is something I have to tell you, and *please* don't trip. I've been through enough."

"As long as you don't tell me you fucked her. You tell me that, and I'm going smooth off."

"I didn't." Darius proceeded to give Bo the rundown about the night at the party when Melody had tried to seduce him. Throughout the story, he maintained his innocence and his word that he didn't so much as touch the girl.

"Why did you take your damn clothes off if you weren't going to do anything? And don't you know my writing by now? How are you going to let some note from a sixteen-year-old get you arrested?"

"Baby, think back to that night. We'd been playing around, cuddling on the couch. You know it's not unusual for us to try out the rooms of strange homes. It was so typical of something we'd do that I wasn't looking for it to be a trap. I wanted you so badly that as soon as I stepped in the room, I started taking off my clothes. But come to think of it," Darius continued, "I might have something that can be used as evidence. Have you taken clothes to the cleaners' recently?"

"Not in the last couple weeks, why?"

"Because that note Melody wrote, inviting whoever had sex with her into the room, should still be in those pants pockets."

"Well, baby, that might help whoever gets charged. That is, if you want to help them."

"Knowing how bearing false witness feels from this personal perspective? I'll help anybody I can."

Bo reached over and hugged his lover. "I admit, this jail shit ain't my territory. But we're going to get through this, and we are going to put up one helluva fight. Johnnie Cochran ain't here, God rest his soul, but we're going to have to find somebody who will get people to understand: if the dick don't fit, you must acquit!"

49

She Said You Did

A week later, Darius sat in Pastor Derrick's office. Melody's parents, Mr. and Mrs. Anderson, were also there. The tension was so thick it could have been cut with a knife.

"First of all, I'd like to thank you all for coming to this meeting. I think we are all deeply shaken by what's happened, and as the pastor of everyone involved, I feel a personal responsibility to this situation."

Mrs. Anderson shifted in her seat and stared at Darius. "Yes, well someone else *didn't* act responsibly, and your sinful soul will now rot in a jail cell before it rots in hell, praise the Lord!"

"Now, Mrs. Anderson, I understand we are all upset. But there's no use having this discussion if one isn't going to listen with an open mind and a Christ-like heart. Jesus said, 'Judge not, lest ye be judged,' and the law says a man is innocent until proven guilty. I'm not taking sides in this matter. I'm just trying to uphold the Christian doctrine of going to one's neighbor if you have aught against them."

"With all due respect, Reverend, how are you going to hold up Christian principles with a homo leading your choir? God forgive me, but it's the truth, and you know it."

Derrick took a silent, restraining breath. Maybe this meeting wasn't such a good idea. Darius had been resistant from the beginning, but since the Andersons had been members in good standing since Derrick had taken this ministry a decade ago, he thought they could at least hear one another out. Maybe he was wrong.

The usually docile and quiet Mr. Anderson spoke into the silence. "Pastor, we're sorry. My wife and I here, well, as you can understand, we're powerful upset. But we respect you as our man of God, and we *will* sit here like good Christians and hear what you have to say."

Mrs. Anderson cut her husband a sharp glance, and for only the second time in the past five years, Mr. Anderson met her stare with equal resolve. Finally Mrs. Anderson nodded curtly, and Pastor Derrick continued.

"As I said, I feel personally connected to this unfortunate situation, not only because you're my members, but also because the church will be linked to this as well. Darius is a public figure, and this story will be major news. I'm surprised it hasn't run nationally already, but *LA Gospel* contacted the church for a statement, so believe me, it will be on all the wires before the month is out, if not sooner.

"This is why I've called you all here, not to take sides or offer my opinions as to the allegations that have been made, but to call on all involved to practice restraint and to realize this affects not only you personally but the entire Kingdom Citizens family. I am also asking that what is stated in this room stays in this room. That we agree to keep this particular discussion private. Is it agreed?"

Everyone nodded.

"Now, before we go any further, let's pray."

After Derrick finished praying, he asked who wanted to make the first statement. After a short silence, Darius spoke.

"Pastor, I'd just like to say," he stopped and turned to the Andersons. "Mr. and Mrs. Anderson, I'd just like you to know, and I say this before God, I did not touch your daughter."

"She said you did," Mrs. Anderson answered quickly. "And I believe her."

Darius knew it would be of no use to recount the actual events from that evening, so he went another route. "Were you aware, Mrs. Anderson, that I had a conversation with your daughter on New Year's Eve morning, telling her she could no longer run my fan club? I honestly believe that's why she made up this story, to get back at me for releasing her."

"I saw the blood; my daughter was raped. And the doctor confirmed that she'd had—that she'd been violated. My daughter was pure, saving herself for marriage. I've drilled that into her head since she was five years old. There is no way she would have willingly laid down with any man!"

"As far as you know," Derrick interjected. He held up his hand to stop the attack that was about to spew from Mrs. Anderson's mouth. "I'm not calling your daughter a liar. Again, I'm neutral here, I don't know what happened. But in the spirit of being objective, and I'm speaking from personal experience here, we parents don't always know our teenagers as well as we think we do."

"Melody was a virgin before this here sinner violated her. And he's going to pay. That he lies down with men is already an abomination, but that he would then plant his filthy self into my baby . . . and then to sing in church, actually lead our choir . . . ? It's blasphemy, I tell you. And a shame before the living God."

Mrs. Anderson put her head in her hands and began sobbing loudly. Mr. Anderson placed his arms around his wife, trying to console her. She only cried louder.

"Pastor, I'm sorry, but maybe this wasn't the best idea. My wife has been inconsolable since this happened. It's all too much. Excuse me, but we're leaving."

With that, he half pulled, half pushed his still sobbing wife out of the chair and headed toward the door.

"Mrs. Anderson, I did not rape your daughter," Darius said again as she passed him.

Mrs. Anderson stopped crying and stopped right in front of him. "You and your scandalous behavior are sure signs that we are living in the last days. You saw what God did to Sodom and Gomorrah, and worse is going to happen to you. If I weren't a Christian woman, I wouldn't wait for Jesus to assign you to hell. I'd choke the life out of you and send you there myself!"

Before anybody knew what was happening or had time to react, Mrs. Anderson took the hand that had been raised toward heaven and slapped Darius hard across the face. Darius, shocked, reeled back in his chair as Derrick and Mr. Anderson quickly ushered a tongue-talking Mrs. Anderson out of the office.

After a few moments, Derrick returned to his office. "I'm sorry, man," he said as soon as he walked in. "I knew Mrs. Anderson was upset, but I never thought she would have gone off like that."

"Don't sweat it, Pastor," Darius said, still rubbing his cheek. "Mrs. Anderson is probably angrier with her daughter than with me, though she'll probably never admit it."

"I don't know, Darius. It seems that while Mrs. Anderson can see everyone else's faults, she's blind when it comes to her daughter. She was in her forties when Melody was conceived, way past the time either of them thought they'd have children. She's spoiled that girl from the beginning, and unless someone can get through to them, I'm afraid their daughter is in for a difficult life. Everyone isn't going to put up with Melody's bratty ways."

"This goes way beyond bratty," Darius said. "This could affect my career and my life. Pastor, as God is my witness, I did not have sex with that girl. One time, in this very office, Cy joked with me that sixteen could get me twenty. Well, according to my lawyer, it can get even more than that. But I'm not going down for something I didn't do. And I didn't do it!"

Derrick sighed. "I believe you, Darius. But someone did. Because I also believe what Mrs. Anderson said about the doctor's report. And there's more."

Darius's head shot up. "More? What more can there be?"

"I didn't get a chance to tell the Andersons this, but according to the reporter at *LA Gospel,* there's a tape."

"A tape—you mean videotape?"

Derrick nodded.

Darius smiled for the first time since the meeting had begun. "Well, that's good news, man! One look at the tape and anybody will be able to see it's not me on it."

"Maybe, maybe not."

"What do you mean?"

"I haven't seen it—understand. But the reporter who has seen it says the quality is grainy, and, because the only light in the room was coming from the lights by the pool outside, it's hard to get a definitive look at the man. But she said the person in the tape resembles you, at least enough to where it *could* be you."

Darius stood. He'd heard enough. And after hearing there was a tape floating around, he decided not to even share the little piece of evidence he had—the note from Melody that Bo had indeed found in the pile of dirty clothes.

"Look, Pastor, I appreciate your having my back. But if you're through, I've got to go. I need to get my hands on a copy of that tape and pass it on to my attorney."

"Wait, Darius. There is one more thing. This was a difficult decision, but one that I feel is necessary. While I sympathize with you, my concern has to be for the entire congregation. It's unfortunate, but I have to try to shield the family from any potential scandal connected to Melody's allegations. Until this situation has been resolved, I'm going to have to ask you to step down as minister of music and to cease directing, playing keyboards, and all other activities relating directly to the Kingdom Citizens ministry."

50

Believe That

Hope sat on the couch looking at her stomach. "I can't believe there's a baby in here. And I'm getting big so fast!"

"I never thought I'd see the day where my cuz was actually excited about gaining weight!" Hope gave her an exasperated look. "But I admit, you better slow down on those Oreos, or you'll still be carrying baby weight when the child goes to college!"

"Oh, hell to the no," Hope countered. "Cy's already agreed to give me a personal trainer as a baby-mama present. I've got to get back into my size sixes when this is over."

"You will, girl. I'm just jerking your chain. You know I'm happy for you."

Hope noticed a hint of sadness under Frieda's carefree attitude. "What about you? Are you happy?"

"You know how I roll: can't let nothing get you down, and if it does, you can't stay there."

"How is it with you and Shabach?"

"Cool, I guess. He's been spending a lot more time in LA since getting me the apartment. The closest thing I've had to a steady since Giorgio."

"Isn't that a good thing?"

"You know a girl can't feel too tied down. He's been hangin' on a sistah like he's got papers."

"I know you always say otherwise, but, Frieda, don't you want to get married, have children? And please don't get defensive, because I'm not judging your lifestyle. But ever since I've known you, especially since we reconnected almost five years ago, it's been one man after another. When you were with Giorgio, I thought maybe he was the one. And then before his plane had left California airspace, it was on to Jonathan. And now it seems like you're hot and heavy with Shabach, but at the same time, concerned that he might want to get serious. Isn't that what you want, to find a man who will be your one and only?"

"One and only can cost too much sometimes," Frieda said in a rare reflective and serious moment. "Plus, I learned a long time ago to protect the heart at all costs."

"But what happened to make you so calloused toward love?"

Frieda looked at Hope a long moment. Then she got up from the couch and walked to the patio doors that offered a full view of the Pacific Ocean.

"There's something I never told you," she began with her back to Hope. "Never told anybody."

Hope watched as her friend's shoulders went up and down with a deep breath. Frieda kept looking straight ahead, away from Hope.

"I was raped."

It was said so softly, Hope wasn't sure she'd heard correctly.

"Frieda, did you say you were raped?"

Frieda nodded her head. "By a friend's older brother when I was eleven. He was twenty, and I thought he was cute. Had a schoolgirl crush on him, you might say. He used to give me candy and tell me I was pretty—one of the first men ever to do so. One day I went over to my friend's house. She wasn't home, but he was there. Told me I could come in and wait for her. He complimented me on my outfit, told me I was rockin' my acid-washed mini and rainbow-colored tube top. When he asked me to sit next to him and watch videos, I was so happy. And when he asked me to come up to his room and get a mixed tape he'd made of my favorites—Janet Jackson, Lisa Lisa, and my boy Bobby—man, I was in seventh heaven. Little did I know I was actually climbing the stairs to hell."

"And you didn't feel you could tell your mom or anybody?"

Frieda turned around then, her eyes dry and vacant. "That's just it, Hope. I enjoyed it. Even though it hurt when he penetrated me the first time, sex felt good to me from the beginning. He said if I told anybody, I'd be sent off to a girls' home, and he would go to jail. But more than the threat was the feeling of acceptance. He told me he loved me, that I was beautiful and more mature than the other girls. No man had told me I was beautiful before. A part of me knew what we were doing was wrong, but the bigger part of me felt it was worth it to make me feel good about myself. By the time I was fifteen, we had stopped messing with each other, but he'd shown me the ropes. I quickly discovered that sex was a powerful weapon, and with it, I could get almost anything I wanted."

"Except happiness." Hope stood and hugged Frieda.

Frieda shook off the moment of vulnerability and returned to her sarcastic self. "You know what, girl, happiness is my bills paid, money in the bank, and a big dick between my legs—real talk. Happiness is being in control instead of letting some nuckah control me. That's why I have to get a handle on Shabach's ass. Make him understand I'm the one who handles my business. No one else."

"But true love isn't about that, Frieda. True love is give and take."

"Girl, you know I don't believe in that true-love, soap-opera, happily-ever-after, fairy-tale bullshit. But I will say this though: if Shabach plays his cards right, we can roll deuce for a long minute. 'Cause the man knows how to please a woman, has hella paper, and looks good to wake up to. Yeah, I'll keep 'Bach in my bed if he acts right, believe that."

51

Take Care

Two weeks after their meeting, Derrick's words proved prophetic. The March issue of *LA Gospel* printed a week early. A smiling, debonair Darius was on the front page. Underneath was the caption in bold black letters: GOSPEL SENSATION CAUGHT IN SIN SCANDAL!

Darius's publicist worked overtime doing damage control by conducting interviews and submitting counter press releases to the statements from various "anonymous sources" who had provided information to the *National Enquirer, Charisma* magazine, and *Gospel Today,* among others. Following the advice of his attorney, Darius had answered every question thrown his way with a terse "No comment." In order to insulate himself from the more jarring personal intrusions, he'd canceled all but the largest concerts and enclosed himself in the studio to work on his third album release.

That's where he was when Stacy called.

"Darius. I just read *LA Gospel.* What is going on?"

"Definitely not what they're saying in that article."

"I didn't believe it for a moment, Darius. You'll barely even *be* with a woman, so to rape one? Uh-uh. But I've seen you a couple times since New Year's. You didn't say anything."

"I figured you had enough problems to deal with."

"What are you going to do?"

"Fight back; it's the only thing I can do."

"Can you tell me who it is?"

"It's Melody Anderson."

"Oh, my goodness, not Miss High-and-Mighty Bernadette Anderson's child."

"The one and only."

"Oh, Darius. I am so sorry. That woman can't stand you."

"Don't I know it."

"But wait. She knows you're gay, so why would she believe you've been with Melody?"

"Obviously where her mother is concerned, Melody's word is gospel. You didn't know?"

"The article said there was a tape going around. Have you seen it?"

"No, it's still pretty underground. But one of Bo's connections is supposed to have a copy by the weekend. I can't wait to get my hands on it so it can help my case. Hopefully this will be the evidence I need to be fully exonerated. It's not me in that video, Stacy."

"I wonder who it is?"

"Maybe a classmate, another church member, who knows? But I'm not taking the fall for whoever it is, trust me on that. I'm not going to jail over this bullshit. I'm innocent. And so is whoever was in the room with her that night."

"How do you know that?"

Darius told Stacy about the note that had led him into the lion's den.

"It's a good thing you kept it," Stacy said when he'd finished.

"Yeah, I gave a copy to Bo, made a couple more copies, and put the original in a deposit box. It might end up being my ticket to freedom out of this madness."

"Darius, I know you didn't do this, and it goes without saying that I'm praying for you. Let me know if there's something I can do."

"Thanks, Stacy. I'm praying for you too. How are the treatments coming?"

"Thank God I have only two more weeks to go. Radiation is nothing nice, and fortunately my doctor believes I can stop after the fifth week. At least I don't have to do the full-blown chemotherapy and lose my hair. As it is, I'm nauseous, tired all the time, and have bouts with diarrhea. But it could be worse, so I'm just grateful things are as well as they are. And the nursing assistant you hired to come help me is a huge help. I really appreciate it, Darius."

"I told you, Stacy, I want to always make sure the mother of my child is taken care of."

"Well, it looks like you need to focus on taking care of yourself."

"Oh, I'm going to do that," Darius said with firm resolve. "I've worked too long and too hard to get where I'm going. And I don't believe God has brought me this far to leave me."

52

I'm Okay Now

The ringing phone pulled Stacy from what felt like layers and layers of thick fog. She'd been dreaming, something about a playground full of kids and big birds swooping down and carrying the kids away in the clutches of their large, wrinkled claws. One was flying toward little Darius. She was trying to reach her son before the bird did. Then the phone rang.

"Hello?" she asked in a voice filled with sleep.

"Oh, I'm sorry. I've obviously awakened you."

"It's okay. Who is this?"

"Stacy, it's Dr. Livingston. I'm calling to see how you're doing and to answer any questions you might be having about your treatment."

Stacy sat up, still trying to clear the birds out of her brains. "Oh, thanks for calling, doctor. I'm doing okay, just really tired. And sometimes I feel congested but not quite like it's a cold." She repeated the other symptoms that she'd shared with Darius.

"All of what you've described are normal side effects of this type of treatment," Dr. Livingston explained. "You may also experience dryness in the area where the radiation is being focused. Should that happen, please let me know, and I will prescribe a special type of cream to help alleviate that discomfort. I also wanted to let you know that once you've healed from the lumpectomy procedure, you may be interested in having reconstructive surgery. You were fortunate in that only a small amount of tissue was removed, a void that can be effectively camouflaged with padded bras. But you're a young woman with a long life ahead of you. I just want you to be aware of all your options."

"I appreciate it, doctor. Actually I haven't been thinking about too much of anything lately besides getting through this radiation treatment. Once I recuperate from that and have some time to just feel normal again, I'll probably be more open to additional surgeries."

"That's totally understandable, Stacy. I just want you to know you are doing extremely well. I'm proud of how you've handled this whole crisis."

Stacy lay back against her pillow. She wasn't as concerned with how well she was handling the crisis as she was in knowing the crisis would truly be over.

"Doctor, what are the chances of the—of me having to go through this again?"

"That's something that can't be diagnosed, unfortunately. I will tell you this, however. Chances for any type of disease can be diminished by a healthy diet and state of mind and by regular visits to the doctor. We'll talk more about that on your next visit. For now, just concentrate on getting better."

"Thank you so much for calling, Dr. Livingston. Your encouragement makes me feel better. Hey, do doctors still make house calls?"

The doctor laughed. "I don't think that will be necessary, Stacy. But do call the hospital if you have any questions or need to combat issues dealing with the dry skin that may develop in the area being treated. Okay?"

"Okay, doctor. Good night."

Stacy had barely put her phone down when it rang again. She looked at the number and smiled. "What's up, Tony?"

"Not you, from the sound of it. Are you asleep already, woman? It's just now eight o'clock."

"I was, but I'm up now," Stacy said. She got out of bed and headed downstairs. "What are you doing?"

"I've got this little situation I'm trying to figure out, and I could use some womanly advice."

"Oh, really?"

"Yeah. See somebody at the church has been leaving notes on my car, little flirty one-liners and whatnot. At first there was a lipstick kiss on it or perfume sprayed on. But tonight they upped the ante. I came outside, and there was a pair of thong panties on my windshield!"

"Tonight? After bible study?"

"Yep. So now I'm trying to figure out whether the person is an admirer or a stalker."

"Sounds like a little of both. C'mon, now, Tony. You've got to have some idea of who it might be."

"Not really. I thought it might be your friend Tanya, but then I heard she was dating one of the dudes who works security."

A thought occurred to Stacy but was forgotten once she looked in her refrigerator. "Dangit!"

"Don't go getting upset now. I'm not worried about it. Not yet anyways."

"No, it's not that. My brothers have been over here and ate up all the food."

"Oh, okay. So what do you think I should do?"

"About what?"

"About finding out whose putting notes on my car."

"I don't know. Maybe speak to security, talk with Greg, have the guys keep an eye out for you. Or else you could leave a note on your windshield for her, along with your phone number, and tell her to call."

"I don't think I have anything to say to a churchgoing woman who'd leave panties on my hood."

"C'mon, Tony. For the father of two children, you sure are sounding like a prude."

"No, but I'm not the man I was back in those days. I handle things differently now, or at least I'm trying to."

"That's good, Tony. It really is. But look, I gotta go. I'm feeling weak and need to scramble up something to eat."

After washing her face and brushing her teeth, Stacy called Tanya to check on her son. She looked for something to eat but, not finding anything, decided to drink a large glass of orange juice and go back to bed. She was midway up the stairs when her doorbell rang.

She smiled, instantly knowing who it was. *Tony—so thoughtful.* It didn't look like a romance would ever develop between them, but it was nice to have male friends.

"Hey, there . . . oh! Doctor Livingston?"

"Just wanted you to know that sometimes doctors do still make house calls. May I come in?"

"Of course," Stacy said, her mind reeling. She never thought the doc would take her serious and end up in her living room!

"I know you're resting, so I'm not going to stay long. It just so happened that an errand I needed to run put me near your house." He walked over to Stacy, looked in her eyes, felt her neck and pulse, asked her to open her mouth, and then nodded. "You're doing well. Are you still nauseous?"

"It comes and goes. I'm okay right now."

"Good. You also may want to limit the amount of dairy products you ingest right now. That could lower the mucous that sometimes builds up as a result of the radiation. And you may want to consider that a long-term goal—limiting both your dairy and meat intake. Build your diet around green, leafy vegetables and lots of fruit. A great diet and steady exercise program will go a long way toward maintaining optimum health."

"I appreciate that, doctor, but God is who I look to for my well-being."

"Is that so? Then why didn't you schedule an appointment with Him instead of coming to the hospital?"

"What, you don't believe in God?"

"I believe in a Higher Power, but, no, I am not religious. Listen, I'm not against religion, I just think we are the masters of our destiny and play a big role in how our lives look. It certainly wouldn't hurt for you to add these sensible exercises to your faith, would it?"

"No, I guess not."

"Good." The doctor stood. "I'll be going now. Continue to get good rest and we'll see you next week."

The doctor walked to the door while Stacy turned her back to adjust her robe.

"Oh, excuse me," he said as he opened the door.

Oh, that's Tanya with my son. Seeing Darius Jr. always made her happy. She turned around with a smile on her face.

"Tony! What are you doing here?"

53

House Calls

For a moment, the two men sized each other up. Stacy quickly made introductions. "Dr. Livingston, Tony Johnson. Tony, this is my doctor."

"I didn't know doctors still made house calls," Tony said, looking the doctor up and down.

"Only for very special patients." Dr. Livingston turned to Stacy. "Don't hesitate to call if you have any concerns—any concerns at all." He turned back to Tony and didn't flinch at the hard stare. "If you two will excuse me."

Tony brushed past Stacy and walked into the kitchen. After locking her front door, she followed him in.

"Ooh, Tony, you brought me something to eat. That was so nice of you. I'm starving!" She walked over to the bag Tony had set on the counter. "What's this?"

When she got no answer, she turned around. Tony was leaning against the sink, brows creased, arms folded.

"What's your problem?" Stacy asked and then turned back around.

"What's up with you and the doctor?" he asked brusquely.

"Who are you, my daddy?" Stacy joked. "I've already got four brothers. I don't need you sticking your nose in my biz. This soup is good, where did you get it?"

Again, she got no answer.

She turned around to see Tony looking at her somberly. Stacy walked over to stand in front of him.

"What is the matter with you?" she asked, hands on hips.

"Nothing that what I'm about to do won't cure," he responded. Then he lowered his lips to hers and seared them with a kiss.

Stacy opened her mouth in shock, and Tony immediately took advantage, plundering his thick tongue inside her mouth. He wanted to crush her to him, but to be careful of her bandage, he stroked her shoulders and back instead. An intense heat flared in Stacy's core and spiraled up through her body. She deepened the kiss, swirling her tongue around his and placing her hands on his massive chest. After several long moments, they came up for air.

"What was that about?" Stacy asked breathlessly.

"It's how I feel about you."

"But we're friends—you know, buddies. Not an hour or more ago, you were asking for dating advice."

"What can I say, your answers impressed me."

"Okay, this is crazy." Stacy turned back to the food. She needed to put some space between them and collect her thoughts. "You want some of this?"

"Yes."

Of course he's talking about the food. "You want some crackers to dip in the soup?"

Lord, have mercy, I'd like to dip something somewhere, all right. "Uh, yeah, that's cool. So what's up with the doctor? Is he trying to prescribe some sexual healing?"

Stacy handed Tony his bowl and led them into the dining room. "He's a nice man—thoughtful, very good at what he does. But he has this 'spiritual but not religious' stance. I don't know how Jesus fits into that description, and you know I'm sold out. Why, do you think he's husband potential for me?"

"Yeah, if you want to marry Dr. Doolittle."

It was three hours later when Tony left Stacy's home. As usual, their conversation had flowed easily, and after dinner they had watched a movie. While their casual banter and comfortable camaraderie returned, something else had entered their relationship as well—desire. And for Tony, one more thing: love.

54

It Hurts

"Hey, hos, wuzzup!" Frieda waltzed into the Taylor penthouse carrying bags filled with P.F. Chang's Chinese food.

Hope walked over to help with the bags. "Cousin, how many times do I have to tell you, I don't play that *b* or *ho* nonsense. That so many women feel comfortable with that label is beyond me."

"Ah, bitch, chill out!" Frieda answered, nonplussed. "If it's said in love, it's all good. What do you think, Stacy?"

"I think that's an *A* and *B* conversation, and I'm going to *C* my way out of it."

"Girl, that line is so tired, it needs to be *retired*," Frieda said.

"Whatever, I'm not getting into y'all's mess," Stacy said.

"It's the same with the *N*-word," Hope went on. "It's been *lovingly* used in hip-hop for the last fifteen years, but if a White redneck spewed the word as he raised a gun from the window of a Confederate-flag-decorated pickup truck, nobody would be talking about love."

"Yeah, but if he said it *without* the gun . . ."

Hope rolled her eyes. "You are simply ig-nor-ant. What's in these boxes?"

As Hope arranged boxes of kung pao chicken, lemon pepper shrimp, beef with broccoli, and all the trimmings on the dining room table, Frieda joined Stacy on the couch in the living room.

"You look good, girl. How you feeling?"

"Better every day," Stacy said. "I have only one week of radiation to go."

"That's great, Stacy. I'm so glad this is getting ready to be over for you."

"Let us pray. And I have some more news, ladies. Tony has stepped up his game. He's let me know in no uncertain terms that he's interested."

"So did he git with that split?"

"No, Frieda, and he won't be getting with anything anytime soon. He and I are both committed to doing things the Godly way, no matter how unpopular that is right now. We've both been hurt in relationships; we've both got kids. We just want to continue taking things nice and slow. But," she added coyly, "he's a great kisser."

"Which lips did he kiss?" Frieda asked innocently.

"I'm not even going to dignify that with a response!"

"I'm fixing my plate if anybody wants to join me!" Hope shouted from the other room. Since her morning sickness had subsided, her appetite was enormous. "Stacy, you want me to get yours?"

"I'm not an invalid," Stacy said, rising. "I hope you remembered the spring rolls," she said to Frieda, who was right on her heels.

The women fixed their plates and settled into the living room. They ate silently for a while and then Stacy spoke.

"Frieda, I think you're about to set a record. I haven't heard you talk about anybody but Shabach in almost a month. Could it be that you're turning into a one-man woman?"

"He's laying the pipe like a plumber, what can I say?"

"It's got to be about more than that," Hope said. "You guys do make a nice couple, though."

"What about Giorgio? You still talk to him?"

"Of course, that's my boo. Giorgio will always be my boo. He likes Shabach's music, feels he's a good hookup for me. Meanwhile he's all up in some girl's grill that he's modeling with. I think she's from Sweden or Russia or somewhere—you know, blond, blue-eyed. He said she sucked dick like a Stanley Steemer vacuum cleaner."

Stacy almost spewed her food. "Girl, you have no sense!"

"I don't get it," Hope said. "How you guys can sleep with other people and then hook right up where you left off when he comes to town."

"That's because you don't understand a friend with benefits. Giorgio and I understand each other. At the end of the day, we're friends—that's it."

"You're right." Hope sighed. "I don't understand."

Once she'd finished eating, Frieda made an announcement. "All right, you bi—okay, Hope, ladies. I've got the hottest DVD in the country right now, hot off the streets." Frieda retrieved a DVD from her purse and walked back to the entertainment center. "Hope, help me work this complicated-ass system."

"Now?" the still eating Hope asked around a mouthful of vegetable fried rice.

"Yes, Hope, now."

"What is it?" she asked as she popped the DVD into the player and turned on the television.

"You'll see."

After several seconds of static, a dark room with a bed emerged on the screen. Seconds later a naked woman lay down. She got up, and after obviously adjusting the camera, lay back on the bed.

"Is this the Melody tape?" Stacy asked.

"Yep."

"Where'd you get it?"

"You know I've got connections."

Hope shifted in her seat. "I don't know if I want to see this."

"Shhh." Frieda pressed play and joined the other women on the couch.

A man walked into the frame. "Is this what you want?" he asked.

"Yes," was the shy reply.

"Baby, this is a lot of . . . You have to be sure you want it. Do you?"

The conversation was low and for a moment couldn't be heard.

"Huh?"

"Yes!" The young-sounding voice was tentative but firm.

"That doesn't sound like Darius," Stacy said.

"You can't even really see them," Hope added.

"Why would she want this taped? That's my question," Frieda said. "If you ask me, this isn't about nothing but money. Watch them come up with some ridiculous out-of-court-settlement scheme."

After a bit more conversation and a little foreplay, the man entered the woman on the tape. The woman moaned loudly. "Awwwww. That hurts."

"Uh-huh, hurts so good, don't it?"

"This is disgusting," Hope said. "I'm not too sure how well hearing about his big beef goes with my shrimp."

But all three women continued to watch, as though mesmerized. As the sexual intercourse continued, the woman's groans turned to moans. The man was moaning too.

"You tight as hell, baby," he said. "Were you a virgin?"

The woman's response was garbled, swallowed up by another loud moan.

After another moment the man quickened his pace; his breathing became labored, and a low growl erupted from his chest. He rolled them over in bed until they ended up nearer to the window. He lay on top of the woman, breathing heavily, stroking her hair.

"Thank you, baby. That was good. Real good."

"That was nasty," Hope said.

"If this is all the evidence, I don't see how they can finger Darius," Stacy added.

"Where's the remote?" Frieda grabbed it from Hope. "How do you push rewind?"

"Oh, please, Frieda. We've seen enough."

"Just push rewind, damnit! Back it up a few frames!"

Hope and Stacy looked at Frieda, and then Hope did as she asked. Once again the man's orgasm was heard before he rolled them over to the other side of the bed. The light from the pool glistened off his back. Frieda sprang from the couch and got directly in front of the television.

"Stop it! Freeze it right there!"

"What is it?" Stacy asked. "What are you seeing?"

After a pause, Frieda slowly turned around. She looked from one friend to the next and then plopped into the chair opposite the couch.

"What am I seeing? I'm seeing the tattoo that's right above my man's ass." She looked at both women a long moment. "That isn't Darius. It's Shabach."

55

New Friends

Frieda got into her Mitsubishi Eclipse and zoomed out of the complex. She was furious. Fumbling with her Bluetooth, she dialed Shabach's number. It went to voice mail.

"I saw the tape, muthafucka. How are going to play me and let me find out like this? If you're in Atlanta, you might as well keep your punk ass there. And send me an address so I can mail you your shit!"

Frieda hit the 405 and put the pedal down. She raced in and out of traffic like she was in the Indy 500, trying to run away from what she'd seen at her cousin's house.

See, this is the very reason I don't develop feelings for nuckahs. All they bring is pain.

And she'd been so close to letting her guard down and totally letting go, allowing herself to be vulnerable with a man. She hadn't done that since lying on her friend's upstairs bed listening to Bobby Brown and empty promises while a man took her prize. After then she'd decided never again. She'd vowed she would be the predator, she'd be the one chewing them up and spitting them out. But Shabach convinced her he was different, made her feel special, bought her things, got the place in LA. He'd even talked of getting her a ring and the both of them moving to Atlanta. She'd been so close to believing the hype.

Frieda saw the 10 freeway and shot over four lanes to make the switch. She gave the middle-finger salute to honking horns and cursing drivers.

Once she exited and hit Beverly Boulevard, the dense Saturday afternoon traffic forced her to slow down. She drove listlessly, aimlessly, with no clear destination in mind. Then she saw it—the Beverly Center—and remembered she still had Shabach's American Express. A sinister smile broke out on her face as a plan began to unfold.

As soon as she parked, she whipped out her cell phone.

"What's up, baby?"

"Hey, Giorgio. Shabach just played me, and I'm mad as hell. I'm about to spend up his money with a turn in the mall and a trip to New York. What are you doing tomorrow?"

In less than an hour, Frieda had enhanced her wardrobe by almost ten thousand dollars. She looked down at her brand-new Jacob the Jeweler designer watch and saw that if she hurried, she could get to her favorite nail salon. Hurrying around the corner while looking into one of the bags, she didn't see people coming. And the next thing she knew, she was sliding on her backside with her legs in the air.

The man she'd barreled into hurried to help her up. "You were in quite a hurry there. Are you all right?"

"I was in a hurry? You ought to watch where you're going with your blind ass. Can't you see through those glasses?"

The stranger grew rigid, not at all used to being spoken to in such a crass manner. "Excuse me, but I thought you ran into me. At any rate, here, let me help you up."

Frieda came to a standing position and began gathering her bags. The stranger helped her. As he reached for the last bag, she caught a glimpse of his backside, ensconced nicely in a pair of faded jeans. Making the journey up from there, she discovered a narrow waist and nice shoulders. The man needed someone to help him dress, she decided, but he had potential. Then she looked again and remembered. The doctor!

"There, I think that's everything," he said.

"Okay, thank you. Sorry I went off on you. I'm having a rough day, doctor."

"Do I know you?"

"No, but getting to do that might be interesting." At his confused expression, she went on. "You operated on a friend of mine recently. Stacy Gray."

"Ah, yes, Stacy. How's she doing?"

"Like nothing was ever wrong. But I'm trying to be your patient now. What's your name again?"

"Gabriel. Gabriel Livingston. What's yours?"

"Frieda Moore."

"Well, what seems to be your problem, Frieda?"

"My heart's broken, and I might need an operation. You in here buying something for the missus?"

Gabriel laughed. "Why don't you simply ask if I'm married?"

"Why don't you simply answer my question and then I'd know?"

"You're pretty feisty for someone who just moments ago was sliding on her rump."

"Well, tell me something, Gabriel, did you like the view?"

Gabriel shook his head. It had been a while since he'd had someone challenge him. The nurses and other females at the hospital treated him with the deference his position afforded, and the peers that were often lined up as blind dates were too busy matching pedigrees to show such unrestrained fire. After working fourteen straight days, the change was refreshing. And the person breathing the fire was easy on the eyes. He answered her question with his own. "Tell me, are you always this forward?"

"I speak my mind, if that's what you're asking. Life is too

short to put on airs. I'm the only one who can do Frieda Moore, you feel me?"

"Is that a proposition?"

"No, fool, it's slang. I can see you don't get out much. Why's that?"

"It's my profession. Keeps me busy."

"Well, Mr. Busy, it's Saturday night. I've had a bad day, and you need to get your mind off your profession. So how's about buying me a drink so we can cry in our beer together?"

"You are as bold as they come, I'll give you that."

Frieda invaded his personal space. "Don't worry, I can think of other things besides that for you to hold against me."

Fifteen minutes later, Gabriel had assisted Frieda to her car, they'd chosen a place to meet, and she was on her way. En route to the bistro and bar on little Santa Monica Boulevard, Frieda warred with her emotions. She was hurt at Shabach's betrayal. And she was angry that she was hurt. She'd worked for over twenty years, since she was eleven, never to be hurt again.

When her phone vibrated she expected Shabach. It was Hope.

"No, I'm not going to kill myself."

"Well, I certainly hope not; not over some dust."

"Where are you, though? You left rather abruptly and haven't answered your phone."

"Did you call?"

"Right after you left."

"Oh, I missed that. I was at the mall."

"Now that's a good way to get over being angry."

"Trust, my anger is what had me spend ten g's of that nuckah's money."

"Frieda, please tell me you didn't do that."

"Okay, I won't. But I can't talk now, I'm getting ready to have a drink with a new friend."

"What new friend?"

"Stacy's doctor. He's kinda dorky, but he's tall with big hands. Maybe some potential there."

"How did you meet? Never mind."

Hope knew Frieda couldn't see her shaking her head, but she shook it anyway. Thinking back to the recently revealed story about rape, she had to ask. "Frieda, are you sure this isn't just a way for you not to have to deal with your emotions? With the hurt and anger you must be experiencing about Shabach?"

"Hell, yeah. That's exactly what it is. Now rub that stomach and think about your child instead of trying to treat me like one. I'm handling my business."

"I know you are. I didn't mean—"

"Girl, I know, that's just love talking. But I'm going to be okay. And like I always say, there's nothing to make you get over an old flame like a new one. Love you, cuz."

Gabriel switched gears in his fully restored Jaguar XKE Coupe. He rarely drove his beloved baby in dense traffic, but as he'd planned to go only to the mall and then home, he thought it would be okay to blow the cobwebs out. He liked to take it out once every couple weeks just to keep it purring properly.

As he turned onto the boulevard and up to valet parking, he thought about the intriguing woman who'd almost run him over. Granted, she wasn't his usual taste—in fact, he couldn't remember ever meeting anyone like her. *And therein may lie the mystery,* he thought, *of why I want to get to know her more.*

56

WTF

It was Darius's first time at church in over a month since being relieved of his ministerial duties by the senior pastor. He wasn't sure how he'd be received by the parishioners, but Derrick had told him in no uncertain terms that he was still considered family and was welcome at Kingdom Citizens anytime. Derrick assured him that he believed what Darius said to be true and that as soon as he was cleared, his minister of music job would be waiting, should he want it back.

This conversation from the past week and Stacy's recovery from cancer were just two of the reasons Darius felt it was past time to darken the doors of a house of God. While the past month had been stressful, there had also been some sunshine between the clouds. One ray was the news he was getting ready to confide to his pastor.

He and Bo rode in a black town car with tinted windows. They were chatting casually as the driver turned the corner. And then conversation ceased.

There, on the corner, stood about fifty people—some with signs, others waving bibles, still others holding crushed copies of Darius's CDs.

IT'S IMPOSSIBLE TO BE GAY AND LOVE GOD, one sign read.

PERVERTS GO TO HELL, read another.

NO MO' HOMOS was being lifted by a woman who looked about eighty years old.

GAY AIN'T THE WAY!

REMEMBER SODOM AND GOMORRAH.

And one of the biggest signs, DEN OF SIN, was being touted by the woman who seemed to be the ringleader—Mrs. Bernadette Anderson.

Bo was the first one to find his voice. "What the fuck?"

Darius sat stunned, sitting back and trying to melt into the leather seat, even with the windows tinted. "Oh, my God," he whispered.

As the driver turned into the parking lot, Darius turned to see some of the protesters walking in a scattered circle, while others walked back and forth across the street. When he turned back around, his eye caught the head of security, Greg, talking into his two-way and hurrying across the street toward the chaos.

"I should go knock the wig off that bitch!" Bo snapped. "In fact, let me out of this car. She don't know who—"

"Bo, please," Darius said as he wrestled Bo's hand away from the door handle. "You'll only make it worse."

"But she's calling you a rapist, baby. That shit ain't right!"

"Don't give her the satisfaction of seeing you upset." Darius sighed. "I guess coming to church wasn't such a good idea after all. Drive around to the executive offices, Wayne. I'll speak with Derrick and then we can ride on."

Darius was quickly ushered into Derrick's office. He caught a few eyes of pity; others wouldn't look at him at all. He felt like getting a shirt that read I'M INNOCENT, but at the end of the day he knew people were going to believe what they wanted.

"Man, do you see what's going on out there?" Darius asked Derrick as soon as he was inside the office.

"I just found out," Derrick said. He wearily rubbed his brow. "Have a seat, man."

"Why didn't you tell me this was happening?"

"The you-know-what just hit the fan this past week. Mrs. Anderson and I had a meeting. She barged in with all sorts of outrageous demands, including a list of people in the church she thought were gay she insisted I kick out of the church. She accused me of taking your side in the rape case and wanted me to testify on behalf of her daughter, who, outside of church, I barely know. When I said no to her ultimatums, she resigned her membership from the church and told me I'd be sorry I crossed her. I guess this is what she meant."

"I'm sorry, Pastor, this has gotten crazy."

"It's not your fault. Melody is the one I want to talk to. But Mrs. Anderson refuses to bring her in. Well, now it doesn't matter, because they're no longer members of this church. And if you want to know the truth, I think this was just an excuse for Mrs. Anderson to remove her membership. She's had a dislike for me since I took over this church ten years ago, was opposed to me changing the name from Good Lord Baptist to Kingdom Citizens. She resents when I teach the prosperity message, wasn't too happy when we changed the music to have a more contemporary flow, and fought Vivian's creation of the Sanctity of Sisterhood."

"How can any woman be against SOS? It's one of the most popular conferences in the country!"

"Oh, she was all for it until Vivian refused to make her president or give her a role with status."

"If she was so unhappy, why didn't she leave a long time ago?"

"Mr. Anderson. He's been here even longer than Bernadette. I think his mother went to this church. He finally agreed to leave, but I wonder if deep down he has doubts as to what his daughter told them."

"If he doesn't, he should," Darius said. "That's one of the reasons I came here today—that and actually go to church, which, considering the chaos outside, is definitely not going to happen. But I'm here because we now know who's in the video."

Derrick's brows shot up in question.

"Shabach."

"Shabach? How do you know?"

"Someone who's been intimate with Shabach recognized a tattoo on his lower back."

"And will this person testify?"

"My lawyers are working on that now. Of course Shabach is denying everything, and unless Melody admits it's him, it's hard for us to force him to cooperate. We're just hoping it's enough to get the system off my back. So I can get my life back."

"Yeah, man, I heard they pulled you from the Stellar awards show and also from the Nation's Family Reunion lineup. The bible says judge not, but people can't help it, and they don't want to be guilty by association."

"I understand."

"Is it affecting record sales?"

Darius nodded. "A little bit. But I'm trying to ignore most of the madness, stay focused on my album about to drop next year. In fact, I'd been stuck creatively; this fiasco has unleashed a torrent of emotions I think will make this one of my best efforts yet."

"Oh, yeah? You got a name for it yet?"

Darius looked his pastor in the eye. "I'm thinking about *From Trial to Triumph*."

The dark gray sedan pulled up to the curb in an area of Atlanta called Little Five Points. Two men got out of the car and walked up to the business that shared the block with a record store and pizza place. Its front looked like a Tahitian hut with colorful letters spelling out the name URBAN TRIBE.

The two walked inside. "Hey, Bastard, what's up?"

Anyone listening may have thought the man behind the counter would get offended, but that's what he called himself—Philthy Bastard. The goateed, earring-wearing redhead nodded his head in greeting and reached out for a soul-brother handshake.

"What's crackin', 'Bach?" he asked pleasantly.

"The world's still mine," Shabach replied. "I need you to hook me up on some business. I need you to remove a tattoo and then cover the spot with another so no one can see the other ever existed. Can you do that?"

"Can you rap?"

Shabach smiled. "Yes, I can."

"Then that's my answer."

57

The Truth

Bernadette Anderson was tired. At fifty-nine, she was way too old to be trying to rein in a teenager with fire between her legs. She hadn't wanted to believe the things she'd heard about her Melody, had sworn to defend her to the death. And she'd believed her daughter, even when her intuition thought otherwise. But the anonymous package she'd just received in the mailbox could not be ignored.

"Melody, I'm asking you for the final time, and you'd better not lie to me: did you write a note to one of Kingdom's members?"

Melody sulked as she weighed her answer. Normally a few tears and a cute pout were enough to get her old, out-of-touch mother off her back. What would that old fogy know about love, much less sex? Melody was still convinced that she might have been a product of artificial insemination!

"Mommy, I . . . Okay, I did write the note. But it was just a joke! A joke my friends and I were playing on Tony because he—"

"Tony?" Mrs. Anderson finally showed Melody one of the photocopies that had been included in the package she'd just received. "According to the letter, this note was given to Darius Crenshaw, the man you said raped you. Now who's Tony?"

Melody had assumed the note her mother possessed was one of several she'd left on Tony's car. She never imagined that Darius would have kept the note she'd had delivered to him the night of the party.

"You remember Tony, my friend at school? I thought you found one of the notes I wrote to him."

"I didn't *find* this note, Melody. It came in the package that was delivered by special messenger this afternoon. Now did you write it or not?"

"I didn't write a note to Darius."

"You didn't."

"No, ma'am."

"But you wrote one to Tony, your classmate at school."

"Yes, ma'am."

"What class do y'all have together?"

"English," Melody hastily replied, telling the lie without missing a beat.

The letter in the package said Melody had written notes both to Darius Crenshaw and Tony Johnson, a professional football player, and that a handwriting analysis confirmed that both notes, as well as a copy of a school English assignment, were by the same writer. The English assignment had been turned in by Melody Anderson and according to the letter, had been obtained through one of Melody's classmates.

Bernadette Anderson didn't know whether it was Darius, Tony, the person who'd written the letter, or her daughter, but somebody was lying. She leaned back against the door, needing its support to ask the final question.

"Melody, did that man Darius rape you like you said he did?"

Melody's pout deepened into a frown. "Why do you keep asking me that? It was hard enough him sticking that dirty thing into me, and you have to keep bringing it up!" She pushed her eyes together until a semblance of wet that could be mistaken for tears formed. "I'm telling the truth, Mommy!"

Bernadette looked at her forlorn-looking daughter yet resisted the urge to go envelop her in her arms as she did every time she scraped a knee, lost an animal—even if it was an ant—or shed a tear.

"Melody, for twenty-five years I prayed for God to send me a child. I endured nine excruciating months and a painful cesarean to bring you into this world. But as God is my witness, if I find out you're lying to me about this rape, after I've asked all these many times just to tell me the truth, I'll do like the Father and say, 'Depart from me, I know you not.'"

Bernadette walked slowly to the bedroom she'd shared with Clyde Anderson for those twenty-five years. She shut the door and then locked it. For a moment she just stood there, staring at the last piece of evidence sent in the anonymous package.

"Lord Jesus, help me, Lord Jesus," Bernadette repeated several times. Finally she reached for the DVD, walked to the twenty-five-inch console from where she and Clyde mainly watched three things: the news, *The Price Is Right* (even though she thought it a form of gambling), and *Sanford and Son* reruns. Her favorite character—the tall, bible-toting, God-fearing Aunt Esther—could still illicit a laugh with her powerful, "Watch out, suckah!"

Bernadette's arthritic hands curled around the disc as she slid it into the DVD player Clyde had bought her two years ago for Christmas. She reached for the remote and pressed PLAY. Within minutes, her worst fears were realized. She could barely make out the dim figures on the screen, but she would recognize her daughter's voice anyplace, anywhere.

"Yes."

"Baby, I got a lot right here. You have to be sure you want it. Do you?"

"Yes!"

"Lord have mercy, Jesus," Bernadette moaned. She clasped her hands to her chest as tears rolled down her face.

"Now, listen," the voice on the tape continued. "I'm not going down for no rape case or some extortion or some bull-shit. So say it nice and loud. And tell me exactly what you want me to do."

"I want you to do it."

"Do what?"

"You know."

"No, I don't."

"C'mon, yes, you do. 'I want you to . . . you know. Do me.'"

"Jesus!" Bernadette covered her eyes, but the words on the tape hit her heart like a fist.

"No, I don't know. Now spell it out!"

"I want you to f-u-c-k me!"

Bernadette stumbled over to the player and blindly pushed at buttons until the movie stopped. She could take no more. Falling back on her bed, she let the tears flow freely. She'd prayed to God that he would forgive her for her sins, but it looked as though the sins of the mother were being visited upon the child. She covered her ears with her hands as she tried to drown out the voices playing inside her head. Voices from more than forty years ago.

"Bebe, you in here?"

"Is that you, Tyrone?"

Tyrone climbed up into the attic. "You know it's me, girl. And I ain't got much time. Now show me what you flashed up at my window yesterday."

"What?" she asked in an innocent voice.

"Why you playing dumb? That what I saw when you laid down on the grass without no panties."

"What did you see?" Bebe said, enjoying the chase and Ty-rone's discomfort.

Sixteen-year-old Tyrone was like a bull at a rodeo ready to crash the gate. "You know, girl, that sweet-looking poontang."

"What am I going to get out of it?"

Tyrone laughed. "Whatever you want!"

This conversation had been the beginning of a string of men Bernadette had entertained in her young teenage years. Looking in all the wrong places for love, acceptance, and the things her parents couldn't afford. Sex had been an easy way for her to get all three, if even for a moment. Sex became a drug, an aphrodisiac, a necessity.

Bernadette's heartbeat increased, and she grabbed at her chest as the memories continued.

"You been with that boy again, huh?"

"No, Mama."

"Get in there and take your clothes off. I'm getting ready to beat the hell out of you. No child of mine is going to practice fornication!"

Bernadette's mother had beaten her to within an inch of her life that day with a corded switch and, when it had shredded, an extension cord. Had it happened in today's time, her mother would have been arrested. But back then it was "spare the rod, spoil the child," and in Mississippi back in the fifties and sixties, they'd beat you for what you were getting ready to do.

That's why when she'd found out she was pregnant by the boy for whom she'd taken a beating, she knew her mother could never find out. Her mother was a staunch, upstanding member of the community, head of the usher board and faithful church member who, after her husband had died, had vowed to remain married to the Lord until the end of her days. Her mother would not understand why Bebe had done what she had done. Would not, Bebe was convinced, know anything about love. So she'd had a back-alley abortion that had torn up her insides. It was therefore a miracle from God that years later she had become pregnant again. And when she had found out she was pregnant, it put a song in her heart. That's why she'd named her daughter Melody.

But now the song of joy was one of sorrow. And while her mother's influence had given Bernadette her strict, biblical interpretation on all things sexual, which precluded her from seeing any joy in the act or any use for it besides procreation (she and Clyde hadn't had intercourse since Melody was born, and Bernadette acted like she didn't know about Josephine, his mistress of the past fifteen years), that was where her resemblance to her mother ended. She wouldn't beat her child. But she wouldn't support her in being wrong either. If only she'd gotten this package last Wednesday instead of this one, before she'd resigned as a member of Kingdom Citizens and organized the Sunday protest outside the church. "Haste makes waste," her mother had used to say. The saying wasn't in the bible, but it was the truth.

Bernadette reached for the tissue on the nightstand. She wiped her eyes, blew her nose, and straightened the collar of her floral-print dress. There were a few calls she needed to make, a few things she needed to do. With a weary heart but a made-up mind, Bernadette pulled herself off the bed and headed for her purse and her address book.

58

Remember That

Hope sat at the dining room table looking as if she were back in college. She wore a light pink warm-up, her hair was pulled back in a ponytail, and she was surrounded by books, papers, sticky notes, and files. With legs up in an adjacent chair and crossed at the ankles, she was engrossed in her second reading of *What to Expect When You're Expecting*. Hope may never win any mother-of-the-year awards, but it wouldn't be because she hadn't tried to be prepared.

She was about to turn on the television when the elevator door opened. Her eyes widened when Cy walked in carrying a large 3-D mock-up of their dream house, the one that was supposed to have been a surprise, but which was now a totally open and collaborative effort between Hope and Cy.

"Baby, come look!" Cy said, his eyes sparkling. "Stan is on his game, baby. This mock-up is exactly what we put on paper."

Stan Connors was the architect Jack had recommended to design the Taylor home. He had more than lived up to the hype.

"Look, baby," Cy said as he rubbed his woman's ever-widening bottom. "The veranda wraps around the entire house. And this gate here, where it ends," Cy opened a miniature replica of a gate that actually swung back and forth, "is the entrance to the backyard and pool area. It's even better than I envisioned."

They spent the next half hour poring over the mock-up for their ten-thousand-square-foot, seven-bedroom, ten-bathroom home that combined elements from several architectural styles: contemporary, Italianate, Spanish, and chalet.

"Are you hungry?" Hope asked. "I think I'll grab a bite." She rose from the table. "Ow!"

Cy was on his feet in an instant. "Baby, what is it, what's wrong?"

Hope was almost doubled over. "I don't know, it feels like a cramp. Help me to the bathroom."

Cy picked her up and carried her into their master suite. As soon as she pulled down her pants, fear jumped into her heart. Blood covered the lining.

"My baby, Cy, what's wrong with my baby!"

"We're not waiting to find out. Let's go!"

Within minutes, Cy was breaking speed limits as he headed toward St. John's Health Center in Santa Monica. En route, he conversed with their doctor, Vimba Chanakira, who tried to keep Cy calm and get him to slow down. Hope sat in the other seat trying to manage the pain with rhythmic breathing. As soon as they pulled up to the emergency entrance, Dr. Chanakira was there with a stretcher and assistants who whisked Hope inside.

Cy didn't want to leave his wife's side, but Dr. Chanakira insisted. "Please, Cy. We need to be focused in there. You'll only be a distraction."

"But what can I do?" Cy was near tears.

"Pray," was Dr. Chanakira's response before she hurried through the double doors.

Cy whipped out his phone and punched in Derrick's number. "Man, you need to pray with me. I'm at the hospital. Hope's bleeding. We can't lose the baby!"

Derrick knew the words *calm down* would be useless and insensitive. So instead he went straight to prayer: "Heavenly Father, who art in heaven, hallowed be thy name. Thy kingdom come, thy will be done, on earth as it is in heaven. And we believe that it is your will, God, for Cy and Hope's child to come through this trauma by your grace and mercy. So we ask now, dear God, to calm this storm, we utter the words of our Lord, peace be still, into this situation. . . ."

Derrick prayed for almost fifteen minutes. As he did, Cy's heartbeat slowed, and his breathing calmed. He began praying in the holy language, underscoring Derrick's words with his soft entreaty before the throne of grace. He reached for the simple gold cross Hope had brought him for his birthday. Fingering it, his faith grew until he could honestly add his belief to Derrick's words.

"And so, Father God, we thank you right now for what we believe you've already done. We thank you that this child will grow to call you Lord. We thank you that this seed will be like the tree planted by the rivers of water and will not be moved," Derrick said.

"Yes, God, we thank you. Thank you, Father God. Thank you, Lord." By now, Cy was in the corner on his knees, not caring how he looked or who noticed. He was praying for his joint heir. Nothing else mattered.

After he got off the phone with Derrick, he sat in a chair, leaned back, and closed his eyes. He forced himself to continue in the calm that had come over him while his brother had prayed fervently for their child.

What's your wife's name? a voice asked in his mind.

Cy knew His voice. Smiling, he whispered, "Hope."

Remember that.

"Hope," Cy whispered again, fingering the cross. "Hope."

A soft hand touched his shoulder. "Mr. Taylor?"

"Dr. Chanakira," Cy said, standing quickly. He still believed, but concern shone in his eyes.

"Your wife is fine, and so are the babies."

"My wife is—what? Babies?"

"That's right," Dr. Chanakira nodded, smiling. "You're having twins. Your son *and* your daughter are fine."

It seemed Cy couldn't keep his hands off Hope's stomach. They'd arrived home an hour ago, and after running a warm bubble bath in their master-suite Jacuzzi, he'd decided to join her. He washed her gently, lovingly, toweled her dry, and then carried her to the bed.

"Cy, they said I'm okay. I can walk."

"The doctor has put you on semi-bed rest. And even though she concluded you experienced severe spotting from a premature contraction, I'm not taking any chances." He adopted the African-sounding accent Eddie Murphy used in one of their favorite movies. "I will carry my queen wherever she needs to go."

"Okay, Prince Akeem." Hope laughed. "Are you going to spread rose petals too?"

"Yes, because," and he broke out in song just like the movie, "you're my queen to be. . . ."

They both laughed as he stood her up just long enough to pull back the covers. Then he picked her up once again and placed her on the bed. He ran his hands over the pooch now evident in her abdomen.

"You've never been more beautiful than this moment," he said, his eyes shining with tears. "My hardest job is going to be not making love to you for the next couple weeks, as the doctor recommended."

"There's making love and then there's making love," Hope said, her eyes going to his manhood as she licked her lips.

"Okay, Mrs. Taylor, behave. We remained celibate for the three months you lived here before we married. We can handle two weeks."

"With you, I can handle anything."

Cy lay on the bed beside her and cuddled her in his arms. "Can you believe we're having twins?"

"No." Hope giggled. "Two for the price of one."

"Exceedingly and abundantly above all we could imagine."

"Plus one of each sex. It's perfect!"

Cy nuzzled her ear. "Are you sorry we found out?"

"No, baby. I'm glad I know. I want to help them stay safe, talk to them, call them by name. So now we can start choosing." She paused for a moment. "I already have a girl's name in mind. It's from the bible."

Cy tried to guess. "Rachel? Elizabeth? Sarah?" Hope shook her head to each name. "Ruth? Mary?"

Hope started to laugh.

"Delilah? Jezebel?"

She laughed louder.

"Rapunzel?"

"That's not in the bible!"

"Okay, what then?"

"Acacia."

Cy pronounced it slowly. "That's beautiful. I like that," he added. "I wonder what it means."

"It's a type of tree," Hope explained. "One that is sharp, strong, with thorny points."

"Wait, how are you going to call our child a thorn?"

Hope kissed Cy. "Here's my take. Trees with thorns have to be handled with care. You can't just rush up on them, you know? You have to show them the proper amount of respect. And while roses have thorns, they are still beautiful."

"And so is Acacia's mother. Now, what about our son?"

"I've done my work," Hope said as she nestled into Cy's hard body. "It's your turn."

59

Shall We?

Tony held the door as Stacy walked into the Getty Museum. He followed, trying hard not to notice the swaying backside deliciously filling out her Apple Bottoms jeans. She wore a lightweight red angora sweater with a pair of red, studded, cowboy-type boots. She looked amazing.

"I can't believe I've never been here," Stacy said after they'd left the information booth and stood reading the maps outlining the five wings and over one thousand sculptures and pieces of art. "This place is beautiful."

"Hmph. None of these pieces can match the artwork I've got on my arm," Tony said.

Stacy smiled. "Good answer."

It had been only three weeks since Tony and Stacy's relationship had gone from friendship to dating. The shift had been seamless, and what she'd heard people say was right: friendship was a perfect foundation for a good relationship. Tony and Stacy were on the same page and wanted the same things out of life. They'd both recommitted themselves to God and were determined to handle this relationship according to His principals.

The myriad of rooms and massive outdoor garden gave them plenty of time to talk.

"You know, there's something I haven't asked you yet," Stacy said.

"What, another question about my babies mamas?"

Stacy swiped him playfully. "I haven't asked much about either of those women. Only the stuff that pertains to your being with *another* baby mama! But seriously, when did you know? When did it click for you that you had feelings for me beyond friendship?"

"Honestly? When I saw the doctor at your house and wanted to jack him up for being around you. I kept telling myself you were like a sister to me, but that emotion doesn't come up for somebody who's just a friend. I always found you attractive, from the first time you sat next to me at the Montgomerys' dinner table. But I'd also been hurt too many times to get caught up with a woman who's heart was elsewhere. I never thought I'd have reason to thank somebody for being homosexual, but Darius—good lookin' out, man! What about you? Never mind. Don't tell me. It was love at first sight."

"Pretty much. When I saw you at church, I liked the way you carried yourself. And when Hope told me you were going to the Montgomerys' . . ."

"Oh, so now we're finding out the truth. You had this whole thing planned, huh, plotting and positioning yourself to get in my good graces."

"Okay, now you're pouring it on a little thick."

"So you weren't attracted to me when we had that first conversation at the table?"

"I'll put it this way: the baked snapper wasn't the only thing making my mouth water."

After walking around the grounds for two hours, Tony directed Stacy to an area of the courtyard where a jazz trio provided an elegant backdrop to the evening. A small grouping of tables for two was set with fine linen and silver. Next to one table, a bottle of Martini & Rossi Asti Spumante chilled in a silver bucket on a stand.

"Shall we?" Tony asked.

Stacy looked around. "We can sit here?"

"Why not?"

"It looks like it's reserved."

"Baby, my knee is acting up. If it is reserved we can sit down until whoever's got the table gets here."

They sat down at the center table, and soon the couple were taken to paradise on the wings of smooth jazz. A card on the table informed them that the group, the Musical Messengers, were on a twenty-five-city tour and would be at the Getty only this weekend. When they broke into a jazzy rendition of Marvin Sapp's "Never Would Have Made It," Stacy unexpectedly teared up.

"They're playing gospel," she whispered, wiping her eyes. "I love that song."

"Me too," Tony said. He kept his arms around her as the band played. After the bridge, the saxophone player stepped to the mic and began reciting an original poem:

"Never would have made it without God in my life,
And now I don't want to go on without you by my side,
You are the air I breathe, the sun that shines,
And I'd be so grateful if you'd be mine because . . ."

Tony, getting down on his knees, began speaking with the saxophonist. The saxophonist dropped out, and Tony continued.

"I never would have made it, and I don't want to take it.
I know we just started this dating thing, but
you're my best friend, so please take this ring.
You have my heart. I love you. Will you marry me?"

He reached into his pocket and pulled out a ring. Stacy could barely see it for crying.

"Tony!"

"I know it may feel like I'm moving too quickly. But I've waited my whole life for you. I know we can work. Because even now, before we're lovers, you're my best friend. Marry me, baby. And make me the happiest man on the planet."

"Yes," Stacy whispered and then again, louder. "Yes! I'll marry you!"

"You'll be my wifey, baby?" he asked as he slipped the ring on her finger.

"Yes, baby, I'll be your wifey."

60

Doctor's Orders

"Doctor? Doctor?" The pretty, petite brunette nurse hurried to Gabriel Livingston's side. "Good work. You were amazing in there."

"Well, thank you. Good assist."

"Look, you must be exhausted and hungry. Do you want to grab something in the cafeteria? Or maybe shake this place for half an hour and go across the street for a bite?"

"Thanks, but no, Amber. I'm still on call for another four hours. I think I'll just go shower and take a quick nap."

Gabriel wearily rubbed his eyes and chin as he continued down the hallway. Being an oncologist brought him great joy. He considered it a privilege to be at the forefront of the fight to stave off and eventually find a cure for one of the nation's most insidious diseases. His beloved grandfather had died from colon cancer, and Gabriel had sworn then, at the age of sixteen, to do whatever he could to help others not feel the pain he'd felt at the loss. At other times practicing medicine brought the immense challenge of trying to remain impersonal in the operating room. The woman they'd worked on tonight was a fighter, and even though her ovarian cancer was in a critical stage, he remained optimistic. He always did.

He stepped into his office and dropped into the swivel-back leather chair. Taking a long swig from a bottle of water, he tapped on the computer and brought up his e-mails. Then he quickly checked his phone messages. He was pleased to find Frieda had left a message both places. The girl had moxie, he'd give her that.

He and Frieda had spoken on the phone several times, but Gabriel's schedule had been too full for them to go out.

"If you don't have time to go out with me, you're too busy," she'd said.

"You're beginning to sound like my mother," he'd responded.

On more than one occasion, Mrs. Livingston had reminded him that she wasn't getting any younger and expected to be able to hold grandchildren from him soon.

"I'm only thirty-seven," he'd said the last time she went into the grandchild mantra.

"And when *I* was thirty-seven," she'd responded without missing a beat, "you were ten years old!"

Gabriel smiled as he shot off an e-mail response to Frieda:

Just finished surgery. Need a nap. Will call you later if it's not too late.
PS: Stop talking dirty. It's not ladylike. :)

He answered a few more e-mails, returned a phone call, took his phone off vibrate, and placed it on ring so that once he stepped into the shower he could hear an emergency call. Then he walked out of his office and down the hallway to the locker room where the shower stalls were located. He quickly stripped out of his clothes and stepped into the steamy, hot water. He stood directly under the pulsating shower head until he felt his shoulder muscles relaxing. Then he lathered and washed, mindful not to waste time showering that could be used for sleep.

Back into his office, he walked past the fluorescent over-head light switch, opting instead to turn on the orange Himalayan salt lamp he'd recently purchased. According to the colleague who'd talked him into buying it, the lamp had been scientifically proven to increase the negative ion count in the air, which was supposed to boost the room's air quality and make you feel more relaxed. While he wasn't ready to offer up his own personal testimony, he did like the subtle lighting and the chilled-out mood it created.

Gabriel checked his watch, placed the phone on the table next to the sofa, and stretched out on his back. Almost immediately, he fell into a light sleep, an ability he'd honed as a sleep-deprived intern. A slight, clicking sound caused his eyes to flutter.

The next thing he knew there was a knee on his chest and a hand on his crotch.

"Don't move, doctor. I'm getting ready to operate."

Gabriel's eyes shot open as he sat upright. "Frieda!" he whispered harshly. "How did you get in here?"

"Never mind that. It's not where I came from but what I'm getting ready to do that's important." She dropped down on the floor and buried her nose in his chest. "Mmmm, you smell like soap. Clean. That's good."

Without hesitation, she reached into his drawstring pants and wrapped her hands around his penis.

"What in the—Frieda, really. You can't be in here."

"In here? Or in *here*?" she said, expertly massaging him into a quick erection.

"Look, I'm still on duty—"

"Well, baby, you better get ready to work!"

Frieda whipped off the white nurse's dress she was wearing that zipped down the front. She was naked underneath. She almost sat on his face as she buried her head in his pants and let her mouth replace what her hand had been doing.

"For heaven's sake, Frieda," Gabriel gasped. "What—are—you—doing?"

I think you know.

His hips began grinding of their own volition, and while he willed himself to push the luscious buttocks away from him, his hands had a mind of their own. Before he knew it he was pulling Frieda's furry paradise toward him.

"Ooh," Frieda gushed as Gabriel proved his oral skills matched those of his scalpel. "Yes, baby, do that, do that!"

Frieda flipped around, yanking Gabriel's pants down in the process. She lay on top of him, and before he could protest, drove her tongue into his waiting mouth. Gabriel gave up the fight and wrapped his arms around Frieda's taut waist, moving his hands to cup her breasts and thread his fingers into her hair.

Knowing they didn't have long, Frieda reached into the pocket of the white dress and pulled out the strawberry-flavored condom she'd placed there. She placed it on his tip and, with surgical precision, used her tongue to unroll it, sending shards of sensation racing through Gabriel's body as she rolled the condom into place. And then she began to ride.

Their lovemaking was frenzied and desperate: Frieda reached toward tomorrow as she filled the empty places left by Giorgio and Shabach, and Gabriel released a month's worth of tension and patient concerns into the willing heat of this willful, savvy sistah. It was just what the doctor ordered.

Frieda gasped as she experienced a mind-shattering orgasm. Gabriel climaxed hard, with an extended shudder, then dropped heavily on top of Frieda.

"Thanks," he whispered. And fell asleep.

Frieda rubbed her hand over his sweaty body, feeling his slender shoulders and small, firm butt. She tried to move, an impossibility with his dead weight, but she didn't care. She'd come to the hospital determined to see the doctor. And he had most definitely filled her prescription.

61

Lover of My Soul

Derrick leaned back against the leather love seat in his executive office. His eyes were closed, and his head bobbed to the beat. The sound was clean, simple, almost acoustic; the slow tempo—poignant—and Darius's pure, baritone sound floated between the musical notes effortlessly, filled with passion and yearning:

> *"Jesus, lover of my soul, let me to Thy bosom fly.*
> *While the nearer waters roll, while the tempest still is high.*
> *Hide me, O my Savior, hide, till the storm of life is past,*
> *Safe into the haven guide, oh, receive my soul at last."*

Darius sat in the chair opposite his pastor, also listening to the sounds. At first he listened professionally, detached from the song itself. But by the time the last verse rolled around, he got caught up, just like he had when God had dropped this song into his spirit. Darius sang along with his CD:

> *"Plenteous grace with Thee is found, grace to cover all my sin,*
> *Let the healing streams abound, make and keep me pure within.*
> *Thou of life the fountain art, freely let me take of Thee,*
> *Spring Thou up within my heart, rise to all eternity."*

By the time the last note sounded, both Derrick and Darius were wiping away tears. They sat in silence a moment, letting the presence of the Holy Spirit wash over them. Finally Derrick spoke.

"Man, I can't remember the last time I heard that song. I think it was back at my grandmother's church when I was, oh, I don't know, nine or ten years old. And I've never heard that last verse. It's beautiful, man, simply beautiful," Derrick said.

"Charles Wesley, 1740. People these days are happy if a song lasts ten years, twenty. But these English brothahs were putting it down almost three hundred years ago and counting—and still powerful. Now *that's* when you know your words are anointed. Let them be singing 'Looks Like Reign' in 2310. That's what I'm talking about."

"How'd you decide to put this on your CD and to go this route? This is the most traditional I've ever heard you sing, and I like it."

"God dropped it on me, man, when I was at a low point. I was praying, and before I knew it, these words were pouring out of my mouth. They sang it at my grandmother's church too. I'd forgotten I knew it."

"Well, I'm not one who's quick to give a word of prophecy. But I wouldn't be surprised if this classic, and not one of your R & B contemporary numbers, is your next hit."

Both men jumped as the door burst open. Mrs. Anderson, followed by a harried Lionel trying to overtake her, rushed into the room.

"Pastor, I told her she needed to make an appointment," Derrick's assistant stated. "She just barged right past me. Should I call security?"

"You don't need to call nobody," Mrs. Anderson said. "I've come here with something to say to Pastor Derrick, and I'm gonna say it. And then I'll be on my way, never to darken these doors again."

Lionel gave his pastor a haggard look. Derrick nodded slightly and waved Lionel away.

Darius rose from his chair. "I'll wait outside," he said.

"You might as well stay. It concerns you too."

Darius looked at Derrick and returned to his seat.

"Would you like to sit down?"

"I won't be that long." Mrs. Anderson took a moment and softened her demeanor. "I've come to ask you, to ask both of you, to accept my apology."

Darius sat up straighter in his chair. *She could not have said what I think she said.*

"I stand by my Christian beliefs. Sin is sin, and some sins are more dire than others. But even so, in these past few weeks I've said some things and did some things that are not becoming to a child of God. And, Darius." she turned to look directly at him. "While I don't agree with your lifestyle, and will never agree with it, two wrongs don't make a right. And I was wrong. This is hard for me to say, but my daughter—" Mrs. Anderson paused as tears threatened to erupt.

Pastor Derrick reached for a tissue and handed it to her. She took it and continued.

"You said something one time in this here office, Pastor. About my daughter. I told you I knew her, and you said I *thought* I knew her. Well, now, I know my child. But I didn't know everything *about* my child. Sin is sin, and lying is sin. And my child has lied on this man here." She pointed at Darius. "And come first thing Monday morning, we're getting with our lawyer to set it right."

Derrick looked from Mrs. Anderson to Darius, too stunned to reply.

"That's what I came to tell you," Darius said to Derrick. "That the tape proves it's not me on there. Whoever ra—violated Melody had a specific tattoo on his back. I don't have any tattoos."

"So that's what I came here to say," Mrs. Anderson continued. "And now I'll be on my way."

"Bernadette—Mrs. Anderson—let me just say that while
we don't always see eye to eye, you have been a staunch sup-
porter of this ministry for almost thirty years, and it would be
a shame to lose you. The body of Christ has different parts for
different reasons. The arm can't do what the leg does, and the
eye can't work for the nose. What I'm trying to say is you have
many choices of where to worship, many fine churches in this
city run by some of my very good friends. You would be more
than blessed to join any one of them. But I want you to know
that you are also more than welcome to stay right here."

"Well, Pastor, I appreciate that, surely I do. Clyde, he sure
doesn't want to leave. But I've caused such a ruckus, I don't
know if I can come back here."

"Oh, a good old ruckus never hurt nobody," Derrick said,
rising and coming over to hug this church mother. "You talk it
over with Mr. Anderson. Better yet, let me call Vivian and see
what her plans are for dinner tomorrow night. We normally
try to keep the schedule pretty light on Saturday evenings, so it
should be all right if you two join us. And I for one would really
enjoy that."

It took determination and a dip in her pride, but Bernadette
also shook the hand of the man she'd sworn never to touch—
Darius Crenshaw. She couldn't quite look him in the eye, but
she didn't beat herself up too badly. This was new territory, and
she'd have to take one step at a time. In her mind touching
him, and not knowing where his hands had been, was already a
huge leap of faith.

Walking to her car, Bernadette let the tears fall. Her heart
felt lighter already. She'd be forever grateful to Faye Moseley,
the member in whom she'd confided after being unable to
bear the burden of Melody's actions alone, afraid to tell Clyde
lest he die from the pain. Melody was his little girl. To know
she'd been raped had almost killed him. If he found out she

had been the initiator, he might kill her. So she'd turned to Faye—Mother Moseley, as she was called—and Faye had given her straight-up, sistah-girl advice.

"Bea, you ain't the only one who's ever acted a fool in church, and if you be truthful, this ain't your first time acting one. Like my boy Donnie says: fall down, get back up. That's what saints do."

"But where did I go wrong, Faye? I tried so hard to keep Melody from making the same mistakes I did, tried to keep her on the straight and narrow, to know where she was and who she was with. I don't even know how long she's been lying to me! How could she do that?"

"Girl, please. You told your parents everything? That's what kids do. Lie, cheat, steal, do whatever they can to break out of their parents' shadow and come into their own. I'm not trying to say you shouldn't be hurt and angry. But you can't blame yourself either. At any given moment, we're all doing the absolute best we can. And who knows? God can turn this thing around and still get glory!"

I hope you're right, Bernadette thought as she headed back to her house. The apology to her pastor wasn't the end but the beginning of the actions she was taking to make things right. And what she was getting ready to do now would be the hardest.

She opened the door and climbed the steps quickly before she lost her nerve. She stopped at the door to Melody's room. It was quiet. *Probably got that iPod stuck in her ear.*

She tapped once and then opened the door. Melody, bobbing her head and text messaging, pulled out the earbuds when she saw her mother at the door.

"Hey, Mommy."

"Melody."

Oh, Lord. What's that tone about? "Are you okay? You seem tired."

Bernadette walked into the room and closed the door.

"No, Melody. I am not okay. But I will be, and so will you. Everything is going to be all right."

Melody began to get a bit nervous. Her mother was acting weird! "Why? What's going on?" she stuttered.

Bernadette sat on the bed, reached into her purse, and pulled out a brochure. She silently handed it to Melody.

Melody took it and saw a picturesque country scene with trees and flowers. Inside a caption box were the words she read aloud, "Angel House. What's this?" She looked at her mother, who only stared back at her. Melody's nervousness deepened. She opened the brochure and began to read. The nervousness was replaced by fear. "Boarding school? Why are you giving me something about a boarding school?" Her attempt to sound lighthearted failed miserably.

"Because, Melody, that's where you're going."

"Mommy," Melody whined, falling into the familiar voice she'd used to wrap her parents around her finger for years.

Mrs. Anderson held up her hand and spoke in a stern voice. "My heart is fixed, and my mind is made up. I can't give you the guidance you need. There's too many things here to distract you, too many temptations to help you fall. Now, I've been on the phone with the people at this school, and they are powerful men and women of God. They've got a program to get you back on the right track. Once you turn eighteen, you'll have to decide which track you stay on."

"Eighteen! You want me to go away for two years? No, Mommy! I won't! I can't leave you and Daddy. How could you send me away?"

"You left the night you lay under that man and asked him to do those nasty things to you."

"But, Mommy, I was raped—"

"Stop lying to me! I saw the tape, Melody."

Melody's eyes widened.

"Uh-huh, sure did. Hurt me to my heart too, but I watched enough to learn the truth."

How did she get her hands on the tape? And then a worse thought followed. "Did Daddy . . ."

"No, thank God, because it would be the death of him as sure as I'm born. And that's why you're leaving. I don't want him ever to see it. And I don't want you to put no more hurt on him than you already have. For twenty-five years, I bowed down on my knees in prayer and supplication for a child. And God answered my prayer. And while this will hurt me to my heart, I'm going to give you back to Him now."

Now both women were crying.

"He can do for you what I can't. And I've got to trust that when the time is right, He'll give you back to me again. It's a good, Christian school, founded on Christian principals. I've talked to the head of the school, some of the teachers, and the pastor of the church that you'll be attending while you're there."

Melody looked at the brochure again. "Mommy, this place is in Louisiana!"

"Yes, in the South, where you'll be surrounded by Christian people with strong Christian values." Bernadette almost wavered as she watched the tears roll down her daughter's cheeks. "Plus it will give you a chance to learn something new, live someplace different. You might like it, Melody."

"But, Mommy, I don't want to go!"

Mrs. Anderson stood and looked down on her daughter. Love mixed with pain filled her eyes. "In life, we don't always get what we want. But God always gives us what we need."

62

Right Here

"Girl, he seems to get bigger every time I see him," Hope said as she handed Stacy's son a breadstick. The ladies were enjoying their first Saturday powwow in a long time.

"And so do you!" Frieda said, rolling her eyes at Hope's round stomach.

"I am, huh?" Hope agreed. She rubbed her belly lovingly.

"How far along are you? Five months?"

Hope nodded.

"And already looking like a Butterball turkey," Frieda said. "Hey, waiter! Cancel that order of calamari and bring this girl a salad!"

The other patrons joined in the laughter.

"You know I'm messing with you, girl. Get your eat on like you want to."

"I have to. I'm eating for three."

"And you've decided on the names for sure?"

"Yes, Acacia and Camon."

Stacy scrunched up her nose. "I like Acacia, but that boy's gonna have to whoop booty for days. I can hear the teasing now: 'C'mon! C'mon!'"

"But it's pronounced like Damon; the emphasis is on the first syllable."

"That won't matter to seven-year-olds."

"And it won't matter to my son. He'll be above such things."

Stacy rolled her eyes. "Oh, here we go, Miss Perfect Mom thinking she has all the answers. Girl, it don't matter that you've read enough books to teach a college course on childhood development; it all changes when they get here."

"We'll see."

"Yeah, you sure will."

"Enough baby talk. Let's talk about dicks."

One of the women at the other tables turned around with a surprised expression on her face. Her lunching companion showed chagrin.

"Good Lord, Frieda. We can't take you anywhere!" Hope shot the table next to them an apologetic smile.

"What? I could have been talking about anything or anybody—uh, Dick Gregory, Dick Clark, and what's that one rerun . . . *The Dick Van Dyke Show*." She looked pointedly at the table of judgers. "It *is* okay to talk about Dick, isn't it?"

The two ladies beside them turned their heads and became very interested in their food.

"I see hanging around the doctor hasn't improved your social skills," Stacy said.

"He's not complaining."

"That is still so crazy that you're dating the man who performed my surgery."

"Yeah, and don't think I'm gonna forget that he handled your titties! So when I bring him around, y'all chicks back the bump up!"

"You are a fool!"

The ladies stopped their banter long enough for the waiter to deliver their meals.

"Have you thought any more about the reconstructive surgery?" Hope asked as she dipped her calamari liberally into the chunky sauce.

"We're going to wait until after the wedding," Stacy said.

She gave Darius a chicken finger and continued. "But Tony has been really helpful making me feel okay with it, whether I get the surgery or not."

"Uh-huh. I knew I'd find out he's been dippin'." Frieda laughed loudly around a mouthful of burger with bacon. "Y'all church girls always trying to act like you ain't getting the lickety-split. But I know better!"

Stacy got ready to protest, but Hope shook her head. "Don't even try it, Stacy," Hope said. "I went through the same thing. The girl is going to believe what she wants to believe, and that's that."

"Tony and I are adamant about staying celibate until after we say, 'I do.'"

"And when will that be?" Hope asked.

"We're thinking a June wedding."

"A whole year from now? Hmph, lickety-split, lickety-split."

"Licky spit," Darius Jr. chimed.

Stacy covered Darius's ears playfully. "Girl, you're corrupting my son. Shut up!"

"Acting corrupt is how you got him. *You* shut up!"

Stacy's cell phone vibrated on the table. She flipped it open. *It's Darius,* she mouthed while listening.

Both Hope and Frieda stopped eating. For a minute. It wasn't long before Hope was biting into her entrée, a jumbo-lump crab burger with steaming hot fries.

"Yes! Oh, praise God. You have got to be beside yourself right now. Who's that screaming in the background? Oh, I should have known. Okay, well, call me later. Congratulations!"

Stacy beamed as she flipped off her phone.

"His case was dismissed," Frieda said.

"Yes!"

"Hallelujah! Our God is an awesome God!"

"And that attorney ain't too shabby either!" Frieda said.

"Oh, man, I can already tell you've been hanging around Dr. Livingston too long."

"I know, isn't that something? All the fine men in our church, and she has to go get another heathen." Hope lowered her voice and leaned toward Stacy. "Now we'll have to try to drag two people to church on Sundays."

"Hmph, you'll have to drag us out of bed first!"

"But what about the case?" Hope said, going back to Stacy's news about Darius. "Doesn't the state take over when there's a rape claim, even if the parties dismiss it? Remember R. Kelly and how even though the girl's parents said he didn't do it, they still tried him?"

"I don't know all the ins and outs of the thing, but with Melody gone and Darius cleared . . ." Stacy shrugged.

"And that punk-ass Shabach." Frieda's tone changed. "Walking around like nothing happened."

"You know what the old folks say. That you might get by, but you don't get away. And I'm not excusing anything he did, but the tape proves it wasn't by force."

"Talk about ironic. What are the chances that Tony would have talked to you about the love letters he was getting? Thank goodness you mentioned it to Darius. Otherwise he may never have put two and two together with proof that would stand up in court."

"Don't give me too much credit. I just casually mentioned the anonymous notes the second time Darius brought up the note *he'd* gotten from Melody. He told Bo, and that's who asked to see a copy of Tony's notes."

"I'll give Bo one thing," Stacy said. "That man takes care of his man better than some women! He holds it down!"

"It still isn't right what Shabach did," Hope said. "He knew she was underage."

"You're absolutely right. But like I said, every dog has his day."

"I don't want to talk any more about him," Stacy said. "My son's father has been cleared. I feel like celebrating."

She motioned the waiter over, and a short time later Frieda

had a glass of chardonnay while both Stacy and Hope savored sparkling cider.

"To your daddy," Stacy said as she kissed Darius Jr.

"To yo' baby daddy," Frieda said.

"To God be the glory," Hope chimed in. They raised their glasses in toast.

"You know, life is full of ups and downs, but if we just keep breathing, a change has got to come. Look at us. Barely six months ago I was ready to drag Darius through the court; now I'm happy he's been *cleared* by the system. Hope, you've been begging for a child, and God has given you two. And, Frieda, you're with a good man, a doctor! Maybe you've finally found your Mr. Right, instead of Mr. Right Now."

"Well, since he's Mr. Got Money and Mr. Got House and Mr. MD and Mr. Big Dick . . . you might be right!" Frieda laughed, but secretly prayed—yes, prayed—that Dr. Gabriel Livingston was here to stay.

Hope sat back in her chair, fat and happy. "You know what? Life is feeling pretty good right now. And they say this doesn't compare to the glory. I can't imagine what it will be like when we get to heaven."

"Girl, you better smack Mistah upside the head and worry about heaven later," Frieda teased in her best Sophia from *The Color Purple* voice. "Seriously though, I for one am not trying to die to find out about the hereafter. If you ask me, I'd say we've got heaven right here!"

Hope smiled at her crazy cousin. "You know what, Frieda, you might be right." She lifted her cider. "To heaven right here, y'all."

"To heaven right here!" Stacy and Frieda echoed.

"Heaben here!" Darius Jr. shouted.

It seemed no one wanted to be left out of paradise.

63

Talk to Me

A month ago she'd been happy. Now Hope lay spread-eagled in the middle of her king-sized bed with two pillows under her and one on the side, trying to find comfort. There was none around. She turned to her side slightly and grimaced. One of her children was bearing down on her lower intestine, the other on her bladder. There was a constant ache in the small of her back, and she had to pee every five minutes. There was a reason she had wanted children, and Hope vaguely remembered that at one time she had actually prayed to get pregnant. Now she was starting to believe Frieda was right, that anyone wanting another human growing "on top of her pussy" was out of their blankety-blank mind.

Hope plumped the pillows behind her and tried to raise herself to a sitting position. The babies really began acting a fool then. One of them kicked her on her side, and the other one (or was it the same baby but now using its hand?) was making an imprint on the top of her stomach. And she had to pee . . . again.

Huffing, Hope threw back the covers and marched to the master bathroom. She was almost there when the phone rang. Thinking it was her mother, who she'd called earlier, she rushed

back to the phone, grabbed it, and made a beeline for the restroom.

"Mama?"

"No, baby, it's me."

Hope rolled her eyes. "What?"

Cy paused, and then said, "How are you feeling, baby?"

"How do you think I'm feeling!" Hope yelled. "I'm feeling
like a stuffed potato—which I can't eat, by the way, because
starch gives me gas. My back is throbbing, and I've spent most
of the morning on the stool. How is your fucking day?"

Cy pulled the receiver away from his ear and stared at it
like he would a foreign object. Who was he talking to? Surely not
his loving, positive-minded, Christian wife. Using the F-word?
This must be her evil twin.

"Uh, look, baby, I can see I caught you at a bad time."

"Yeah, whatever." *Click.*

Cy frowned and hit the redial button. He got voice mail.
"Hope, I'm worried about you. Call me back and let me know
you're okay and if you want me to bring you anything. Matter
of fact, I can cancel my last two appointments and come home
early if you want. Call me. I love you." Cy ended the call and
speed dialed another.

"Hey, father-to-be. What's going on?"

"That's what I called to find out."

"Hold on a minute, man." Derrick motioned his assistant
to leave the office and to close the door behind him. "Okay,
talk to me."

"Hope just cursed me out."

"Who?"

"Hope."

"That's what I thought you said."

"Man, I don't know what happened. When I left her this
morning, she was fine. Up until last month she was fine. Now
I don't know who I'm going to wake up to in the morning."

Derrick chuckled under his breath.

Not far enough under. Cy grew rigid. "You'll understand if I fail to see the humor in this situation."

"It's called pregnancy, bro. Nobody schooled you on the multiple personalities a woman can take on when they're expecting? When Vivian was pregnant with our son, I spent several nights in the guest room."

"Really? It got that bad?"

"Worse, but that's all I'm going to tell you."

"All I know is she's driving me crazy. In and out of bed all night long. I barely get any sleep. Crazy mood swings, running me to the store every other hour as her taste buds swing between craving sugar and sweet. And why isn't it ever something we have in the fridge? We haven't had sex for weeks, she keeps threatening to move her mom in, and she's harping on me every day to finish the house before the kids come. I'm tired of it!"

Derrick leaned back in his leather chair. "So what I hear you saying is you've never felt more blessed in your life and you never thought you could love someone as much as your wife. That about right?"

Cy smiled into the phone. "That's exactly what you heard, my brother. I'm blessed beyond measure, and the woman who is carrying my son and my daughter? I love her more than life itself."

64

Runaway Child

Melody was still pouting, much as she had been for the past two months, going on three. This act alone used to be enough to melt any amount of anger her mother had against her. But not this time. Even her father, normally putty in her hands, had turned a deaf ear to her pleas not to be shipped off to another school in another state. In what she'd hoped would be a turning point, she'd pseudo run away from home the week after Bernadette had delivered the decision that she would be attending a Christian, girls-only school. "Pseudo" because she'd actually only gone over to Natasha's house and refused to answer her cell phone.

Things had turned, all right. When she'd arrived at school the following Monday, she was summoned to the office and met by a police officer and a social worker.

"You've been listed as a runaway, and we're taking you in," the officer had said as she'd led a tearful Melody out of the office.

When Melody had jerked her arm away in an act of defiance, the officer had turned her around and had her handcuffed before Melody even saw silver. When they reached the police department, they took off the cuffs and allowed Melody her one phone call. Of course it was to none other than Bernadette Anderson.

"Mom." Melody didn't have to fake the tears. "I—I—I'm at the police department. They're saying I'm a runaway!"

"Isn't that what you are? After being a liar and a whore?"

The caustic comment had taken Melody's breath away. Her mother was showing a tough side the daughter had never known existed.

"I'm sorry, Mom. If you come and get me, I promise I'll do right. Go to Louisiana, whatever you want. But please come and get me. I'm scared."

"Let me think about it."

"Huh?"

"I *said*, let me think about it. Now put the officer on the phone."

Melody's hand trembled as she called out to the police-woman. "Excuse me. My mother wants to talk to you."

The officer gave Melody a stern look. She shuffled a few papers around and took so long Melody began to doubt if she'd take the call. "Excuse me?" Melody said timidly.

"I heard you!" The officer marched over and snatched the phone away. "Officer Ladd here." She shot another withering glance at Melody, who scuttled over to a bench in the waiting area.

"I know you can't talk, but I just want to thank you." Bernadette fought to stay composed. "This hurts me more than it hurts her."

"I understand."

"Your mother raised you right, Becky. All those years she and I worked together . . . I know it was God that had me run into her in the store this weekend. I'm in your debt."

"Not at all, Mrs. Anderson."

"Well, I won't keep you. Please take care of my baby while

she's in there. She's done wrong, but deep down she's a good kid. You'll keep her a few hours?"

"That's correct."

"Well, God bless you, child."

"Right, I'll keep you posted."

From the time Bernadette and Clyde had picked up their daughter from the downtown juvenile center, Melody had been reserved yet respectful. The only thing she maintained of her old, spoiled, selfish self was the pout and the absolute belief that she was the victim and the one who'd been wronged.

Melody threw down the magazine she'd only been pretending to read, snatched the earbuds out of her ear, and jumped off the bed.

"It ain't fair! I don't want to leave California," she hissed through clenched teeth.

She continued talking to herself as she pulled her phone from her backpack and angrily punched buttons. "If I've got to go through this bullshit, I'm not going to be the only one who suffers."

65

Good Lovin'

"Hope!" Frieda threw her purse on the living room couch and headed to the master suite. "I know you've got your lazy self in bed even though it's five o'clock. Get your butt—ow!"

Hope's timing was perfect. The pillow she'd thrown as Frieda came around the corner from the sitting area had hit Frieda squarely in the face.

"You'd better be glad you're my cousin and I love you. Otherwise I'd kick your—"

"Yeah, whatever. Go get those SunChips on the counter for me. And there's some dip in the refrigerator. Please."

Frieda crossed her arms. "I thought the doctor said to watch your food intake. That's part of the reason you're miserable."

"No, I'm miserable because, as you'd say, I have two people sitting on my pussy. Now go!"

Frieda was stunned and then let out a whoop of laughter. "Oh—my—God! Did I just hear Miss Church Girl use the P-word?" She turned to exit the room. "There's hope for you yet, girl," she threw back over her shoulder.

Hope knew Frieda was trying to be helpful, but no matter what anybody around her did these days, it pissed her off. Yet no one but her knew the real reason: she'd snuck onto Cy's e-mail account and saw that Millicent still e-mailed him. The mail seemed innocuous enough. Most referenced Jack or their ministry or the house or Darfur. But why did she have to keep e-mailing her husband? True, they'd broken bread and had a kumbaya moment, but so what? The warm fuzzy of that evening was long gone. Why couldn't she just leave Cy alone?

"What, are you hurting?"

Frieda came around the corner with a tray containing a large bowl of cut vegetables, a small plate of chips, and the dip Hope had asked for.

"I'm okay."

"Well, let your face know because you're looking evil as hell. What's up?"

"Nothing."

Frieda sat on the couch with the tray between them. She reached for a celery stick and dipped it in the creamy blue cheese. "So tell me about nothing."

Before she knew what was happening, the tears came, as did the news she hadn't shared with anyone else. "It's Millicent," Hope said wetly and reached for a chip. "Like I said, nothing at all."

Frieda left the room and came back later with her arms full. "Here," she said, putting down chips, cookies, a liter of 7UP, and a tin of leftover baked chicken.

"I've got to go, so here's a spread for when you get hungry. But just so you know, it's not the food you're craving. You need some good loving." She went on before Hope could interrupt. "Don't even try to protest. Just give Cy some tonight. It will make you both feel better and keep me from having to put my foot in your stuff the next time you hit me."

Frieda bent down and hugged her cousin. When she left, the smell of Frieda's Prada perfume wasn't the only thing she'd left behind. So was the feel-good vibe yet no-nonsense energy with which she had filled the room. Hope reached for a chip and a piece of chicken. She felt better already.

★ ★ ★

Cy reached for his briefcase. He was going home. Nothing in life was more important to him than Hope and how she was feeling. He couldn't imagine how hard it must have been for her right now, emotionally as well as physically. Before they'd gotten off the phone, Derrick had suggested Cy go online and purchase a couple books on pregnancy so he'd be able to empathize with his wife's roller-coaster mood swings. He'd done that, as well as called his favorite LA chef and ordered a gourmet meal for two that would be delivered later that night. There was just one call and stop he needed to make before going home and doing whatever it took to make the mother of his children feel better.

He was just reaching for his office phone when it rang. "Taylor," he said.

"Hey, Cy."

"Millicent, I was just getting ready to call you. I'm going to have to cancel our meeting today."

"Oh, no, I'm already en route."

"It can't be helped. Hope needs me."

There was a slight pause on the other end. "Is anything wrong?"

"Nothing a little TLC won't take care of."

"You're a good man, Cy Taylor. But I'm sure Hope knows that. Of course you're going to cancel on me and take care of your wife. And that's how it should be. When would you like to reschedule?"

"I'll call and let you know."

The house was quiet. Cy stepped into the living room and placed the packages on the sofa. Bypassing the master suite, he walked into the guest room, stripped, and stepped into the shower. Afterward, he walked back into the living room, took the gifts out of their noisy packages, and went into the master suite.

Hope was sleeping, curled into a fetal position on her side. Her arm lay protectively around her stomach, as though holding the babies as she rested. *Conversations with Carla* was muted on the television, and various baby books were splayed across the covers. Cy stood silently a moment, in his glorious nakedness, staring down at his wife.

He walked over to the nightstand and picked up a tray of uneaten food. Once he'd come back from placing it in the kitchen, he opened the first box. It was a glimmering tennis bracelet of yellow, pink, and white diamonds totaling seven karats. Then he sat and waited. Within minutes, Hope shifted and moved her arm to the side. Cy smiled and eased the bracelet on her arm. She frowned, and her eyes fluttered, but she didn't wake up.

Next, he placed the outfits he'd purchased from Nordstroms on the chest at the bench at the foot of the bed, and he placed the large vase of perfectly grown bird-of-paradise on the dresser directly opposite the bed. After him, they'd be the first thing she saw when she opened her eyes. *Or maybe the bracelet,* he thought, smiling.

He eased into bed next to her and cuddled spoon style, placing his arm under hers and around her growing belly. He planted kisses along her shoulder and at the nape of her neck. "I love you," he whispered.

Not quite an hour later, Hope stirred. Unconsciously she rubbed her booty against Cy's hardness. She placed her hand on top of his and nestled deeper into the pillow. And then her eyes flew open, and she looked down at the hand she held.

What is Cy doing home at this hour? He had meetings. Oh, my gosh, what's wrong?

She struggled to turn over her growing body. When she did, two dark brown eyes shining with emotion stared at her.

"Hey, beautiful."

"Cy, what are you doing here?"

"I live here, remember?"

"But it's early, you have meetings—"

"*Had* meetings. But I decided another meeting was more important." Cy tweaked Hope's nipple to show just what type of meeting he had in mind. "You were sleeping soundly; do you feel rested?"

Hope reached for pillows to put under her back. Cy was right there, helping, holding. "I do. Frieda came over. You know she's good for changing a mood. And then I took a long shower. There's still a little throbbing in my lower back, but the hot water helped a lot."

"Hmmm. I just showered too." Cy reached over and gently lapped Hope's nipple with his tongue. He fully expected her to rebuff his advances, as she had for the past two months, but he wanted her to know she was still his sole desire.

To his surprise and delight, Hope took his hand and placed it at the apex of anticipation. She opened her legs, and he quickly eased a finger along already wet folds. His moan was involuntary and genuine as he enveloped Hope in a lingering kiss.

But his lips didn't stay there long. He positioned Hope in a comfortable position, almost sitting up, and gently spread her legs. And then he began a journey from her upper lips to her lower ones.

"But wait, Cy. I want to pleasure you too," Hope protested.

"Later," Cy breathed. "Right now, it's all about you."

Cy took a long time bathing Hope's body with his tongue and talking softly to his children as he planted kisses along Hope's stomach—and on the foot that made an imprint on that stomach.

"Ooh!" Hope exclaimed.

"Is that for what the baby is doing, or for me?" Cy asked.

"Both," was Hope's breathless reply.

Cy spread her legs farther. Hope eased her body down to a more reclined position for easier access. She was rewarded with a warm, wet tongue separating her feminine folds and probing her love button. Her writhing, grinding body told him she was close to release. He intensified the thrusting with his tongue and let his fingers join in the symphony.

Hope's orgasm was violent, shattering her sanity and ripping a yell from her throat. She began to cry and reach for the man who'd given her the type of pain release a pill couldn't duplicate. She was glad she'd followed Frieda's advice. Cy, coming home early, had obviously followed someone's advice too. *Maybe God's?* she thought.

"My turn," she whispered as she eased into a kneeling position, straddled Cy's legs, and took his large, hard manhood into her hands. She began slowly, lovingly returning the favor, trying to lavish her eternal love from tip to base. She got as much pleasure from giving as receiving; she'd forgotten how much she loved satisfying her man. And she forgot something else too—the remembered joys of pleasure made her forget all about her back pain.

66

Another Beat-Down

Shabach and his crew sat around the studio, heads bobbing in unison as they listened to the track play through the speakers.

> *"Beat-down, beat-down for the devil,*
> *Got a fist for the mist who is always causing trouble,*
> *Got a . . . beat-down, beat-down for the devil . . . yo!*
> *No, no, no, no, no, no mo'—Go!"*

"Man, that track is screamin'!" the producer yelled, jumping up from his chair and playing an air guitar. The other men in the studio nodded their agreement while the engineer kept playing with the knobs on the board.

"Yeah, yeah, yeah, pump that bass," Shabach instructed. "I like that."

He was the most subdued in the group, sitting back in a black, leather recliner with a hood pulled over the Braves baseball cap he wore over dark shades. A toothpick dangled at the side of his mouth as he studiously listened, barely moving. Every now and then he'd point a finger, emphasizing a key or tempo change, and then sit back in the recliner. He was pleased with the remix and could already hear it jamming in clubs across America.

The vibrator on his Blackberry went off at the same time the door opened. He hit the text-message button: **Police, man— get out the studio!**

But it was too late. They were already parting the men in the studio like Moses did the Red Sea. Even Shabach's bodyguard moved like a punk, raising his hands in a "Man, what can I do?" gesture.

Shabach was cool. Whatever this was couldn't be that serious. Probably a warrant on a traffic violation. It wouldn't surprise him if his accountant had failed to pay the speeding ticket he'd recently gotten in Atlanta. *I'll dock Junior's pay for this, for real!*

The engineer stopped the music just as the first officer reached Shabach's chair.

"Yes, officers," Shabach said as he smiled and looked from one officer to the other. "What can we do for you?"

"Are you Joseph Reubens?"

Shabach looked around at his buddies and laughed. Only a handful of people outside Atlanta knew his real name. A couple joined in with nervous laughter of their own.

"I'm Shabach, baby, you heard?"

"Are you Joseph 'Shabach' Reubens?" Their was an underlying sarcasm to the officer's voice. The second officer's hand went to the handle of his gun, and rested there. Two more cops entered the room. *This is a lot of heat for a traffic warrant.* Normally the room was considered large for a studio, but right now it felt so crowded Shabach could hardly breathe.

Shabach stared at the cop who'd asked the question. The cop next to him began easing his gun out of the holster.

"Yeah, yeah, whatever man. I'm Joseph. So what's up?"

"You're under arrest."

"For what?" Of course, Shabach already knew about the ticket, but he wanted to make sure his buddies understood to stay cool, that he had this.

"For sexual assault against a minor. Now get up!"

"Sexual assault—what the hell? Man, get these handcuffs off me. I haven't assaulted anybody!"

"You have the right to remain silent. Anything you say can and will be used against you in a court of law. You have the right to an attorney—"

"Call my attorney, man!" Shabach shouted to his bass player.

"If you don't have an attorney, one can be appointed—"

The silence screamed as the door slammed behind the officers who'd just taken Shabach away.

"Man, that's fucked up," someone finally said.

"This is some bullshit, man. All the pussy that gets thrown at your boy? Ain't no way he's going down for something like this. Just some female trying to make rent next month, take a brothah down as usual."

"You right about that," the bass player said as he took out his phone and headed for the door. "I'm getting ready to call his lawyer now. He'll probably be out by morning."

The engineer nodded and reached for a knob. Soon Shabach's defiant voice filled the room.

"Beat-down, beat-down for the devil,
Got a fist for the mist who is always causing trouble . . ."

67

Counting Blessings

Stacy watched as Bo played with Darius Jr. Every time Bo made a face, her son would squeal with joy.

"My son really likes you."

"Well, you know what they say," Bo quipped. "Like father, like son."

"Oh, God, don't make me lose my lunch."

"C'mon now," Darius said, putting a casual arm around Stacy's shoulders. "Bo spent too much time slaving in the kitchen for you to throw up his food."

"Girlfriend knows she better not act a fool. That lobster was twenty dollars a pound!" Bo said.

"Forget you, heifah!" Stacy replied.

"No, you're the cow."

"All right, all right, that's enough. None of that arguing and name calling in front of my son. Come here, little man. Come here to Daddy."

Darius Jr. squealed and ran over to his father, who was sitting next to Stacy and Bo on the couch. Darius picked him up and placed him on his lap as Stacy watched. Bo reached for a magazine and began idly flipping through. It wasn't the typical family scenario playing across America on this late May afternoon, but it was the one that now seemed perfectly normal in the Crenshaw household.

Stacy was content, something she thought she'd never be in a house with both Darius and Bo in it . . . at the same time. But her life had seldom played out as expected. Next to getting cancer, getting Tony—or any other man besides Darius—had been the last thing on her mind just a little over six short months ago. And now here she was, about to get married, and actually getting along with not only her baby daddy but his "wife" too.

"Where's the remote!" Bo's high-pitched question shattered the peaceful mood.

Stacy and Darius looked at the television, which had been on mute, at the same time. Shabach's face was on the screen behind an anchorwoman reporting a story.

Darius reached between the cushions for the remote and turned off the mute.

". . . best known in gospel hip-hop circles for his platinum-selling album, *Beat Down for the Devil*. If found guilty of these sexual-assault charges, Joseph Reubens could spend the next twenty years behind bars. Reporting live from downtown Los Angeles, I'm . . ."

"God don't like ugly, and ugly just got his." Bo was pacing back and forth in the living room. "I told you, baby. I told you they'd get his sorry behind."

Darius turned his stunned look from the television to Bo. "Did you do this, Bo? Did you talk to somebody and get 'Bach arrested?"

"Hell, no! But I would have if given the opportunity."

Darius shook his head. "That's messed up, man."

"Why? What he's experiencing now is exactly what he was ready to put you through—bad press."

"No, what he's experiencing is worse than my coming out

could ever cause. Cy once told me sixteen could get you twenty. . . ."

"I can't believe it," Stacy mumbled.

She hugged Darius Jr. as he crawled from his father into her lap. Moments like these made her count her blessings and remember that no matter how bad it had ever looked for her, somebody somewhere was facing something worse.

68

A Different Appetite

Gabriel laughed. Frieda was at it again, mimicking the nurses and other associates he worked with at the hospital. Her impersonation of Amber was spot on, the way she batted her eyes while sidling up to Gabriel at the nurses' station in an overt flirtation she tried to pass off as nonchalant. Problem was, everyone in the entire hospital knew Amber was in love with Gabriel and longed to assist him with more than surgery.

"Gabe, are you *sure* you don't have time for a salad?" Frieda aped in a pseudo-suburbanite flair. "I could bring it to your office." Frieda finished the statement with an exaggerated wink. That she did these impersonations nude in his locked facility office added to the preposterousness of the situation.

Gabriel's pager buzzed. He didn't even have to look at it to know it meant time was up. Back to work. He followed Frieda into the shower, and after a quick yet thorough performing of ablutions, swatted her playfully on the behind.

"Come on—out, you. I have to go." Gabriel stepped out of the shower and began toweling off.

"You go ahead," Frieda said. "I'll lock up."

"How many times do I have to tell you I prefer not to leave you in the office. This is not a social suite, and if the wrong person found you here it could mean trouble for both me and/or the hospital."

"All right, all right." Frieda quickly rinsed off the soap, grabbed the towel Gabriel had abandoned, and dried herself. As usual, dressing was quick. She purposely wore as little as possible on these visits, allowing the time-constrained doctor easy access for the office quickies he'd come to look forward to with anticipation and enjoy. Not even the fact that he was fodder for the rumor mill was enough to discourage Frieda's visits, though he did try to limit them to thirty minutes or so. No, the truth was, Frieda energized him, and the sexual release provided a release of tension that led to greater focus when he went back to work. In short, she was good for him. Even if he did have to limit her on-the-job pick-me-ups to short doses.

"And just for the record, I'm still quite angry with you."

"Why?" Frieda asked coyly.

"You know why. I always practice safe sex; you're a bad in-fluence."

"I told you I'm not fucking nobody but you."

"Frieda . . ."

"Okay, screwing, making love to, having coital relations with—is that better?"

"That's not the point."

"No, the point is you pulled out, nuckah. Ain't no baby-daddy action happening here. Life's too short, and I've got too much to do."

Gabriel opened the door. "Really, Frieda. Let's go."

"Wait." Frieda struggled with the straps on her four-inch sandals. "Go on, Gabriel. I have to pee anyway. I'll be out in five minutes, promise."

Gabriel's huff was more chagrin that he had to leave than anger she was staying. "Look, just don't forget to—"

"Lock the door," she finished.

Frieda blew him a kiss, finished fastening her sandal, and

hurried into the bathroom. When she was ready to pull up her lacy thong panties, she had a second thought, took them off, and smoothed down her tight, midthigh skirt. She turned off the bathroom light, walked over to Gabriel's desk, left her present in a drawer she knew he'd open, and sashayed out of her man's office, locking the door behind her.

Minutes later, Frieda eased her new BMW into Beverly Hills traffic. She loved this recent gift from Gabriel—the smooth way it handled in traffic and most importantly how good it made her look while navigating the streets of LA. The custom beige color was a perfect complement to her mocha skin, and she always made sure to wear colors that coordinated with the vehicle. She was the significant other of a doctor. Baby girl had to represent!

She turned on the satellite radio. Tupac's voice filled the car's interior and took her back to Kansas City and a much different time in her life.

"Me against the world, I got nuttin to lose
just me against the world baby . . ."

The memories this song invoked were from another lifetime when she'd lived in a small apartment in an increasingly neglected area of Kansas City, near 27th and Paseo, and dated men who's annual salaries were half of what Gabriel made per month. When her hangouts were clubs on Prospect and Troost, and if anybody got cut, it was not in the throes of surgery. Frieda hadn't been unhappy then. She just hadn't known there were levels to happiness and that she could aspire to and achieve a higher level. Frieda changed the channel—much like the move to California had changed her life.

"Speak, fool." Frieda turned down the music as her Bluetooth beeped.

"I'm in town, baby."

"Giorgio! You were supposed to call me."

"I wasn't sure I was coming. My agent didn't reach me until this morning."

"Oh, and where were you, between somebody's legs?"

"I'd rather be between yours. I'm at the Four Seasons waiting on you. That's what's up."

"No, what's up is that log between your legs. Meet me in the restaurant."

Frieda made a U-turn and headed back down Beverly Boulevard. Only now did she realize she'd worked up an appetite. She hoped Giorgio was hungry as well and that he'd believe her when she told him the food on the menu was all he was going to eat.

69

The Proverbial Straw

"Oh, girl, thanks so much for rescuing me. I couldn't take being in that house one more day!"

"Please, no worries. It just gives me an excuse to shop."

"And your going shopping gives me an excuse to surprise Cy at the office."

Hope smiled and looked back at the lunch she'd prepared for her busy hubby. She was blessed and knew it. He was caring and attentive and had shown real interest in understanding what pregnant women went through. That he'd read several of her baby books had won him brownie-and-chocolate-chip points. She'd responded by trying to control her feelings more, stop yelling at him, and practice prayer and meditation as a way to keep her feelings positive. She'd also hired a yoga instructor and chiropractor, both of whom had employed methods that greatly relieved her back pain. Besides constant trips to the restroom and limited walking, she felt almost like her old self again, plus sixty pounds.

Hope turned from the sunny June landscape and eyed Stacy speculatively. "I still can't believe you've changed your plans for a big wedding and moved up the date. Are you sure there isn't something you want to tell me?"

Stacy shot Hope a surprised look. "Like what?"

"Look, girl. I would totally understand if you and Tony have become intimate. Goodness knows my months of celibacy while living with Cy were the hardest months of my life. Even so, we, you know, played around a lot and several times came close to doing the do."

Stacy looked over at Hope but remained silent.

"I guess what I'm . . . Now I feel silly, but . . . is there a baby on the way?" Hope asked.

"A baby? Is that what you think this is about? Tony and I moving our wedding date up because we're pregnant?" Stacy's laugh was genuine and continued until she had to wipe away tears. "If you, one of my closest friends in the world, is thinking that, I wonder who else is thinking it. Have you talked to Sistah Viv?"

"No, I haven't talked to anyone."

"Not even Frieda?"

"Well, we did discuss it a little."

"Y'all heifahs. You've been talking about me behind my back, thinking I'm getting my groove on, when I *told* you we were going to wait."

"I'm sorry, Stacy."

"And you should be." She softened her tone and continued. "But I'm too happy to let a little gossip bother me. The simple truth is, we don't want to wait another six months, either to be married or to have sex. We're both grown and know what we want, and more than a grand wedding, we want a grand marriage. What you don't know because we didn't tell anybody is we've been in counseling with the Montgomerys for the past two months and will continue even after we're married. That's what's most important to us. Not that I have the right ring or the right dress but that I have the right man and that we're getting married for the right reasons."

Now it was Hope's turn to give Stacy a questioning look.

"Yes, sex is one of those reasons."

"C'mon now, 'cause a sistah can only take so much of your

holy hem-hawing before you get real and break it down!"
Hope laughed.

"It's been so hard to hug that body and not be able to—"

"Baby, you don't have to tell me twice. I've been there."

"And then the other night I accidentally walked in on him
after he'd come out of the shower. . . ."

"Uh-huh."

"Girl, I had to leave his house."

"Stop!"

"For real, girl. I couldn't see him for two whole days. That's
how long it took my cootchie to calm down."

Stacy wheeled her car into the Century City office building's circular drive. "You sure you don't want me to wait on
you?"

"Not at all. I talked to Cy earlier, so I know he's here. Besides, you're only going to be a couple hours, right?"

"Tops. I just need to go by my wedding-planner's office
and drop off these swatches. Thank you so much for recommending her; she's been a lifesaver."

"It's the least I can do, as I can't be a maid of honor in the
true sense of the word."

"You're perfect. Now scoot."

Hope waddled through the revolving doors and up to the
elevator. She'd been to her husband's office only a handful of
times, which made every visit that much more special. She
liked to hang out in Cy's world from time to time—feel a part
of the mover-and-shaker environment he experienced on a
daily basis. Hope would be lying if she said she missed corpo-
rate America per se, but there were aspects she missed, such as
the feeling of productivity and accomplishment that came from
seeing a task from inception to completion. *Guess that task will
be my family now,* she thought as she stepped off the elevator
onto the thirty-third floor of the high-rise building. *All in all,
not a bad trade-off with a company's bottom line.*

She eased open the office door and stepped inside his outer

office. His office door was open, which meant he didn't have clients. Still, she didn't want to interrupt him unexpectedly. She repositioned the basket on her left arm and walked wide-legged to his door.

"Hey, baby—what is *this?*"

"Oh, this. This is nothing, absolutely nothing." Millicent scrambled out of Cy's office chair and from behind his desk. "I was just playing a game of solitaire while I waited—"

"Waited for what? Millicent, what are you doing in my husband's office? And why is it you can't seem to stay out of what I thought was his and Jack's business?"

"That's just it. He and Jack—"

"You know, Millicent, I've tried, I've really tried. To be a good Christian, to forgive and forget, to accept you with unconditional love. When it was clear my husband wanted to work with yours, I made up my mind to try to get along—that, like you said, while we'd probably never be friends, we could at least be civil toward one another. We're both adults, and I vowed to act like one."

"Really, Hope, if you'll just let me explain—"

"When I caught you with him at the hotel in La Jolla, I jumped to conclusions. And I apologized. I came to you, woman to woman, and let it be known in no uncertain terms that I preferred my husband's business dealings be with Jack and not you. But every time he turns around, there you are. What's the deal, Millicent? Is Jack not laying the pipe deep enough? Do you still have some crazed and distorted fantasy about being with my man?" Hope slammed the basket down on the desk and stepped up to Millicent.

"I beg your pardon?"

"I don't care how much you try to act like the contented, dutiful wife, you aren't fooling me. You've wanted Cy Taylor ever since I've known you. God gave him to me, and you can't stand it!"

"Wait just a minute, Hope. You are way out of line."

"And you'd better get in line. Because if you think I'm going to let your string-bean, fake-Christian, flat-butt, no-forehead, cross-eyed-looking jealous self come between me and my husband, you've got another think coming."

Hope was standing toe to toe with Millicent, separated by only a large belly. Millicent was trying to maintain her composure but was precariously close to losing her temper as well. She held a hand to Hope's chest to stop her advance.

Hope jerked back as if she'd been singed. "Get your trifling hands off me!"

"Hope, calm down!"

"I will not calm down until you get out of my husband's office. That's it! Get out! Now!" Hope reached for Millicent, swung her around, and pushed her toward the door. Millicent grabbed the purse that was in a chair.

"That's right. Get your designer shit and get out!" Hope screamed at the top of her lungs.

Millicent backed toward the door. "Once again, you've got this all wrong, Hope."

That was it, the proverbial straw that broke the camel's back. Hope rushed toward Millicent, her hands ready to strangle the neck of the woman who dared utter one more word before obeying her command.

Millicent ran around Cy's desk, putting the massive piece of wood between them. Hope would not be denied; she shifted and ran the other way.

Or at least that's what she had in mind. But as she took a step to her left, a massive rush of warm water gushed into the lining of her pants. It stopped her midstride. Fear replaced anger as she looked at Millicent.

"My water just broke."

Millicent immediately went into organizer mode. "Sit on the couch. Try to stay calm. I—I'll dial nine-one-one."

Hope took a step toward the couch and was met with excruciating pain. "Ow!" She doubled over and reached blindly for anything that would hold her. *"Ow!"* she said again, holding the word like a note in a song.

Millicent rushed from behind the desk and came to Hope. "Can you walk? Let me try to help you to the couch."

Hope felt intense pressure on her lower abdomen, as if one of her babies had a saw and was trying to cut their way out. "I—I—I can't move."

The pain intensified as Hope sank to the floor. Another sharp pain racked what felt like the entire lower half of her body, from her stomach to her knees. Tears sprang from her eyes. She wanted to say the Lord's Prayer, but the only thing that would come out was "ow."

"Shhh, deep breaths, Hope. The ambulance is on its way."

Hope's eyes grew bigger. "Oh, God help me. Something's happening down there! Oh, I feel, I feel . . ." Hope began thrashing, trying to get up.

"It's important to stay calm," an increasingly panicked Millicent said as calmly as possible. "If you can just . . . Oh, my God. You're bleeding."

Millicent raced to Cy's desk, pressed the speakerphone button, dialed, and raced back to Hope.

"9-1-1, what's your emergency."

"She's having the baby!" Millicent screamed.

"Argh!" Hope seconded in the background, pulling frantically at her pants. She rolled to all fours, and, as God was her witness, if she could have made it in that moment, would have jumped out the window to end the pain.

"Ma'am, where is the patient?"

"She's rolling around on the floor!"

"Okay, stay calm. The President of the United States is in your area, and roadblocks are everywhere. But the ambulance is on its way. We're going to need your help, here."

"My help! How can I help?"

"What's your name?"

"My . . . what? It's, uh . . ." *Lord, have mercy. Jesus, what is my name?* Millicent paused and took a deep breath. "It's Millicent. Millicent Kirtz."

"Well, Millicent, get ready. It sounds like you're getting ready to deliver a baby."

70

Push

"What are you doing?" Hope battled with Millicent even as she tried to help remove the pants.

"You're having the baby," Millicent said through clenched teeth.

"No, I'm not. Not until the ambulance gets here."

Millicent jerked off the pants. A fuzzy black head between Hope's legs was the sight that greeted her.

"I see the head!" she barked into the telephone.

"Okay," the EMT operator replied calmly. "Tell the patient not to push until she feels a contraction."

"Don't push—"

"Don't you dare tell me what to do!" Hope screamed.

"—until you feel a contraction," Millicent finished.

"Lord Jesus, please. Just take me now, take me now!"

"Try to take your finger and insert it between the vaginal walls and the baby's head," the operator said.

"Take my who and do what?"

"I'm gonna kill, Cy," Hope panted. She shot a dagger look at Millicent. "He did this, you know. This is what he did to me!" Another contraction ripped through Hope's abdomen.

"Push now!"

"You just wait until I have this baby," Hope panted. "I'm gonna kick your butt."

"Well, don't wait until the battle is over, sistah, shout now!"

Hope couldn't roll her eyes; they were already in the back of her head. Instead she tucked her chin into her chest and pushed down with all her might.

". . . Five, six, seven, eight, nine, ten," Millicent counted. "Good job. Now breathe."

" 'Good job,' " Hope mimicked. "What are you doing down there? Get your finger out of. . . . ooh . . . Just pull it out. Grab it by the head, the neck, I don't care. Just get it out!"

"The head is out!" Millicent announced triumphantly.

"Okay, the shoulders are the hardest," the EMT instructed, still on speakerphone. "Slowly move your finger around the rim, expanding the opening. Have the patient hold her knees in the air and bear down in her pelvic area."

"This is way too close for us to ever be," Hope panted as she felt Millicent's finger inside her. But she was in no position to demand change. Sweat was now dripping from her face, and while only a few minutes had gone by, it felt like years.

"Where's the ambulance!"

"It's coming. Concentrate, Hope. And when you feel another contraction—"

"Urgh," Hope growled as she bore down again.

"Keep going! Keep going!" Millicent's breath became shallow as amid the sticky, whitish goo she saw a neck and tiny shoulders—and then a whole body slid out.

Just then the door opened. In ran the paramedics, followed closely by Cy and Jack.

"Hope!" Cy cried, falling down by his wife. "Oh, my God!" He looked down at what Millicent was holding.

"Cy Taylor," she said, beaming as if she herself were the mother. "Say hello to your son."

71

Down the Aisle

Everything was perfect. The weather, the setting, the gathering of fifty or so friends and family seated to witness the moment. Stacy stood quietly, just out of view, taking it all in. Here she was, in the garden restaurant at the museum where Tony had not long ago proposed . . . perfect. The past six months had felt like a dream, and this day, an ultimate fantasy.

Granted, it was not the wedding she'd envisioned. She'd always seen herself walking down the center aisle at Kingdom Citizens with the entire congregation looking on. Of course, there had also been another man in that scenario. Which made it all the more fitting, as she continued to ponder the moment, that nothing had followed her script—especially the man waiting at the altar. Her mother had used to say that life was what happened while you were busy making plans. Stacy certainly felt that was true because right now, in this incredible moment, Stacy Talisa Gray had never felt more alive.

"You ready, baby girl?"

"Yeah, lil' sis—you've still got time to make a quick getaway."

"Man, I say she runs while she still has the chance."

Her younger brother came to stand directly in front of her.

"This is the happiest I've ever seen you, big sis. You get ready to walk to your man. We'll be right beside you, now and forever."

Stacy's eyes shone with unshed tears as she hugged her brothers. Sean's words were almost her undoing; the teasing from her other three brothers was much easier to handle. She hugged each one of them and remembered these protectors who'd always been her shield—how after their dad had died, they had all stepped in to fill his shoes. And during Stacy's dating years, much to her chagrin, how they'd chased off many a nuckah who didn't mean well and threatened a few more who wouldn't leave her alone. They were a pain in the neck, but she couldn't imagine life without them. It was the only appropriate action that all four of them accompany her down the aisle.

Her mother waited at the altar, along with Tony, serving as her maid of honor. Dr. Montgomery looked resplendent in a tailored tuxedo, as did Tony's NFL-playing best man. Frieda, Vivian, and Mother Moseley were among those on the front row. As Stacy walked down the aisle to an original wedding march played by the Musical Messengers, she eyed several relatives, members from the church, and coworkers from her former job before resting her eyes on her beloved and keeping them there.

As for his part, Tony could barely contain himself. He wanted to run down the aisle, meet her halfway, scoop her up, and carry her off to a place where it was only the two of them. The six months he'd waited to make this woman his had been the longest six months of his life. In fact, it had taken a lifetime, he thought as he watched his beautiful bride in her palest of pink confections approach him. She reminded him of cotton candy, soft and sweet. Her beautiful brown eyes were hidden behind a short veil, and the simple yet elegant halter design with trumpet lace emphasized her small, lanky frame and added the illusion of curves with its flared hem. He couldn't wait for her to melt in his mouth.

He looked at his parents sitting in the front row on the other side of Frieda, Vivian, and the others. Their look said it all. They knew what he'd gone through with the others: the model who had left him for his teammate and the college baby mama who brought drama all day long. Fortunately, for once, both acted like women who had some sense when Tony's mother called and requested her grandchildren attend their father's wedding. He winked at Shea and Justin, looking loving and mindful between their "mawmaw" and "pawpaw."

"Who gives this woman away to be married to this man?" Derrick asked in a clear, firm voice.

"We do!" was the unanimous reply.

And so it began, Stacy's official journey into becoming Mrs. Stacy Johnson. Later, the entire day would seem a dream. After the traditional ceremony—where the sometimes controversial words *honor* and *obey* were used in the vows to her husband—the entire wedding party and all the guests enjoyed a sit-down dinner of tenderloin beef, lobster claws, rosemary potatoes, and a fresh green salad. The three-tiered wedding cake was Tony's favorite: carrot, covered in Stacy's favorite frosting, a creamy white buttercream dusted with crushed pecans.

A few dances were as long as Tony and Stacy could linger. After they'd dutifully danced with brothers and mothers and taken a swirl around the room, they exited amid bubbles and blessings and headed to the first stop of their eventual Parisian honeymoon, the Beverly Hills Four Seasons grand luxury suite, compliments of the Taylors. Stacy had felt the prize in brothah man's package on more than one occasion. Leaning into her husband's solid chest, she seared him with a kiss as the limo whizzed them toward their destination. The waiting was over, the party was starting, and both Tony and Stacy were thinking the same thing: they couldn't wait to experience a little heaven.

72

The Ladies

Stacy Johnson, Hope Taylor, and Frieda Moore sat enjoying the breeze coming off the Pacific Ocean. Two-and-a-half-year-old Darius Crenshaw Jr. sat cooing and clapping in his high chair, obviously enjoying the late September weather. It was the first time in months the ladies had hung out together, and for all three the good food and great conversation was just what the doctor ordered.

"You're looking good, Hope," Frieda said as she eyed her cousin critically.

"Well, thank you—"

"Your booty is still as big as a Broadway marquee, but your face is starting to lose that chubby look."

"—I think," Hope finished. She ignored her favorite relative and dug into her perfectly cooked lasagna.

"Don't listen to her," Stacy said as she speared an asparagus tip with her fork. "You look marvelous, darling. Three months after twins and still nursing? Please! You are doing *fine*."

"Oh, please, chick. Everything has been fine with you since you started having sex again. It's working for you though. Your face is glowing!" Frieda studied Stacy as she nibbled her garlic bread. "Sure there isn't something you want to tell us?"

"Actually, there is." Stacy swallowed her food, wiped her

face, and put down her napkin. "Tony and I are moving to Phoenix."

"What?"

"You lyin'."

"Why?" Hope asked.

"Football. You know the Raiders released him. Thank God the Cardinals gave him a one-year contract. He's hoping to parlay it into a multiyear deal, but even one year is enough for us to get a nice place, put some funds away for Darius's college and whatnot, and adopt a lifestyle out of the fast lane."

"What does baby daddy think about that?"

Stacy shrugged. "He wasn't too happy at first, but I think he's slowly coming around. He said he might buy a condo there, have a place to chill out of the limelight himself."

"Here's a bigger question," Frieda said. "What does Uncle—no, *Godfather*—think?"

"Well, for once, Bo and I are on the same page. I think there's a few fellas here after Darius that Bo would be more than happy to put some distance between."

"You and Bo in cahoots. Now that *is* some mess."

"No, what's some mess," Stacy said as she turned her attention to Hope, "is Millicent delivering this woman's firstborn. I still can't get over that irony."

"You and me both," Hope said. But the grin belied her rough tone. Truth of the matter was, since Camon and Acacia had come into the world, her joy at their arrival had covered a multitude of other faults. She was too blessed to be angry, stressed, or depressed, although a touch of postpartum had hit her in the weeks following the delivery.

"So how is that—you and Cy living so close to them?"

"Well, we aren't close, per se; there are a good five miles between us. Still, like it or not, that woman will never be out of my life."

"Why, because Jack and Cy are so close?"

"No, because she's Camon's godmother."

"What?" Stacy and Frieda exclaimed simultaneously.

"That's why I waited to tell you cows, and I don't want you mooing what you think about it. She delivered him and was very helpful after Mama left and during the times when neither of you could make it down. Whenever I can see my way past the past, she's really not a bad person. I'm not saying we'll ever be BFFs, but lately I've been neighborly. And so far no one's died."

"Well, there's one thing for sure: for as long as you waited, your babies' entrance into the universe was anything but dull!"

"Can you believe it? Having one in Cy's office and the other in the ambulance? That was insane! I'm just glad they were healthy and, yes, that Millicent was there. But I still feel bad I wasn't there for you," she said to Stacy.

"How many times do we have to have this conversation? You couldn't help when your babies were born. That they chose to come the same week as my wedding is the best gift you could have given me—my play niece and nephew. Besides, I never thought to ask Mama to be my maid of honor, but when I did, she was thrilled. She was meant to be standing there, really."

Frieda scooped up the last of her manicotti, sopped up the sauce with her bread, and relished the bite. Then she sat back in her seat and crossed her arms.

"Do you realize that all the two of you talk about is marriage and motherhood? See, that's what happens when you settle down. You get dull and boring."

"Oh, is that so?" Hope asked.

"Yes, it is."

"Well, if your life is so bright and exciting, why don't you liven up the conversation?"

"Yes, Miss Free-as-a-Bird Frieda, tell us what's been going on in your fast-lane life."

"I'm pregnant," Frieda said calmly, motioning the waiter over for dessert. "Your children's holy-terror cousin is on its way."

HEAVEN RIGHT HERE

LUTISHIA LOVELY

ABOUT THIS GUIDE

The following questions
are intended to enhance
your group's reading
of this book.

DISCUSSION QUESTIONS

1. Did Stacy have a legitimate argument for keeping her son away from his father? And on the flip side, did Darius have a legitimate right to sue for full custody of Darius Jr.? Why or why not?

2. Stacy was obviously hoping that her love would be enough to change Darius's sexual orientation. Do you think it's possible for someone who is gay to become straight, and totally leave the gay lifestyle behind?

3. Did Mother Moseley know that Stacy was coming to dinner at the Montgomerys'? Do you think she plotted this Sunday showdown between Darius and Stacy?

4. Was Cy wrong to re-establish a relationship with Millicent? Given the circumstances, was he wrong to try to surprise Hope with their new dream home?

5. Do you feel Millicent had an ulterior motive in encouraging the business relationship between her husband, Jack, and Cy?

6. How much of a part did Hope's emotional state play in preventing her from conceiving? How big a role do you feel emotions play in conception overall, or the inability to conceive?

7. What are your thoughts on seeking counseling from psychiatrists, mental health professionals, etc.? Do you think it is okay to seek alternative "holistic" treatments, such as what Dr. Whitmore offered Hope?

8. What do you think about Frieda? Is she a "ho," or simply someone who feels in control of her body, and her life?

9. In what variety of ways did Frieda having been raped as a young girl affect her adult choices?

10. Do you think someone like Frieda deserves someone like Gabriel? Do you think they should get married? Why or why not?

11. What do you think about gospel music crossing over into the secular world? How should this be handled by gospel artists, and how should they interact with their secular peers?

12. Was sixteen-year-old Melody the perpetrator or the victim? Why or why not?

13. Did Darius in any way encourage Melody's flirtation with him?

14. What about Shabach? Was he a villain or victim? Is there any instance where a sixteen-year-old can be held responsible for having sex with an adult?

15. Is Tony a good match for Stacy? Do you think she should have gone after the doctor instead?

There's more scandal on the way . . .
Don't miss
Reverend Feelgood
Coming in February 2010 from Dafina Books

1

Generations

Nate Thicke yawned, casually stretched his six-foot-three-inch frame, and gave the woman beside him a kiss on the forehead before getting out of bed. He strolled from the king-sized bed to the master bath in all his naked glory. At twenty-eight, he was in the best shape of his life, thanks to a mindful diet and the recent addition of a personal trainer to his church's official staff.

His administrative assistant and the woman in his bed, Ms. Katherine Noble, admired his plump, hard backside and long, strong legs as he left the room. She especially loved how his dark brown, blemish-free skin glistened with the fine sheen of sweat that had resulted from their lovemaking. They'd been lovers for a long time, and while she knew their relationship would never be more than that, had known from the beginning, she had fallen in love with him, anyway. Even though she knew the day would come when he would take a wife and start a family. Even as she hoped he could continue to be her spiritual covering, her sexual satisfaction, as both his father and grandfather before him had been. Katherine had been a Thicke woman for generations.

Katherine rose and walked to a floor-length mirror that occupied a corner of the elegantly decorated bedroom, the black, tan, and deep purple color scheme her design. She eyed herself objectively, critically, turning this way and that. At fifty-three, her body still held its firmness, her butterscotch skin still smooth and supple. The stretch marks from her single pregnancy thirty-two years ago were long gone, rubbed away with cocoa butter and the luck of excellent genes. She tossed her shoulder-length hair away from her face and brought her image closer to the mirror. The fine crow's feet around her eyes and on her forehead were deepening slightly, she noticed, and she detected a puffiness that hadn't been there five years ago. There was a slight sag to her chin, and even though she'd been the same weight for twenty-five years, it looked as if her cheeks were sunken, hollow, and not in a good way. These imperfections were not noticeable to the average looker. Most people who saw Katherine either admired or envied her for the attractive woman she was.

She turned to the side and continued her perusal, a frown accompanying her critique. Her butt had never been big, but it had always been firm. Not now. Now it hung loose and soft, like a deflated balloon, obeying the gravity that she tried to defy. A discernible dimpling of unwanted cellulite challenged her vow not to age. She cupped her cheeks, pushed them up, and thought about butt implants.

"Get out of the mirror. You're still fine." Nate walked from the bathroom into his massive closet and began to dress.

"I'm sure you say that to all your women," Katherine responded, without rancor. "But even if you're lying, it sure sounds good."

Thirty minutes later, a showered and dressed Katherine sat across the desk from Nate in his roomy, masculine home office. She looked the epitome of decorum in her black skirt, which hung below the knee, and pink-and-black-polka-dotted blouse with a frilly lace collar that tickled her chin. Her hair was pulled back in a bun, and black, rectangular reading glasses sat perched on her nose. Anyone entering would see a scene of utmost respectability.

The "matronly" older woman who had known Nate since he was born, Katherine had been considered the perfect choice as his assistant when he became senior pastor four years ago, the perfect barrier between him and all the young, single female members who clamored for his "counsel." Her position was the perfect cover for their ongoing liaison. No one ever questioned why she was in his home; no one guessed that she spent as much time in his bedroom as she did in his office. Of course, Nate's residence in a gated and guarded community was beneficial as well—few eyes could pry.

"You had something you wanted to discuss with me?" Katherine asked after Nate had finished a call with a church deacon.

"Yes," he answered.

Katherine waited. In bed, at first, she had been the teacher, he the student. She had been the older woman, he the enthralled teenager. She'd been in control. But those roles had reversed a long time ago. Now he was her boss, and the more experienced lover. He was now clearly in control. So now, even though she could tell that his mind was in turmoil, she didn't push, but waited until he was ready to speak.

Nate cleared his throat and began toying with a paperweight on his desk. It wasn't so much that he was getting ready to talk with Katherine about what God had told him; often she'd been a sounding board. It's just that this time he wasn't sure how she'd react to what he had to say.

"The Lord has spoken to me," he began in a tone of authority. "He has given me confirmation on who's to be my wife."

Katherine let out the breath she'd been holding. *Is that all?* she thought. At once, she quelled the surge of jealousy that rose to the surface, determined not to deny this woman what she knew she could never have, Nate's hand in marriage. It was why she'd denied her own feelings when Nate came to her four years ago and said he'd been led to become Simone's biblical covering. How could she protest his decision to have sex with her daughter? Katherine, along with the older Thicke men, had been Nate's mentors, his example, encouraging him to indulge his conjugal rights as a spiritual leader in their church. That's how he had wound up in her bed. And now, this is how she would always have a key to his home . . . as his mother-in-law.

Katherine was certain of God's message to Nate that Simone was to be his wife. After all, she was perfect. The two were good friends, had practically grown up together. At thirty-two, Simone had never been married and had only one child. Like her mother, Simone was a stunner, the family's Creole blood prominent in her features. Three inches taller than Katherine's five foot six, Simone had beautiful hazel eyes, a full, pouty mouth, large breasts, and long, black hair. She was educated and cultured, perfect "first lady" material for a prominent, up-and-coming minister. And, to top all this off, Simone had the voice of an angel. Beyoncé, Rihanna, Mariah: these younger women had nothing on her daughter, either in looks or voice. This is what she'd envisioned on that first night when she knew Nate and Simone were sleeping together, when she had to make room for her daughter in her pastor's crowded bed. And now her dream was coming true!

She reached over and placed her hand over Nate's. "Don't worry, Nathaniel. I knew this day would come. Everything is going to be fine, trust me. Simone is going to make a beautiful bride and a fabulous wife."

Nate's dark brown eyes met Katherine's hazel-green ones. He forced himself not to squirm or break the stare. He had heard from God, and knew in his heart that his decision was right. For the first time since walking into the office, he blessed his longtime lover with a dazzling smile of straight, white teeth set against skin so dark and creamy smooth, one wanted to lick it.

"Katherine, you're right, as usual. The woman God has

chosen for me will make an excellent wife and be the perfect first lady. But it isn't Simone."

Katherine snatched back her hand, stunned into silence. Within seconds, however, she found her voice. "Well, uh, I mean, who could it be, if not my daughter? There's nobody in our congregation who compares to her!"

Katherine thought back to Nate's busy schedule, and the increasing amount of time he spent ministering in other churches.

"Oh, my God, that's it. You've found someone outside of Palestine. Is it someone from Mount Zion Progressive, or one of those silicone-injected, weave-wearing minister chasers in LA?"

Katherine stood and walked to the window behind Nate's desk. And then she stopped, put her hands on her hips, and swirled his chair until he faced her. "You know I respect your anointing. I've never questioned your ability to hear God's voice. But, Nathaniel, I have to question it now. I'm positive that Simone is the woman you should marry."

"And I'm positive that it's her daughter, Destiny. Katherine, your granddaughter is the one who will be my wife."

Don't miss Lutishia Lovely's
A Preacher's Passion
and
Love Like Hallelujah

Available now wherever books are sold!

1

Is That You?

People say Passion was fast from the womb. That when she heard men talking, she'd make a motion in her mother's belly that felt like a tickle. When she heard women, her mother got gas. Even before Passion was born, she decided that men were to be loved; women, tolerated.

She had one real girlfriend growing up, Robin Cook. They got along like two peas in a pod from the moment they met at Martin Luther King Jr. Elementary School in Atlanta, Georgia. For one, they were big tomboys, bigger than most girls their age. For another, they both hated their female classmates and constantly baked up evil schemes to right some imagined wrong done to them. Whether it was putting cayenne pepper in a girl's food, glue on her seat, or beating somebody up at recess, they were always getting into trouble, and usually together. But Passion and her family moved from Georgia to California when she was fifteen years old. She hadn't seen Robin since.

Passion sat in her living room, flipping through an *Essence* magazine and watching the MLM channel, a new, progressive,

Black-owned network that was finally giving BET some competition. A minister, Derrick Montgomery, was speaking at a convention hosted by a group called Total Truth. Passion decided he looked as good on TV as he did in person. *That man is fine forever,* she thought, as she turned up the volume.

Passion wasn't a member of Montgomery's church, Kingdom Citizens' Christian Center, but the church she belonged to, Logos Word Interdenominational, fellowshipped with KCCC often. Passion loved Pastor Montgomery's fiery style, not to mention the way his body blessed a designer suit. She could always expect a good word plus some men worth watching when she visited Kingdom Citizens, and was one of many who'd visualized Pastor Montgomery sans suit or wife. Either him or Darius Crenshaw, KCCC's hot minister of music whose latest hit, "Possible," had spent months at the top of both gospel and secular charts. Pastor Montgomery was fine, but Darius could sing, play several instruments, *and* looked like "thank you, Jesus." Add the fact that he was single, and as far as she knew, available, and he was the obvious choice.

For all her salacious wonderings, Passion couldn't see herself actually sleeping with Pastor Derrick or anybody else's husband. She admired Pastor Montgomery's wife, Vivian, who was good friends with her first lady, Carla Lee. Even after news broke that Pastor Montgomery had an older son from a previous relationship, a son he supposedly knew nothing about until two years ago, his and Vivian's marriage remained strong. Word had it that the boy was even living with them now and playing basketball at UCLA. No, Passion would never act out inappropriately with Pastor Derrick. Well, other than the lusting in her heart for which she was already guilty. She'd probably not send love notes or nude pics to Darius Crenshaw either. But he was definitely daydream material.

An hour after the television program went off, Passion pulled into her favorite strip mall. It housed an inexpensive clothing shop, video store, nail salon, Chinese food restaurant, and the reason for her trip, Gold's Pawn Shop. Passion loved this store. Pawning had kept her lights, gas, or phone on many times right after her divorce, when she'd been struggling to raise her new-born daughter. She'd pawn gold, diamonds, anything she could to make it to payday. She prided herself on the fact that she al-ways bought back her stuff and in the process would some-times find a couple bargains, enough to where she continued to make regular visits even after her finances improved.

She stepped inside the store. As she'd expected for the mid-dle of the day, it was quiet. Lin, the Korean owner, was behind the counter, helping his one, lone customer.

"Hey, Lin," Passion said cheerfully.

"Hey, Passion," Lin said. "What you buy today? I got tennis bracelet you like—just came yesterday."

"How much you want for it?" Passion asked. "I might be interested if you give me a good deal."

"I give you very good deal," Lin said. He unlocked the show-case and pulled out a bracelet set with tiny diamonds, effec-tively shown off in a black, faux-velvet case.

"This is nice," Passion said. She put it on her arm, turned it this way and that.

The other shopper, a woman, looked at the bracelet as well.

"It's pretty, huh?" Passion said to her, being friendly. "You think it's worth two hundred dollars?" That's the deal Lin said he'd give to Passion, because "she good customer."

The woman didn't answer, just stared. Passion looked up and stared back. The face was familiar. Then it dawned on her.

"Robin? Robin Cook? Girl, is that you?"

Robin was shocked, her response subdued. "Passion Perkins?"

Both women were incredulous. It had been twenty years.

"What on earth are you doing in LA?" Passion exclaimed, stepping forward to grab her former best friend in a bear hug. As she did so, she felt something cold, hard, pressing against her stomach. She pulled back, looked down. "And why are you buying a gun?"

Robin looked at Passion, then down at the gun, almost as if she didn't know how it had gotten in her hand.

"I, well, uh, girl, it's good to see you!" Robin placed the gun on the counter and hugged Passion with fervor. This had been her best friend back in the day. She was genuinely glad to see her again, but still couldn't have a sistah all up in her business.

Passion didn't miss the fact that her question had been diverted. But this was Robin, her homegirl from the ATL!

"Oh my God, Robin, I swear I thought about you just today. Listen, we've got to grab something to eat and catch up; you got time?"

"Of course." Time was all Robin had had for the past eighteen months.

Both the gun and the tennis bracelet stayed at Gold's Pawn Shop as Passion and Robin headed for the Chinese food restaurant three doors down. They quickly ordered, paid for their food, and sat down.

"Passion Perkins, or is it something else now?"

"No, it's Perkins again. I've been divorced almost five years, got a little girl. What about you; are you married, divorced, kids? Are you living here or just visiting? Girl, I still can't believe I'm looking at you!"

"Me neither," Robin said, taking a large bite of her egg roll. "Um, this food is good."

"Good and greasy," Passion countered around a forkful of chicken fried rice. "Just the way I like it."

Passion and Robin were silent a moment, devouring their tasty dishes, and then Passion probed again. "So, Robin, tell me wuzzup?"

Robin smiled as Passion mimicked the voice of their teens. She felt she could maybe share a few things with an old friend.

"Well, for starters, I'm divorced, no kids." Robin filled Passion in on her ten years in Tampa, Florida, after leaving Atlanta, her turbulent marriage and its equally turbulent end, the split-second decision to stay in Los Angeles after visiting almost two years ago, and her current employment.

"You've been here two years?"

"Off and on." Robin didn't want to tell Passion or anyone else where she'd actually resided during most of her LA stay—in prison for identity theft and credit card fraud. "I took some time off to, uh, visit family . . . came back a couple months ago."

"Wow, girl, you must be rolling to be able to take off work like that." Even as Passion said this, her thoughts returned to the gun left lying on the pawn shop counter.

"Hardly," Robin replied. "But sometimes you gotta do what you gotta do."

Like shoot somebody? "So, where are you staying?" Passion asked.

"Downtown," was Robin's short reply.

Passion studied the face of her former running buddy. Twenty years was a long time; maybe she shouldn't expect the two girls-turned-women to be as close as they once were. Still, Passion didn't understand the guardedness she sensed in Robin's demeanor—eking out conversation as if words cost money.

After an awkward silence, Passion reached into her purse and pulled out her cell phone. "I stay over in Leimert Park. Let's hang out one day soon. What's your number?"

They exchanged phone numbers and then Passion rose to leave. "You coming?" she asked Robin.

"Uh, in a minute, girl," Robin said, looking up at the menu, prominently displayed along the restaurant's back wall. "I think I'm going to get me something to go."

Passion leaned over and hugged Robin. "Well, it was good seeing you, Robin. Take care, and let's talk soon, okay?"

"Okay."

Robin waited until Passion walked out the door, and then placed a take-out order. There was just one other purchase she needed to make before leaving the area.

Passion wasn't sure why, but she didn't leave the strip mall when she got in her car. Instead, she sat watching the door to the Chinese restaurant. A couple minutes later, Robin came out of the restaurant, looked around briefly, and headed back to the pawn shop. She looked around again before going inside.

Passion waited until she saw Lin unlock the gun case and hand something to Robin. "I knew she was going back to buy that gun," Passion said to herself as she started the car and left the parking lot. "What is going on with you, Robin Cook? What is *really* going on?"

2

In the Way

Robin sat on the sagging bed of her dingy motel room. It was almost midnight, and her workday began at seven A.M. Still, she sat there wide-eyed, watching reruns of *Good Times,* eating Cheetos dipped in peanut butter, and washing it down with malt liquor beer. This was her ritual almost every night. After spending eighteen months locked down, where every move was ordered and every moment scheduled, Robin fully appreciated being able to have lights and television on after nine P.M. The one good thing the motel had was cable TV. Watching reruns of J.J. badger Thelma or a preteen Janet Jackson cozy up to her TV mom, Willona, saved Robin's sanity, such as it was.

Robin finished the bag of Cheetos and, licking the cheese off the fingers of one hand, picked up the gun with the other. She palmed the simple, semiautomatic Cobra compact, satisfied with the comfortable fit. Eyeing a crude, hastily drawn picture on a piece of paper taped to the opposite wall, she aimed the unloaded gun and fired off five shots in quick succession. V-I-V-A-N, the misspelled name on the paper identifying the drawing's inspiration, was safe. Along with being on the antipsychotic drug Peridol, Robin was near-sighted. She thought she'd hit the target perfectly, but had the gun been loaded, no one would have died. *Gonna get bullets as soon as I get my check on Friday,* Robin mused, as she shot Vivian a couple more times before tossing the gun carelessly on the floor beside her.

Robin stared at the drawing, mentally replaying the events from two years ago. How she'd come to LA to reclaim her man, Derrick Montgomery, and after a failed coup d'état of Vivian's domain, been tossed out of their church like a sack of potatoes by a burly security guard. She thought back farther, to the beginning: Lithonia, Georgia, and Pilgrims' Rest Baptist Church. That's where she and Derrick first met. She'd been his assistant with aspirations to be much more. But somebody named Vivian had gotten in the way. Robin's smile was sinister as she imagined the future according to her plan. If it worked, Miss High-and-Mighty wouldn't be in the way for long.

Robin stumbled into the bathroom, shook three Peridols into her hand, and swallowed them with the remaining beer. She turned out the lights, and after peering at the moonlight spilling through the torn, stained curtain, closed the window on the loud sounds of brass-based banda music drifting in along with the cool, autumn air.

As she waited for the drug to take effect, Robin thought about Passion and smiled as dim recollections of a happier time flitted across her mind. Her smile turned to a frown as one of the faces in her reverie became that of a young Vivian Montgomery. She flopped over on her stomach, letting the dulling effects of drugs and sleepiness overtake her.

Robin kept repeating something over and over, until her snoring blended with the muted Mexican music and a steady, rhythmic creaking sound from the couple's bed above her. *I'm gonna get her. I'm gonna get that prissy muthafucka. . . .*

From *Love Like Hallelujah*

I

Remember to Forget

Cy moved with calm precision, feeling perfectly at home among Victoria's Secret's wispy feminine apparel. Not the most traditional gift to give his soon-to-be wife, but Cy couldn't think of anything he'd rather see her in than a silky negligee, except her bare skin. He knew her body would show off to perfection the diamond necklace he'd just purchased at Tiffany's, and he wanted a delicious piece of lingerie to complement the eight-carat teardrop. He couldn't help but smile as he fingered the delicate fabrics of silk, satin, and lace, unmindful of the not-so-covert glances female shoppers slid his way. It hardly mattered. His fiancée, Hope Serenity Jones, had captured Cy's attention from the moment she'd appeared at the back entrance of Mount Zion Progressive Baptist Church, a piece of sanctified eye candy wrapped in a shimmering gold designer suit.

Female admirers ogled Cy as he continued his deliberate perusal. He stopped at a hanging negligee, red and pink flowers against a satiny white background. The top had thin spaghetti straps that held up a transparent gown hitting midthigh. The thong had an intricately designed rose vine for the string, a trail he would happily follow once it was on Hope, first with his fingers, then with his tongue. . . .

A perky, twenty-something salesclerk came over with a knowing smile. "Are roses your favorite flower?" she asked, flirting.

"They could become my favorite," Cy countered easily, "if worn on the right person."

"That's a very popular design," the salesperson offered, encouraging the purchase.

"I'll take it," Cy said as he casually handed the lingerie to her.

"Will this be all?" she asked, unconsciously moving closer to the live Adonis who had walked into the store and (blessings abound!) into her area.

"No, but I'll keep shopping on my own," Cy murmured as he eyed something on the other side of the store. The salesperson followed without thought. "I'll let you know if I need any help," Cy said with emphasis.

"No problem. I'm here if you need me." The salesclerk turned around, a look of regret barely concealed behind her cheery smile. Cy was oblivious to the wistful stares his six-foot-two frame elicited from the saleswoman and other shoppers. His naturally curly jet-black hair may have been hidden under a Lakers cap, but his raw sexuality was in plain sight. He had no idea that his sparkling white smile lit up the room like the noonday sun or that the dimple that flashed at the side of his grin was like a finger beckoning women closer.

Cy picked up a bra and panty set that had Hope's name written all over it. It was a soft, lacy, yellow number. The panty was designed like a pair of shorts—very short shorts—and Cy reacted physically as he thought of Hope's bubble booty filling them out. He quickly added this set to the black and beige more traditional sets he'd selected earlier.

While making his way to the perfume counter, another

outfit caught his eye—the perfect backdrop for the diamond pendant. It was a lavender-colored sheer nightgown with matching floor-length jacket. The beauty was in its simplicity, and he smiled again as he thought of how Hope would look wearing this purple paradise. He held it up and closed his eyes, mentally picturing her ebony splendor wrapped luxuriously inside the soft material rubbing against her silken skin as he kissed her sweet lips.

Cy felt the presence of someone behind him. Figuring it was the attentive saleswoman, he turned to apologize for taking so long to make his decisions, and for the growing pile of lingerie she'd collected on his behalf. The smile died on his lips, however, as did the clever banter he'd thought to deliver as he completed the turn and stared into the eyes of the person he'd most like to remember to forget . . . Millicent Sims.

Or so he thought, initially. The woman could have been Millicent's twin sister; that's how much alike they looked. But after the initial shock subsided, Cy realized it wasn't she. The eyes were similar, but this woman's nose and lips were larger. Her face was a bit fuller, the cheekbones less prominent. One thing was definitely the same, though; the woman looked at him as if he were a chicken nugget and she the dipping sauce. He quickly excused himself and went around her, making a beeline for the cash register. A close encounter of the Millicent kind had cooled his shopping frenzy.

Moments later, he closed the rear door of his newly purchased BMW SUV. It had been hard to get him out of his Azure, but looking back it hadn't made sense for a Bentley to be his main driving vehicle. As the salesman had promised, Cy found the BMW to be a perfect ride for jetting around the city. He fired up the engine, hit the CD button, and zoomed out of the parking lot. The sounds of Luther Vandross's greatest hits, redone to perfection in snazzy jazz styles as a tribute to his memory, oozed out of the stereo. Cy bobbed his head as Mindi Abair got ridiculous with her alto sax version of "Stop to

Love." As he crossed lanes and merged onto the 405 Interstate, his thoughts drifted back to Millicent. His heart had nearly stopped when he thought he saw her; it had been a while since she'd crossed his mind. He wondered how she was doing, where she was. Even after "the incident," he wished her well.

The incident. It had been a while since he'd thought about that too. But seeing Millicent's near twin in Victoria's Secret had brought the memories back with a vengeance. That crazy Sunday when, out of the blue, and in the middle of a regular church service, Millicent had wafted down the aisle in full wedding regalia. It had shocked everyone in the sanctuary, him most of all.

Cy had had months to replay those events in his mind, and they'd mellowed with time. Now, he thought about the Millicent Sims he knew before she'd lost her mind that Sunday morning. He remembered the way he felt when he first saw her, tall and regal with beautiful hair, flawless skin, legs forever, and a smile that made his heart skip a beat. He'd quickly asked her out, knowing those fine looks would test the limits of his celibacy vow. But it hadn't taken him long to realize that aside from good looks and Kingdom Citizens' Christian Center, they had little in common. He also quickly felt Millicent's desire to take their relationship to another level, one of the physical kind. Though sorely tempted, he did the right thing and broke it off with her after a couple months. Now, however, he wondered what it would have been like to have those long legs wrapped around him, his dick tapping that flawless skin. His manhood jumped in response to these thoughts, the smaller head seconding the bigger head's thoughts.

As Cy exited the 90 freeway into Marina Del Rey, Millicent's words from that fateful day of their last encounter drifted through the melodies of Rick Braun's rendition of "Dance with My Father." He could hear them as loudly as if they were actually being spoken: *Come! It is our time. . . .* Cy's dick went limp.

A horn honked. The red light he'd reached had turned green. Cy floored the gas pedal as if trying to outrun the memories of Millicent from that Sunday and his wandering sexual thoughts just now. He thought of Hope, physically different from Millicent yet beautiful both inside and out. His dick jumped again. He massaged it mindlessly, even as he once again tried to divert his thoughts and calm "Mr. Man" down. *Man, sleeping next to my baby is gonna be hard tonight!*

As Cy turned into his garage, he smiled. A yellow MG sat parked in the stall next to his. Hope. What an appropriate name she'd been given, because hope was exactly what she'd given him. Hope that he could have the love he'd always envisioned, that he'd seen his parents experience. Hope that he could find someone both spiritual and sexy, who could love God like an angel and love him like a courtesan. He now had no doubt that that was exactly what he had in the chocolate pudding waiting upstairs for him. They'd agreed to remain celibate until their wedding took place, but that hadn't prevented them from getting to know each other. He hadn't played the piano, but he'd definitely stroked the keys.

Cy turned the key and activated the elevator to the penthouse floor. Humming to himself, he looked at the lingerie packet and Tiffany box he'd concealed in a plain brown bag. He wanted to see her in something different every night of their honeymoon, before he saw her in nothing but his arms.

The house was quiet as he went inside. "Hey, baby," he called out, noting the silence of the almost always playing stereo. He entered the large open space that was the living, dining, and den area. No Hope. He continued to the kitchen, where he saw the note as soon as he turned the corner:

Hey, Baby, tried to reach you on your cell. I'm with Frieda. Hollah.
Love you, Hope

He set down the packages, pulled the cell phone from his briefcase, and noted a couple of missed calls. Belatedly, he remembered how poor the cell phone reception was in some of the mall stores. Smiling, he hid Hope's honeymoon package in the closet and decided to fix a protein drink before calling his baby. Yes, Hope was the woman he wanted to be thinking about, the one he wanted on his mind. He hoped Millicent was happy, but she was his past. The woman occupying number one on his speed dial was his future.